SOUTH
OF
NOWHERE

ALSO BY JEFFERY DEAVER

NOVELS

The Colter Shaw Series

Hunting Time
The Final Twist

The Goodbye Man
The Never Game

The Lincoln Rhyme Series

The Watchmaker's Hand
The Midnight Lock
The Cutting Edge
The Burial Hour
The Steel Kiss
The Skin Collector
The Kill Room
The Burning Wire

The Broken Window
The Cold Moon
The Twelfth Card
The Vanished Man
The Stone Monkey
The Empty Chair
The Coffin Dancer
The Bone Collector

The Kathryn Dance Series

Solitude Creek
XO

Roadside Crosses
The Sleeping Doll

The Rune Series

Hard News
Death of a Blue Movie Star
Manhattan Is My Beat

The John Pellam Series

Hell's Kitchen
Bloody River Blues
Shallow Graves

Stand-Alones

The October List
Carte Blanche *(A James Bond Novel)*
Edge
The Bodies Left Behind
Garden of Beasts
The Blue Nowhere

Speaking in Tongues
The Devil's Teardrop
A Maiden's Grave
Praying for Sleep
The Lesson of Her Death
Mistress of Justice

Collaboration

Fatal Intrusion *(with Isabella Maldonado)*

SHORT FICTION COLLECTIONS

Dead Ends

More Twisted

Trouble in Mind

Twisted

Triple Threat

SHORT FICTION INDIVIDUAL STORIES

The Broken Doll, a Four-Story Cycle

Swiping Hearts, a Lincoln Rhyme Story

The Deadline Clock, a Colter Shaw Story

Scheme

A Perfect Plan, a Lincoln Rhyme Story

Cause of Death

Turning Point

Verona

The Debriefing

Ninth and Nowhere

The Second Hostage, a Colter Shaw Story

Captivated, a Colter Shaw Story

The Victims' Club

Surprise Ending

Double Cross

Vows, a Lincoln Rhyme Story

The Deliveryman, a Lincoln Rhyme Story

A Textbook Case

ORIGINAL AUDIO WORKS

The Starling Project, a Radio Play

Stay Tuned

The Intruder

Date Night

EDITOR/CONTRIBUTOR

No Rest for the Dead *(Contributor)*

Watchlist *(Creator/Contributor)*

The Chopin Manuscript *(Creator/Contributor)*

The Copper Bracelet *(Creator/Contributor)*

Nothing Good Happens After Midnight *(Editor/Contributor)*

Ice Cold *(Co-Editor/Contributor)*

A Hot and Sultry Night for Crime *(Editor/Contributor)*

Books to Die For *(Contributor)*

The Best American Mystery Stories 2009 *(Editor)*

SOUTH OF NOWHERE

A COLTER SHAW NOVEL

JEFFERY DEAVER

G. P. PUTNAM'S SONS
NEW YORK

PUTNAM
— EST. 1838 —
G. P. PUTNAM'S SONS
Publishers Since 1838
An imprint of Penguin Random House LLC
1745 Broadway, New York, NY 10019

Book design by Laura K. Corless

Hardcover ISBN: 9780593717493

Printed in the United States of America

If there is magic on this planet, it is contained in water.

—Loren Eiseley

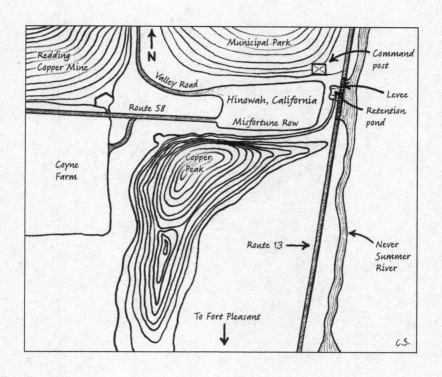

SOUTH OF NOWHERE

WEDNESDAY, JUNE 20

1.

Three vehicles had the bad luck to be atop the Hinowah levee when it gave way.

At the front was a late-model Chevrolet Camaro, nicknamed Big Blue by the woman driving it, Fiona Lavelle.

She was twenty-six years old and had recently left a teaching job and was using the newly allotted time to devote herself to her passion: writing a fantasy novel.

Traveling from Reno to Fresno, for a spa getaway, she had taken this more demanding but picturesque route through the mountains.

In jeans and a red crop top under a gray sweatshirt, Lavelle gripped the wheel firmly, her car countering the lashing wind. The vehicle's engine was big, but the body light.

The highway, Route 13, was two-lane asphalt except for the hundred-yard stretch on the dirt levee, where it was surfaced with cinders, gravel and—today—mud.

Guardrails, she thought, mentally putting sardonic quotation marks around the words. They looked like they wouldn't stop a bike, let alone a muscle car like hers.

A sign on her right, where lights and the outline of the town of

Hinowah were visible a hundred feet below, said SLOW UNPAVED ROAD.

As if one needed the warning.

On the left, where the river raged: NO FISHING FROM LEVEE.

Odd capitalization.

As the car progressed, bits of stone clicked as the tires tossed them into the undercarriage even at this slow speed. It was an odd counterpoint to the powerful drumbeat of the rain on Big Blue's roof.

"Well," she gasped, as a wave splashed from the river into the air and spattered the windshield.

The Never Summer was relentless, racing downstream, south, a speeding train, nearly even with the top of the levee. The rain had been torrential for the past hour. The velocity of the river had to be twice hers, which was about twenty miles an hour or so. On the opposite bank was a steep cliff, craggy and dotted with small caves.

She noted an old graffitied heart, in red. In the center: LM + DP. 4EVER . . .

What are you doing? she thought. Concentrate on the road!

A flash of light appeared in her rearview mirror. The headlights of a vehicle behind her.

Was the driver irritated at her slow pace? She was in a sports car, for heaven's sake. The underbelly was inches away from the messy ground.

Be patient, she thought to him, automatically assigning a gender.

Unfair, she reflected.

And then noticed that she was wrong altogether. He wasn't flashing the lights at her. The pickup had hit a pothole and the beams dropped and rose.

"Sorry." She actually whispered the word aloud.

As she approached the end of the levee, where the slick but dependable asphalt resumed, she began to relax.

The clock on the dashboard read 6:14 a.m.

The second vehicle on the levee was an F-150, piloted by Louis Bell, the self-described "best drywall man" in the town of Hinowah, California, if not all of Olechu County. He was listening to Taylor Swift and admiring the bright blue Camaro in front of him. Some Cams came with 600 horses. Man, to hit the Hawk's Canyon straightaway behind the wheel of that beautiful machine . . .

Take your time, he thought to the driver. Driving over this crap in a car like that?

Take. Your. Time. . . .

The fifty-year-old, moderately and not irrevocably rotund, was smoking and would remove the Marlboro long enough to sing along with an off-key but robust voice. He would also occasionally glance up at the low clouds as if that would give him some indication of when the downpour would let up.

What a storm! This part of the state—east central—had been in the grip of a drought for the better part of two years. Not good for the number one producer of fruits and vegetables in the country. Would this cure it? He didn't think so. He'd heard that downpours made only a small dent in solving the problem, as the water tended to vanish into places where it wasn't particularly helpful.

On the seat beside him was a McDonald's bag containing three basic Egg McMuffins. He never went for the fancy things. Simple was better. Normally he had four but was trying to cut down, and was exercising his willpower, resolving not to start on the first until he hit the city limits of Fort Pleasant, the Olechu County seat, about fifteen miles ahead.

Though maybe he would celebrate getting off this damn mud slick ten stories above Hinowah and eat half a sandwich. As if having to wrestle the wheel in the muck counted as exercise.

Ah, the games we play . . .

Bell's thoughts dipped to the job he was on his way to, plasterboarding one of the multigazillion-dollar houses in a new development west of the city. How the hell people could afford them, well, that was beyond him. Maybe some of the new companies moving here from the Bay Area and Sacramento. Then his attention faltered and he was drawn to the rushing water. The Never Summer was showing some balls today. Normally it was a modest stream pacing along a rocky bottom, some feet below the road he was presently on. You could hike along the bed all the way to Fort Pleasant and never dampen a toe.

Tense from the driving, Bell stretched and momentarily laid his right arm across the passenger seatback.

Thinking of a few years ago, him and Nancy, then his bride of six months, parked in this same set of wheels, watching the sunset behind Gold Claim Hills. She'd nestled against him, and his arm, on the seat, dropped to her shoulders and he pulled her close. They'd kissed. She'd said, "You know one thing I never heard of?"

"What's that?"

"Making a baby in a pickup truck."

He hadn't heard of that either. But they both decided it was a topic that deserved more consideration.

The recollection—and the smile it engendered—occurred at precisely 6:14.

The third vehicle on the levee road was a white Chevrolet Suburban, driven by George Garvey, who was glancing at the water cascading out of the bed of the pickup truck in front of him. It never occurred—as he'd never owned one—that pickups would need drainage. A day like this, they would fill up fast with what was probably a ton of water.

He mentioned this to his wife, Sonja, who looked up from her knitting.

"Hm."

George was owner and operator of a small business that his great-great-grandfather had created and had remained in the family, nonstop, for more than a hundred years. He was the front man and manager; Sonja ran the business office. As between the two, she was the silent type.

George's eyes strayed from the flooded pickup truck to the dark gray sky, the clouds speeding west to east. *Scudding,* he thought, was the word. They'd had the option of taking interstates and four lanes from Sonja's mom and dad to the 5 and then south. But a family conference had resulted in the decision to take this, a more picturesque, route. He negotiated with Google Maps and after some minutes—during which the algorithm seemed to ask, "Are you sure?"—they got these directions.

His wife said, "That town we passed, ten miles or so. Hibbing. Wasn't there another one? That somebody famous came from?"

"*Somebody?*" George asked as if it were an insult that she didn't know instantly. "Bob Dylan."

"Right." Back to knitting and purling.

George called to the most musical of the Garveys, "Kim. Who's Bob Dylan?"

"Who?" asked seventeen-year-old Kimberly. The blonde more cute than exotic, to Garvey's immense relief, was examining a chipped nail. Neither she nor her friends could keep all ten tips in pristine polish for more than a few hours.

George—who had been a folk singer years ago—said, "The best songwriter who ever lived."

"Not than Drake or Taylor." Maybe a question, maybe a statement.

"Hands down better than them."

"What does that mean?" Kim asked with teenage exasperation.

"Yes, better than them."

No response.

Beside her, skinny eleven-year-old Travis was lost in his phone, linked in via Airbuds. The jeans and hoodie kid was capable of playing a game and texting simultaneously on a screen the size of a deck of cards.

And, while spelling and syntax were sometimes off, those errors were intentional; he never mistyped.

He noted Sonja's gaze now turn from the rustic town of Hinowah, below them to the right, to the river. "Never Summer. Funny name." She grew quiet. "Honey?"

"What?"

Whispering, "I don't like the looks of that."

He too took in the torrent once more.

"I think the level's gone up just in the last few minutes. It could start coming over the top, it looks like."

"Wish they'd hurry up." George nodded toward the pickup truck and the blue sports car in front of it.

He smelled the sweet scent of fingernail polish.

Kimberly, the far more energetic—and fidgety—of the children, glanced up. "I'm bored. When're we going to get home?"

"About one or two."

A huge exhalation. "It's like only six-fourteen."

And George Garvey marveled at the teenage skill to make a sigh sound like a veritable groan of pain.

The world changed in an instant.

At exactly quarter past six, the battle between the Never Summer and the Hinowah levee was decided in the river's favor.

The top two or three feet of the embankment vanished, as if sliced by a huge knife.

The individual with the best view of what happened to the travelers was Louis Bell, in the middle of the procession. Ahead of him, the driver of the Camaro apparently saw the collapse coming. She gunned the engine—the wheels sent up rooster tails as she made an effort to launch the car the ten feet or so to the asphalt, where the levee ended and the highway proper began again.

He didn't see if she made it, and he couldn't afford to wait to find out. He dropped into low gear—to get purchase in the dissolving muck beneath him—and floored the engine. The truck bounded forward, though only a few feet, before it slowed and began to sink as the river simply washed away the ground beneath the tires. The truck listed toward the furious waves.

Behind him, the Suburban containing what he believed was a family of four, took the brunt of the disaster. He observed the vehicle rock sideways, back and forth, and then roll upside down over the edge.

His truck listing harder, he waited for a fate similar to theirs. He tried the handles on either side, but the water and muck held the doors firmly in place.

Louis Bell found himself curiously calm as he considered options.

There weren't many. In fact, he saw only one question: Was it better to dive into the river and be battered to death on the rocks lining the Never Summer? Or drown inside the cab of his truck?

Bell debated merely a few seconds before rolling down the window and gazing, as if hypnotized, at the icy tide that flooded over him.

2.

Colter Shaw had his enemies.

In his profession of rewards-seeking, he avoided bond enforcement—tracking down bail jumpers—but over the years he had found more than a few men and women who emphatically did not want to *be* found.

Nearly all rewards involving criminals were offered for "information leading to their arrest or capture," with the first word of that phrase always emphasized. The last thing the authorities wanted was private cops engaging in tactical work and bringing the bad guys in, zip-tied. But whether Shaw simply offered up "information" on the whereabouts of a fugitive or physically took him down himself (he'd been a championship college wrestler), the opponents were not pleased.

And they often held grudges. Some of the more sociopathic ones had actually sent him graphic descriptions of what they intended to do when they were out of prison. One had illustrated the torture, and the drawings were surprisingly good.

The incarcerated also had friends and family who roamed the land freely, often with nothing better to do than track down the man who had sent Papa or Mama, or a sibling, to jail.

So Colter Shaw had created an early warning system of sorts. People he knew—personally or professionally—would be in touch when someone suspicious inquired about him.

Which was why he was presently in his late father's office in the mountain house of his youth, working his way through five thousand sheets of the man's notes and correspondence.

He was searching for a reference to a particular individual, and having zero luck.

The lean, six-foot Shaw was dressed for the outdoors, in black jeans, 5.11 tactical boots, and two T's under a sweatshirt for insulation. It was nearly summer but this June was in March mode, drizzling, cold and windy. None of this would have stopped him from hiking the hundreds of acres that made up the Shaw Compound in the Sierra Nevada Mountains, an activity that was to have been on his agenda today.

But instead, he was chasing paper.

And coming up with nothing.

He tested the coffee. It had lost its last hint of warmth, and he set the mug aside. He'd get more—a pot was in the kitchen—but not until he hit an arbitrary milestone of another half inch of documents.

Stretching, he slumped in a chair in whose back was carved the face of a brown bear—a grizzly. Young Colter had been fascinated with the bas-relief in his youth and had once done a rubbing of it, like people do on the gravestones of the famous dead. The result, on gray newsprint, was presently hanging, framed, on a wall in his home on the East Coast.

He now looked around the room where he'd spent many, many hours with his eccentric father, as Ashton imparted endless rules about survival. Shaw recognized dozens of the objects and books that had absorbed his youthful attention like the chairback: maps, Native American weapons, lacquered boxes, books on politics and philosophy, paintings, one of his sister's model locomotives, a bowie knife that his older brother and their father had forged.

Some good memories and some tough ones.

Then, it was time to tuck the past away. And return to the hunt for the threat—if indeed a threat existed.

The early warning message had been ambiguous. It was from a political science professor at the Bay Area university where his father had taught, in Berkeley, though not the famed Cal. The professor had been a student of Ashton's and was well aware of the cranky man's mission back then—and the enemies he'd made. The text the man sent read:

Colter, You should know. Someone called the university, asking about Ashton and his family. Directed to me because I knew him. My assistant took the call. A woman gave the name Margaret. No last name. She knew about the Compound but didn't know where it was and was looking for it. She wouldn't leave a number or say why she was interested. Said she'd call back but never did. My assistant said the woman seemed "edgy" and "blunt." Maybe nothing but thought you should know.

Margaret . . .

The name meant nothing to Shaw, and as this had happened just an hour ago, he had not had a chance to pose the question to his mother, who was working in the garden.

He slogged on through the documents—the process slowed by the fact that anything Ashton generated was written by hand.

One preliminary question: *Who* exactly was at risk? He was the logical front-runner, given the number of suspects and escapees he had rounded up. Yet the mysterious caller had been interested not in Shaw himself but the "Compound" and the "family." Maybe the danger was to someone else: His sister, Dorion, three years younger; his brother, Russell, six years his senior; or their mother, Mary Dove. Or even the Shaws as a whole.

And why might they be targets?

A very likely answer: because of the patriarch, Ashton Shaw.

It was here to the Compound that Ashton had fled with his wife and children years ago when the man had learned of threats against him due to research he had engaged in. He had poked the bear of corporate and government overreach and corruption, and learned that people were gunning for him.

Ashton had not been able to outrun the threat, though Shaw and Russell had teamed up to make sure that the main actors would never be able to harm anyone again.

But the enemies' reach had been vast, and it was not impossible that some successors in interest might wish to pay a visit to the Shaw Compound to exact revenge on the family.

More documents. And more after that.

Ashton was the master of what he called the Never Rules, a list of prohibitions he formulated as the consummate survivalist.

Never be without a means of escape, never be without access to a weapon . . .

And a vital one.

Never write anything in any electronic medium now or in the future created . . .

A rule that Ashton had followed religiously. Hence the twenty pounds of paper before Shaw presently—covered in handwriting so small it would be described by graphic artists as "mice type."

Completing his milestone half inch of documents, Shaw ran his hand over his short-cropped blond hair and stretched once again. He glanced out the window to see his mother planting seeds in the half-acre garden, the early start intended to beat a predicted inundation later that day. Mary Dove had the touch, and she would be raising a crop large and varied enough to keep herself, family visitors and neighbors in staples for a year. Colter Shaw enjoyed vegetables and fruit as much as anyone. You couldn't argue with vitamins and whatever else they contained, but tending a plot of dirt from season to season remained an alien mystery to him, as it would to anybody who clocked more than 300K miles, give or take, in a Winnebago every year.

The Restless One . . .

A slim woman in her sixties with long white hair, today in a single braid, Mary Dove was pulling off her gardening gloves and walking toward the cabin. He had not yet told her about the early warning. He would now get a second cup of coffee and ask her if she knew of anyone named Margaret from the days when she and Ashton were in Berkeley, and if so was there anything concerning about her and her interest in the Compound.

Maybe it was a family friend who'd lost touch. Nothing more than that.

Of course:

Never assume what appears innocent is not a threat.

He heard Mary Dove in the kitchen, the water running, plates clanking. Shaw picked up his coffee cup and started out of the office, happening to glance down at the next sheet of paper on the stack.

He froze.

It was a draft of a letter Ashton had been composing. There were cross-outs and additions, the typical edits one would make in an effort to refine the final product.

Unremarkable in every way, except for one word.

Dr. Sheridan Tillis
Assistant Director of Curriculum
San Francisco Consolidated School Board

Hello, Sheridan:

Thank you for the recommendations of grade schools for my daughter Margaret. It was most helpful and I will keep you apprised of our decision. If you can think of any schools in Marin or Contra Costa as well, they would be appreciated.

*Please send to the address below. And, again, discretion
would be appreciated.*

 Hope all is well with you and yours.

Kindest regards,
Ashton

The shocking word: *daughter.*

All right. Assess.

Shaw had never heard any talk that Ashton had been married before Mary Dove or that he had fathered a child before the marriage. In fact, Shaw knew, his parents had gotten together when they were young, meeting by coincidence in a prohibited area of a national park.

Was there some explanation that this letter was *not* evidence of an affair he'd had?

Well, the timing wasn't going to clear him. The date indicated that it had been written after Ashton had been married to Mary Dove for fifteen years. A child going to grade school at that time meant that she had been conceived well into Shaw's parents' marriage.

And the address the recipient was supposed to send the recommendation to was a safe house in San Francisco whose existence Ashton had kept secret from the family; it had been discovered by Shaw and Russell only recently, long after the man's death.

And there was that telling admonition regarding discretion.

"Colter, are you all right?"

Mary Dove stood in the doorway.

His heart thudded.

"Fine. A little tired."

The universal response that people used as a fencing foil to parry a question. Men, mostly, Shaw believed.

She held a pot of coffee and lifted it. "More?"

Covering the letter as she walked up would be too suspicious.

His mother had an eagle eye. So he strode quickly to her instead, and she poured. He liked milk but was concerned if he went to get some from the kitchen, she might wander to the stack of documents. He'd drink it black.

She turned, was saying something about neighbors coming for dinner.

Shaw's mind was on the letter. "Good," he said.

Mary Dove laughed.

He raised an eyebrow.

"I just said that we're not doing mushrooms because Kathy's violently allergic to them. And you said, 'Good.'"

"I mean good that you're not serving them."

His nieces—Dorion's daughters—would have responded to his comeback as "lame."

Which it certainly was.

Mary Dove gave him a questioning look but let the matter drop. She never pushed. If he wanted to talk to her about something, she knew he would. This was true about everyone in the Shaw family. Of course there were secrets. But if one clearly wanted them to remain hidden, none of the others pried.

It made for a curious but effective genre of familial harmony.

Setting down the coffee he'd lost all taste for, he stared at the letter, flipped through a dozen sheets below, but none were related to the "Margaret" note.

A secret half-sibling . . .

Mary Dove had been through a great deal in her marriage to Ashton Shaw. She was a talented, in-demand academic, researcher and physician; she'd supported his crusade against corrupt politicians and corporations; and she had endured, if not relished, the move to the Compound, where she, like the children, learned the art of survivalism.

It challenged her body, her spirit, her mind.

And ultimately his actions had left her a widow.

But in her heart, all the offspring knew, she believed in the same values and thought his decisions were the right ones. The couple was in unity, and always had been.

Or so it seemed.

Infidelity?

Beyond the pale.

Another two dozen sheets of paper.

Frustratingly, nothing.

All he knew was Margaret's present age—mid- to late twenties. And probably Anglo, given the name, though an ethnic minority was certainly a possibility.

Why not give Ashton's colleague in Berkeley her full name and relationship and number if there was nothing to hide?

And why not contact Shaw through his website, where people desperate to find missing loved ones left messages about rewards they were offering, which his business associates back in Florida, Teddy and Velma Bruin, monitored several times a day. They would have instantly forwarded notice.

What did she want?

Never speculate. Once you have sufficient facts, your process is analysis—not speculation.

Well, the sole answer was to go through the entire stack—now "only" seventeen or eighteen pounds of documents—one by one. Looking for *Margaret* or the words *daughter* or *girl* or *child*.

He bent forward and began again, when he was interrupted by a text.

The first words were arresting.

Need help. Now.

He read the full message, and his mind was instantly transported to a different place altogether. His father's infidelity became a secondary issue, as did Margaret and her mission.

After sending a brief response, he charted a route to the destination provided in the text.

His eyes took in the documents once more, and he came to a decision. Gathering the stack up, he shoved the sheets into an empty orange gym bag sitting under a nearby table. He wouldn't abandon the search for Margaret altogether. He placed a call to his local lawyer, Tony Rossano, whose office was a few miles away. The man sounded shocked at the news, which Shaw relayed nearly in a whisper. The attorney, sworn to secrecy, agreed he would continue the search for Margaret in the maze of Ashton's writing, in Shaw's absence.

After disconnecting, Shaw collected his black backpack from the floor beside the desk and walked into the kitchen, where he told his mother he had to leave immediately, and gave her what details he knew.

"Oh, my, I'm sorry to hear."

He told her that he didn't know how long it would take but to count on his missing the mushroom-free dinner.

They embraced and then he hurried out into the morning.

He fired up the white-and-tan Winnebago and headed down the lengthy drive.

GPS assured him his destination was forty-five minutes away.

A quick trip.

But as to the question: Would he be too late?

That was another matter entirely.

3.

anlon Tolifson walked to the end of what had been Route 13, a darkly auspicious number to some. Though he was not a superstitious man, he felt the digits appropriate, reminiscent of the election in which he'd won the mayoral race by 666 votes.

He looked down at the rushing torrent of water that had just sliced off the top of the levee as smoothly as a supervillain's blast would have done in the apocalyptic movies his grandkids watched. It had been a long time since he'd been tested like this.

It wasn't like when his wife passed. He simply had to be strong for his children and theirs.

And it wasn't like fighting in county board meetings to win money for Hinowah.

Nor taking on parents who resisted the hiring of a gay teacher.

Those were moments you had to be strong. You stood up.

But this was a different kind of test. You met the challenge because there was something *you* wanted, something that moved you forward in life and you needed to prove yourself.

A test . . .

He looked back over his burg. An old mining town dating to the 1800s, Hinowah had been settled because of its silver, not because the topography represented a safe environment for its citizens. The place was as vulnerable as could be, a deep bowl surrounded by low hills to the north, west and south, the levee in the east. The earthwork, built more than a hundred years ago, was now a waterfall, twelve inches deep and thirty feet wide, pouring over the mudslide that had been the top of the levee, and into a grim retention pond. From there it gushed into a spillway that diverted the water around the village.

The spillway—a concrete chute ten feet wide and three feet deep—had not, in his decades as a resident, been a conduit for a single drop of water from the Never Summer. There was constant talk about breaking it up and putting a bike trail in.

Thank God for bad-tempered, unyielding and environmentally skeptical residents.

Hinowah was protected for the moment, but the flow was increasing as the waterfall ate away at the top of the remaining levee. He wondered how long it would be before the spillway filled to the brim and water invaded the town.

Tolifson was dressed in a long, bright yellow coat that was called, he believed, a sou'wester, as in "southwestern"—which was a wind or storm or something in New England, he thought, even though the outerwear's name and that part of the country were in direct opposition. In this part of the state, given the annual rainfall, he had worn the outfit once in six years. The matching floppy hat looked silly, and he'd replaced it with an Oakland Athletics cap.

Tolifson was six two and weighed one hundred and seventy-three pounds, hardly imposing. But his eyes were keen and he had learned to identify and deflect BS without a hem or a haw. He was mayor by election and now police chief by default, as Hiram Folk had ended a twenty-one-year career to take care of his aging parents in Florida. A meeting of the town council had been planned to hire a new chief, either promoting one of the two senior officers—TC McGuire or Leon Brown—or hiring from outside. Résumés were currently being accepted.

And then there was the testing.

As a youngish widower—he was fifty-three—the job of running the only home inspection company in this part of the county had never excited him.

Then he jumped at the chance to run for mayor.

He won easily—by the devil's sign margin—and he was good at being mayor. Fighting those fights and juggling what needed to be juggled came easily to him.

But still, there was a gap.

The something-missing stuff.

And so town procedures for selecting a new head law enforcer would be followed and candidates for chief would be interviewed and voted upon.

But he had decided that he himself might give it a shot, going after the job permanently.

He liked the badge. He liked the way people looked at him different. And, he had to admit, he liked the gun. (Tolifson never met a Hollywood Western he didn't adore.)

He liked waking up every day knowing there'd be a new challenge.

There had even been a few crimes to investigate. A little meth selling, a little oxy selling, a domestic, a drunk teenager with his father's scattergun.

And while he hadn't been trained formally in any law enforcement school or academy, he was picking up tricks of the trade steadily, if slowly, from TJ and Leon. Even cute little Debi Starr, their traffic girl, offered some decent suggestions on occasion.

But now he was faced with an opportunity to move his cause forward.

The test: how he would handle the levee collapse. The disaster wasn't really something that a police chief would deal with, being more in the realm of the fire department—Hinowah's population of seventeen hundred souls did not allow for a civil defense or disaster relief office. But Tomas Martinez, head of the volunteer FD, as well as being town council chair, had no more experience in levee collapses than he did. Nor had Buddy Soames, the pumper truck operator and second-in-command at HFD.

And so the task fell to Tolifson.

He felt uneasy at first, but then kicked himself, thinking: The heck is the problem? Here's your chance. It's a test. Do a good job and the council'll vote you in as police chief by a landslide (all seven of them).

So, step one: save the immediate victims, those on the road atop the levee when it collapsed. What might have possessed them to take that route when the Never Summer was nearly level with the road was a mystery, though to backtrack on other roads in this part of the state would have added over an hour to their journeys. Then too, while hardly a miracle of engineering science, the levee was an exceedingly large lump of earth and would appear strong enough even to handle the renegade waves.

In any event those in the three vehicles flipped mental coins and took their chances.

One, described as a young woman in a blue sports car, had apparently made it off safely.

The driver of the pickup behind her, Sheetrock maven Louis Bell, had resigned himself to death but had, with little effort it seemed, climbed out the window and waded to safety before the southern portion of the levee fully collapsed.

But some people had not been so lucky: according to Louis, the occupants of a Chevy Suburban—seemingly a family of four—had rolled upside down into the fierce gray river.

Had they drowned in the car by now? Had they forced open a door or rolled down a window before the electrical system shorted? Swimming in the river seemed impossible; they would have either died by drowning or being torn apart on the rocks.

But he was assuming they were alive.

And Police Chief Pro Tem Tolifson was going to do whatever it took to find them.

Pacing back and forth before the gushing waterfall, he thought of the family, the bloating spillway, the eroding levee, and his town.

And he thought, of course, of DRB.

"Han? You reading me? Ten-four." The radio on his hip clattered. Tomas Martinez was heading the search party of six volunteers looking downriver for the missing family.

"Tomas, let's not worry about codes, okay?"

The truth was, Tolifson didn't *know* the codes anyway. Well, 10-4, sure, but that was from *Blue Bloods.*

"Fine."

"Where are you?"

"Two miles and change south of the levee."

"Anything?"

Why bother to ask? He'd have said, wouldn't he?

"No. But, Lord, the depth's got to be twenty, thirty feet here. No, more! Swear to God. Hard to spot anything."

The Never Summer was relatively clear under normal circumstances. Now, it had churned up curtains of mud. You couldn't see three inches below the surface.

"We're moving, but slow."

For miles the banks of the river were similar to where Tolifson now stood. Steep rocks and thick pine, most of the trees alive, some dead and gray. Tough going for the search team, plodding along on the banks, with their chain saws, axes, ropes and medical gear.

Martinez was continuing, "We ought to get a boat—"

"Boat? In that current? We'd end up rescuing *you.* Keep going as best you can."

This seemed like a good response to the police chief test: try to save the victims but not at the expense of your men's lives.

People's lives. Two women volunteer firefighters were in the party. Something else to keep an eye on.

Martinez said crisply, "Ten-four . . . Sorry, can't help myself. I'll check in later."

"Okay." Tolifson disconnected and stared at the turbulent waters, wondering who the family was, where they'd come from and where they'd been going.

Had the SUV floated? Was it stuck somewhere, in one of the many caves or a shaft of an old silver mine from the 1800s, most of whose entrances they had no way of sealing off? (And those that were sealed sometimes got unsealed—by idiotic teenagers who went exploring and weed-smoking and sex-having just for the thrill of it.)

He glanced down again at the town.

His town.

Yes, the family was important but he could hardly imagine what would happen if the rest of the levee went. If so, the crushing flood would be horrific.

"Han? Help here?"

He turned away from the breached highway and walked to a grassy area atop the northern hillside, the highest point in town. It was the municipal park; fifteen feet above the levee and therefore the perfect site for a disaster response command post. The voice belonged to petite and pert and somewhat-round Debi Starr, in a brown Public Safety uniform, under a translucent rain slicker. Her trooper hat was protected too—with a clear plastic covering that the men, only them, of course, called a rubber. She was muscling a tent into position, fighting against the ornery wind. Debi was the most recent addition to the police force, a teacher for the county laid off in recent cuts. She joked that she was a "patrol officer third grade" since that was the class she'd taught at the town's elementary school. "Not a lot of difference between the kids and the motorists, except the youngsters were easier to catch and didn't give you quite so much crapola."

Not a real cop, but no matter—the city needed ticket revenue and she was good at the job.

Also, it was helpful to have a gofer. Coffee and packages and batteries . . . and putting up command post tents on high ground. Two were already open; he joined her to tug up the poles of the last tent, against a wind that kept turning the direction of the rain from vertical to horizontal. He grabbed and pulled, while she pounded stakes into the ground with solid, and accurate, thwacks of a steel mallet.

He and Debi then pulled two six-foot-long fiberboard banquet tables out of the back of her pickup, along with folding chairs. Her husband, Jim, managed Sierra Restaurant and Catering. They served damn good food, put together events at the last minute and did it for a song. "These were for Edna Zale's baby shower." She looked up. "Got the shower part, but no babies."

Setting up the tables, kicking the legs into place and sending globs of mud flying, Tolifson said, "You bring the cute tablecloths? Moana? Nemo?" Thanks to the grandkids he was getting an education in what was culturally relevant.

"Ha."

He eyed the tight switchback leading from the village in the valley up to the CP.

No sign of DRB.

A bit of relief.

He knew it wouldn't last.

Debi now eyed a stake straining against the rope. The tent was like a sail. She picked up the mallet and thwacked some more.

As she did, she glanced his way with a concerned look on her pretty, round face.

"Any word on the family in the SUV?"

"No. Tomas and the crew are about two miles south. Nothing."

"That's harsh—kids, Louis was saying." She was the young mother of twins.

Another pickup appeared, slightly less spattered than the others. Marissa Fell washed her vehicle every other day. Polish was involved too. The paste kind, which few souls on earth now used. It was largely how she ran the administrative side of the police department, clean and orderly, everything in its place, if not spit shined.

Climbing out, the solid, curly-haired woman zipped up her blue quilted parka.

"I got 'em." Her eyes danced Tolifson's way, then took in the levee. "How's it holding?"

"No idea."

From the backseat of her Silverado, she collected wires and power strips, and Tolifson a gas-powered generator. Marissa had also brought paper towels. Tolifson started to wipe down the table. Debi took over. And when they were dry-like, she ran the cables to the generator and fired it up.

Marissa said, "Ruth's manning nine-one-one. She's just telling everybody who calls we're on top of the situation." Her troubled eyes were on the white torrent of the river's surface and the cascade. "But seeing that? I'm not so sure . . ."

Tolifson nodded at the tents. "Might be safer up here."

She snorted a laugh. "Have the landlines. Can't run a police department via mobiles and Zoom."

"Suppose not."

"What a day. What a day. You holding up?"

Haven't failed the test yet, he thought. "So far . . ."

They shared another glance, then Marissa climbed into the truck, made a three-point turn and headed down the hill.

Tolifson was startled by a woman's voice from behind him, snapping, "Mayor. There are people taking selfies, right under the breach! You really need to get on top of this."

His lips grew into a tight line.

DRB was back.

4.

DRB.

Tolifson's nickname for the athletic blond woman who had arrived in town a mere forty-five minutes after the levee had collapsed.

The initials stood for *Disaster Relief . . .* And a *B* word he had never uttered aloud and had thought only with regard to a few individuals, all well-deserving of the designation.

"Look." She was pointing to the base of the levee.

A dozen residents were recording themselves as the waterfall flowed down the mudslide into the spillway. Two kids were skipping rocks over the retention pond, which was, oddly, more appealing now than it was in its typical shallow, scum-covered state.

Tolifson ordered, "Debi, call whoever's in the fire station and have them shoo those folks off."

DRB didn't seem to think "shoo" was strong enough. She said, "Announcements need to go to the media and cell provider alert system."

The woman and her associate—a trim man named Eduardo Gutiérrez—had arrived in Hinowah with such authority that Tolifson had initially thought she was law, until he recognized their tan

SUV as a commercial rental, not an official vehicle. Hair in a taut ponytail, wearing a forest-green baseball cap, orange-brown Carhartt jacket and black rainproof pants, DRB had announced that she did disaster response for a living and happened to be nearby. She would take the lead now and then stay to assist, when teams from the county and state arrived.

As DRB watched—schoolmarm-like—Tolifson placed a call to the Olechu County Fire Service, which ran the civil defense system. It was making emergency broadcasts about the collapse and potential flooding of the town and he told the dispatcher who answered to add to the warning that no one should take selfies—

"No, no, no," DRB said sharply.

He turned, frowning.

"The minute you say that, they go out and start taking selfies."

How was he supposed to think of that?

"Tell them to say it's too dangerous to approach. They'll be buried alive. That gets people's attention. I've used it before."

It certainly got his. Tolifson was morbidly claustrophobic.

He relayed the information and the OCFS dispatcher said he would get the announcement out, and they disconnected.

"The county responders, state? What's the status? They should be here by now." DRB was nodding to the three tents, set up to house about a dozen emergency personnel.

Tolifson explained that he'd spoken to the county earlier. All available men and women were stacking sandbags around Fort Pleasant, the county seat, which sat at the juncture of the Never Summer and the Little Silver Rivers, around fifteen miles south. As long as the levee hadn't come down all the way, he'd been told, Hinowah would have to wait.

DRB's glare signaled she did not like this news, and he thought: It wasn't *my* decision . . .

The wind then upended a stake and Debi leapt into the task of securing it once more.

"Call them."

"Call them?"

"The head of the county. Who is that?"

"The head?" Tolifson repeated again.

"Of the county," DRB snapped back.

"The whole county?"

She sighed in response.

Tolifson continued, "Prescott Moore. But he's probably pretty busy . . ."

Her look was withering.

"I want to see him."

"See him?" the mayor asked.

"Virtual's fine. Zoom, FaceTime, Teams."

"Well."

"I can do that," Debi said. "Did it just the other day with Sheriff Barrett."

Tolifson waved toward her. At least *he* wouldn't be on record as distracting a very busy county supervisor at a time like this.

In five minutes, Debi had propped her phone up and he and DRB were on Zoom.

"Han." The slightly paunchy, pale man, around fifty years of age, pushed his glasses up his broad nose. His tone was that of an overworked senior government official. "What's up?"

DRB interrupted, identifying herself by name.

A pause from the other end of the call. "Well, hello, miss. Uhm. Have to say it's pretty busy here."

Tolifson said, "Don't doubt it, Pres, but we were—"

DRB fired off, "We need responders here now, in Hinowah. A dozen at least."

"And who *are* you exactly, miss?"

"I run a private disaster response company. I was nearby and came to assist."

"I see. And you've had experience at this sort of thing?"

"You want my creds?" DRB was as exasperated at Moore as she was with the mayor himself. It gave him a bit of comfort to have the abuse spread out some. "It's wasting time. But if you *have* to know, the Jenkins Canyon blaze, the Stoddard Petroleum oil tanker spill, the San Diego Westland's fire, the Harkins Bay bridge collapse . . . and a nuclear incident I can't talk about. And if you were about to ask, I'm not charging for my services. Now, I was saying we need people here immediately. Minimum a dozen. And sandbags. I can start with fifty tons. But I'll need more pretty soon."

A pause. "Well, I can't really help you out. Like I was telling Mayor Tolifson."

"Why not?"

"It's a question of allocation of resources. Hinowah's one of a dozen towns in the county and—"

"Are any of *them* on a collapsing levee?"

Ouch.

"Not yet, no, but Fort Pleasant's between two rivers and it has a population twenty times bigger than Hinowah. We have to go with priorities."

DRB held up her phone screen, on which appeared a box.

TIME ELAPSED FROM INITIAL COLLAPSE: 1 HOUR

She said solemnly, "Hinowah and everybody in it's living on borrowed time. Every minute that goes by means we're that much closer to the whole thing collapsing."

The man's eyes shifted. He didn't seem to care for the dramatics. "You know, Han, I have an interest in helping you. I'll do what I can." He looked up and had another conversation they couldn't hear. "I'm sorry. I should go. I'll be back with better news when I know more."

The screen went dark.

DRB scoffed, tucking away her phone with its countdown clock still visible. He wondered if she'd make it her screen saver. She muttered, "What did he mean 'an interest'?"

"He used to live here," Debi said. She pointed to a two-story house in an overgrown, untended yard not far from the levee. "Moved to Fort Pleasant after his wife passed last year. He still owns the place. Wouldn't want to see it washed away, I'm guessing. So it'd be hard for him to hold off on help."

Tolifson added, "And he owns the biggest mortgage brokerage outfit in town. That's right in the path too."

But Prescott Moore's sad personal history and commercial connection to Hinowah were clearly matters of only marginal interest to DRB. She was focusing now on her associate Ed Gutiérrez, who stood fifty feet away, on the shattered edge of the northern side of Route 13, aiming his phone toward the waterfall levee with an app open. It was measuring "situational erosion"—how fast the stream was eating away at the remaining top and sides of the levee. He looked toward her and shook his head.

"It's dissolving the levee faster than we thought."

Debi was staring at her, the mallet poised motionless in her hand.

DRB said, "We need to evacuate."

"*What?*" Tolifson brushed raindrops from his cheeks.

"Now."

"All of Misfortune Row?" Tolifson was pointing to the low-lying strip of the village beside the spillway.

"No," DRB said, absently scanning the levee once again. "The entire valley. The whole town."

His snort of laughter was the wrong response.

She glared.

"But . . ." Where to start with the challenges? he thought.

"Mayor. This town is one big cereal bowl, just waiting to fill up to the brim."

"But the spillway. It's moving water around the town."

"For now. It won't last, and if the levee goes, it won't mean a thing. I want the town empty ASAP. We need your people going door-to-door. That search team from your fire department, looking for the SUV that went into the river?"

"They haven't found . . ."

"Of course not or we would have heard. Not my point."

B . . .

"Pull the team back, all except one."

"I'm not going to do that. It's a family."

She blinked at the response. "I know it is. You told me. We have to make choices in this line of work. Four people against a thousand. The math is easy."

DRB strode to the nearest tent, relocated the stake Debi Starr was pounding into the ground and said, "That's loam. You want clay. Computers?"

Debi fixed the stake and glanced at TC McGuire's pickup plodding up the hill. Debi nodded. "TC does our computer stuff. That's him now."

McGuire climbed out and pulled on a rubber-protected hat. He was dressed the same as Debi—in a brown Hinowah Public Safety uniform, though his rain shield was a clear poncho. It was a souvenir from a concert, the Kiss Tribute Tour. He was a big man who could glare you down with the best of them. Fearless too—he'd climbed into a burning Jeep to pull a drunk driver out of the wreckage. He was also knowledgeable about the law, and was the frontrunner for the chief position. Apart from himself, of course.

If Tolifson came through this test and took the job, he would be most troubled about passing over McGuire, who he knew was also hoping for the spot. But in Tolifson's opinion McGuire lacked "vision," though he wasn't sure exactly what that meant in the context of being chief of a small town like Hinowah. "Computers?" DRB encouraged in a mutter.

Tolifson told McGuire to hook them up and get online.

"Will do." The officer took two laptops and Verizon jetpacks from the backseat and booted the units. As he did, he glanced at the river and said, "We may have a break. They say the rain's going to let up by noon."

A pair of small binoculars had appeared in DRB's hand and she scanned the west side of the village. She was saying absently to Mc-Guire, "It's not the rain. It's the *melt*. Record snowpack in the mountains from November fourteenth through January twenty-fourth. Record heat in the past four days. And *that's* only going to get worse."

"Oh."

Tolifson was thinking again—evacuate a whole town? How?

His phone hummed. Marissa Fell. "Hey," he said, picturing the woman hunkered down at her desk back in the Public Safety Office.

"Han. Just heard from the Army Corps of Engineers. They're sending a team. One that specializes in flooding."

"Thank God. ETA?"

"They just said soon."

He thanked her and turned to DRB. "Looks like Prescott Moore came through after all. He must've called the army engineers." He found himself eager to defend the local government.

"Who's in charge, the engineers?"

"Uhm, I'll get a name."

He called Marissa Fell back. She couldn't remember the name. "A sergeant. A woman."

He relayed this to DRB, who nodded. "All right. She got the number, I assume."

After posing the question he said to DRB, "Not exactly."

Her reaction was "Ah." The neutral sound nonetheless was thick with displeasure. He guessed it meant, Either you got the number or you didn't. What's the point of hedging?

Debi said, "City's been talking about getting landlines with caller IDs for ages. Just doesn't end up in the budget requests."

DRB said, "Might want to think about that."

Yes, Mother.

McGuire announced he had the computers up and running. DRB ordered, "Map of the area. One that's got topography with elevation. All roads, paved or not. And I'm not talking Google. I want state survey maps."

"I'll get it," McGuire said with a who-the-hell-is-this glance to Tolifson.

DRB's binoculars now scanned Misfortune Row. "South side of the spillway."

McGuire nodded like he got it but he didn't.

"I want to blow it from twenty feet past the levee to that big oak tree there." She was pointing.

"You mean . . ."

"The oak. The big one!"

"No, you mean, 'blow'? With . . . explosives?"

A glance his way. "Whoever did your public works did a crappy job with the levee and a good one with the spillway. But it's not made for this volume. It'll start to overflow. You've got an hour before the water reaches that power substation." She pointed to the large metal shack bristling with wires. "Maybe less. We need power for as long as we can. Communications, medical. I know a demo man but he can't be here in time. It has to happen now. So? You have any dynamite?"

Tolifson was about to say, Not on me, but knew that DRB would not appreciate the slightest hint of humor.

McGuire said, "There's the mine."

"Well, it's private. We can't just use civilians like that." Tolifson was frowning. "Not with explosives. Can we?"

Ed Gutiérrez had joined them. "What mine?"

Tolifson explained that the Redding copper mine was a mile or so west of town. Most such mines were open pits but this was a traditional shaft mine and used explosives to break up the rock at the face, deep underground. Every couple of weeks you could hear the warning whistle then feel the thud beneath your feet.

Apparently DRB believed that one *could* use civilian explosives with no problem. She said, "I want a dozen sticks of dynamite, with a weight strength of at least sixty percent. Make it eighteen sticks. Gelatin would be even better."

Tolifson was pausing. DRB glanced and he lifted his phone. "I'll see."

"And rock drills too. With fresh bits. You'll burn through them fast but tell the owner or manager, whoever you're calling, you'll reimburse him the cost. It won't be much."

Easy for you to say . . .

Tolifson called the mine and got through to Gerard Redding.

The gruff voice: "Hanlon. I heard about the levee. What's going on?"

He explained about the partial collapse and said the rest of it was holding for the time being. But they needed some explosives to divert runoff.

A pause. Redding asked, "From us?"

"From you, from somebody."

"Well, I'm sorry, Han. I don't do that myself. I use an outside company."

"You have dynamite or something called gelatin there?"

"No. When we're blasting, the company comes in, sets the charges and blows it, then leaves. Takes with them what they don't use."

"Thanks. You safe there?"

"I shut down. Got some volunteers sandbagging the perimeter fence. Man, I want to keep water out of the shafts. If it's more'n two or three feet, I can say goodbye to the pump bearings. What're the odds the whole levee'll give?"

"I don't know. It's not looking good."

DRB interrupted bluntly, "Mayor? Explosives."

"No, he doesn't have any."

Another neutral yet damning "Ah." Then: "Does he know where to get some? In the next twenty minutes?"

Tolifson posed the question.

Redding said, "The company we use is in Eureka. I'll give you the name, but it'll be three hours to get here. And you know there're regs. You need permits. Inspections."

"Okay." Tolifson was going to push back if DRB gave him any trouble. He said firmly, "No. Nobody close."

She shrugged. The gesture he took to mean: It's *your* town I'm trying to save.

He thanked the miner again and disconnected the call.

She looked over at the levee, standing with her hands on her hips.

"Let's get that evac underway. Are those searchers—the ones looking for the family—on their way back?"

A reminder that he hadn't yet done anything about it. Stepping away, getting a bit of shelter under a tent, he gave a chill smile and placed a call to Tomas Martinez.

"Got a woman here, runs a disaster response company. She needs your people back to evacuate the town."

"It's that bad?" Martinez asked.

"Lookin' that way. One person can stay on the search for the family and the SUV. But everybody else back."

"One person? Who decided that?"

Tolifson only repeated, "One."

"Okay. I'll keep at it. And send the rest back there."

After disconnecting, Tolifson walked up to DRB, who was looking over the map on the computer. She announced, "For the evac center we should use Hanover College. It's on high ground and has room for the entire village. Those needing shelter, at least. The younger, the healthier can stay in their vehicles for the time being. And it's got an ROTC department, and those kids love to volunteer in these situations. Can you call them and set it up? News like that comes better from locals."

"I guess."

"Now. I've called a sporting-goods chain and got them to deliver a hundred tents."

"They'll just do that?"

"Publicity. You'd be surprised. I'll need you to find vehicles to transport people who don't have cars or can't drive. Any in-patient medical facilities in the town itself?"

"No."

Debi said, "But there are in-home care residents."

"We'll have to make sure they're taken care of. What's your physical civil defense warning system?"

Tolifson said, "Physical?"

"For the residents who aren't online or watching *The Price Is Right*."

Tolifson and McGuire looked at each other. The mayor said, "Only the siren, I think. Right?"

McGuire nodded.

"Which is for what?"

Tolifson said, "Tornadoes. I think the switch's at the fire station. You want to let it rip?"

She blinked. "Well, we hardly want to do *that* now, do we? Send people into their basements when they're facing a flood? Get all town vehicles with loudspeakers. I need the announcement to say, 'Everybody has to get to the college immediately. And tune in to the local station and any online newspapers for details.'"

McGuire asked, "Uhm, what would those details be? I mean, exactly?"

"The orders—and say that, quote 'orders'—are to evacuate to the college and bring only cell phones, chargers, computer if they want, one change of clothes, medicines. That's it. Absolutely no weapons."

Tolifson scoffed. "No guns? This is rural California. That's going to be tough."

"The order," she said firmly, "is—"

"No weapons. Got it. What about food?"

"You really want people debating whether to bring tomato or beef barley soup?"

His face burning, Tolifson said, "No food."

"And get a copy of the evac order to the big mobile service providers so they can send it out on the text alert system."

"'Copy of the order'?" he asked. "There's something I should get official, from the state?"

"No. You don't need legal language."

Looking at the waterfall, smooth, fast, glistening, Debi said, "All my days, never seen anything like this."

DRB said, "Last time the Never Summer was this high was in nineteen thirty-eight. But back then the levee was a foot higher and two wider. Nobody's done anything about the erosion since then."

Damn. The woman sure did her homework, no arguing with that.

A glance his way. "So, that evacuation?"

"The thing is, don't some authorities need to declare an emergency before issuing an order?"

"Exactly right. Under Government Code Section 8630."

Silence.

"Well . . ."

"Oh, that's *you*, Mayor. You're the authority. And in the announcement, make sure to add that under the code anyone who violates the mandatory evacuation order can be fined up to one thousand dollars and imprisoned for six months." As she scanned the levee once more she added, "Be sure to add the prison part. It gets people's attention as good as burial alive."

5.

olter Shaw urged the Winnebago up to eighty.

Windy, yes.

Hydroplane risk, yes.

But this was a straightaway, and he was largely in control.

His mindset presently was similar to that during motocross racing. Those who won stood right on the edge between control and what was called the "yard sale"—where the rider and pieces of the bike lay everywhere.

That speed was for the thrill. Whereas the reason for his speed now was because lives depended on it.

Shaw occasionally wished for a helicopter. But that seemed impractical.

Never squander your resources on efforts that have minimal benefit.

That was what his father called one of his *Crackpot Idea Rules*.

He was ten minutes from his destination, and finally getting a feel for this particular camper.

This one was new, its predecessor having been burnt to the rims by two inconsiderate men who took issue with his involvement in their hunt for several people they wished to murder. It was the third motor home Shaw had lost in the course of his reward-seeking business. Or was it the fourth? He wasn't concentrating on much but the road.

And the job ahead.

Some people in his line of work—admittedly a small body—used the job description "rewardist." One had even described their activity as "rewardism," which Colter Shaw found absurdly pretentious. He kept to the more modest, and perfectly accurate, "reward seeker."

People offered rewards for all sorts of reasons: Prison officials for an escapee (didn't happen often).

Police for criminals they couldn't find (happened *all* the time).

Then private citizens posting rewards for missing children, missing spouses and partners, missing parents. Missing business associates. Missing documents and even the occasional rare object (like the sacred Ashanti holy stool hiding in plain sight in the rec room of the offeror's larcenous business associate).

While Shaw's efforts to find a missing person or thing were sometimes astronomically complicated, the business relationship between Shaw and his clients was simple. A reward is a unilateral contract in the eyes of the law. One individual makes an offer—please find our missing fill-in-the-blank—and another individual, the reward seeker, endeavors to find him or her or it.

At that point there's no contract, no obligation. The person who makes the offer can pull the plug without any expenses being due. And the reward seeker can simply walk away.

But once Shaw delivered, an "acceptance" to the offer occurred and a contract miraculously came into being. It was dues time. Most offerors paid up immediately, though there were sometimes complications. Shaw sometimes had to sue offerors who suddenly decided the missing person (a husband hiding out in Cancún with his lover) wasn't worth the $20K. Being shot at and driven off the road, and losing a $140K camper to fire, to pick one example, for someone else's benefit had to be compensated for.

At other times, he might have been successful but would either drastically reduce the reward or refuse to take it at all, much to the distress of Teddy and Velma Bruin, especially the latter, who would patiently explain that however generous he felt, he should at least collect enough of the reward to cover his outlay. Gasoline and ammunition were expensive, she would point out.

Then there was another type of "reward" job.

When no reward was being offered at all.

And they were just as valid as the others. Because a reward's existence represented what to Shaw was an addictive drug: a problem that no one else could solve. After all, the very fact that a reward was offered meant it was a situation of last resort.

Unsolvable . . .

That was catnip to Colter Shaw.

Having been dubbed "the Restless One" by his family when young, he was true to that moniker; a man who needed challenges. His father's lesson to the children was of physical survival, tricks of staying alive in the wilderness. But in a different, a broader sense, it was challenge that let Shaw survive *emotionally*.

And what challenges would this particular job—another fee-free one—pose?

That was another thing about the reward business.

You never knew . . .

Shaw now eased the camper to a stop on the shoulder of the highway amid rocks and forests and swampland.

He stepped outside into the sheeting rain and surveyed the scene around him.

It was clear immediately, yes, that the enraged Never Summer River was more than powerful enough to have seized a full-size suburban utility vehicle containing four helpless souls, pulled them underwater and swept them downstream hidden from searches by its gray, turbulent surface.

And it had now fallen to him to do what he could to find them.

6.

S haw returned to the camper and grabbed two large black suitcases from a storage area near the kitchen.

As he approached the end of the highway, he opened them.
From one suitcase he took out an orange float, in the shape of a do-
nut, about eighteen inches across, like a child's pool toy. It would
flow with the current, and if the device lodged against a log or rock,
its sensors would shoot out jets of water to free it.

From the other case he removed a VidEye drone. He assembled
it quickly and took out his phone from a pocket. He pulled up an
app and typed in a command. The drone's four motors came silently
to life.

It was a heavy craft, about fifteen pounds, and would remain
fairly stable even in this wind and slashing rain. He turned on its
camera, radar and other sensors and sent it into the air. The craft
rose and hovered patiently like a guest at a front door waiting to be
admitted to a party after ringing twice.

He walked to the edge of the highway and pitched the orange
float into the current. It sped off immediately, as did the drone, ten
feet above. They were connected via a radio link to stay invisibly

tethered as the float followed the current, roughly the same route the missing SUV would have been tugged in.

The drone contained software that could recognize a large metal object like the vehicle, on the surface or submerged. If it came across one, Shaw would get a message with the GPS coordinates and the device would then go on to continue the search. The float dragged a small sea anchor to keep its speed down and give the drone a chance to zigzag across the entire breadth of the river.

Shaw had come up with the system himself and Teddy Bruin, former military, knew a drone technician, who had built the device. It was the second one that Shaw had used on the job. The first, employed to track an escaping bank robber, had been destroyed by a damn impressive—or unbelievably lucky—pistol shot.

Was it guaranteed to spot the vehicle? No. The Never Summer was wide in places, and it wasn't possible for the device to cover every square inch. The radar wasn't as reliable as its eye. He put the odds at twenty percent that it could miss something even as large as an SUV.

Still, in reward seeking when persons were missing and clearly endangered, you did everything you could.

Shaw returned the suitcases to the camper and checked his phone. The float was already fifty feet away and the drone had reported no sightings.

He recalled that the algorithm would also recognize human figures.

Alive or dead.

Climbing from the camper again, he walked down a hill into a park sitting atop a hillside overlooking the town of Hinowah. He had loaded some Wikipedia and website information into a reading-aloud app and listened to it on the drive here. The place was a mining town that dated to the Silver Rush days, the 1840s and '50s, the same era in the same state as the more-famous Gold Rush. While the latter ore was more valuable than the former, the evolutionary template was the same: discovery, astronomical population growth, bloody battles over claims, the genocide of the Indigenous population and then quick departure after the mines were played out, leaving behind environmental scars that persisted to this day.

While some townspeople lived outside the immediate area, the bulk of them made their homes in the village, which nestled in a bowl directly in front of the levee. The majority of houses were wood-framed. The commercial structures too. Very little stone or brick. The older were more solid than the prefab and just-get-it-done structures from the last forty or so years. If the levee collapsed altogether, the village would be hit with a ten- or twelve-foot wall of water, he estimated. Some buildings would survive, he assessed, but others would be splintered to pieces and some carried away altogether. California was not the land of basements, and buildings' foundations did not embrace their ascendant structures tightly.

And the flood would not stop with the initial impact. The Never Summer River was fed by a massive source: a currently dissolving pack after record snowfalls.

A survivalist must be aware of all types of natural disasters, and Shaw had looked into the dangers of floods. The majority of victims drown, of course, but many deaths and injuries occur from blunt force trauma, after being slammed into what's in the flood's path—or being struck by detritus: furniture, parts of buildings, heavy equipment, vehicles. One flood he'd read of hit a lumberyard and set thousands of planks and boards shooting downstream into a village at lethal velocity.

There is nothing compromising about water.

Some techniques allow you to fight—sandbagging or blowing new pathways with explosives—but the best chance of survival is to flee.

Which was clearly the—literal—marching order in Hinowah.

A fire truck and two ambulances were driving slowly through the streets, giving orders to evacuate to a college named Hanover, several miles northwest of town. Scores of vehicles—pickup trucks and SUVs mostly—were migrating in that direction on a two-lane road that rose through forest and rock to a hillside. The route was packed.

He now walked toward three rainswept tents, the flaps snapping sharply in the wind, beside which was a cluster of vehicles. Dominating was a white pickup, on whose door was printed HINOWAH PUBLIC SAFETY. It was topped with a blue and white light bar. Nearby was a camel-brown squad car with the same logo. The other vehicles were off-the-rack SUVs.

Shaw walked up to a large redheaded man wearing a clear plastic rock concert slicker over his brown uniform. His trooper hat was also rain-protected. Shaw could see a name tag on his chest: TC MCGUIRE.

"Officer."

"How can I help you, sir?"

He introduced himself and the men shook hands. "I'm here to help look for the family in the SUV that went into the river."

"Oh, sure, heard somebody was coming." He looked Shaw over. "You law?"

"No. Civilian. I'm a tracker."

"Like with dogs."

"Without dogs."

He shook his head. "We had six people looking for them, went south about two, three klicks, but no sign. Have to tell you, sir. It's a big river, and moving fast."

"I've got a drone looking for them."

"Ah. My boy and me play with one of them some days off. They do searching?"

"Mine does."

A fiftyish man, tall and quite slim and wearing a sturdy yellow fisherman outfit and sports cap, approached. He wore a badge but the younger officer called him "Mayor." Then blinked. "I mean,

Chief." McGuire grinned. "Keep forgetting. Chief, this fellow's the one we heard about. Like with dogs but he doesn't have any. He's got a drone he's using. Can you imagine?"

"Drone. Really." The man glanced up the hill at Shaw's Winnebago and then back, saying, "One thing I need to say up front. I heard you do this for money. Public Safety's a small office and our budget—"

"No charge. I'm volunteering."

"Really? Well, appreciated, sir." He glanced over his shoulder. "Oh, word of warning. See that woman there, coming this way, the blonde. Do *not* cross her or get on her bad side. There'll be hell to pay. I don't use the 'B' word but with her, fits like a glove."

Shaw gave a shrug. "I think I can handle it."

The mayor's expression was priceless when she walked up and threw her arms around him.

"You two know each other?" he whispered.

Shaw said, "We do. She's my kid sister."

7.

In the command post, the canvas sides fluttering, the top aclatter with raindrops, Colter explained to Tolifson and Officer TC McGuire that he had been visiting his mother, along with Dorion and Eduardo Gutiérrez, who'd just finished up at a conference in the Bay Area. His sister had heard of the collapse from her employees and she and her coworker hurried here. Colter did not add that he probably would have come earlier but Dorion didn't learn of the SUV washing into the river until she'd arrived. As soon as she'd heard she'd texted the Need help message.

Tolifson looked like he wanted to make up for the B-word faux pas but couldn't find an entrée. He needn't have worried. Colter wasn't going to dime him out and he—like all the Shaw siblings— was not inclined to hold grudges.

Never waste time on revenge.

As the firefighters and other town employees were spreading the word about evacuation door-to-door, there was a meeting in the command post of the strategists: Hanlon Tolifson, the mayor/police chief, TC McGuire, Colter, Dorion and a short, sturdy blond woman officer. Debi Starr was not young—thirties—but clearly a newcomer to law enforcement. An apprentice, or intern, Colter could tell, from the way Tolifson and McGuire spoke to her—and from her agreeable nodding and scurrying off to do what she'd been assigned.

Efficient assistants ruled the world.

Ed Gutiérrez was presently on the ground, among the crew marshalling the evacuees. His wife and children were flying in from the East Coast tomorrow for some time hiking in the Sierra Nevadas, which were at their most beautiful this time of June, weather allowing. Well, that had been the plan. Now? Who knew?

Dorion said, "We've got the Army Corps of Engineers en route. Standard procedure is sandbagging. Let's hope they're bringing plenty." She nodded to the crest of the levee over which tens of thousands of gallons were pouring every minute.

Colter found it curious that while the feds were sending the army engineers, there were no county or state responders. He asked about it, and Dorion muttered, "California Water Resources responds to floods. One of its main missions. But there's a wrinkle."

Her dark expression matched that of Tolifson's and McGuire's. The mayor explained that those resources had gone exclusively to the city of Fort Pleasant, the Olechu County seat. The supervisor himself, Prescott Moore, had been approached directly, and though he had personal and professional reasons to shift resources to Hinowah, he had declined to do so.

Tolifson said, "They're treating us like the runt of the litter. We're on our own. I don't know why. The river's wider in Fort Pleasant. Flooding'll be gradual. Damage, sure, but no loss of life."

Dorion nodded to the town and then glanced at her brother. "Evac's moving slowly. Lot of remainers." The word for those who because of obstinance, denial, laziness or political leaning were not inclined to do what the authorities told them to. Convincing people to leave their homes was one of the most difficult tasks of disaster response, Dorion had told Colter. Barring a massive wall of wildfire flames speeding toward your house at twenty miles per hour, when flight was the only option, owners vastly preferred to stay and fight to protect their homes, however improbable the odds of success. Family photographs and souvenirs and heirlooms? People just don't want to give them up. She had once asked Colter to guess the number one thing in a house that kept people from evacuation in a forest fire.

When he said he had no idea, she'd answered, "Fish. You can get your dogs and cats into a car, you can grab a hamster cage. But aquariums you have to leave behind."

Looking thoughtful, Tolifson sighed and said, "The family? In the Suburban. Hate to say it but, I mean, wouldn't you think they'd be, you know, gone by now?"

"No," Colter said. "Not at all."

"But . . ." The mayor cast a glance toward the river.

"Late-model cars and SUVs are all sealed pretty well for sound and temperature. What's the riverbed?"

"Dirt," Starr said.

"Good. Now it's mud. A natural sealant. A six-thousand-pound vehicle, with passengers, would settle into the bed fast and that'd seal most of the bottom vents and intakes. There'll still be water coming in. No vehicle's watertight. But the air pressure and window and door seals will keep most of the air inside. If they have anything else they can seal it with, that'd be a plus."

"How long until they run out of air?" the mayor asked.

"The issue isn't running out of air," Colter said. "It's running out of *oxygen*."

"Aren't they the same?" Tolifson asked.

"No. Air is a mix of nitrogen, oxygen, CO_2, argon, neon and hydrogen. It's the *proportion* of those gases that's critical. What we breathe is mostly nitrogen and 21 percent oxygen. CO_2 is only 0.03 to 0.05 percent. Exhaled air has a big jump in carbon dioxide—to about 4 percent. The oxygen in a closed space decreases while the carbon dioxide goes up. Suffocation isn't lack of air. It's poisoning by CO_2. When it hits 8 to 10 percent, you die."

Starr was frowning. "How much time?"

Colter said, "I looked it up—a Chevy Suburban has about a hundred and fifty cubic feet of cargo space. With the passenger compartment, call it another fifty. So two hundred. The time-to-limit-level of CO_2—that 8 or so percent—is around six or seven minutes per cubic foot—for one person. There are four people inside?"

"That's what Louis thought."

"Assume small children—the younger the better—so three hours plus for the whole family. There are ways to extend that a bit. Wet carpet will dissolve some CO_2. If you're trapped, you can pee on the rugs. That helps. Though only temporarily. In this SUV the carpet's sure to be plenty wet already."

"If we can't get to them in time," Tolifson said grimly, "I guess at least they'll go to sleep peacefully."

"That's only true if you pump the air out of a space altogether, both oxygen and carbon dioxide. CO_2 poisoning is not a good way to die. At 4 percent CO_2, you start to get restless, have headaches, hallucinate—and the survival mechanism is to get the body out of there. So you start to have panic attacks. Bad ones. Then thrashing. By 6 percent you're gagging uncontrollably."

"Lord, I had no idea." Starr whispered this.

Colter was looking at a map of the area on a large laptop, running off a generator. He located their position and studied the topography. "I'll head south along Thirteen, so I'll be closer to the drone if there's a hit."

He explained that for speed he would take the dirt bike. His backpack carried basic rescue equipment, including a glass-break tool, supplemental oxygen and respirators, hose, a diamond-tipped saw and a drill, first aid gear.

In his thoughts was a fact that went unstated. He also had six body bags in the camper.

Which he would not take with him.

Dorion said, "The town council president—he's also the fire chief—is downstream, searching."

Tolifson nodded. "Tomas Martinez." He added, "Ms. Shaw pulled back the rest of the search party. Left him. By himself."

The chill in his voice was obvious.

Dorion had no reaction, but said to McGuire, "If you could get back on evac detail. And remember to threaten to arrest anybody who doesn't comply."

Tolifson said, "Uhm, Ms. Shaw, I don't know that we can. Isn't it just a misdemeanor?"

"You can arrest them, sure," Colter said. He was the one Shaw child who had considered law school. He could answer Tolifson's question, though, not for that reason but because he himself had been arrested for misdemeanors on several occasions. It went with the reward-seeking territory.

Dorion pointed to the Public Safety building. "You've got a prisoner transport van. I can see it."

Starr said, "We only use it to take DUIs to County. And meth cookers, once in a blue moon."

Dorion said, "Just throw a couple of the more arrogant ones inside and make sure people see it. Word'll spread fast. Then release 'em."

Tolifson said, "Can't they sue for wrongful arrest?"

Debi Starr said, "In this podcast I was listening to, somebody tried that, and the judge laughed the stinkers out of court."

McGuire climbed into his pickup, three-pointed and descended quickly into town on the tight gravel switchback.

Colter said, "Dorion mentioned there was a witness who saw the SUV."

"Louis Bell. That's his pickup stuck at the other end."

"Did he say if the Suburban was upside down or not?"

"Upside down, he thought, but it all happened fast. He just glanced in the mirror and saw it go in. He had to pay attention. There was a car in front of him."

"What car?"

"We don't know anything about it, except a blue sports car, woman driving. Driver made it off the levee and just kept going. She wanted to get the hell out of Dodge."

Colter asked, "You have no idea who the family is or about the tag on the SUV?"

Starr shook her head. "All we know is it's not local. All the white Suburbans registered here're accounted for."

This was unfortunate. If they had a name he could contact other family members about the incident—and learn if they had any particular skills that might help in survival.

Colter consulted his phone. The drone and float were now several miles downstream. Dorion, scanning the evac progress, didn't bother to glance his way. The two had worked together from time to time and they tended not to pepper their conversation with unnecessary queries like "See anything?" Or "You're okay?" On the theory that if the other had seen something or was not okay, there'd be an announcement.

A flash of dark motion took their attention. Another trough opened at the crest of the levee and more water gushed downward, adding to the flood in the spillway, and sending a brown tidal wave over a large retention pond.

A huge flash filled the western portion of the town, near the spillway, then a crack like a gunshot, as the substation exploded.

"Lord," Tolifson muttered.

Dorion's voice was dark. "Wanted to blow the south side of the spillway but the copper mine here didn't have any gel. Hate it when comms go down."

At that moment, Shaw's phone gave a trill. He looked down. A small red dot had appeared on video feed from the drone. "May have a hit." The others turned quickly.

"About three miles downstream." He looked at the screen. "Could be a vehicle roof just under the surface."

He sprinted up the hill to the camper, pulled his backpack from beside the front seat and, running to the back, pulled the Yamaha bike off the rack. He climbed on and fired up the engine. He didn't bother with the U-shaped switchback road that offered a gradual descent into town. He went straight down the north hillside into the village and toward the spillway bridge, feeling a faint chill down his back as above him the levee disgorged another massive wad of mud. It slid near but not into his path. The flow of water increased once more.

Then he was climbing up the opposite hill, catching air and landing on smooth asphalt.

Soon, he was heading south at seventy miles an hour, weaving through an obstacle course of branches and patches of leaves that would be slick as ice.

8.

Dorion and the six employees of Shaw Incident Services, LLC, regularly engaged in studying natural disasters to better understand the behavior of fire, oil, wind, rain, snow, metal fatigue, electricity, toxic waste and myriad other substances and devices—all of which posed an infinite and, sometimes, insidiously clever threat to human beings.

She felt that they were like the criminal perps her brother sometimes pursued: individuals with motivations that some might see as evil but was hardly that at all (murderers, after all, are the heroes of their own stories).

Water was one of these creatures too.

As she looked over the fragile town of Hinowah, California, she was thinking of the Boxing Day 2004 earthquake and tsunami, whose epicenter was in Indonesia, and the 2011 Tohoku earthquake and tsunami in Japan. Those terrible disasters left huge death tolls: nearly 250K dead in the first, and 20K in the second, with the vast majority dead from the water, not the collapsing buildings from the earthquakes.

Floods are particularly tricky. While the water set in motion by an earthquake can travel at five hundred miles per hour under the surface in a deep ocean, it is barely noticeable on top; those on ships sense only a slight swell. When it reaches shore in shallow water, the speed slows to twenty to thirty miles an hour, still far faster than a person can run, and like a car in low gear, the force behind it has the power to destroy buildings meant to withstand hurricanes.

In Hinowah, the wall of water would not reach the hundred-and-twenty-five-foot waves in Tohoku, but it would have a similar speed and the same force.

You could not ride out a flood of this sort. Escape was the only sure method to save lives.

Dorion recalled the story of ten-year-old Tilly Smith, visiting Thailand with her parents from the UK in 2004. The girl noticed the sudden recession of the resort beach water, and she announced to her parents that a tsunami was coming. She had learned in school how the phenomenon often sucks water from a beach before the deadly waves slam into the land. Tilly simply would not be ignored and talked her parents into warning the resort. They closed the beach and got everyone off—minutes before a tsunami did indeed hit. It was one of the few beaches in Thailand where no deaths occurred during that storm. She was credited for saving more than a hundred lives.

Dorion was amused to think that here, today, she herself would have to be as persistent as a ten-year-old girl.

She, Tolifson and Debi Starr stood at the command post, looking down at the evacuation effort.

The mayor sighed. "The minute the storm hit, I heard the Never Summer was rising. I should've closed the damn highway."

"Don't beat yourself up," she said, her tone soft. "The volume of the snowpack melt surprised everybody. It's a once-in-a-lifetime occurrence. I know this part of the country. And you've never had to deal with anything like this. You just happened to be at the wrong place at the wrong time, Mayor." She smiled.

His face flushed, and she guessed he was regretting his first impression of her.

Which was not unwarranted. She could be a real bitch when it came to saving lives.

Just then two black SUVs with U.S. government plates appeared on the south side of the levee. They pulled onto the shoulder. Two men in olive-drab military uniforms got out, each a driver of his respective vehicle. They walked to the end of the asphalt and surveyed the scene. Pointing, conversing, nodding.

Dorion's phone hummed. A number she didn't recognize.

"Hello?"

"Dorion Shaw?"

"Yes. Who's this?"

"Sergeant Tamara Olsen, Army Corps of Engineers. I got this number from Police Chief Tolifson."

"I'm looking at you now. From the hillside across the valley."

A pause. "The tents. Got it."

She saw a trim woman also in an OD uniform climb out of the passenger seat of the first SUV and walk around to the front of the vehicle and gaze at the levee. She said a few words to the two men, then returned to the call. "My corporals say the integrity of the levee's good for now. I'll drive over."

Olsen returned to her vehicle and the Ford Expedition drove down the south hillside, crossed the bridge over the spillway and made its way through town. Then it wound up the switchback road to the city park that was the command post.

She climbed out. The woman with standout red hair had intense, focused green eyes and a firm handshake as she greeted Dorion first, then Tolifson. A brief nod at Debi Starr.

In a firm, low voice, she said, "I'm not promising anything, but we've got a battle plan. And I think we're going to save your town."

9.

Olsen set up shop in the command post, opening a computer of her own—and powering up a jetpack. She was happy, though, to take advantage of the town's generator.

Her phone hummed and she took a call. "Be a sec," she whispered to Dorion and Tolifson and stepped aside.

Dorion regarded her own phone for texts. Nothing from Colter yet. Eduardo Gutiérrez reported that he had recruited twelve townspeople to root out residents from their homes. Per her instructions, he had given each of them her phone number with instructions to text with regular updates about the evacuation. The sweep was starting at the most dangerous area—directly under the levee, in front of the broad, flooding retention pond—and proceeding west.

She was troubled to learn that several scores of remainers were refusing to budge, ignoring or even firing snide comments toward the evac team. There was a bar near the levee, occupied even now, in this early hour, and people were making the monumentally bad choice to steel themselves up for disaster, rather than simply avoiding it.

TC McGuire's text said he had threatened arrest, and a number of the patrons laughed at him.

She texted back:

Arrest the loudest. Use cuffs.

She judged he was not a smiley-face kind of guy. But the words "With Pleasure" were an equivalent.

Dorion eyed the levee and the soldiers across the valley on the south side of shattered Route 13. She knew a little about the Corps of Engineers, and had worked with them on several previous disasters. Their authority was far more extensive than most people thought. They supported troops in combat by building bridges and battlements and the like, but that was only a minor portion of their job. They also built and maintained all of the U.S. military installations around the world, and managed most of the country's inland waterways and dams. The Corps was also one of the biggest providers of energy in the country, and the nation's largest source of outdoor recreation, operating thousands of parks.

Given its jurisdiction over waterways, one of its specialties was flood control. A law from the 1930s gave them primacy over the subject. And she was encouraged that they were here. Their presence was far better than county responders who might be hardworking and diligent but who would have little, if any, expertise in water disasters.

Olsen disconnected and offered a smile to Dorion. "You're civilian, I understand. Disaster response."

"That's right. Normally I'd have a full team on a situation like this. But it's not an official job. I was nearby on a personal trip and our monitoring system picked up the incident. I got an alert from my office back home."

"She's doing it for free," Tolifson said. "Bless her."

Dorion was amused; there was a faintly uncertain element to his voice as if he wanted to remind her that that was the agreement.

Olsen lifted an impressed eyebrow. She would undoubtedly have had plenty of experience with contractors in the disaster relief business who milked the situation for every penny they could.

"Any injuries?"

Debi Starr said grimly, "Probably. An SUV went into the river." The woman had appeared behind Dorion. She kept forgetting about the police officer, who seemed timid to the point of being invisible. Dorion thought, entirely unfairly, of "bring your child to work" days—when her own daughters would sit in an unoccupied office, organizing papers to be copied and untangling comms cords.

Dorion said, "We had a lead on the SUV about fifteen minutes ago. Downstream. Somebody's gone to check it out."

Tolifson said, "It's a family inside."

"Oh. That's rough."

It was.

But irrelevant.

As she gazed over the levee, Olsen glowered. "Don't care how rare floods are around here. Whoever built the levee should've done a better job. They could've spent another week and added six extra feet. If so, we wouldn't be here. But they never talk to us until afterward, do they?"

When Tolifson took a call, Olsen said to Dorion, "Let's walk."

The women climbed the incline to the north side of Route 13, where Dorion's brother's camper sat. Olsen examined the waterfall coursing over the levee. "I've ordered sand and bags. We'll need a lot of them. Starting there." She pointed to the far end of the levee, where the pickup truck sat. "I'll need a half dozen volunteers for the bagging detail."

"Hate to pull them off evac but I agree."

"How's that going? Evacuation?" She looked over the line of traffic.

"Too many remainers. They see a pretty waterfall. Let's take selfies."

"Always the way, isn't it?" She placed a call and said, "ETA of the sand? . . . No. Sooner. Now . . . And Hydroseal? Okay . . . Yeah, the three of us. But there's a civilian disaster response person here. She knows what she's about."

Dorion was the more extroverted of the siblings, the first to question, the first to push back when she had doubts, even when she was young. Oddly, though, compliments unsettled her.

After disconnecting, Olsen said, "My corporals'll supervise the sandbag op and place the bags themselves. I don't want civilians at risk." She glanced at Dorion once more. "So you do what I do, only you get paid a lot more."

"But you can retire after twenty years."

A laugh. "Retire? And then what? Play pickleball and bake cupcakes on a YouTube channel?"

So true . . .

The sergeant added, "But doesn't matter who writes your paycheck, right? It's a pretty good gig."

"None better." Dorion was tempted to tell the woman about the survival training of the Shaw children's youth. About their father too. There was certainly something of a drill sergeant in Ashton Shaw. Maybe the noncom standing beside her had had a similar upbringing. But that was a conversation for another time.

"What's that you mentioned, Hydroseal?" Dorion asked.

"Amazing stuff. Underwater-drying sealant. Like the undercoat car dealers're always trying to sell you. Only *this* works. We'll pour it along the interior face of the levee. That'll slow the erosion a fair amount."

"I know underwater polymers work on wood and concrete." A nod toward the levee. "But dirt too?"

"The way we apply it, yes."

"That's good to know. I'll have to look into it."

"Give me your email and I can get you the details."

Dorion recited her contact information and the officer put it into her phone. "I'll get one of my men underwater to check out the weakest spots and mark them. Where're the evacuees going?"

"A college on high ground about a mile or so from here. I've got Safeway delivering water and a dozen fast-food places doing their thing. Sporting-goods chains providing tents and a porta-potty outfit bringing in two dozen. A mobile hospital too, and I've alerted all the local medical ops they may be seeing patients and better prepare for blunt trauma, electrical shock and water in lungs. Eye injuries too."

One of the biggest problems in flooding was damage to eyes and mucus membranes from chemical substances released from service stations, car repair shops and other industrial operations in the flood's path.

"A portable morgue too. Refrigerated."

Olsen was nodding. "You are one on-top-of-it woman. Usually I fly solo in disasters. Good to have a partner." She gave another warm smile.

They returned to Tolifson, who was still on his phone, and Debi Starr, looking over the map. The officer glanced up and she said, "Mr. Martinez called in. He got to Fort Pleasant. He didn't see any sign of the SUV or the family. He's turning around and going north to meet Mr. Shaw."

Dorion squinted into the wind. "We need a half dozen volunteers for sandbag duty. Working with Sergeant Olsen here. Could you track some down?"

"You bet." Starr pulled out her phone. "Got some in mind. They'll hop to. Some fellows owe me for being on the lenient side with tickets." She frowned. "Never DUI, mind you. But you're twelve miles per hour over the limit, I'll knock it down to five." She began to place a call. "Or make it a warning."

Olsen looked over at Dorion. "Mr. Shaw? Your husband?"

"My brother."

"He works for your company too?"

"No."

"But he's in a related line of work?" the sergeant asked.

"You could say that."

Olsen looked at her wristwatch, a big model, bulky. She sighed. "They have to be dead by now, wouldn't you think? The family?"

"I don't know. Colter gave us a formula about air in a vehicle underwater."

She paused, processing this. "But . . . won't it fill up?"

"You'd think so," Dorion said, her face grim.

"But your brother doesn't believe that?"

"No. He doesn't think that way. To him, they're still alive."

10.

Luck was not a word George Garvey would use under the circumstances.

But now that the initial shock from the roller-coaster ride when the levee collapsed had faded, he was feeling slightly differently.

No one had been badly injured.

Kimberly's nail polish had spilled onto her face, just missing an eye. Trav's phone and tablet had whacked him on the head. He had jammed his thumb. And one of Sonja's knitting needles had jabbed her side but not broken skin; he could only imagine the injury that might have caused—and how ill prepared they were to do anything about the wound. There was probably a first aid kit somewhere in the SUV but it would be as useless as they all were: gauze, Bactine and Band-Aids.

Luck . . .

And while the engine had stopped, the battery was still functioning. He didn't see how this could be the case but Trav—the science person—said something about the lack of salt content and how fresh water was a very bad conductor of electricity. They had the flashers on and one of them would take turns beeping the horn—Trav had the duty at the moment, leaning past his father from the driver's-side second-row seat.

And then there was the air situation. After the Chevy had righted itself, it had bobbed, not sinking right away. With the electricity still working, George had rolled down his window, planning for the family to escape that way. But they were riding too low for him to risk opening it farther. Still they had a good five or six minutes of fresh air flowing into the SUV before he'd had to roll the window up once more, and they sank below the surface.

There would have to be people looking for them, he believed. He was not far behind the pickup truck and it was likely, if he'd taken even a glance into the rearview mirror, the driver would have seen them tumble off the road. Of course, he might not have survived but assuming he did, he'd have called in about the Suburban. There'd been another car too—a blue sports car in front of *him*, and between the two surely someone had gotten a glimpse of the big white SUV.

Luck . . .

But what was the luckiest of all would seem like a disaster to anyone else. The vehicle was sunk deep in mud, which provided a nearly airtight seal. There was only minor seepage. Thank you, General Motors.

"Can't we," Trav asked, "like, break a window and swim out?" He loved action movies, where breaking glass and gunshots and improbable escapes often substituted for plot.

George told his son, "No, even if we could break one, we'd flood before we could get out. We need to keep the windows up. Don't worry—they'll be looking for us."

Sonja had tried all four cell phones and both iPads. No signal.

Hardly a surprise.

She set them on the dash. Travis again tried the more primitive form of communication.

Honk.

Maybe someone was nearby and—

Suddenly, startling them all, Kim began to scream. She was thrashing in her seat.

She accidentally walloped her brother on the nose.

"Ow, bitch."

"Travis," Sonja warned and she spun toward the backseat and said to her daughter, "Honey, no! It's okay. We'll be all right."

The screaming continued.

"Mom, make her stop!" Travis was crying now.

In his profession George often saw such emotion. But his role then was conciliatory. He was kind, he was gentle, he was persuasive.

He presented the same George Garvey to the children, day in, day out.

And conflicts worked out. Harmony returned.

But now. This was different. He had only one thought in his mind. That they survive.

And screaming away the little oxygen they had was not acceptable.

He spun around, grabbed his daughter by the shoulders and raged, "Stop it now!" He shook her hard.

She gasped, her eyes wide. "Daddy!"

"Now!"

Sonja and Travis stared in shock.

This broke his heart. And, if they survived, it was possible that he'd just created an irreparable rift between them.

But a parent's role wasn't to coddle. It was to raise, and raise right.

He would rather she hate him and live than love him and not.

"You're hurting me!" Another scream.

"You understand? Stop it!"

"Honey . . ." Sonja was speaking to him now. She touched his arm. He didn't brush it away but he stiffened and she removed her fingers quickly.

"Understand?" he growled, struggling to keep from bawling like his son.

And he controlled the urge. Because his family needed him. George had thought that a husband/father's role was to be a bread-winner, and—along with coaching and attending plays and the like—that was all he was put on earth to do.

But those missions seemed trivial, even silly.

Now, he had to become somebody else. A despotic king.

And with a sharp sudden breath, his daughter controlled the panic. She continued to cry, but softly. She nodded.

He released her quivering shoulders.

"Thank you."

She ignored him and hugged herself.

He glanced toward Sonja, who regarded him with an undefinable expression, and he had no desire to try to decipher it.

"Now, I need you all to move as little as possible. And take shallow breaths. It'll feel weird but you have to." He looked throughout the interior of the vehicle, the dome light was on. Did that use oxygen? He didn't see how. And darkness would only lead to panic.

Examining the windows and doors, the dash. The seal was pretty good, but water was trickling in.

"We need something to seal us up better. Do we have any ideas?"

Having a task, even one as minor as this, seemed to calm everyone down.

Sonja spoke first. "Don't you have that stuff in the trunk for tires? If there's a flat you can spray it in to fix the leak? It probably has some goo inside."

"Maybe." He sent Travis to the back to see if he could open the trunk and get the Fix-a-Flat.

"Nail polish," Sonja said.

Would that work?

He remembered the horn.

Honk . . .

"Try it, Kim."

She glowered and remained still for a moment. Then picked up a bottle from the floor with shaking hands, opened it and applied a streak to a window seam.

Yes! It took a moment to dry but it did stop some of the trickling.

"Good! How many bottles do we have, you stylish ladies?"

Sonja smiled. Kim, of course, did not.

Six, as it turned out.

The three each took two and used the brush to slather on the sweet-smelling liquid. The scent reminded him of the happier moments—forever ago, it seemed—when he smelled the same aroma as they drove blissfully along Route 13, oblivious as to what was about to happen.

Who's Bob Dylan?

Eerily, blood red was the most common selection of polish they had brought.

"I can't get the trunk open!" Travis was calling.

George looked back toward Travis. In the Suburban—an SUV—there was a trunk of sorts, where the jack and other tools were kept, but it was not meant to be opened with the liftgate down. He called the boy back and handed him one of the fingernail polishes.

Travis's hands too shook as he opened the bottle. He was still crying.

"It'll be all right," George said. "I know they'll be looking for us. The man in the pickup? We had our lights on. He would've seen us."

Not adding that just because they didn't see him slide off the levee didn't mean he hadn't fallen in a few seconds after they went over.

And drowned minutes after that.

The polish bottles were nearly all depleted and the interior of the vehicle took on a psychedelic look—a thought that struck George hard; he realized that he was lightheaded from the lack of oxygen and seemed to be slipping into and out of a dreamlike state.

Honk.

The muffled sound seemed pathetic, probably audible no more than five or six feet away.

He had a ridiculous thought that every time he honked somehow a bubble was released and it rose to the surface and blared away for the world to hear.

Crazy. A scene from a Road Runner cartoon.

Is this what depleting oxygen did to you?

Apparently so.

"Good job," he said to Kim.

She didn't glare. It was worse. She didn't even acknowledge him.

He noted that Sonja was manically rubbing her fingers together.

"Just . . ." Her eyes were wide. She whispered, "I don't know. Feel weird."

He assessed and realized that he did too, in addition to the sense of tripping.

Another symptom apparently, anxiety—being fidgety in the extreme.

Honk.

It was then that another smell joined that of the polish.

No . . . He closed his eyes in despair.

He found Sonja looking at him.

The scent was of gasoline.

He quickly killed the light. They would just have to risk the panic that might ensue.

"Dad!" Travis called, his voice cracking.

"What are you doing?" Kim raged. It was clear that his words of reconciliation had had no effect.

"The gasoline. We can't afford a spark."

"Lights don't fucking spark," the girl shot back.

No language corrections now.

"We're not taking any chances."

There'd be no more honking either.

"There's nothing more we can do. Breathe—"

"Shallow, yeah, yeah, yeah," their daughter said.

"Kim!" Sonja said sharply.

Odd not seeing anyone's faces during an emotional exchange.

Sonja said, "Should we tell a story?"

No," George said. He felt an urge to gag, but controlled it.

More symptoms of the lack of oxygen, he guessed.

"Just sit back, relax."

"And enjoy the flight," Sonja said. "What the flight attendants tell you before you take off. Like what else is there to do?"

George gave a faint laugh, and squeezed his wife's hand. He had no idea if the children smiled. They gave no verbal reaction.

Was that the last time the two of them would laugh together?

He reached for the seat control to recline it, so he could lie back some.

But then thought: Spark.

The gasoline fumes were stronger now. Would *they* kill the family before the lack of oxygen? They had to be poisonous.

Again a fierce burst of panic.

Travis gagged, then it stopped.

"Son."

"That smell."

Sit back . . .

In the silence he closed his eyes, then opened them. The blackness was actually more intense with his eyes open. When they were shut, phantom light bursts wandered in his vision, which was oddly comforting.

Relax . . .

He had a thought.

So this is what it's like to be in a coffin.

He didn't share those words with anyone, of course, but he allowed himself a faint manic smile.

And enjoy the flight . . .

11.

Shaw was driving quickly, but not motocross fast.

A decision dictated by the slick surface of Route 13, south of Hinowah.

Tomas Martinez, HFD chief and town council chairman, was ten miles south and heading north toward him, on the way to the geotagged spot; Shaw's drone and float had spotted something.

The camera offered only a vague image of a discoloration in the water, which he hoped might be the roof of a vehicle otherwise embraced by the mud of the riverbed. The radar, similarly, showed nothing beyond a shape.

Had the family escaped? Were they currently hiking through the woods or even along the shoulder of 13 somewhere for him soon to see, drenched and exhausted, waving him down?

Martinez had discovered nothing on his search so far; he had had to rely on his eyes and ears and much of the Never Summer was hidden by trees and brambles and its course created a constant rush of noise that would obscure all but the loudest shouts.

And what of his calculation about oxygen?

From what he'd seen on the drone images, the vehicle might have been sealed in mud up to a point, but above that, water would leak in.

Had they drowned or suffocated?

Both would be hard ways to die, but suffocation was slower and accompanied by the agony of CO_2 poisoning.

He put those thoughts aside and continued the drive. He was one mile out from the geotagged spot.

He reflected on Dorion's decision to pull off the other searchers and rely on Shaw's drone-floatie system, alongside Martinez's physical search.

Shaw himself might have gone with a larger search party, but she made the call that an evacuation was more important.

He couldn't argue.

Like rewards-seeking, disaster response required difficult decisions.

Besides, having seized the operation from the out-of-his-league mayor/chief, it was now her show.

He took a call from Martinez, tapping the hands-free bud to answer.

"Yes?"

"Mr. Shaw? I'm about seven miles south of where you had that hit on your drone. I can be there in about ten minutes. Are you there yet?"

"About two minutes."

"Does it look like a vehicle from the camera?"

"Likely, but impossible to tell for sure."

"Just to let you know, I've searched all the way down to where the Never Summer meets the Little Silver at Fort Pleasant. There's flooding but it's a broad watershed, only four or five feet deep, even now. Definitely no vehicles."

Moving the needle a few degrees closer to the likelihood that the ambiguous square on Shaw's video feed was indeed the family's SUV.

"Almost there. I'll call you."

He drove over a bridge and braked fast; he was close to the flashing red dot, to his left, fifty feet through the dense woods, the ground swampy. Under the bridge, however, ran a shallow stream from the forest into the Never Summer. He skidded to the right, nosing down a hill, and stopped on the bank of the stream. He could hike along the bank to the geotagged spot and avoid the tangle of the plants. He killed the engine, dropped the bike and sprinted east toward the river.

He thought of the rescue gear in his backpack. The diamond-edged circular saw, diamond-tipped drill, steel glass-break tool, hoses, a scuba pony tank holding nineteen cubic feet of air, enough to keep someone alive for twenty, thirty minutes. There were regulators too—mouthpieces. But that would require cutting a larger hole in the roof and the water would pour in, drowning them. It would have to be a hole the size of the tube—a half inch.

Hurrying through rushes and muscling aside branches, negotiating the slippery rocks as best he could, he made his way to the river.

Yes, the glint was of metal, exposed briefly as the waves dropped, then vanishing again underneath.

He forced his way through an infuriating tangle of brush and reeds and saplings and clabbered onto the shore.

Breathing hard, Shaw looked down.

He sighed.

Why on earth would someone go to the trouble to toss away a refrigerator into a river?

Why not go the extra distance and dispose of it in the county dump?

And not waste his time.

He texted Tomas Martinez, copying Dorion.

False alarm. I'm continuing south after the drone. Should meet you soon.

He received back two texts.

Thomas's was a simple:

K

His sister's read:

Got the txt. Army engineers here, sandbagging starting soon.
Bringing in sealant to shore up levee as soon as weather's clear
enough to fly choppers.

Now it was Shaw who gave the single letter acknowledgment.

He started back up the gulley, under the bridge, getting a whiff of the mold and fungus that were coating the old stones. Then to the Yamaha.

Shaw was no more than four feet from the bike when he heard two things.

One was the snap of a twig behind him.

The other was that nearly imperceptible sound that someone makes drawing a breath when they're about to swing a deadly weapon—say, a pipe or baseball bat—your way.

12.

Dorion Shaw felt an urge to salute, though, of course, she did not. Both the large corporal—L. WILLIAMS, on the chest—and the considerably smaller and paler one—identified as R. MCPHERSON—stood at attention in front of a dump truck that had just off-loaded a huge mound of sand. Strewn here too was a sloppy pile of burlap bags.

She told them, "I've got a half dozen people on their way up here now."

"Thank you, ma'am," Williams said in a baritone.

Again she felt the urge to lift a flattened hand to her temple, although her only experience with the military was watching movies like *Saving Private Ryan* and *Crimson Tide* with William and wine, after the girls had gone to bed.

Damn, they had good posture. She was always after her daughters to sit up straight; today's youth was developing what she called a "texting slump."

The men turned back to the supplies and began laying out the bags for the fillers of what must have been fifty tons of sand.

This sounds like a lot but people are always surprised when they order a ton of topsoil or sand or gravel. The pile in the driveway isn't nearly as big as they'd expected. Mother Nature is heavyset.

This rain-darkened and pocked mountain of sand, though, dominated the southern end of broken Route 13.

The state and county had marginalized Hinowah but the feds had not. Usually the opposite was true. Dorion was impressed that the engineers had gotten the supplies here so quickly. She suspected this was due to the blunt touch of Tamara Olsen, the definition of a no-nonsense woman.

Sandbags prepared in a factory—and presumably within the military—came filled and stitched on both ends. But these bags were empty and sealed only on the bottom; the townspeople would fill them and use zip ties at the top. Corporal Williams had made a few now—so he could illustrate how it should be done. They looked like bags of loot from a stagecoach robbery.

Dorion thanked them both and asked about the arrival of the Hydroseal.

Williams answered crisply, "I don't know, ma'am. Sergeant Olsen would have that information."

The vehicles of the "volunteers" Debi Starr had recruited began to arrive from town. Two men climbed out of the first one, a dually pickup. One of the them, in a crew cut and of military retirement age, fifties, actually *did* salute Williams, who mirrored the response. Dorion believed there was a wistful look in the townsman's eye, hinting at cherished memories. Another vehicle arrived, an SUV with two more men, followed by a battered sedan with a man and woman.

The rain and wind persisted and it was clear that these people, accustomed to arid climes, had not experienced these types of conditions. They wore multiple jackets, ski parkas and one man a Burberry raincoat, as if he'd been interrupted on his commute to his job as bank vice president.

Soon an assembly line was going, and it broke down according to natural order. The slighter men and the woman would fill the bags and zip-tie them closed, while the beefier carted them to the edge of the asphalt, where Williams and McPherson would place them in the water.

The goal was to build a wall to slow the erosion of the top and keep it intact until the Hydroseal arrived. It seemed to Dorion that the flow was too powerful and the cascading water would simply launch the sandbags down the town-side of the levee. But she would let Tamara Olsen make that call.

The sergeant's SUV arrived and she climbed out. She offered another fast smile to Dorion, then walked to the edge of the highway and looked down. She called over her shoulder, "Make the bags four wide, Corporals."

"Yes, Sergeant," McPherson called.

The sandbag wall grew slowly, and so far it was holding. To Dorion it seemed that the roiling water that struck it was more energetic than on the rest of the banks, as if it was angry that its path of least resistance—down into the town of Hinowah—was being thwarted by human interference.

She drove down the steep road along the south side of the valley, over the spillway bridge and into the center of the village. She parked near Ed Gutiérrez's Explorer, climbed out and found the man just exiting a large frame house. A family of four followed, with gym bags and backpacks. Each of them—husband and wife and two elementary-school-age daughters—gave nervous glances at the levee and then climbed into their SUV and fled west, to the two-lane road that would take them to the college and safety—a route already badly congested.

"Sandbagging?" Gutiérrez asked.

"Moving along."

The most cowboy of her employees—lean, denim-wearing, easy-moving—Gutiérrez offered, "had some luck. Somebody posted on a town watch website that God is going to bring down the levee for the miners' sinful ways during the Silver Rush. Guess it was kind of a bawdy place. Somebody else posted that it's divine retribution for stealing Indigenous land. Which set off a troll war online. But whatever your evil deed of choice, divine wrath is motivating people to leave. Their ancestors' bad behavior was a long time ago, sure, but there's no expiration date on sin."

"Add that to our evac playbook. Next brush fire, maybe we should start some rumors that God's pissed off. Where do you need me?"

He pointed to a neighborhood. "Nobody's been there yet."

She returned to her SUV and drove to the blocks he'd indicated.

She slowed at a cluster of residents standing on a corner, talking, four women and two men, early to late middle age. Most held coffee mugs or cardboard cups. They must have appreciated the risk—their faces were troubled—but they weren't moving.

"You have to leave," she shouted. "Hanover College! Now!"

Two of the half dozen looked her way and walked off, to grab their belongings and leave, Dorion hoped. The others remained where they were.

She called, "You can be fined or arrested!"

A woman in her forties snapped, "The government has no right to tell us what to do."

Other than telling us to pay taxes, register cars, get a driver's license, not to commit crimes, build according to code, how we can buy alcohol and guns . . .

But she didn't engage, only drove on to urge more cooperative souls to save themselves.

13.

As he rolled to the ground, out of the path of the short shovel, a host of his father's rules came to Colter Shaw's mind.

Never strike with your fist if there's a risk of hitting bone; use your palm, elbows and knees.

Never back yourself into a corner.

And of course the most important rule of them all:

Never fight unless you have no other choice.

His present situation was a prime example of the last rule. Not fighting wasn't an option; for some reason the assailant—big and ruddy and bearded, with soupy hazel eyes—was clearly dedicated to stoving in Shaw's skull. The man's facial and head hair were red and unkempt. He was dressed in a quilted camo outdoors vest and a green plaid shirt, which was stretched taut at the belly by a roll of flesh. Jeans and ankle boots made up the rest of the recluse/mountain man look.

"What are you doing?" Shaw asked impatiently.

Another lunge.

Shaw dodged. He foresaw a possible move from the man, but chose not to engage. It would have been risky, given the man's bear-like bulk and strength.

The assailant muttered: "Son of a bitch."

Another chance—a takedown tackle. But again Shaw waited.

Never act prematurely when you're being attacked. Assess.

He did this now, noting that while the man might have had other weapons, none were visible—and therefore could not be easily accessed.

Then, scanning the ground. No vines or rocks or branches to trip over.

And no one else seemed to be present.

Never assume assailants are acting alone.

Part of assessment in combat was always to determine why one was being attacked. That could decide the response. But as to this question: no damn idea. He called again. "Who are you? What's this about?"

"Shut up, asshole."

All right. Time to move things along. There was a family to save.

Another swing, and now Shaw dodged but remained in position, and parried with an open palm to the ear—a very painful blow that can deafen if done right.

The man grunted and winced. "Oh, you're going to pay for that," he said, and moved in again.

Shaw feinted forward, then when the tool swung, he dodged back and grabbed the handle. Bear—a good nickname, why not?— was expecting him to try to pull it away and leaned back ready for a tug-of-war. But Shaw did the opposite, pushing it hard in the man's direction, throwing him completely off balance.

Bear had to turn to stay upright, which gave Shaw a chance to plant his sole behind the man's knee, pushing hard. Bear went down on his back, but before Shaw could move in and get his wrist in a come-along—or, safer and more satisfying, simply break a bone or two—he rolled away surprisingly quickly. And leapt to his feet. He was in good shape for a man in his forties and overweight.

They circled for a moment.

Shaw tried again. Sounding almost comically reasonable, he gauged. "I'm serious. You going to tell me?"

Bear leered. This probably had some effect on tipsy or intimidated opponents. But to Shaw it revealed both that the man had no strategy and that he was growing uneasy, pulling out his psychological warfare chops, meager as they were.

The man tossed the shovel far away—played for drama, and a very stupid idea.

Never give up a weapon.

Then he came in fast. Shaw took a glancing blow to the cheek, the man's knuckles landing near a scar left by a far more competent combatant.

The slug gave him the chance to clutch his face and groan, bending over. The script called for an "Oh, shit," which he muttered convincingly, and he spat, as if he'd lost a tooth. And when the overconfident man charged at him, Shaw stood and delivered an open-palm blow to his unprotected nose. He felt a snap and stepped back from the gusher of blood. The curiously high-pitched howl was loud.

Snorting and wiping blood, enraged, Bear got ready for another charge.

The poor man didn't have the benefit of Ashton Shaw's rule:

Never fight from anger.

Shaw was looking around the area. The shovel was out of sight but he noted a branch about two inches in diameter, the size of a good cudgel, protruding from a tangle of brush.

He looked back to Bear, who noticed it too.

A beat during which neither man moved.

Suddenly Shaw took a few steps toward the branch. But the attacker lunged forward, driving Shaw back, and he leapt to where the weapon awaited.

He grabbed it.

But it didn't move; its other end was stuck in the brush—as Shaw had noticed, and he'd decided to use its immobility as part of his tactic.

Bear had expected to rip it free, but pulling tugged his body forward, off balance.

Shaw's father never taught the children any Asian martial arts. It took too much time to master—and was not always helpful in street fights, since opponents rarely play by the same rules. So he instructed them in grappling—a form of wrestling. (In the latter sport, Shaw himself nearly went to the Olympics. He scored points mostly from his lightning takedowns, though he was known to be a talented "rider" too, controlling the opponent and keeping him from escaping, which also added to your score.)

Shaw now moved in fast and caught him again in the back of his knee. This time he had leverage and the blow was harder.

Bear teetered—and Shaw executed a classic takedown, slamming the man onto his back. He rolled him over and gripped his right wrist in a come-along hold.

Bear struggled to escape but found himself trapped. This was a new experience, Shaw could tell. Bear most likely picked opponents who under weighed him and were easily intimidated.

Weight, of course, was only one factor in hand-to-hand combat. Leverage and surprise—and a working knowledge of human anatomy—counted more. For him to try to move now would result in broken bones.

"You're dead," Bear said.

How many times had Shaw heard that expression or a variation of it?

And yet here he still was.

On occasion, like now, Shaw was tempted to share that observation. Or quip: "You had your chance. Didn't work." But a rule he himself had coined came to mind.

Never banter.

A careful frisk revealed no weapons.

But curiously Bear also didn't have on him a wallet or any identification. Money, yes—five hundred or so in rumpled bills—but nothing else. Not even car keys, and this was a place where no one was without a vehicle. Odd too: Shaw smelled aftershave that he happened to recognize as expensive, not of the drugstore variety.

"Now. You're going to tell me. What's this all about?"

A little more pressure.

And a resulting groan. "You going to fucking torture me?" A scowl. As if Shaw were the bad guy.

"I don't have time for this," Shaw said in a matter-of-fact voice. "If you don't talk to me, yes, I will break the wrist—and that's a long recovery time."

Yet more pressure.

"Ah, all right. You're trespassing."

Was he joking? "Twenty-five feet in woods, on land that's not posted? I want the truth."

"It's private property. And we don't want you here. Trespassing's a crime."

"So is assault with a deadly weapon and battery. I need a better—"

Shaw's phone dinged.

Bear took this as a welcome distraction he might use to escape. But Shaw instinctively tightened his grip. "Settle."

"Ah," he groaned in pain. "You're in so much trouble . . ."

Fishing out his phone. Reviewing the screen.

The drone had made another sighting. About two miles south.

He looked down at his captive.

Shaw was without zip ties. He often carried them but hadn't thought they'd be necessary on a search-and-rescue job.

In his pocket was his locking knife. He might have sliced the man's jeans into strips and tied him to a tree for Tolifson and TC McGuire. But this was no time to play cop.

He would have to let the matter go. He released his grip and lifted his phone to take Bear's picture, but realizing what was coming, the man leapt to his feet and sprinted away fast.

Was he in a facial recognition criminal database?

That too was curious.

Even if he was not, Shaw's private eye in D.C., Mack McKenzie, had access to some of the best facial rec databases in the world, and she could get him an answer within an hour. But the missing family was his priority and he let Bear vanish.

Shaw fired up the bike and shot back onto Route 13.

In just a few minutes he was at the site where the red dot told him the nimble algorithm had identified what might be an SUV in the water.

The visual image suggested the vehicle was just underwater, like the refrigerator he'd spotted.

He leaned forward and twisted the throttle for the final sprint, glancing into the river at his left.

There!

He could see it from the road.

Sixty seconds later, backpack resting heavy on his right shoulder, he was climbing down the hill toward a faint shiny patch in the river about five feet from shore. The Never Summer was much wider here and the current was moving more slowly.

He strode to the edge.

Paused and stared down.

And found himself shaking his head.

As he wondered how *two* household appliances—this one a Kenmore dryer—had managed to end up in the waterway.

A white pickup approached and parked. Climbing out was a man with short dark hair and mustache. He wore a navy windbreaker and orange safety vest emblazoned with the letters *HFD*.

Shaw climbed to meet him.

"Mr. Shaw?"

A nod.

"Tomas Martinez." He seemed to note there was nothing urgent about Shaw's behavior and lifted an eyebrow.

"Appliances."

Martinez's face fell. A sigh. "Where do you think they are, sir?"

"Stuck somewhere the drone couldn't see it. A cave maybe. I saw a lot of them."

"That's right, and some are definitely deep enough to hide a car, even an SUV. Old mines too." He sighed again. "And if they got washed into one of them, we'll never find 'em."

Shaw typed commands to untether the drone from the float, and sent the UAV back north, toward Hinowah, to continue searching in case it had missed the vehicle on the way down. It would eventually land beside the Winnebago—or ditch in the river if the batteries didn't hold.

Martinez asked, "I'm wondering if we should move from rescue to recovery at this point. I mean it's been a few hours."

The pivot point where you admitted the objects of your search were dead and the mission became one of finding their bodies.

"No," Colter Shaw said with hesitation. "Not yet."

14.

The aftermath of a mass disaster can be heartbreaking.

Dorion Shaw had witnessed firsthand the hollow gazes and tear-soaked faces of families as they stared at the ash-filled foundation pits that had once been their homes, and the repositories—naively considered impregnable—of mementos that represented sometimes centuries of family history.

She recalled one family sifting through flattened ruins searching for the tiniest object to salvage—only to find that the devastation was so great on the street that they'd been searching the remains of a *neighbor's* house.

Dorion Shaw absolutely did not want the citizens of Hinowah to face that fate, but her priority was to make certain they were safe from far worse: the deaths and injuries themselves.

She was going door-to-door, delivering the warning in her stern voice. William and the girls had learned that her "mean look" was mostly inadvertent—or a bluff—but to those not in the know it could be quite intimidating. Mary Dove had said once that her children could make up the Police Force of Shaw. Russell would be SWAT and intelligence.

Colter the detective.

And Dorion would be the no-nonsense traffic cop.

Sir, I do not believe you only had two beers. Please step out of the car . . .

She had learned much about building and infrastructure in her years on the job, and she recognized an irony in Hinowah that was true in many places. If the levee were to go, the Never Summer tidal wave would most likely destroy the newer houses. Thinner studs and economical Sheetrock meant vulnerability. But the older structures had been built according to the conventions of the day: your house was to be passed down for generations—hundreds of years—and that meant tamarack and cedar and oak construction. Some houses in Hinowah were log cabins, but the settlers here, like most in the 1800s, preferred their wood hewn into flat planks, which were stronger in support and lasted longer than the raw, round timber used by early pioneers.

Over the next half hour, she dislodged two dozen families and individuals and, with a metaphoric butt-swat, sent them on their way to Hanover College.

She walked past a transformer station, a twin to the one that had blown up earlier; Dorion had texted or emailed everyone who was or might be a responder about the dangers of electricity in a flood.

These rules had been learned long before she thought of starting a disaster response company. In the Shaw household years ago, Ashton had taught the children about the dangers of the invisible force.

Never touch an appliance in a flooded area, even the outer housing.

Never stand in water that has risen above the level of electrical outlets.

Never trust that there are ground-fault circuit interrupters, as there might still be live outlets and wires not connected to them.

Never approach downed power lines.

So much to safeguard against . . .

She passed a house that had been pointed out to her earlier, the darkened residence of the county supervisor. What was his name again? It was distinguished . . . That's right: Prescott Moore. It was in disrepair and the yard even more badly overgrown than it had seemed from the command post. She recalled the man had moved to Fort Pleasant, presumably—and understandably—because of his wife's death last year. Why had he kept this house, though?

She paused, noting that there appeared to be fresh footprints leading from the sidewalk around to a side door, then back again. She walked up to the front and peered in. It was a mess, almost as if it had been ransacked, but more likely abandoned quickly by the last surviving occupant.

There was no answer when she knocked loudly so she turned back to the sidewalk.

Noting the flickering light from a TV inside the next house she came to, a single-family home squatting on a lot not much bigger than the structure's footprint, she approached and rang the bell.

A young mother—her two toddler sons were in front of the TV, watching Pixar—greeted her with a cautious smile that vanished when she saw Dorion's name on a lanyard. It was hardly official, just her laminated company ID with a picture, but the card, along with Dorion's demeanor, suggested stern authority.

The woman blinked in shock at the news.

"Oh, those voices, the loudspeaker. I couldn't understand them, then the car or truck was past. I thought it might be an election thing."

Dorion told her to leave immediately—either to friends or family outside of the valley or to the college.

"It's that bad?"

"Yes."

"My God . . ." She ducked her head out and looked at the waterfall that the levee had become. The gray sky glinted in the surface of the water as it flowed relentlessly over the side. "My parents're in Salinas but I'm not driving in this stuff." A nod at the stormy sky. "I'll go to the college."

"Okay, get there now. And when you leave, lock up."

The woman frowned. "We don't really bother with that. It's Nowhere."

"It's what?"

"Nowhere. That's the nickname for Hinowah. It's a nice place. Nobody'd break in."

"Lock up anyway . . ."

"You mean, people would actually rob somebody? A time like this?"

Yes, people actually would. Dorion told her so.

"Good Lord."

Marshaling the children up, the young woman said over her shoulder, "You're going house to house?"

"That's right."

"Two doors up, to the right, that big house? It's Mrs. Petaluma. She's Indian. I mean Native American. I don't think her English is real good. Never says a word. Might be deaf and mute."

Hadn't one of the local officers mentioned the woman?

"I'll check on her. Take only a change of clothes, medicine, computer, phone and charger. That's all."

"But . . ." The woman's stricken face looked at a wedding photo on the wall. Her husband was in uniform.

Dorion said, "It's okay. You can take the picture."

Then she was outside and headed up the street. She suddenly got it. Hinowah. Hi-*nowah*.

Nowhere.

She looked around her at the town. Modest, rugged, rustic, scuffed.

Dorion allowed herself a rare moment of the sentimentality that was virtually unheard of in the Shaw household. She thought:

But it's somewhere to me.

And I'm doing whatever I can to save those who call it home.

Mrs. Petaluma's house was an old hewn-log structure, much like the others surrounding it, though it was more ornate. And there were two stories. Most of the others in downtown were one.

The style was what Dorion's mother, Mary Dove, called "gaudy gingerbread." Wooden scalloping and frills and ornate frames surrounded the door and windows. The house itself was dark red, the trim yellow and green. The porch sported a number of hanging flowerpots in bloom. They rocked in the wind. Some beer barrels, cut in half, rested open side up and were filled with dirt. Flowers grew in these too. This was the largest lot in this portion of town—about a half acre—and the entire backyard was devoted to a garden. Now, June, some of her spring sowing was showing results as rows of green sprouted up, ankle high.

The Compound featured a similar garden, though bigger; it provided vegetative sustenance for the family all year long. Their father was insistent they stay true to the spirit of his favorite book, *Self-Reliance* by Ralph Waldo Emerson. The Shaws lived primarily off the land and streams. Pike, trout, bass for fish. Venison from the fields and forest—the term usually was taken to refer to deer, but in fact it meant the meat of any game: deer, elk, moose, caribou, antelope, pronghorn, for instance. They had a small cornfield and Ashton ground meal for bread that he himself baked. Dorion recalled the first time she ate a piece, covered with unsalted butter, declaring it the best thing she had ever tasted. And since then, few delicacies had come close.

Dorion approached the woman's house and rang the bell, which sounded inside, suggesting the young neighbor's thinking that the woman might be hearing-impaired was wrong, although some systems for the hard of hearing include a light as well as a bell to announce visitors.

A moment later a slight woman in her mid-sixties opened the door and looked at Dorion with an expression that was, she decided, unfathomable. Not hostile, not curious, not suspicious, though hardly welcoming.

"Mrs. Petaluma?" Dorion looked past her at the unlit interior of the house, filled with pictures of family and largely Native memorabilia and artwork, much of it cloth.

There was Indigenous blood in the Shaws. Mary Dove's ancestry traced back to the Ohlone, who once inhabited California from San Francisco down to the Monterey Peninsula. Their mother was fluent and had passed a few words on to the children but Dorion had forgotten every one of them.

She said, "I'm working with Mayor Tolifson, the police and fire department. The levee's in danger of collapsing and we're evacuating the town to Hanover College. On Route Ninety-four, west of town. Do you know it? We need you to get there now. Is that your truck outside?"

Still no word.

The woman leaned forward and looked toward the waterfall of the levee without a hint of reaction. Then she eased back.

So language and hearing were not issues.

"I need you to leave now. I can help you pack." She stepped inside.

Mrs. Petaluma drew back her apron revealing an old-time pistol in the waistband of her skirt. It was a cap-and-ball model, a muzzleloader. The gun didn't use brass shells, but round balls were squeezed into each cylinder from the front and sat atop a charge of gunpowder.

A Colt Dragoon, Dorion was pretty sure. A classic.

And extremely powerful.

A moment of silence.

The woman simply stared.

Dorion said, "You have a nice day now."

And returned to the sidewalk to continue her role as town crier.

15.

nside their coffin, black as black can get.

Nearly silent, except for the faintest sound of streaming water above the car.

And a drip from somewhere.

The panic was starting. The fucking CO_2 was filling George's lungs. His skin crawled and his muscles were cramping from not getting enough of the magic O.

Hands shaking and sweating. Gagging.

He gazed down and stared at the pill bottle on the floor. Empty.

He had wanted to make sure there was enough for Sonja and the children. To take them away from the horrors they were experiencing.

But that meant no pills for him.

He was—he reflected with giddy irony—keenly drowsy. Meaning his thoughts arose and then petered out, following his consciousness somewhere, who knew where. But when he was alert, it was like a knife in his heart.

If only they had left the rest stop a bit sooner—that was on him. He'd wanted to use the toilet, even though he probably didn't need to. He could have waited.

If Kim had not debated the extra sixty seconds about what additions to get to her flavored coffee at Starbucks.

If he'd set the alarm to awaken five minutes earlier or later.

They would not have been on the damn levee at just that moment. Kim had sighed right before it happened.

6:14 . . .

But why even bother to . . .

He lost his thought.

Ah.

Wait. It came back: But why even bother to speculate. Historians called it counterfactual. A fancy name for alternative history. If the Treaty of Versailles had been more generous to the Germans . . .

Where was this going?

Fate had led them here, and fate had killed them all.

And why was that so appalling, even remarkable?

In every compelling story—real or fictional—there has to be death, or its possible appearance. It's what keeps us humans forging ahead to survive in real life and keeps readers turning pages, praying that the author will not betray them and snatch away a beloved character.

And if death does arrive, it engenders anger and resolve and motivation to find who is responsible and, in the end, cobble together some justice.

Or an opportunity to reflect on what the deceased's life was all about.

George Garvey could write a book about death.

He kissed the motionless head of his wife and those of his two children, noting—just beyond the scent of gasoline and body odor and nail polish the distinctive odor of each. Different variations in soaps, shampoos and hair spray. He could differentiate them in the dark from these alone, though of course, he knew this from their positions where they lay, in stillness, in their coffin.

To Kim he thought, I'm so sorry, honey. I said what I said because I love you.

And he told himself: Well, get to it.

George clambered over the second row of seats—the third was folded down to make the storage area in the rear larger.

Boxes, clothes, food, a six-pack. He pulled off a can, cracked the tab and gulped down the warm Coors.

Why not?

Then he found what he was looking for.

Sonja's dry cleaning, two blouses and her green dress with a sexy slit up the side.

It was not the garments he had any interest in, though, but the plastic wrap.

This is not a toy . . .

What would the sensation be like after he wrapped it around his head?

Hell, probably not a lot different than right now, he decided. He was half-suffocated anyway.

He took another sip of beer and said to his family, "I love you. Goodbye."

Words, of course, that they could not hear.

16.

Colter Shaw was returning to Hinowah with a new mission.

He sped toward the south end of Route 13, which was bustling with a sandbag-filling party.

A woman noncommissioned officer from the army engineers and two corporals were supervising a workforce of about eight townspeople. He'd never heard of putting sandbags on top of a fragile levee but that was hardly his area of expertise, and the fact was, it seemed to be having some effect.

Most of the eyes turned to him as he skidded off the asphalt and down the hill on the south side of the valley, using the road to the village proper. He could have negotiated the hill by himself, off-road, but the only way across the torrent-filled spillway was the bridge.

Once over he picked his way through the soupy mess that the south side of town—Misfortune Row—was becoming, thanks to the overflowing spillway. It had been hours since the levee's collapse, and the erosion at the top had turned the spigot up higher. The waterfall was far stronger—and louder—than when he'd left town. He continued north until he came to the hill on which the command post was situated.

Here, he didn't bother with the switchback and gunned the engine to plow straight up the grass and over the crest. He got more speed than planned and needed to brake fast, so he skidded to a sideways hockey stop, just shy of the main tent.

Debi Starr, the young officer, watched and nodded with approval. She looked as if she spent her days in knitting clubs and the kitchen, not in the garage tinkering with a Harley, but Colter had learned long ago not to make baseless assumptions.

In addition to Starr, Mayor/Chief Han Tolifson was present. He sat at a table, looking exhausted as he typed, two fingers at a time, on his laptop keyboard.

He said a perfunctory, "No leads to the family, I assume."

"No."

Starr's face tightened at this.

Tolifson said, "Isn't looking good."

This was true and there was no reason to dispute, or elaborate on, the comment.

But he did have something to say.

It was about his new mission.

"My drone's been up and down the river all the way to Fort Pleasant. Tomas Martinez and I have covered it too. Nothing."

The rain persisted but was less insistent and the wind less fierce. The drumming on the canvas ceiling was softer.

Tolifson asked, "Where's the drone now?"

"In the drink. Almost made it back, but the batteries went."

"I'm sorry. Must've been expensive."

It was, but hardly worth even thinking about. "One last thing I want to try—the caves on the east side of the Never Summer. I think that's the only place left to search."

"Some are big, sure," Tolifson said. "But an SUV?"

"I still want to check."

Never equate a long shot with a no-shot.

"How would you do it, sir?" Tolifson asked.

"Boat. Pontoon. Double outboards ideally."

"I guess it might work. But ask our resident fishergirl. Debi, those caves?"

Starr said, "I'd go with Daddy and my little sister and we'd canoe into some of them, after trout and pike. But inside, about four feet, the clearance shrinks to nothing. Any vehicle, especially a Suburban, you'd see from here. Easy."

So.

That took care of his mission.

Rescue vs. recovery . . .

An SUV approached. Dorion's rented Nissan Pathfinder.

She climbed out and joined the others in the tent. "I saw you come back. Didn't hear anything, so . . . bad news?"

"*No* news. Couldn't find it. But, yeah, that's bad."

A wave of anger swept through him.

Could he have done anything differently?

Nothing occurred.

Which didn't take away the tragedy of a loss like this—and its related burn of failure on his part.

Unreasonable? Maybe. But it always happened when he wasn't successful at a reward job.

Starr asked Dorion, "How's the evac going?"

"So-so. Still dozens of remainers. We're threatening jail time and fines. We get laughed at. Or threatened back with Dragoons."

"Oh, you met Mrs. Petaluma." Tolifson looked at Colter. "She's a town institution. And I guarantee she didn't say a word to you."

"No, just showed me the grip of her weapon."

Colter said absently, "Nice handgun. Accurate—for a black powder piece."

Starr pointed out her property to Colter. "It's the one there, with the big garden."

Tolifson said, "Her ancestors were some of the original people here. Early eighteen hundreds."

Starr said, "The nation—they prefer that to 'tribe,' I found out. They did fine when the miners were here—the Silver Rush hit this part of the state a little after the Gold Rush. But when the ore dried up, the miners moved on; the Native people had to sell off all their land and move away. That property of hers is all that's left. Out of more than a thousand acres."

Tolifson offered, "Wonder if her attitude is: If I lose the ancestral home and land to a flood, what's the point of going on?"

Colter felt a tight grip in his heart at these words. He was a survivalist and the son of a survivalist. You might risk your life at various activities from professions to sport, but you never gave up the game voluntarily.

He said, "We could pick her up and drag her."

Starr said, "Hm. That'd be illegal. And there *is* that pistol thing . . ."

Motion from the levee caught Colter's eye.

The streaming water had done what he'd suspected it would, knocked several sandbags off the crest and sent them tumbling toward the spillway.

Then his eyes took in some of the garbage and rubble at the base, sitting in front of a wide retaining pond.

He felt a blow, as if Bear had landed a gut punch.

Colter turned to Tolifson. "The man in the pickup, Louis Bell? He said the family's SUV went into the river, right?"

His voice was urgent and the mayor frowned. "That's right."

"Did he see it happen through the rear window, looking back, or in the mirror?"

"Mirror, he said."

"So it seemed to him like the SUV went to the left, but it might've gone *right*." He nodded to the base of the levee. "I think they're trapped in the retaining pond, not the river."

17.

Colter Shaw surveyed the mud- and water-filled pond, which resembled a huge murky swimming pool, twenty-five by forty feet.

He then scanned the town and noted a fire department pumper moving through the streets of Hinowah, slowly, making the PA announcement about the evacuation.

"Get him on the radio for me," he called to Tolifson.

"Who?"

"The fire truck!"

The mayor looked around. Starr handed him the Motorola, and he hit a button.

"Buddy, you there?"

A moment later came a clattering response. "Han. Yeah. Go ahead. I'm prying 'em out. Just, a lot aren't leaving."

Colter reached his hand out and took the unit.

"Buddy, this is Colter Shaw. Your tank full?"

"My—?"

"The water in your fire truck," Colter snapped.

"Oh, yessir. Who exactly are—"

"Get over to the base of the levee. Now! The retaining pond."

"Well, the thing is, the levee . . . the pond's right underneath and it's looking worse. I—"

"If you're not going to drive it, I will."

A beat of a moment: "Who are you, sir?"

A bellow from Tolifson, "For God's sake, Buddy, get the fucking pumper where he says."

"Well, Han . . . never heard you talk like—"

"Now!"

"All right. Geez."

Colter saw the big vehicle turn.

While Tolifson, Officer Starr and Dorion ran to their vehicles, Colter did his motocross run again, straight down the hill.

He nearly wiped out in the "puddle" at the bottom; it was a foot deep. But he yanked back on the bars and lifted the front wheel just before it slammed into the far side, and he went over. He drove thirty or forty miles per hour until the mud slowed him and he had to stop. He didn't need to set the Yamaha down. It got stuck straight up in the goo.

He jogged to the retaining pond. Bubbles? Impossible to tell. Water continued to cascade from the levee into the pond and then on into the spillway.

With a groan of the powerful diesels, the fire truck approached. A truck of this sort would weigh twenty thousand to thirty thousand pounds. The engines were massive.

Behind it were Dorion's SUV and the police department's pickup, driven by Tolifson. Debi Starr was in the passenger seat next to him.

Colter gestured the muddy pumper to a spot where there was the most access to the pond.

Buddy, a balding and rangy forty-year-old in overalls, climbed from the cab.

Colter asked, "What's in your tank?"

"Eight hundred gallons."

"And capacity?"

A hesitation.

Tolifson muttered, "Tell him, Buddy. The man's in charge. My Lord. It's not trade secrets."

"A thousand gallons per minute."

"Your attack line?"

"One and a half inches."

"So you can pump about six minutes' worth."

Buddy frowned in curiosity. "Well, that's right. Say, you fire service?"

Colter said nothing about the fact their father's survival education was, to put it simply, comprehensive. He said, "Nozzle the line and bring it with you."

"Whatever you say, boss." His attitude had flipped, fast, one-eighty. The man fitted a brass nozzle to the metal end of the canvas attack line and dragged it from the spool, jogging toward the retention pond.

Colter called to Tolifson and said, "Have the team up there drop a dozen sandbags and get them over here."

Without questioning why, Tolifson fired up his pickup and, with Starr in the vehicle, sped to the south side of the levee. A moment later, the larger of the corporals and a massive townsman were flinging the bags over the side. They cleared the spillway and landed with a sucking thud in the mud.

Colter looked to the top of the levee, noting where Louis Bell's pickup truck was still stuck. The family's Suburban had been behind it, and like the pickup and the blue sports car, the driver of the SUV would have accelerated to try to beat the collapsing roadway behind it. Using the pickup as a reference point, he estimated where the family's SUV would have ended up.

He pointed to a spot in the center of the pond.

"Buddy," Colter called to the fireman. "What you're going to do is shoot into the water there." He pointed. "And zigzag. We're looking for an SUV."

Buddy blinked. "The family! They're here, not the river! Never thought of that! Yessir."

The truck arrived with the bags and Tolifson got out and dropped the gate on the bed.

Colter called, "Keep them there for now."

Tolifson nodded.

To Buddy, Colter said, "I'll rev and hit the supply."

"Yessir." The fireman gripped the hose and walked closer to the pond. He aimed toward the area indicated.

Colter returned to the fire engine and climbed into the cab. He pulled the hand control for the engine throttle and pushed the revs up. The engine growled impatiently. Climbing out, Colter shouted, "Ready?"

"Go!" was Buddy's response.

Colter yanked the chrome supply lever on the side of the boxy red vehicle and almost instantly the hose went rigid. Given where they were and what was happening, he couldn't help but think: The power of water.

"Everybody!" he called. "Look for metal or glass!"

The stream blasted through the several inches of water on the surface.

Colter stared at the swath it cut.

Buddy was making good progress, firing the stream into the soup everywhere that Colter had expected the SUV to be.

And where it was not.

Everyone stared at the stream, looking for any hint of the vehicle. Nothing.

The mayor walked up to Colter and as both men looked at the pond, Tolifson said, "I get the rearview mirror thing, but what gave you the idea they might be here in the first place?"

Colter pointed to a sign, entangled in the metal posts, concrete footers and cable from a guard fence that had once protected traffic from falling into the river.

NO FISHING FROM LEVEE

It took the man a moment. Then he exhaled a sour laugh and shook his head. "Goddamn. The sign was on the *river* side of the road. If it ended up here, the SUV might've come this way too. I saw that very sign hours ago. And didn't think a thing of it."

"Losing pressure," Buddy called.

Colter glanced at the gauge. Twenty seconds of water remained.

And just then Debi Starr cried, "There!"

It was definitely the roof of a vehicle.

As the nozzle sputtered to silence and the line went limp, Buddy called, "What do we do now?"

Colter gestured back to the fire truck. "I need a ladder."

18.

The Hinowah Fire Department vehicle did not feature a power ladder but rather two extendable manual ones. Buddy and Tolifson grabbed one and pulled it to its full length—about thirty feet. They placed it where Colter indicated: from the levee side of the mudslide to the shore of the retention pond, making a bridge about a foot above the flowing surface.

He called, "Need a chain saw!"

"I'll get it." Buddy ran to the truck. To Dorion and Tolifson, Colter shouted, "Sandbags."

He hefted one himself and walked over the bouncing ladder to the vehicle and stepped into the water onto the Suburban's roof, careful not to slip. A fall would mean a difficult extraction from the mud.

Or, if one went in headfirst, a very unpleasant four- or five-minute death.

He set the bag in the center of the roof and gestured for the others. Dorion, Tolifson and Starr formed a bucket brigade and passed the heavy sandbags to Colter, who placed them two deep on the roof, making a rectangle with an interior about three feet square. This was to keep the water from flooding into the Chevy when the hole was cut. Without the bags to stanch the flow, water would pour in and fill the van in seconds.

Colter called, "Saw!"

Dorion, Starr and Tolifson backed off the ladder—and Buddy made his way to the improvised sandbag well Colter had created.

Colter said, "Do the honors. Keep it shallow."

Buddy fired up the tool, which clattered to life instantly. It was old, but Colter could see it had been perfectly maintained and the chain was new. He gave the fire department credit, and guessed that while the police rarely saw much felonious action, the fire service was kept pretty busy, even in a quiet town like Hinowah.

The man dropped the blade into the water, sending up a fierce spray—and filling the area with the huge sound of grinding. The teeth were sharp and dug readily into the sheet metal of the Chevy's roof. Buddy was careful to cut no deeper than three or four inches in depth.

The instant of the first slice, the water drained inside, but the bags were doing an adequate job of keeping the rest of the pond at bay.

Soon he'd cut a U and was working on the final edge. Colter gestured to the saw and Buddy let it idle then gave it to him, while the fireman himself gripped the impromptu hatch in his gloved hands. "Ready!"

Colter revved the saw and completed the final cut as the firefighter lifted away the metal rectangle and pitched it into the pond.

Shutting off the saw, Colter rested it on one of the sandbags and pulled his tactical flashlight out of a rear pocket and clicked it on.

He wondered: What're we going to find?

Dropping to his knees, he was hit by the scent of body odor and gasoline. A fuel tank leak! Had the fumes combined with the lack of oxygen killed them? There was no sign of life.

Directly beneath him were the empty front seats. He aimed at the second row.

There reclined a woman in her late thirties and two children, a teen girl and a boy a few years younger.

None of them were moving.

Their eyes were closed.

Colter dropped into the space and set his flashlight on the dashboard, pointed toward the rear of the vehicle. He turned to the three occupants.

He gripped the woman's collar and pulled her forward.

With a gasp she startled awake, and gazed at him groggily.

Her movement jostled the daughter and she too stirred.

Colter noted something on the floor. An empty bottle of over-the-counter decongestant, and he understood that the family had cleverly tried to minimize their oxygen use by "overdosing" themselves to sleep.

Smart.

Though it would be a hell of a job to get the three largely unresponsive passengers out of the flooding vehicle fast.

And where was the fourth person Louis Bell had reported seeing?

No time to consider that further. Just get them all out.

"Who . . . ?" The woman's eyes were unfocused, and her voice slurred.

"Let's go," Colter said and muscled the woman into a sitting position. "You're going to be okay."

"No . . . children . . . first . . ."

Colter didn't object. He helped the daughter sit and then pulled her to the front seat and, careful to avoid cutting her on the jagged edges, lifted her up to Buddy.

The girl was more or less conscious but the boy, smaller framed, was still out. Colter wondered how many pills they'd each taken.

"My . . ." The woman frowned and lost her train of thought.

As the boy was passed through the freezing stream of water, he began to revive and gasped at the freezing bath. "Mom . . ."

"I'll . . . be . . . there . . ." Her words stumbled out before stopping. She blinked fiercely against the flashlight beam. They would have spent the last few hours in the dark. He helped her into the front seat and then handed her up to Buddy, far stronger than his slim build suggested. He simply plucked her from the front seat.

"My husband . . . George. My . . ."

She muttered some more words, but by then she was outside.

Colter shone his light into the back, playing the beam over the interior, noting that they had sealed the door and window seams with fingernail polish.

This too was smart.

Improvised survival techniques.

The water inside was now up to the bottoms of the seats, slowly rising. Toys and luggage and clothes and boxes and food and cups floated everywhere. In the rear was a man lying on his back, feet pointed upward.

Colter crawled closer. Was he unconscious?

Or dead?

"George!"

He couldn't get close enough to the man's head or chest to see if he was breathing or otherwise responsive.

The water was rising fast. Soon, Colter would be in danger himself. If the man was in fact deceased, Colter would have to escape.

But he needed to know for certain.

Colter tugged the man's right shoe off. He used the handle of his unopened knife and ran it firmly along the underside of the foot. The maneuver, known as the Babinski reflex, will elicit a response in even comatose patients—though not with the dead.

His big toe curled and the others spread wide.

He was alive.

"George!"

He grunted and shifted.

"I . . . Sonja!"

"Your family's okay, George. You're okay. But we have to get out of here. It's going to flood any minute."

"I . . ." He began to cough. And, Colter believed, sob.

He was not groggy in the same way the others were, and Colter guessed he had not taken any of the pills, leaving those for his family. He had probably just passed out from the depleted oxygen and carbon dioxide poisoning.

"You're going to have to move on your own."

The man began to work his way over the second row of seats. Once there, Colter could help him. As they made their way into the front row, Colter noted that he was hampered by holding something in his right hand.

"That?" Colter asked. "Just drop it."

The man stared at what he gripped and Colter realized it was a wadded-up bouquet of plastic film—the sort that dry cleaning is wrapped in.

Ah, he understood.

He recalled Tolifson's words about Mrs. Petaluma's possibly choosing not to go on in life without her house and garden.

That was an end Colter simply could not reconcile.

But here? George's debate was to sacrifice himself and give his family a few more minutes of air, in hopes that rescuers would get to them in time.

A universe of difference between the two mortal decisions.

George had probably passed out before he could enwrap his face.

He released the wad and it floated away.

With a boost from Colter, the man climbed out of the hole and onto the ladder as Buddy took him by the arm and steadied him. He stopped, looking around, a gaze of astonishment on his face as he saw the reality of where they were.

Colter followed, and a few seconds later the inrush of water slowed and the interior was completely filled.

Starr joined them and helped the man make his way off the pond, her walking backward on the ladder, holding his hands.

Once off the ladder, he staggered to his family, who were with two medics in the back of an ambulance.

Buddy collected the chain saw and he and Colter followed. The fireman and Tolifson pulled the ladder to shore, and collapsed and reaffixed it to the fire truck.

Then the husband and wife lifted their eyes and, in identical poses, stared at the sandbags that sat atop their vehicle.

Like tombstones above their putative grave.

Colter laughed to himself: wondering where on earth the bizarre, if poetic, phrase had come from.

Debi Starr called, "Everybody, back to high ground."

Wise. He reflected. Better not to lose sight of the fact that a thousand tons of lethal mud and water, at any unannounced moment, could come raining down upon them.

19.

A brief shower in the camper.

First, Colter, then his sister.

The Winnebago could handle the water; Colter had had an extra tank installed, not wishing to have to rely on finding a campsite hookup if a job turned urgent.

He wondered, however, how sturdy the filtration system was. It was processing an excessive amount of mud from the SUV rescue.

Colter had plenty of clean clothing. Dorion also had gym bags in the back of her SUV. She was planning on getting a motel room later, but that was not a priority. The Never Summer still poured and splashed and roared, and the levee gave up its bulk inch by inch, moving closer by every minute to the destruction of the town of Hinowah.

As for the family of the hour—the Garveys from Bakersfield— they had been examined at County North Medical Center and released, having sustained no serious injuries. The only changes of clothing they had were at the bottom of the Chevy Suburban watershed, but as part of her disaster preparation, Dorion had arranged for scores of dry outfits in all sizes to be shipped from several emergency way stations she knew about in Northern California. They could shower and change in the college gymnasium. Sonja's mother and brother, whom they'd just visited in Oregon, would arrive to take them back north to sort out insurance and find new wheels.

And gadgets too. Colter imagined, with some amusement, the horror the children faced because not a single electronic device had survived.

George had used a borrowed phone and offered Colter boundless gratitude. He said if there was anything that he could ever do for Colter, he need only say the word. He would be happy to offer his family-owned business's services to Colter and his family for free.

And what exactly was that? Colter was thinking food service or computer repair or accounting.

No, the man was a mortician and proud of it; his funeral home had been in the Garvey family for three generations.

Laughing, Colter took the info, reflecting that the man's profession and the art of survivalism were largely in opposition. But perhaps the man's skills might come in handy if he ever needed research into the nature of the business. He recited his email address and they disconnected.

Colter and Dorion were watching the sandbag team when he heard a man's voice. "Not good." It was Ed Gutiérrez, who'd just been to the edge of the north side of Route 13 and measured the width of the levee again with an app on his phone. "Situational erosion's taken another two inches off the interior in the past hour, three on the top. Water's like a damn sandblaster."

Dorion called Sergeant Tamara Olsen. From her reaction, it was clear the news she was getting was not to her liking.

After they disconnected, she said, "Helicopter with the superglue's still grounded. I asked if they could truck it in, but she said it has to be applied from the air."

"Any ETA?" he asked.

"No."

Maybe soon. The rain continued to grow less fierce and the

drumming on the canvas roof was bordering on pleasant—or would have been, if not for the circumstances.

It was then that Starr noted Colter's battered cheekbone. "Hey. You all right? You banged into something in the SUV?"

"No. Earlier when I was checking out the drone tag, off Route Thirteen."

Dorion, who had studied first aid extensively for her job, examined the torn skin. "Wash it."

He knew she was right and did as she'd said—using bottled water and a small packet of liquid soap he pulled from his backpack. The pharma industry makes huge money off antibiotic lotions and sprays. But most minor wounds are best treated with simple soap and water. Anything stronger often destroys tissue and makes the healing process much longer and more painful.

"Accident?" Tolifson asked.

"No. Battery."

A frown from the mayor.

Starr said, "I don't think Mr. Shaw means that like Delco, Mayor. He means he got attacked."

"My God." He seemed shocked. Hinowah was probably not known for barroom brawls.

"What happened?" Dorion asked.

"Went to look at the place my drone geotagged as a possible hit on the SUV. Then he came up behind me. Probably forty-five years old. White, six two, two twenty, beard. Red hair. Took off before I got a picture. Objected that I was trespassing."

"Where?"

Colter explained about the bridge and the creek.

Tolifson was frowning. "Don't know that's anybody's property."

"Maybe Mr. Redding's," Starr said.

The mayor said, "Gerard Redding. Owns that copper mine." His brow furrowed. "Not a particularly pleasant person."

"And that's putting sugar on it," Starr said. "A good percentage of the town works for him. But the man you described, your battery-er? I don't know anybody who fits that description—anybody who's a troublemaker, that is."

Dorion asked, "What would he want to protect? I mean, copper's valuable, but . . ."

The mayor flipped drops of rain from his face. "Industrial secrets? Copper mining's low margin. And they have to purify the ore at the source—before it ships. Has all sorts of secret techniques. Probably thought you were a spy from a competitor."

Starr said, "That land's not posted. He can't do anything without trespassing you first."

On private property the owner can throw you off for any reason or no reason at all. But you can't be arrested until you've been "trespassed"—meaning a formal complaint has been filed against you.

"And he can't take matters into his own hands, no matter what," Starr offered. "My guess, he's a squatter and just plain wacko."

Tolifson asked, "You want to file a complaint?"

"No. Just get word around to your folks. He's dangerous. No idea if he's armed or not."

"Handle that, wouldja?" The mayor glanced sideways.

Debi Starr nodded and began typing into her phone. "What was he wearing?"

Colter described the clothing.

"Wedding ring or other jewelry?"

"Didn't really notice."

"Okay. Smell like he'd been drinking?"

Tolifson said, "Debi, give the man a break. Just get the word out. Big guy with a beard. Nobody's going to be sniffing any suspect's breath."

She lifted an eyebrow. "Well . . . Was listening to a podcast. True crime. Detective in L.A. solved a murder because he smelled whisky on the suspect's breath and on the victim's too. Meant they'd been drinking together even when the killer had an alibi. He's in jail for life; the fake alibi-er is doing fifteen."

Colter added, "Funny thing about that. His aftershave. Expensive. Even though he looked like a mountain man."

"Now, that's worth jotting. Anything else you can remember?"

"After I suggested he get down on the ground—"

Starr laughed.

"I searched him. Money, but no ID. No car keys. Nothing."

Tolifson considered this, and came to no conclusion.

But the younger officer was nodding, taking this information in. "That was on a podcast too. Pros sometimes leave all their identifying stuff at home when they get an assignment to kill somebody . . . Maybe he was on the lam. Hiding out here. Hm."

Tolifson was shaking his head. "Come on, Debi."

"Stranger things've happened. Can't think of any at the moment but they must have."

Ed Gutiérrez said he was going to continue the evac operation and returned to his SUV. Dorion said she would join him, but Colter received an email and saw the sender. He told his sister to hold on a minute.

The note was from his lawyer Tony, who was reading through all the material Colter had dropped off as he sped to Hinowah.

Someone—bless them—had brought a Keurig coffee machine. He nodded toward it with a querying glance. "Let's take five."

"Sure."

He and his sister each made a cup and, at Colter's suggestion, stepped to the end of the third tent, the one at the bottom of the downward slope of the hill. Maybe Tolifson and Starr were expecting a horde of responders from the county and state; as it turned out, the first tent was sufficient. This and the one in the middle were empty except for a few chairs. "Something I need to tell you."

Dorion eyed him closely and remained silent.

"I heard from one of Ashton's associates."

"The university in Berkeley?"

"Yes. He told me a woman had contacted the school, looking for the Compound. First name Margaret."

"She knew about the place?" Dorion frowned, concern growing on her face. Its existence was a carefully guarded secret.

"She didn't leave her number."

"There's something about the way this story's unraveling, Colt. What's the punch line?"

"She's his daughter."

Dorion was still for a moment. "All right."

He explained that when he'd learned about the mysterious woman, he'd gone right to Ashton's study and began his search, unearthing the document about getting the girl into a grade school. "He had an affair with a woman not long after we moved to the Compound. She had a baby by him. I checked the dates. She's roughly your age."

Three years separated the younger siblings. Russell was six years older than Colter.

She asked, "The safe house in San Francisco? The one he kept from us? That's where they met, I guess."

"Probably. I searched it when Russell and I were looking for evidence about Ashton's death. But I didn't notice anything about a Margaret or any woman Ashton might've known."

Dorion stared out over the town. Colter's eyes followed. In the mist the scene looked snowy, quaint, like a Christmas village. Dorion gave no outward reaction to the news. She had had a fine relationship with her father until his final years, when he grew paranoid and hostile. Mary Dove, a licensed MD, kept him on antipsychotic medication, but sometimes, Colter learned later, he palmed the pills and flushed them, presumably believing that they were part of an elaborate plot to poison him or control his mind.

When Dorion was thirteen she and Ashton had a falling-out. His boot-camp survival training included a final exam: rappelling down a hundred-foot cliff at night. The girl was an expert mountaineer— a better climber than Colter and Russell had been at that age—and she'd taken on rock faces scores of times, some even higher than the one he'd picked. But that night she'd said simply, "No." She saw no point, and had a mind of her own even at that age.

Ashton had grown furious and, when Russell intervened, his father pulled a knife on him.

The overwhelming tension finally broke, and Ashton vanished into his room, leaving the children badly shaken.

Some years later, when the subject of that evening came up, Dorion had told Colter she felt that was the moment their father died. "I know it's his mind, I know it's the wiring. I didn't hate him or resent him. It's just that man was not my father anymore. Somebody else took his place."

Now, Colter handed his sister his phone. "Here's what I just got from Tony."

Colter:

Found a letter to your father. Has to be from the woman your father had the affair with, Margaret's mother.

Ashton, I am owing you my soul. I am owing you everything. But it is not safe. It is never safe. THEY are out there. You know who they are. And they are after me. I see a shadow and I cringe. I hear a loud bang and I am jumping out of my skin. I hear a phone ring and I am wondering, will it explode, they can plant bombs in phones you know.

I know what you've told me about survival, and I try to survive but sometimes it just seems so difficult. Overwhelming.

They're out there. Hiding, waiting.

I wish I could stay calm. And tell myself it's my imagination,
but the voices are screaming at me.

You told me I had to ignore them.

But I can't.

And so I did what you told me not to do.

I went to Eddy Street.

You know what I mean.

Yes.

I didn't have any choice.

Forgive me.

But they're after me, all of them are after me.

No choice, no choice . . .

Yours in devotion and love,
Sarah

Tony's message finished by saying he was going to keep searching. He still had about five inches of documents to go through. He
would let them know what he found.

Dorion said, "She sounds like Ashton when he was off his
meds. All right. Margaret, the daughter of Ashton and Sarah, has
surfaced and is now looking for the Compound. Any thoughts on
why?"

"Sarah's mental issues get worse, and she kills herself. Either
because she's completely unhinged. Or—"

"Because she begs Ashton to leave Mary Dove and marry her."

His nod confirmed that that was what he was thinking as well.

"Margaret, now in her twenties, discovers something that makes her think Ashton was responsible for her mother's death. It's time for revenge."

Colter said, "Another scenario. Sarah was married too. She gets pregnant by Ashton and has the baby. The husband finds out and kills her. Margaret blames Ashton."

"Little extreme."

"But look at the syntax of the letter. There's a foreign tone about it. European or Mediterranean or Latin? Relationships can be fiery. Misogynistic too."

Dorion conceded this was true. And added, "Even if he doesn't kill her, though, he might have thrown Sarah out, cut her off completely. She led a terrible life. Ashton won't help because he's married and has a family of his own. Sarah dies impoverished. And that sets Margaret off."

In his reward business, Colter Shaw was well aware of the intricate soap opera plots that were people's lives. This teleplay was no more outlandish than any other that bloomed when the orbits of two people overlapped.

"But get even against who? She has to know he's dead. It's public knowledge. The most basic research would have shown that."

"Which means Mary Dove might be the target."

Colter added, "Or us."

"Positive reasons she's looking for the Compound?"

"Ashton told Sarah and their daughter everything about his other family. But Margaret went off to school to study abroad, got a degree or two and has come back to reconnect."

"Maybe we should have nicknamed you the Optimistic One."

"Just ask me the percentage likelihood."

She lifted her palm.

"Ten percent it's innocent. Why is she asking third parties about the Compound? Any research would tell her about me and the reward business. I'm in dozens of articles and podcasts. And Google takes you right to my website."

"That means ninety percent she wants to kill us and burn the Compound to the ground."

"Not exactly," Colter said. "Remember there's that other percentage."

"The unknown. The percentage that it's something else, something we can't figure out just yet."

"Right. I'd say ten percent innocent, fifty percent she has murder or mayhem on the mind, and forty percent who-the-hell-knows." Colter thought for a moment. He added, "And she mentions going to Eddy Street. What's that about?"

A part of San Francisco's Tenderloin District. Back then it was an unsavory place, to put it mildly.

Dorion shook her head.

He said, "Well, the important thing is to get Mary Dove out of the Compound."

"We can't just call. News like this isn't phone worthy. Let alone *text* worthy."

He agreed. "But we can't get back to the Compound while this"— a nod at the levee—"is going on. And even if we did tell her that her stepdaughter is looking for her— Wait. Is she a stepdaughter?"

"No, no relationship between Mary Dove and Margaret."

Colter could never keep family connections straight. "Even if we did tell her on the phone, you know what she would do."

"Stay and defend the place."

"It's just a matter of time until Margaret finds the Compound."

"We need to get Mary Dove here. Stat."

Dorion's eyes had been scanning the town. She turned back to her brother. "I know how to do it."

"How?"

"Simple. I'm just going to ask."

"And why would she?"

"Oh, she will. Believe me."

20.

"M ayor, we may have a solution to the old-time-pistol-lady problem," Colter Shaw said.

"Mrs. Petaluma?"

There were others? thought Colter.

"That's right."

Dorion offered, "She's Indigenous. Miwok probably, in this area. We know Mrs. Petaluma speaks English—she looked at the levee when I mentioned it. So it's not a language thing. For some reason she doesn't want to leave."

"Our mother is Ohlone. It's a nation related to the Miwok. She can impress on Mrs. Petaluma it's important she leave her house."

And, according to Dorion's plot, this would also get their mother out of harm's way from the possibly homicidal daughter of her late husband.

"Makes sense to me."

Dorion added, "She's also an MD. Which might be helpful depending on how things go here. I called and explained our situation. She's on her way."

Colter noted activity from the northern end of Route 13, near his Winnebago. After pitching the sandbags over the levee to help in rescuing the family, Sergeant Tamara Olsen and the corporals had left the crew of volunteers and driven through town and up the road on the northern side of the valley. Supervised by Olsen, one of the soldiers—the slimmer of the two—had donned a wet suit and, tethered to a tree, was easing into the water as his huge partner paid out the rope slowly. He was making his way along the inside of the levee, trying to ease in a straight line along the surface. But the river had other ideas and was buffeting him right and left.

A mask and attached snorkel sat high on his head.

Olsen left the men to the job and strode down the hill to the command post. She nodded to Tolifson, Starr and Dorion, to whom she said, "Your brother. Some resemblance." She stuck out a hand to Colter and they shook. "Tam Olsen." Hers was a firm grip. She had an attractive angular face and athletic figure. Her skin was outdoor ruddy. The tone appealed to him. Margot—the woman he had more or less lived with for a time, a while back—was an archeologist and preferred outdoor digs; she had a permanent tan. Margot and Olsen shared similar builds, he also noted.

Colter saw that her nails were painted red. He'd worked on a reward job with a woman who was an army lieutenant. He knew that modest and inconspicuous polish was acceptable in the service. As for nail length, there was no skirting that rule. One-quarter inch. Not a millimeter longer. He'd been told that some commanders carried a ruler. The crimson shade was probably out of regulation, but her focused, determined eyes told him she seemed like the sort of soldier who could get away with breaching the little rules because she was so good at her assignments.

Her eyes lingered in his direction. He took in her pose—hip cocked, arms at side, an "open" configuration in body language analysis—and his eyes held hers briefly.

Han Tolifson said, "What's your man doing up there?"

"Checking where it's best to lay the Hydroseal. We can't put it on the whole length. He'll find where it's eroding the quickest."

"Hope he gets hazard pay for that."

Olsen asked Dorion, "Evacuation?"

"We're about seventy, eighty percent. Not good enough. They look at the levee and see the water over the side. They don't get, or care, that it means erosion. To them it's a big solid dam of dirt with a pretty waterfall."

Tolifson scoffed. "And I'm sick of hearing that nonsense about 'government conspiracy.' We want them out of their houses so we can . . . Well, I don't know. Plant bugs inside or cameras. Or look for propaganda from the opposing political party." The man said with a sigh, "Can't take a pill for stupid."

The sergeant laughed, a pleasant breezy sound. Colter found himself taking in her green eyes once again.

The map indicated there were two roads leading west from Hinowah. Route 58 angled south between a large farm and the copper mine. The other, Valley Road, Route 94, veered north and went directly past the college. The latter was a patiently moving bottleneck. Colter wondered how far the concern for fellow citizens would extend if the flood started. Would people try to sneak past or push their way ahead of the crowd? Would there be fighting? California was ambivalent about guns. San Francisco and L.A. were oases of strict control. But much of the rest of the state was cowboy territory. And he guessed that Dorion's prohibition about taking weapons in the evacuation was largely ignored.

Officer Starr slipped her mobile back in one of the holsters on her service belt, which bristled with cop gear. She had washed off much of the mud on her hands and face, from the Garvey family rescue, but her outfit was still soiled badly. Her expression was not happy. "Mayor, we are still getting the short end of the stick here, and I don't care for that much."

"How do you mean?"

"I was talking to my cousin Edna, you remember, Momma's sister's eldest. She's an EMT in Fort Pleasant. She was saying it's like the county fair opening day. They've got forty, fifty people flinging sandbags this way and that. Even where she doesn't think they need to. And the rivers're *nothing* there."

Colter recalled Tomas Martinez, the town council head and fire chief, who'd also been looking for the Garvey family, telling him about the two rivers and that while the flooding risk was significant, it presented little mortal danger, just property damage.

"She had her boss call Prescott Moore—the supervisor you talked to, Ms. Shaw? And he was just like he was before. 'Oh, I'll look into it.' And she said he wasn't going to look into diddly but his own navel."

Dorion had told her brother about the conversation. Moore had to balance when allocating resources, the man had said. Hinowah didn't rate any. Which didn't sound like much of a balance to Colter.

His sister now added that the man probably *did* want to help, as he had a house and a mortgage brokerage company in town, both in the direct path of a flood. She pointed to a gothic, dark, deserted house in the middle of the village. "So maybe some higher-ups are putting the kibosh on any aid."

Half the battles Colter fought in the reward business were with local government bureaucracy—far more than with escaped convicts and kidnappers.

Tolifson sighed, then said, "Debi, be a dear, and get me some coffee."

"Yessir."

Colter decided to get another cup. "You?" he asked Dorion but she waved her hand, passing.

He followed Starr to the Keurig. They were standing shoulder to shoulder and Colter made a cup.

"I can do that."

"No, let me," he said. And handed it to her.

"Hm. Well. Thanks."

He figured she was mostly the coffee maker, and rarely the coffee makee.

Starr doctored with sugar and cream. "Used your head there, sir, Colter. Rearview mirror, that SUV going right, not left."

The art of rewards-seeking required expansive thinking. He didn't offer this somewhat pretentious thought but rather said, "We were lucky."

"Well, there're people who use luck and people who let it slip away. How's that for small-town philosophizing."

"Just the thought for sharing around a potbelly stove at the general store."

"We have one, you know." She shook her head. "No stove, though. Just a store."

When his own cup was ready and the machine sputtered to silence, he asked for the cream. Starr passed him the bowl of tiny half-and-half capsules.

Colter took one and froze.

"Your sleeve. I need to smell your sleeve."

"What?"

He didn't wait but bent down and smelled a patch of cloth.

Oh, hell . . .

He gestured to Dorion, who joined him and the officer.

"Smell her arm."

She did as he said, as a very perplexed Officer Starr lifted her limb. "My deodorant's not to y'all's liking?"

Dorion whispered, "Can't be."

He asked Starr, "You been near construction blasting?"

"No, sir."

"The copper mine?"

"Not in weeks."

Dorion ran to the occupied tent and—startling everyone—grabbed Tolifson's sou'wester off a chair. She smelled it too. "Yep, Colt. Both of them have residue."

"We probably had it on ours too, but we showered and changed right away." Colter was scanning the levee again, looking at the clean-sliced-off top. He should have made more of the dynamics of the collapse.

He shouted to Olsen, "Get your man out of the water now! And tell the sandbaggers to move back from the levee, at least a hundred feet."

The sergeant saw the urgency in his eyes and pulled her phone out, asking, "What is it?"

He gestured toward Starr's stained sleeve. "The mud from the levee? I can smell explosives residue. It didn't collapse on its own. Somebody sabotaged it."

21.

Colter asked, "You have a crime scene lab?"

Tolifson squinted, thinking, and Colter recalled he had only become the police chief by default and, it seemed, recently.

It was Debi Starr who answered when she saw that the mayor wasn't able to. "We farm all that out, if we ever need it, which is hardly ever. Burglaries, we know who's done it usually. And the two murders in the past three years, the state came in, ran the scenes and sent the prosecutor the report. It didn't matter anyway, because both of the suspects confessed. Most courteous of them."

Colter regarded his sister briefly. "A lab'd take too long anyway." She nodded.

The mayor's face grew mystified. "But who the hell would blow it up? You have to be wrong. Maybe the husband, in the SUV? He did construction or demolition."

"No. He runs a funeral home."

"Who on earth would do such a thing?" Tolifson muttered, paraphrasing his earlier comment. "Any chance you might just be wrong? All respect."

"A possibility. But we have to find out for sure. That other officer of yours? McGuire?"

Starr said, "He's down in the village, herding evacuees out."

"Ask him to scoop up samples from the mudslide. Three or four, from different sections. And I need one other thing."

"What's that?" Tolifson asked.

"A beekeeper."

Twenty minutes later, Colter Shaw was in room 117 of the Hinowah Motor Inn, a quarter-mile north of the levee.

The owner/manager, a stocky woman in what Colter believed was called a housedress, of tiny yellow flowers on a purple background, had given him the key and returned to the office, not the least curious why someone had checked in with no luggage other than a grocery bag containing six coffee cups filled with mud.

While most people were sheltering in the college a mile away, up the road from the inn, some of the wealthier citizens of town had decided to go for the private mode of protection, securing rooms here. The guests had arrived in fancier pickups than what was the average set of wheels of the evacuees: these residents were in BMWs, a Jaguar, a Mercedes, two Land Rovers.

The news was playing on the large TV monitor; video footage showed a long string of cars on Route 94. There were also some videos of the levee shown via long-angle lenses. Reporters had tried to come into town but, with Route 13 closed, 94 and 58 were the only access. Town council head Martinez had ordered them roadblocked except for emergency vehicles going in and evacuees going out.

A news chopper from a Sacramento station was hovering. By phone Colter had pointed this fact out to Sergeant Olsen, but she said it was not the weather here that was keeping the helicopters from delivering the sealant but the weather at the base. The ceiling was below minimums to take off.

On the TV, the story about the "devastation" to Fort Pleasant was unfolding. Yes, there was flooding, and a few dramatic images showed basements filling with gray water, but at worst the film crews had found only thigh-high levels, just as Starr's cousin had reported.

There would be significant damage to retail inventory and property, but that was about all.

And, of course, every one of Fort Pleasant's problems would be over the minute the levee failed and Hinowah became the drain, diverting the water from the Never Summer and relieving any risk whatsoever to the county seat.

Shaw was now joined by Tolifson and Starr.

"Who the heck was behind it?" Tolifson asked. "Terrorists? I heard they're looking for soft targets. Like infrastructure grids. Taking out a town from flooding would be a real plum of a statement."

Colter remained skeptical. Incidents of terror, foreign or domestic, were extremely rare.

He knew in the years Dorion's company had been responding to incidents, only one was declared a terrorist attack—a bombing in Pittsburgh that targeted an LGBTQ rally and set fire to a whole block of row houses. Two others—a derailment and a brush fire—might have been terror related but the authorities never found out definitively.

Drowning Hinowah to make a political point?

Ten percent at best.

There was a knock on the door and Tolifson let a middle-aged man inside. Introductions were made. Arthur Simmons, around fifty, was nondescript, with dark skin and a short, trimmed Afro. He carried a bee transport container. He set it on the desk.

"Mayor Tolifson says you're in a bind, the levee and all. Well, I'm happy to help you, sir, but I will not have any of my creatures injured, if that's what might occur."

"They'll be fine," Colter said. "In fact, they're going to get a treat."

This drew curious glances from Starr and Tolifson.

Another knock on the door. Dorion was let inside, carrying a bottle of clear liquid. It was simple syrup—sugar and water. Tolifson had called the owner of a bar in town and arranged for her to get a bottle. The establishment was closed but he'd left the back door open.

Colter picked up the tray the coffee maker sat on. Setting aside the appliance and wiping the surface, he placed the tray on the table. He then drew his Glock, giving the beekeeper momentary pause, then ejected a round and replaced the gun in its holster. Withdrawing a multi-tool and pair of pliers from his backpack, he worked the slug out. He dumped the gunpowder grains on the tray, spread them out and poured a circle around them with the simple syrup.

"Okay . . ." Tolifson muttered uncertainly.

Colter nodded to the beekeeper, who opened the lid and turned it on its side and tapped the insects out. It didn't take long before they sensed the syrup and flew to it.

He glanced briefly at the confused faces—everyone except Dorion, who knew exactly what he was up to. It was she who explained. "Our father taught us hundreds of survival techniques. Some involved ways to detect food, water, severity of wounds."

Colter added, "There are dog breeds that will sit beside a badly wounded person who has a chance of survival, but walk past one who can't recover. Canines can sniff out explosives, everybody knows. Pigs are better. They're used in conflict zones to find land mines."

"That's a sure way to get some bacon for breakfast," Tolifson offered.

No one smiled.

Colter continued, "But mammals need a long period of training. Bees?" He nodded toward the insects at the sweet liquid. "Their proboscis is as sensitive as a dog's nose, and it only takes five minutes to teach them."

Simmons laughed in surprise.

Tolifson said, "Well, darn. Gunpowder and syrup. You're conditioning them to find bombs!"

Then the beekeeper caught the implication of the training session. He looked stricken. "You mean, somebody sabotaged the levee?"

"That's what we're going to find out."

"Why would a soul want to do that?"

Starr said, "We don't know. But I can see his plan unfolding. Whoever it is hears there's a bad storm coming, and knows about snowmelt. Figures the river's going to flood. He hikes to the river side of the levee while the water's low and plants the explosive charges. Then he just waits for the flood. And bang."

Tolifson asked, "Then why didn't anybody hear it?"

Starr shrugged. "The storm. Maybe they'd think it was thunder. And the devices were under tons of dirt."

They watched the insects' long tongues sucking up the syrup. Honey would be their first choice, but sugar worked as well. Colter knew they would go for it, even if they weren't hungry. What they didn't eat they would direct to their second stomach, a storage container, in effect, to take back to the hive.

For five minutes, the humans in the room made phone calls or watched the news. Then Colter announced, "Training day's over." He lifted the tray and the startled bees flew off, spreading across the room. Taking care to make sure none of his consultants escaped, Colter opened the door and set the tray outside.

He then walked to the bathroom and opened that door.

The vanity and floor were littered with paper towels dripping in mud collected by TC McGuire.

Everyone in the room watched the sextet of bees strafing the bed and the TV and heads of those present.

Until one by one they zipped into the bathroom, where they hovered over, or landed to suck at, the paper towels.

"It *was* a bomb," Tolifson whispered.

Colter said briskly, "Call the FBI and Alcohol, Tobacco and Firearms. You have their numbers?"

Tolifson looked to Officer Starr. He said, "Do you?"

"Never needed them. But I'll bet the Justice Department is just like any cable company or hotel chain. They'd always rather you contact them online. But I'll bet there's a phone number on the last page of their website. In nice and tiny print. No worries. I'll track somebody down."

22.

Arana Braveblade thought of herself as a "Somewhat Person."

This was a phrase she had learned from one of the Elders of the Near Realm to describe certain people, and it was this rare quality that was, she prayed to Marthan, going to save her.

A Somewhat Person. What this meant was that she was partly who she seemed to be. And yet, decidedly, partly not. An outer her and an inner her.

It was the latter of these that she kept to herself, hidden deep. And it would be the key to her survival.

So now, when she strode to the gate to the Everscent Garden, on the mountain ledge two thousand feet above the village, one version of her nodded pleasantly to the guards, while the other her prepared in secret for what was coming next.

"Siress Braveblade," said Ebertton Garr, the head jailor of this wing. "This is not a garden day."

Braveblade hated that she was referred to as "siress," the feminine version of "sire." Certainly it might seem neutral on the surface, but in fact it none-theless carried the whiff of inferior station. At least the Court recognized her surname, which she had chosen on her Womaning Day. "Braveblade" was her mother's maiden name, and the preference was for those of her sex to adopt their father's (to promote the appearance of which of the genders was to be in charge), but so far the naming convention had not yet made its way into the Scroll of Rules.

Tugging tighter about her the gray cape that matched the required floor-length skirt, Braveblade summoned a horrified expression upon her heart-shaped face. "My, you are right! Fuddled me! I've done it again. And now I am in dires. What shall I do?"

She looked from Garr to the other guard, Plank the Younger, a silly name for a silly man, too small for the sword that hung from his hip.

Garr asked, "What is the difficulty?" He had a drift for the ladies and the words were offered in a way that seemed sympathetic but was truly a clumsy flirt.

"I told Siress Stodge that I would prepare a Spell-Bind for her, and I must deliver it to her no later than Segment Fourteen today." Her voice cracked as she added, "Two segments hence. Oh, she will not be pleased."

Now both men stirred.

No one wished to have Siress Stodge—whose backname was Siress Strident, though she was occasionally called far worse!—angry with you. It could mean you would spend the rest of your days carting refuse to the Noffin Pit.

She bowed her head and wondered if her outer Somewhat Person could conjure tears. Braveblade was a fine spell-caster but damp eyes eluded her. So she touched the tip of her fingers, dipped in Farood powder, to the corners of her eyes.

The resulting waterworks—and genuine gasp of pain—were impressive.

Garr said, "Siress, is there . . . perhaps something I can do?" *His* backname was LeerMaster.

"Oh, Sire. You would be my savior! I would be forever grateful! If you could go into the garden and collect me drandons of bandiweb, cholaefa and still-gale. Of the first, I need only the yellow leaves. As you know, the green are useless. And they must be a certain shade, the shade of bee pollen. As for the stillgale, be wary of the black seeds. They can—"

"Perhaps, Siress, I think it would be better if you gathered what you need yourself. If you're quick about it."

"Could I? Oh, you are beyond kind!" The outer her beamed toward the man, who smelled of boreroot. Disgusting.

She endured what she knew would be his firm embrace and hand straying down her back—missing, thank Marthan—the contour of what she wore beneath the cape. The Scrolls required women to wear only cambric shirts above the waist. Any other garments were forbidden—especially what she had donned this morning: a warrior's thick leather vest.

She found the embrace against his body repulsive—as was Plank's perverted smile—but that feeling was counterweighed by the thought that they would soon be assigned to Noffin as punishment for this dereliction.

Then, she strode into the garden, the door closing behind her.

And so began the first stage of her escape from the castle of Thamann Hotaks, the reviled dictator controlling the Central Realm.

Yep, thought Fiona Lavelle. *I'd* keep reading.

Sitting in the driver's seat of her Blue Strayer—well, her Chevy Camaro—she continued editing. She had eleven notebooks filled with the novel, which now totaled about a hundred thousand words, roughly half finished.

But she had decided to revise the story somewhat to incorporate current events, one might say—the levee collapsing behind her as she drove along Route 13.

She had just managed to escape and a moment later had found herself plummeting down an old trail at the base of this mountain, where the car ended up stuck in the mud beside the raging torrent of runoff water spilling over the top of the levee.

The storyline might go like this: Her hero—not "heroine" of course—was escaping in the magical Blue Strayer sled from her nemesis Thamann Hotaks. But the man had shot a Melting Spell toward her and it had dissolved the dam, endangering an entire village and knocking the Strayer to the ground in a forest, where it ended up stuck in the mud. And complaining mightily about it. Arana Braveblade's Strayer was more than a means of transport. It had become her ornery yet lovable sidekick.

Amusingly, just at that moment, the car shook briefly in a fierce gust of wind, and rain machine-gunned the roof.

Lavelle yawned and stretched. She was still somewhat groggy. After Big Blue had streaked to a stop where she now sat, Fiona surveyed that scene and decided she was indeed seriously stuck in the mud and thought: Screw it.

And had done what someone else might not, under the circumstances. She took a nap. A glorious three-hour bout of oblivion. Not undeserved, considering she had wakened at three-thirty for the drive from Reno.

Then, waiting for the storm to pass, she'd noodled with the book.

Now, though, it was time to free herself, as Arana Braveblade was doing in her story.

Though Lavelle's magic would come from a different source of spells: YouTube.

On her phone she viewed dozens of clips of men and women getting out of mud. Eventually all the escape efforts seemed to come down to roughly the same technique.

1. Find rough-surfaced material (dry, if possible—not likely here, so she would use the carpet from the trunk and floor mats) and force it under the front of the drive tires—rear, in the case of the Camaro. Not as helpful as the front. It was better to pull rather than push in such a situation. But there you had it.

2. Gently rock back and forth. Drive, reverse. Drive, reverse.

3. Keep doing it until you were free.

Lather, rinse, repeat.

Got it.

One thing remained.

Lavelle checked herself out in the mirror. Her pink-framed glasses, the backward baseball cap, with no makeup, of course. She appeared more pale than she usually did, though her Roman nose provided some Technicolor; the cold had turned it significantly red.

A natural look. Fine.

All right, now, it's lights, camera, action time . . .

She switched to the front camera—selfie mode—and hit RECORD.

"Hello, all. It's stuck-in-the-mud Fiona. I've been following all you dears who've posted advice about getting unstuck. Here I am with Big Blue—my two-year-old, kick-ass Camaro—who is a bit . . . under the weather. Ha."

Switching the camera off, she tucked it away, then pulled on her parka and stepped out into the rain, walking around to the trunk of the car.

Ten minutes later, she was ready and started to record again.

"About to get started!"

She walked to the passenger side and shot the view from there. The car was about four feet from the edge of a low cliff that dropped straight into the raging torrent of water—a flooded gulley that was an extension of a spillway under the levee.

"Reminder to self—avoid that. Don't want to flood the engine! LOL!"

Lavelle set the phone on a low cliff, under an overhang, to keep it out of the rain. The lens was pointed at the rear wheels of the car, where she'd tucked the trunk carpets and floor mats.

"'Gently,'" she called to her audience. "That's the key word."

She walked out of frame toward the driver's door.

The phone recorded the action perfectly in 60 fps high-def video.

It caught the rear left wheel rocking back and forth ever so slightly.

It caught a little more of the car's progress forward—until the wheel got stuck on a branch under one of the carpets.

It caught Fiona's voice as she called, "Just a little more gas. And over the final hurdle!"

It caught the engine revving harder.

And it caught the rear wheels leaping over the branch and spinning madly in the mud as the Camaro slid sideways and tumbled over the edge into the water, accompanied by Fiona's panicked scream, which lasted only seconds before becoming a horrible choking, one final cry, and then silence broken only by the slap and splash of the frantic water.

23.

The team—Colter decided it was a reasonable description—returned from the motel to the command post, where Sergeant Tamara Olsen was sitting and speaking on the phone. When she saw Colter, she smiled, before noting his somber expression.

Colter said, "We confirmed explosives."

"Sabotage," she whispered.

He added that they had not ruled out the possibility that the perps, whoever they were, had placed additional explosives farther down in the levee, which had misfired or were meant to explode later.

"Christ," she muttered as her shocked eyes went to the levee. "And Corporal McPherson . . ."

The soldier who had just been in the water perhaps exactly where those charges were.

She turned her eyes to Colter. "You got him out in time. Thank you."

Tolifson was finishing a call in the cab of his truck. He disconnected and joined the others. "Talked to the FBI. Have to say the response was underwhelming. They asked if we knew there was another live IED, and I had to say no. But we thought there might be. And . . ." He sighed. "When he asked how we knew it was an explosion, I sort of . . ."

No, he didn't.

He winced. "Mentioned the bees. Which was greeted with some silence. They said they'd send somebody. But it was not 'We're sending some agents!' it was 'Yeah, we'll send some agents . . .'"

The lack of emphasis was clear.

"ATF?"

Though still known by that trio of initials, the organization had recently changed its name to the Bureau of Alcohol, Tobacco, Firearms and Explosives.

"Same thing."

Olsen said, "Think it's extortion? They blow the top, send a blackmail note and if we don't give 'em the money or Bitcoins or whatever they want, they blow the rest of it?"

Dorion asked, "But then why are they waiting to send the note?"

Tolifson said, "Hold on." He placed a call and had a brief discussion. He disconnected and looked up. "That was Marissa Fell, in the office. She would've forwarded ransom emails or told me about the phone calls right away. But I thought she should check for mysterious letters or packages. None, though."

Colter asked, "Anybody with a score to settle with Hinowah? You come down hard on a meth dealer or gangbanger?"

Again, Tolifson regarded Starr, who said, "No." Then she had a thought. "But is there something we wouldn't've heard of in Public Safety? Something civil?" She was speaking to Tolifson. "Any runins with land rights issues or zoning with corporations?"

Colter and Dorion shared a look.

Their father had surely been paranoid but one thing that he had not imagined, a particular corporation was headed up by a CEO who was more than willing to murder—in his case to pave the way so that the corporation itself could actually run for political office.

Tolifson considered this. "No, just your basic planning and zon-ing issues. Small time. Mostly residential or retail."

The young officer continued, "Any strike marks against the city? Something racial or ethnic? Prejudice, you know."

"God no," he said. "Hinowah? Why did you think of that?"

"Saw a movie. *Bad Day at Black Rock.* Whole town was behind a racist killing. And, let's face it, Hinowah is not the most diverse town on the face of the earth."

Tolifson said, "Well, no. And don't bring up stuff like that. Ru-mors get started that way."

"Yessir."

Tamara Olsen stepped away and made a phone call. A moment later, still holding the mobile, she said, "I'm talking to my com-mander. If you want I can arrange for some bomb curtains."

Colter was familiar with the huge blankets of chain or steel mesh. They were placed over the ground by construction crews dur-ing foundation blasting to keep stone shrapnel from flying through the air. "It's a good idea. If there *are* more explosives, curtains'll limit the damage. And even if there aren't, they'll slow the erosion."

Tolifson asked, "How soon can you get them here?"

She continued her conversation, then disconnected, turning back to the others.

"Choppers're still socked in. Ceiling goes up another five hun-dred feet, they'll be in the air. They'll pick up the curtains at the depot in Oakland, be here in a half hour."

Then Debi Starr was shaking her head as she gazed out over the levee. "What's *your* opinion, Colter? Misfire or it's still live and somebody's waiting to blow the rest?"

Colter said, "No idea. But I know one easy way to find out."

Tolifson, Starr and Olsen looked his way.

"Figure out who's behind it and ask them."

24.

Vultures," Dorion said.

She was thinking back to some of the jobs she'd had.

Fires in particular.

"Vultures." Tolifson was looking up, expecting birds.

Olsen and Starr kept their eyes on her, suspecting that something more figurative was at hand.

"It's a phenomenon we run into all the time with a disaster. And frankly I think it's an insult to the birds. People appear at the site after an incident where there's been significant loss of residences to fire, flood, tsunami . . . Anything but a toxic spill, since that ruins the ground for a long, long time.

"Well, houses and small businesses are gone, and the vultures descend—brokers and speculators are on the scene almost as fast as first responders. They go into a song and dance about how hard it's going to be to rebuild and deal with the insurance company. 'You'll never recover enough to make yourself whole if you want to rebuild. It's better and cheaper to move someplace else—where there won't be any bad memories. And we'll give you cash. Right now, here's a check!' They buy up the land for a song and put in buildings of their own."

"People really do that?" Olsen's face tightened with disgust.

"And a lot of victims go for it. They're numb, vulnerable. But the money? Whatever the brokers say, it's never really enough to get a leg up in a new life. And, yes, there may be bad memories of the disaster itself but ultimately people *want* to stay where their home was and rebuild."

Starr said, "But we're not talking natural disaster here. This is sabotage and attempted murder. You ever hear of anybody actually *creating* a disaster themselves to buy up the land?"

"The Yuma Vista fire in northern Arizona. Two thousand acres and fifty-seven low- to moderate-valued homes destroyed. Morgan Developments wanted the property for luxury estates. A campfire spread out of control. One of the principals in the company was suspected of starting it. Hard to prove it was intentional. Until the police found he'd already written offer letters to whom it may concern for the lots that burned—a week before the fire. He'll be out of jail in forty years."

Tolifson said, "I suppose so. But, I mean, I love Hinowah. It's my home and my family's been here for donkey's years. But it's hardly the most appealing place in the state. It's an old dried-up mining town. And you've got to drive miles to anyplace worth taking your wallet out for. Why would a developer risk jail to buy up the property?"

Dorion said, "Maybe somebody wants to put in high-end vacation homes. And on the drive here I saw they were constructing a new highway. I assume it'll go to the Five."

"That's right," Starr said.

"That'll bring people from Sacramento, Fresno, the Bay Area."

Starr offered, "I heard this podcast about the mob going into their own Airbnb business to get rich clients to come to their casinos. Stock them with liquor and hookers. Yeah, yeah, it's incorrect. I'm supposed to say 'sex professionals.' But I kind of reject correctness, as a general rule."

Olsen said, "I'm liking that theory. The mob would have easy access to explosives; they control half the construction industry in the state. And they also are pretty happy to blow up their competitors."

Colter said, "I passed a development driving here. A big one. Just north of Fort Pleasant."

Starr said, "I've seen it. My oh my . . . Talk about lavish. And prices through the *roof*."

Colter said, "Maybe he has his eyes on expanding here."

Dorion asked, "Who is he?"

"Theodore Gabris." Starr was reading from some online source. "His main office is in San Francisco. Nob Hill. And that's one fancy place. But there's a local news story that he's working out of Fort Pleasant on this development."

Colter was looking at the computer on which a map was displayed. "The man who attacked me. Bear. You were saying he might be connected with the mine, working security. But isn't Fort Pleasant and Gabris's development near where I was attacked?"

Starr replied, "Not that close but in the same direction. Another seven miles or so further south. But that's not a long drive. You think there's a connection?"

"Don't know. What's Gabris's background?"

Dorion was on her computer too. "Not much online. His company website talks about developments in San Francisco and Silicon Valley. Small projects. Some in Arizona and New Mexico. No bio. And no other news about him. No Facebook or X accounts."

"That's odd," Olsen said.

Colter looked to Tolifson. "NCIC?"

The FBI's crime database, Dorion knew. Even though it's run by the feds, NCIC's vast resources include state criminal cases and suspects too.

Starr looked up from her Dell. "I'm there right now. Nothing. And no record of a name change. That's always the first thing to look for."

Dorion said, "There's a first time for everything. Maybe there was no more good land in Fort Pleasant—it's a pretty rocky place—and this was the closest thing he could find for expanding his empire."

Tolifson said, "Of course, there is one thing working against him as a suspect. The flood. All right, it's a rare occurrence, but with climate change, there'll be more and more snowmelt. That means the floods'll be *less* rare. He buys the property for a song, and then hopes it doesn't flood again."

"He'll fix it," Colter said. "Put in a reinforced concrete levee."

Dorion nodded. "It'll be a selling point. The Hinowah flood can never happen again."

Colter stretched. "You know what?"

Everyone looked at him.

"I'm taking a liking to these here parts. Think I may want to consider buying a house."

Starr was chuckling. "*Undercover Exposé.*"

Dorion was wondering what the woman meant.

Her brother, though, apparently got it. "Podcast."

"Oh, it's a snazzy one. Love it."

Tolifson was frowning toward Colter. "You're going to, what? Look for explosives hidden in one of the construction trucks?"

"I don't know what I'll be looking for. But maybe."

Debi Starr offered, "Too bad we don't have one of those bomb-sniffing pigs. You could bring him along." She frowned. "Though I suppose the story you and Porky have come to town to find your dream house might raise a few eyebrows."

25.

Colter Shaw had with him his phone.

And his notebook.

And his three-hundred-dollar fountain pen.

One more thing.

His slim Glock 42, a six-shot (seven, with one in the chamber). The caliber was .380, a round that was like a stubby version of a nine-millimeter. Coming to Hinowah at Dorion's request, he had believed his main mission—to find a missing SUV—would not require a weapon.

One shovel attack and an improvised explosive device later, he knew it was time to arm up.

The weapon sat high inside the waistband on his right hip.

Per Ashton:

Never cross-draw a weapon. It will sweep along unintended targets.

Going seventy miles per hour, he motored the Yamaha past the bridge where he'd had the run-in with Bear.

A glance to the west, wondering if he'd see the man.

No sign of him.

Again, the attack piqued his curiosity. What was the point? Bear didn't seem like the sort to be a stranger to firearms, and if he had wanted Shaw dead it would not have been a difficult conclusion to arrange.

But a shovel—and risking a beating?

There had to be some reason other than shooing off a trespasser.

Maybe simple psychosis. Growing up with Ashton Shaw, Colter had learned that many words and actions that seem bizarre, and dangerous, to the normal world made perfect sense to those who lived with a turbulent, unstable mind.

Then the man and his issues were gone. He arrived in Fort Pleasant, which passed for a city in this part of the state, with about forty thousand souls. To his left the broad floodplain filled to the brim as the Never Summer River joined its cousin, the Little Silver. The water was flowing into some parts of the city and environs, yes, but it appeared that damage would be minimal. The defense included solid lines of sandbags, which were holding against a two- or three-foot swell.

Why divert all major resources to prevent minor damage here when Hinowah's very existence was threatened?

The continuing mystery.

The GPS now sent him west, away from the water, and soon he came to the Windermere Development, about a hundred acres of single-family homes—big ones—and several luxury apartment buildings of ten stories, skyscrapers in this area.

A billboard in front of a large plain filled with sparse grass and ground cover proclaimed that this acreage would be a "BEAUTIFUL AND CHALLENGING" EIGHTEEN-HOLE GOLF COURSE. He wondered if the promoters realized that the quotation marks might be taken as sardonic, suggesting that the course would be just the opposite. Presently it looked like one big sand trap, but then Shaw had once tackled a reward job in Palm Springs, which was even more desert than this and yet boasted a number of lush, verdant courses. The ground was waiting to blossom. It just needed one thing.

Water.

The substance of the hour today.

Some of the houses in Windermere had been sold, but most were still under construction, with crews nailing up Sheetrock, lifting prefabricated roofs onto frames with cranes, drilling wells and running utility lines, mostly underground. Shaw passed one house whose miniature front-yard billboard reported that it would feature 5,244 feet with seven bedrooms and thirteen baths. The garage could hold five full-size vehicles.

Spacious, certainly. But still claustrophobic for a Restless Man.

He circled the development twice, looking for signs that there'd been blasting to prepare the foundations. He saw no evidence of this, though if the developer, Theo Gabris, was behind a plot to flood Hinowah, he would surely have used explosives from a source different from his own project.

No problem with directions to his destination. Dozens of signs in bold white type read SALES OFFICE, with helpful arrows acting as power-free GPS directions.

He slowed the Yamaha and drove carefully over the shiny rails of train tracks, before steering into the parking lot of the sales office.

Outside, under a porch roof, he brushed the rain off his jacket and slicker pants and shook his baseball hat. Stepping inside, he smiled at a young attractive receptionist. Her black hair was done up high on her head, the way a beauty pageant contestant's might be—if there still *were* beauty pageants. Shaw had no idea.

"Morning. I'm Carter Stone. I called earlier."

"Yessir, Mr. Stone. One minute." She hit an intercom. "Sir?"

A gruff voice asked, "What is it?"

She told him his appointment had arrived. Now the tone softened. "Ah good. Show him in."

She had been given permission to enter, but still she knocked on the double door in the back of the office, and stood still, with a posture that radiated uncertainty.

"Come in!"

The young woman opened the door and nodded for Shaw to precede her.

Theo Gabris was larger than life. The two hundred and thirty- or forty-pound man rose, setting down a cigar he'd been chomping on. There was no smell of smoke in the air, so Shaw guessed the pacifier was a compromise to the state's smoking ban, which he would surely resent.

He wore a well-tailored suit that had to be expensive, and a Rolex watch. The cuffs of his starched white shirt were affixed with—most likely—real gold links. The office, though, was modest—functional and cluttered with scores of files and thousands of sheets of paper. Shaw recalled the man's main office was in San Francisco on Nob Hill.

The most elite 'hood in the City by the Bay.

He was, Shaw guessed, a man who enjoyed nice things in life but when it came to work, he wanted to stay focused. He'd known sales-people like him; closing the Deal was a sacred quest.

The receptionist recited, "Would you like something to drink, sir? Coffee? Water?"

"Nothing, thanks."

She retreated and Shaw walked into the office. "Carter Stone," he said, extending his hand, which was wholly enveloped by the developer's huge meaty digits. He was balding and had a ruddy complexion. Shaw wondered how he'd come by a tan; June was a bit early for such a deep tone in Northern California, but then again he was a real estate developer with three-thousand-dollar cuffs. Baja was not that far away, and California had the second highest level of private jet traffic in the country, after Florida. He could be sipping margaritas under a hot sun in two hours.

And—to keep in mind—Baja and nearby Sonora were home to the Sinaloa Cartel, which was always eager to launder money through legitimate operations like real estate.

"Now, Mr. Stone, what can I do for you? Change your life, make you happy in a million ways, find a nest for you and—you're of a particular age—you and your bride. Children too? I have six. Three boys and three girls. Ask me which I prefer? The ones that are under thirteen."

"A wife, no children." A smile. "Yet."

"Ah, now don't wait too long," the man scolded. Then a glint in his eye. "But maybe she's younger, maybe you robbed the cradle, did you? My wife is a younger woman." He nodded gravely. "We were born in the same year and the same month . . . only she is one day younger than I am!" A braying laugh. "All right, to be serious . . . Let me do what I can to put you in your dream house."

Colter found himself amused; Debi Starr had said much the same, about a dream house, though with a porcine companion.

"You just cruising by on that mini Harley of yours and were impressed by my properties."

So he'd been observed.

He was glad he had intentionally parked with the plate unseen by the front door's camera. A habit of his.

"Nope. I was at a party in San Francisco and someone recommended you. They had bought property in Silicon Valley."

"Evershire. Named after *The Hobbit*. The Shire. You know the books?"

Shaw had read all the Tolkien Middle-earth books. He said, "I've heard of them." A sentence that invariably means no. "I looked you up and found this." He nodded out the window. "Windermere. Maddie and I are in a condo in Mountain View . . ." He closed his eyes, mindful not to overact. "The mortgage, the HOA fees, and the cost of living there? Forget it! So we decided, like taking a deep breath and cutting the cable cord, we'd get out of the Bay Area. Maybe come here."

"A wise move, sir. You'll get ten times the value for your money. You'll be king of your own domain."

Shaw beamed at the validation. "We saw one on your website. The Byron model. We can customize it, right?"

"Interior? Yes, to your heart's content. Exteriors I've designed myself."

"Seriously? So you're an architect."

"No, no. But I will say I have imagination. Then I hand the nitty-gritty over to the experts."

"Do you have a model I could look at?"

"Not the Byron. They won't be ready for another two months or so. Can I interest you in a Shelley or Coleridge? They're similar. But smaller."

"No, our heart's set."

"Well, here's this." He pushed a brochure Shaw's way.

"Nice," Shaw said slowly, flipping the pages. "Oh, the kitchen. To die for. Maddie'll love it. She was going to meet me here, but did you hear? The levee collapsed in Hinowah and took Route Thirteen out."

"No! I didn't! Anyone get hurt?"

"I don't think so. But my wife's stuck in Nevada. Was there on business."

Was the surprise in Gabris's face genuine? The developer's reaction seemed authentic but in his years of rewards-seeking he had learned that depending on their level of skill, sociopaths can lie without detection.

Gabris scoffed. "That levee . . . I always said they should reinforce it."

So he was aware of how fragile the earthwork was.

"But all the county ever said was quote, 'We'll look into it.' And they never did. Of course, in fairness, in recent memory, the Never Summer's always been about two feet deep, tops."

"Let me ask you a question," Shaw began, a hint of conspiracy in his voice. "When they ran the news story about the levee, I saw some footage of the town."

"Hinowah?"

Shaw nodded. "It looked pretty nice. Quaint, you know. You have any houses there, by any chance? Or any plans to build? I frankly like trees a bit more than the desert."

Gabris blew out air and his cheeks puffed up. "No, sir, Mr. Stone, and word of warning: steer the hell away from property in Hinowah."

Shaw shot him a frown. "Why's that?"

"I looked into acquiring some land there. I thought there might be some people who'd like a more rustic home—like I'm hearing from you. You know, tucked away in an old mining town. A certain appeal. But I found out that the land is shit. Pardon my language."

"How's that?"

"It's not a declared Superfund site, but there're problems with the soil. You'll buy a home there at your own risk."

"But there are hundreds of houses there, it looked like."

"Nothing new. Mostly grandfathered in."

"What's the issue?"

Gabris chewed briefly on the cigar. "Runoff from the mines. A hundred fifty years ago, they had no concept of the environment. There's lead, arsenic, sulfuric acid. Bunch of other crap."

Shaw method-acted a frown. "Is there a problem *here*?"

"My God, no. I've had the soil analyzed from every single lot. Cost me a fortune. I'll get the report to you and your inspector. He can take samples of his own. But no, we're ten miles from the closest mine."

Gabris might have very well been a vulture, but Hinowah wasn't his prey.

"And that's not the only problem. Southwest of town there's an oil and gas fracking field. They pollute too. They say they don't but don't believe that bullshit . . ." A grimace. "Ha, you got me going today. I'll have to put two quarters in the swear jar tonight. So forget Hinowah, Mr. Stone. You want to live in Windermere! You play golf."

Not a question. Of course, every man on the face of the earth owned a set of clubs.

"My handicap isn't what I'd like," Shaw told him, with only a vague idea of what a handicap was.

"Well, our course'll be just the place to work on it!"

Shaw shook the man's big hand, and walked to the door, stowing the brochure in his backpack.

He fired up the cycle and backed away from the sales office, then sped off, keeping the license tag out of view. As he navigated back to Route 13 and passed through the ROAD CLOSED—DETOUR barricade, he was thinking: A helpful trip.

For one thing, he had eliminated a suspect.

But more important, the boisterous man had pointed him to another one.

Someone who had possibly blown up the levee to steal not land but something else altogether.

Something definitely worth killing for.

26.

Dorion Shaw's phone hummed with a text.
It was from Mary Dove.

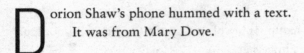

Hello, love. Route 44 closed—mudslide. Will be cleared around
midnight. Too late for these roads. Days Inn here. I'll be there for
the night. I've called the woman you asked me about, Mrs.
Petaluma. Twice. No answer. Left messages—English, Ohlone
and Miwok. I'll try again. And let you know if anything changes.
See you in the morning. MDMD

The last letters were a joke within the family, the nickname being her initials and her professional designation, as she was a licensed physician.

Dorion texted a cheerful and warm response.

Zipping her windbreaker up against a blustery gust of wind, she
walked to the fiberboard table that dominated the main command
post tent and regarded the map on the seventeen-inch Dell. The in-
tersection the woman had referred to was about ten miles from the

Compound, and it was also on the route that the mysterious and possibly dangerous Margaret would have to have taken to get there if she'd learned its location.

Dorion pictured the improbable scenario: Mary Dove was stuck on the northbound portion of 44, while on the other side of the blockage, one hundred feet away, Margaret waited in the southbound.

And they both got rooms for the night at the Days Inn.

No, beyond improbable.

Perhaps . . .

Begging the question: Had the half-sister *already* found the Compound? It would not be easy to track the place down. Ashton had titled the property through layers of offshore companies. But that in itself might be a clue Margaret would capitalize on—a review of local deeds books would reveal a large parcel titled in the name Emerson Trust IV, which would certainly stand out among names of other area property owners like Jones and Smith and Rodriguez.

She turned from these thoughts for a moment and sent texts seeking updates to Eduardo Gutiérrez, Tomas Martinez, TC McGuire and several other townspeople who were designated "evacuators," including most of the waylaid sandbagging team, pulled off that duty because of the risk of another explosion at the levee. She was pleased to learn that the evac was going well. McGuire reported:

Only had to cuff two, and that got the message across, tho one was the coach of my son's soccer team. I suspect my boy'll be sitting out most of the games this season oh well . . .

She calculated about three or four dozen remainers in the direct path of the flood, Mrs. Petaluma included. These would not be the lazy or uninformed, but those with the iron-core attitude that government should keep its hands off citizens.

Pill for stupid . . .

Part of her job, though, was protecting even people like that, and once the evac teams were done, she would descend into town herself and make her final pleas.

Her eyes on the hypnotic flow of water over the levee, she placed a call.

Tony Rossano answered. "Dor. All good there?"

She turned from the increasingly fragile earthworks and said, "Peachy. How's your Ashton homework?"

"I'm into my three-diopter reading glasses. Does anyone have smaller handwriting than your father?"

"Colter comes close."

"Reminds me of illuminated manuscripts from medieval monks." A beat. "Dor, look, I knew your father."

She sensed a defense coming and preempted him. "You're a lawyer, Tony. If the evidence is there, you go with it. And the evidence shows he had a daughter. And to have a daughter, he needed a lover."

"Granted. But I was going to say, he wasn't a serial philanderer. He would have cared about the girl's mother. There must have been . . . extenuating circumstances."

She gave a cold laugh. "That phrase can be used to *try to* justify almost anything, Tony."

She thought back to the night of the fight she'd had with Ashton, ending with her father and older brother facing off, a sharp blade between them.

"Let me ask you this," she said firmly. "You steal a hundred dollars from a bank once, you're still a bank robber, right? You don't need to do it a dozen times to qualify."

A sigh. "The court concedes the counselor's point. Now, I was about to text you and Colter. I found another letter from Margaret's mother, Sarah. It's troubling. I'll quote it. 'Ash, I'm moving again. It's exhausting. But I have no choice. They keep sniffing out my trail. They're EVERYWHERE.' That's in all caps. 'And I keep thinking about one thing: How did they find the last place I stayed, in San

Francisco?'" Tony paused. "'That room we know so well. Someone betrayed me. And I'm going to find out who it was. And then . . . Well, Ashton, as you know, actions have consequences.'"

Silence.

"That's all?"

"It looks like it's one of a couple of pages. I'll keep looking for the others. These are just a jumble. He used to be so organized."

For a brief moment Dorion nearly choked up. She nearly said, "People change." But she didn't, for fear her voice would crack. After a moment she managed, "Colter and I were thinking that maybe Sarah killed herself, and Margaret blames Mary Dove. Or she wants revenge against the whole family. Colter, Russell and me too. It sounds like she's out for blood. It's not just defense that she's about. It's offense too now."

"Not totally far-fetched. I'll keep looking."

After a second Dorion said, "Ashton's essays and letters, some of it? It's pretty crazy."

"Yes," Tony said thoughtfully, "but not aliens-from-outer-space crazy. There's a kernel of truth to what he's saying. Corrupt politicians, corrupt companies, corrupt pharma . . . But he saw it everywhere. I'm a lawyer and even *I* don't think there's that much evil out there."

A brief laugh. "We're out in mining country, Tony. That's the way it used to work, apparently. You panned through tons of rock and mud and dirt to come up with one nugget of gold."

"That was your father, true. Though I wouldn't call the insights he found gold. More like radioactive uranium."

"I'll tell you why I called, Tony. If anybody drives to the Compound, they have to go past your place. Any chance you could swing a security camera wide, so you'll see them?"

"No security cams near the road, but I've got a wildlife camera in the back. Motion activated and infrared, so it works at night. And it's camo, so nobody'd see it. I'll move it to the front yard."

"Thanks."

She disconnected and heard the rattle of her brother's motorcycle. He arrived at the far end of Route 13 and took the hill down into town. Then he sped through the village and up the hill on this side of the valley.

He climbed off and she joined him, wishing to speak in private about her call with Tony.

She first told him that their mother was safely out of the Compound but had been delayed en route. She would be here in the morning. Dorion then told him about the threatening letter that the lawyer had found. "Sarah was upset and suspicious. Talking about somebody betraying her. Almost like it was Ashton himself."

"Betraying her how?"

"No answer that Tony found. I asked him to set up a camera on the road to the Compound."

"Good." He made a cup of coffee from the Keurig. Dorion declined. He said, "Let's talk to the others. I've found a few things."

They joined the mayor, Starr, Olsen and TC McGuire. Just then Eduardo Gutiérrez pulled up in his SUV. He would have seen Colter's cycle, or heard it, and would be curious as to what he'd learned. He joined them too.

Colter said, "We need to confirm something, and if it's true, we can eliminate Gabris."

He told them that the developer had reported that Hinowah's soil was tainted and that he wouldn't even consider a development here.

Tolifson was frowning. "We did have some issues, I remember. I thought it was limited to Misfortune Row. That was closest to the silver mines."

As Debi Starr looked at her phone she recited, "This part of Olechu County, including Hinowah, is a designated brownfield. I'm reading from the EPA."

She was one fast woman when it came to online research.

"Brownfield?" Olsen asked.

Starr said, "Here's a quote. 'A brownfield is a property where expansion, redevelopment or reuse may be complicated by the presence or potential presence of a hazardous substance, pollutant or contaminant.'" She looked up. "There goes your vulture."

Colter said, "Gabris gave me an idea for another possibility, though. Somebody blew the levee to steal the water."

Tolifson asked, "Steal it? Who?"

"There's a fracking operation southwest of town, he told me." Her brother turned the computer so that they could all see the map. He typed a command and it changed from the basic schematic to the satellite image. You could see the town and, to the west, the copper mine and a farm. About three miles south of the farm was a large rectangle of land that was filled with industrial equipment.

He said, "I looked it up online. American Oil and Gas Extraction Company."

Tolifson blew a breath from puffed-out cheeks. "Oh, I'll tell you. Plenty of protests when they leased the land."

Starr nodded. "The hearings? Anti-frackers painted this gloom and doom. Blowouts from gas explosions, earthquakes. The big issue is the water pumped down to do the fracking. It's mixed with chemicals to make it a better quote 'drill' and after it's shot into the ground the flowback comes to the surface and the companies have to do something with it—millions of gallons. Lot of it ends up in local soil."

Dorion had run a cleanup job at a fracking site destroyed by an earthquake—which might or might not have been caused by the well itself. She told those assembled about the job and added, "The company said the chemicals are the same as you'd find in household products. That may be true but they don't tell you that it *also* contains diesel fuel, methanol, formaldehyde, ethylene, glycol, glycol ethers, hydrochloric acid and sodium hydroxide."

Starr grimaced. "The leases went through anyway, no matter all the protests, and I always wondered if administrative folk got paid off." She gave a chuckle as she looked at Tolifson. "Not you, Mayor. I'm talking higher up. At the county level."

Tolifson scoffed and said, "Hinowah is too lowly to even rate a bribe."

McGuire asked, "Why do you suspect them?"

Colter explained that fracking operations used huge amounts of water.

Dorion said, "An average frack uses millions of gallons. Sometimes up to ten or fifteen—for a single well."

Eyes on the map, Colter said, "Just a scenario. Thinking out loud. They blow the levee, the water flows down the spillway, into the gulley in front of Copper Peak." He traced a line. "It hits the copper mine and farm and flows south, ending up here." He tapped what looked like a dry lake bed right next to the fracking company.

Starr clicked her tongue. "Like a huge spigot, straight from the river to the frackers."

Dorion added, "And one thing to know: fracking operations can use explosives in addition to the water for drilling. In fact, the process was invented by a Civil War general who saw that the impact of artillery shells released oil and gas from the battlefield."

Olsen said, "So the fracker could have access to C-four or something else that goes bang." Dorion noted another smiling glance Colter's way. Interesting, she thought, before tucking the thought away.

He said, "I'm going to check the place out."

Starr chuckled. "How's that undercover thing of yours going to work this time? Tell them you want a barrel of fracked oil as a souvenir of your trip to the Sierra Nevadas?"

"I was thinking—"

"Flaw in the plan," Gutiérrez said.

All eyes turned to him.

He looked up from his phone. "I'm quoting. 'AOGE—American Oil and Gas Extraction Company—has suspended its operation in Olechu County, California, citing a miscalculation of the reserves.

The equipment will be dismantled and sent to the company's other facilities in Southern California and Oregon.'"

She looked up. "So."

"Square one," Tolifson said.

Or whatever cliché you wanted to use, Dorion reflected.

But the search for a new theory was interrupted by the curious sight of a shiny black limousine that pulled to a stop above them, on Route 13, parking in front of Colter's Winnebago, just shy of the shattered edge of the highway.

A businessman sort, about forty, with short perfectly trimmed hair, climbed out of the backseat, bending over to say something to the driver. He stood, fired up an impressive folding umbrella, then, with a frowning glance to the waterfall streaming over the levee, spotted the command post and walked down to it, apparently without a second thought about the mud bath that was staining the shoes that Dorion guessed had to have cost five hundred dollars.

27.

Colter Shaw watched the precise man pause outside the tent and carefully shake the umbrella out, as if he had just come calling to the home of someone whose beautiful hardwood floors he would never, in a million years, taint with rainwater.

He entered, set the open umbrella down in the back and joined those present with a cheerful nod.

His name was Howie Katz and he'd driven here—well, apparently, *been* driven—from Fort Pleasant.

"How can we help you?" Tolifson asked, waving him to a chair.

Colter's eyes caught his sister's and they shared a glance of curiosity—tinted with a vague air of suspicion. Some things just didn't smell quite right from the get-go.

"I know how busy you must be so I'll just jump in. I'm head of community relations for a company in Fort Pleasant. You've probably heard of us . . . GraphSet Chips, Inc." A look around. TC McGuire nodded. Tolifson squinted but the others gave no reaction. To them he said, "No? Well, no worries." He smiled. "Chips. Not the potato variety. We really ought to change the name. We're one of the biggest specialized graphics-processing chipmakers in the world, and unlike a lot of the others we make chips exclusively in the United States, not South Korea or Taiwan."

McGuire said, "You need GPU chips for artificial intelligence. AI can't run on CPUs."

Katz's eyes brightened and he stabbed a finger toward the officer. "Exactly! To make a long story somewhat less long, we met in an emergency meeting this morning, the board and the senior staff. We authorized aid for towns in Olechu County affected by flooding. And Hinowah is one of them. You can look at us like a private FEMA."

"Aid? What kind of aid?" Tolifson asked.

"Two forms. Cash payments to each household damaged or destroyed by flooding—that's on top of their private insurance coverage. Insured or not, a homeowner gets the money. And, two, our financing department will arrange long-term, low-interest loans." He added brightly, "I'm talking private residences *and* businesses."

"That's pretty generous," Tolifson offered. He glanced at Starr. "Maybe our guest would like a cup of coffee."

Colter noted Dorion stiffen—and he himself was about to shoot a get-it-yourself glance to the mayor. But before either could react, Katz shook his head. "No, no, I'm good. Thanks." The man smiled. He had a cherubic face. Made sense to look like that, if you were a shill for a big company.

"We want to be a good neighbor. Our employees've fallen in love with Olechu County. And I'm one of them. We were based in Silicon Valley but we decided it was too expensive and congested. And we didn't like the . . . mindset. Too many apps for sushi and wine terroirs. We were a little apprehensive—being outsiders—but you all welcomed us with open arms."

Shaw was six when the family fled from the Bay Area to the Compound. He had little recollection of Silicon Valley, though he was now very aware of its pricey and pretentious nature, having run various jobs there, including one that took him head-to-head with one of the biggest video-game makers in the world. On the other hand, those people you could label inauthentic and pompous had unquestionably changed the world—usually for the better.

The cheerfulness now gave way to a strain of sincerity. "It's not all altruism, of course. We count your residents as some of our best employees, and we want to make sure they have houses to come home to when the day is done."

Colter suspected there was another reason behind the move. Dorion had told him that every disaster response company in the country had a tactical plan for the aftermath of a quake along the San Andreas Fault, which ran nearly the length of California—and right through the heart of Silicon Valley. It was this fault that was responsible for the quake of 1906, which resulted in the destruction of much of San Francisco.

Another quake *would* happen.

Only a matter of time.

Katz placed a large stack of business cards on the table. "Give those away to your residents. And you can make the announcement to look us up online. We have people standing by to take their calls. We can arrange for emergency shelter, food, water, insurance company liaison, get them cash. Your ATMs'll be out, of course."

"Can't thank you enough, Mr. Katz," Tolifson said.

"Giving back. That's what it's all about." He rose, again studying the levee and its growing waterfall.

"Ask a question?" This came from Debi Starr.

"Of course, Officer." He turned.

"What about now?"

"Now?"

"You're talking about help *if* the levee fails."

"That's right. God forbid it happens, of course."

"All very good and kind of you. But Fort Pleasant's got the bulk of the state and county manpower to sandbag and shore up and who knows what the heck else they're up to."

Tolifson was once again shaking his head subtly, instructing his officer to tread carefully.

She either didn't see or—Colter suspected—chose to ignore him.

Katz was frowning. "I'm not sure about that."

"No, no, it's true. All the resources're there. And I'm just thinking, since you've got to be talking millions . . ."

"Tens of."

A finger snap. "There you go, sir. Well, we could use help *now*. We're still not one hundred percent evacuated. And we're not sandbagging the top of the levee because it's not safe."

The officer did not mention why.

"But if we had the manpower, I mean fifty, sixty people, we could clear out all of the population and triple sandbag in front of the town. And get a half dozen bulldozers in here to trench. Won't stop all of the flood, if the whole shebang comes down, but it'll go a long way."

He grimaced. "Well, we looked at the estimated volume and the topography. That would save *some* of the town, but not the south side. And of course, the farmland and the mine would still get flooded."

Tolifson stirred. "I'm sure—"

But Starr ignored him. "Just looking the whole thing up and down, I'd say saving *some* houses is better than saving none. And it'd also save *you* a big wad of that aid money."

Katz looked into the village. "Anybody sandbagging would be in harm's way."

Olsen said, "We're taking precautions to prevent or slow the collapse."

Again, not mentioning that it was tactical bomb curtains that would buy them protection and time.

Katz was nodding. "Of course. It's a great idea. A super one. I like it. Of course, that's not a call for *me* to make but I'll raise it. I'll raise it soon as I'm back in the office."

Dorion said, "I hope your personal home's okay, Mr. Katz. And the company headquarters."

"Both safe, thanks for asking."

Colter had known his sister long enough to spot the stiletto blade of irony.

Which the executive missed entirely.

He retrieved his hundred-dollar umbrella and climbed back up to the Mercedes. There, Colter saw him sit in the backseat, leaving the door open. The driver, a large man with pale skin, walked around the car to him. Katz took off his shoes and handed them to the man, who put them in the trunk, along with the umbrella. He returned with a shoebox. Katz opened it and pulled on brown lace-ups. There was tissue paper involved. The shoes were new.

Debi Starr happened to be looking too. "Hm, I'm going to check and see if we've got money to hire a shoe-replacer man, Mayor."

"You don't think he's going to up and throw the dirty ones out, do you?" Tolifson asked.

Starr said to Dorion: "I guess vultures come in all shapes and sizes."

"Amen," whispered Tamara Olsen. "You think we'll see any of that money and manpower up front?"

"Not a penny," Starr muttered, though with some good humor.

TC McGuire said, "So. What now? No suspects. It's a dead end."

Starr looked from the limo to those around the table. "Thought occurred."

Colter asked, "Inspired by a podcast?"

"Matter of fact, yes. I *do* love them. Jimmy, he likes *Dancing with the Stars*. Mr. Two Left Feet. And *American Idol*. And the twins are sports, sports, superheroes and sports. But I like my pods. Anyway there's a history one I was listening to last year. You ever hear about the Hatfields and McCoys?"

28.

Waylon Foley loved to hunt.

The kick of a rifle was a kind of sexual thing, though he never told anybody that.

He liked the sweet smell of Hoppe's gun cleaner, the even-more-pleasant smell of the smoke from smokeless powder, the sun on the rich warm walnut, and the cold blue barrel of a Winchester or Remington or his own Savage.

The best part of all: He loved the way your target just dropped.

Alive, then not alive.

What a beautiful thing.

Presently Foley was in Hinowah, making his way through the brush, on the south hillside above the town.

He kept his eye on the command post, on the north hill, about three hundred yards away. He was careful that no one there saw him.

The kick of the recoil.

A pause.

Then down went your prey.

On the highway above the command post the limo did a careful three-point turn and vanished slowly. No one else was around and he crouched in bushes and removed his spotting scope from inside his jacket, which was still soiled from where the asshole had cheated and dropped him to the ground that morning, which never would have happened in a fair fight.

Foley played the scope over the conference going on in the larger of the three tents.

He set the crosshairs on the very man responsible for his dirty garment, his aching shoulder and swollen nose. He could still taste the pungent tang of the blood.

Motorcycle Man . . .

There are two telescopes used in hunting. The one everybody who took game or owned a TV knew about was mounted to the top of the firearm. A telescopic sight, crosshairs and all that.

But the second—the one he now held—was just as important. It was known as a spotter scope. Military snipers didn't operate alone. Killing at distance was a process, like a medical operation. You needed a nurse. The spotter used a scope like this on the job.

You had to know distance precisely. Down to the foot. And you needed to see how the wind was blowing around your target—dust going this way or that, grass waving.

That's what this scope did—in addition to scanning for threats (you never used the rifle scope for that).

He winced once again, and gazed through the scope at the man responsible for his pain.

Foley could have taken him earlier. And he would have if the guy hadn't gotten a phone call or text and used that as an excuse to run off like a scared boy.

He swung the scope to take in the levee, which was now a righteous waterfall.

Slowly eating itself to death.

Foley had his weapon with him, in a green, waterproof case. But now was not the time.

The distance was fine—three hundred and thirty-two yards.

But the wind from the damn storm . . . it was too unpredictable.

He'd have to wait. Find the man in a valley, less breeze, and maybe a little closer.

There was also the matter that at the present moment there were a half dozen law enforcers with weapons. Though a shot with a handgun from that distance was unlikely to be accurate, you could be killed by a wild shot just as easily as one aimed with perfect skill.

As he slowly made his way out of the nest, Waylon Foley decided there was another reason to wait. He'd learned over the years the longer you delayed satisfying your desire, the richer the act of achieving it was in the end. And this applied to a shot of whisky, a woman or a kill.

29.

There's this thing called the Law of the River," Debi Starr explained.

Colter had never heard of it, and it was clear no one else had either, even Tolifson, who mayored a town sitting right beside one.

"You hear it most often about the Colorado River—seven states in the basin are in a compact to share the water—but it's a legal principle everywhere. The first person to use water from a source has senior rights. The next is secondary. The next is thirdiary or whatever the word is. The person with senior rights uses what they need and what's left over goes to the second-rights person and so on. That's hunky-dory if there's enough, but in California, usually there isn't, so somebody gets the short end of the stick.

"Well, Nowhere—excuse me, *Hinowah*—is like some town out of an old-time Western. Clint Eastwood flick. Don't you love him . . . Two warring sides."

Tolifson was nodding now. "I see where you're going. The Coynes and the Reddings. Bad blood."

Starr snapped her fingers again. "Bingo. Annie Coyne runs that farm you were just looking at on the map, Colter. And Gerard Redding has that copper mine just north of her.

"All right, Law of the River. We clear so far? Good. I taught third grade, so, sorry. Just want to make sure I see that burst of understanding in everyone's eyes, not a glaze-over. The Coynes, the Reddings. Both families came to Hinowah around the time of the Silver Rush. Eighteen forties. They both used water from the Never Summer. Farming, well, that goes without saying. But copper mining uses a bunch too."

Tolifson said, "I went to a booster club lunch a few months ago, and Gerard was talking about the mining business. He needs the river, because copper miners do the refining on-site. It's cheaper to do that than to ship raw ore to refineries someplace else. And refining's water intensive."

Debi Starr continued, "Well, all was good waterwise between the two during the eighteen hundreds, when it was share and share alike. The twentieth century starts out fine. Oh, a few disputes, because the Never Summer's starting to get lower and lower. Then forty years ago: bad. It's drought city and there just wasn't enough to go around. They go to court, Ezra Coyne—Annie's daddy—and Redding's pa, Henry. They make their claims, but there's no—what the judge called—'credible evidence' about who was first. So the court orders a fifty-fifty split.

"Now, one thing about mining towns. Gambling. *Hinowah* comes from 'gambling bones' in Miwok."

Colter and Dorion shared a glance at this.

"So Ezra and Henry are in a poker game at Butch's. You remember that place?"

Tolifson said he did and his face darkened remarkably, which told Colter two things. One, Butch's was either a biker bar or strip joint, and two, Tolifson was probably a churchgoer.

"Ezra bets four hundred acres of farmland against ten percent of Henry's entitlement to the water. Ezra loses. His daughter goes topsy-turvy. She drives to the mine and confronts Henry and his son and says words I won't repeat to you. Claims he cheated. But there was no evidence of that either. Ezra had no choice but to deed over the land. A whole one-third of the farm.

"Their old men have both passed and Annie and Gerard have inherited the land *and* the feud. I've had to serve a dozen warrants. And respond to complaints from both of them. Water smuggling, diversion from irrigation troughs, sabotaging pipelines. There was a settlement here, a fine there."

Tolifson muttered, "I think you listen to too *many* podcasts, Deb. Call me slow. But how would that work? Annie Coyne—who does not *look* like a killer, I'll tell you. If you've ever seen her. But we'll assume. She brings down the levee, floods the town and the water runs into the mine? Drives him out of business?"

Gutiérrez said, "Or vice versa, Gerard Redding blows it to flood *her* out."

Olsen said, "But they'd each risk ruining their own companies."

Tolifson: "My point."

But Colter was intrigued with the idea. "Could one of them have been building up some savings to live on, and outlast the other one after the flood, hoping they'll go bankrupt? One survives. The levee gets rebuilt and the water supply stabilizes and they get a hundred percent of it."

Starr said, "That means that the guilty party knows what's coming and wants to minimize their damage, so they've been making plans all along for this—and started protecting their place *before* the levee went, maybe, I don't know, sandbagging last night." She looked to Dorion. "Like that arson vulture you were telling us about. The one who started the fire in Arizona—the police found the letters he'd written to homeowners ahead of time."

A solid idea, Colter was thinking. He noted Olsen's striking eyes above that mysterious smile drift his way.

McGuire said, "I know both of them. And they're tough businesspeople, I'll admit. But this is murder you're talking about."

Colter, though, said, "Not necessarily. Look how it's working. Two feet of levee goes. There's a risk of more flooding. The town's evacuated. When everybody's out, whoever's behind it blows the other charges."

Tolifson said, "Nearly killed the people were on the levee this morning."

Starr said, "Six a.m., Han? Probably didn't expect anybody to be driving along it then."

Colter said, "I give it a forty-, forty-five percent chance that's what happened. I can go have a talk with them. Tell them I'm working with Dor's disaster response company. Seeing if they're complying with the evac order."

Tolifson said, "If you find out they started prepping early, then we'll get a warrant, search the property."

Starr turned to Colter. "Keep that toy six-gun of yours with you. That Bear fellow's probably working for one or the other."

Colter understood too that this could have been the reason for the attack that morning. Bear was worried he was investigating the sabotage.

He nodded and rose. "I'll get out there now."

As he was walking down the hill to where his Yamaha was parked, a voice from behind him asked, "Hey, Colter."

He turned. It was Tamara Olsen. He now realized there was something different about her. Ah, right. She had taken her hair down from the bun.

In his experience this was occasionally a message.

She walked up. A bit into his space. He didn't mind. He offered, "Hey."

He received one of her great smiles right back.

She said, "Look, I don't mean to be out of line, but can I ask a question?"

He gave her a smile too. "That's an intriguing opening."

She was hesitating. "I mean here I am, a U.S. soldier, but, with some things, I get kind of shy."

"Understood."

"Well, what I wanted to know . . ."

"Go ahead." Colter's eyes swept from her hair to her taut figure, then to her cheeks, dusted with freckles. Colter Shaw had always liked freckles. His eyes seated on hers, the curious green.

"Your sister? Is she married or seeing anybody?" She looked down.

Oh.

So those meaningful looks were aimed *past*, not at, him, toward nearby Dorion.

A faint laugh. "She'd be flattered, but she's married." He'd almost added, "To a man." But that was, he assessed, both unnecessary and politically fraught. "She doesn't wear a ring on the job."

"Ah." A tightened smile of disappointment. "He's a lucky man, her husband. That's all I can say. All right, go get 'em, Jack Ryan."

Who? Colter wondered. And continued on to the Yamaha.

30.

She wasn't hard to spot.

A determined look on her face, the blond woman was driving a thirty-six-inch black-and-orange Ditch Witch trencher north to south along the front of Coyne Farm, which was about a mile from downtown Hinowah.

In a transparent rain slicker over blue jeans and a brown leather jacket, she was pushing the implement as fast as it could go, dirt flying out and joining its muddy kin.

She was on her third trench and the interconnected ditches were well placed. They would divert floodwaters to the south, around much of the farm. Another line of defense were hundreds of sandbags. Three workers wearing similar gear to hers were filling and stacking the bags.

How much water would these defenses divert? Hard to say, but not enough to stop the farm from getting some damage, he assessed. Maybe a lot. The flood would have the full snowpack melt of the mountains within it.

But that wasn't Colter Shaw's concern. The only question he had to answer here was: When had the work begun?

After six-fifteen that morning, when the explosion sheared off the top of the levee?

Or before? Because, like an inside trader, she knew what was coming?

Vultures . . .

She had dug one trench at the gate but had laid planks to make a six-foot access bridge.

Coyne was looking his way. She nodded into the yard and Shaw accelerated over the bridge, parked and swung down the kickstand. He got off the bike. Coyne clicked the trencher to neutral, climbed off and walked to him.

Her pretty, weather-tanned face studied him carefully. There was a hint of suspicion. "Can I help you?"

He offered one of Dorion's cards and gave his name. "I'm working with Mayor Tolifson and a disaster response company." He nodded to the trenches. "You heard about the levee, I see. The mayor's issued an evacuation order."

"I know. And that there are criminal penalties for not complying." She had a pleasant alto voice. "I'm staying. You going to arrest me?"

"I'm not a law officer."

"A threat like the levee? Either you run or you fight it." A nod at the Ditch Witch. "That tell you my decision? I need a rest stop." She shouted words in Spanish to a worker nearby. He hurried to the machine and continued trenching.

Halfway to the house, she looked over her shoulder at Colter. "You coming?"

Inside, the residence was surprising. Not the least rustic. It was filled with lace throws, overstuffed velvet furniture with carved feet on the legs, tasseled lampshades and Pre-Raphaelite paintings and old photos in ornate frames. Oriental rugs, stained glass. The smell of rose petals and cloves mixed with that of fertilizer.

Seeing his reaction, Coyne offered, "Mining town bordello chic, don't you think?"

He couldn't help but laugh.

She tugged off the rain slicker and hung it on a peg by the door. She left her jacket on.

Coyne looked him over. "Shaw Incident Services. Fairfax, Virginia. You're a long way from home."

She'd glanced only quickly at the card but managed to retain the information.

"It's my sister's company. I'm just helping out."

"You live around here?"

"Family does."

"Not you?"

"I travel a lot."

"Be right back." She vanished into a hallway. A few minutes later she returned. "I heard three to four feet of the levee came down. How's the rest of it holding?"

Did the delivery of the question implicate or absolve her?

Hard to say.

"Not great. Situational erosion's whittling it down."

She frowned.

He explained, "Term of art. It means acute, unexpected erosion. In this case, it's because of a sudden snowmelt about fifty miles from here."

"'Situational.' Hm. Too long for Wordle. You know when the river will crest?"

"Probably not for a day or two."

"Shit. Is the cavalry here?"

"In a way, yes. Army engineers. But the county and state have their hands full with Fort Pleasant."

"I need a beer. You?"

"Not with two wheels on mud and asphalt."

"A cautious man."

"At times. Coffee if there's some made."

"There's a pot. Been there for a couple hours."

"It's still coffee."

"How do you like it?"

"With a little milk if you've got any."

"I have a cow. She's in the barn. Because of the flood I got her to the top floor, which was a feat, I will tell you. So, yeah, I have milk."

She disappeared into the kitchen and he stepped to the hewn-wood mantel above a fieldstone fireplace. There sat scores of photographs in ornate silver frames. He scanned them. A happy family working in the fields and at afternoon Sunday suppers. Parents, Ezra and his wife, their daughters, Annie being the eldest. As the photos grew clearer—higher definition—the population in the pictures aged and then thinned.

And then they stopped altogether. No photos in the past few years.

But several—from ten years ago—were of her in uniform with other soldiers. Army.

There was nothing about being in the service that necessarily made you more familiar with explosives than anyone else. But it did give you better access to knowledge about things that went bang.

And access to ex-military personnel who wanted to keep playing with the tools of the trade for fun and profit after they commissioned out.

Mercenaries.

Coyne returned with a bottle of Anchor Steam and a mug of coffee. Shaw nodded thanks. It wasn't too burnt.

She chugged half the bottle.

Shaw said, "Impressive what you've done." Glancing toward the front of the property. "And in next to no time."

Trying to pin her down.

"I started the minute we heard."

Sidestepped that one, he thought.

"You were lucky to have a trencher."

Wondering if she'd rented it recently.

"Farming is all about heavy equipment." She gave a sour laugh. "You know what it's like—digging the trenches? It's like a reverse moat around a castle—and the water's the marauding barbarian."

"And planks at the gate? Your drawbridge."

Another long swallow from the bottle. "I always thought that levee ought to be replaced. California's the land of special referendums on the ballot. People can vote for what they want. Get a concrete one put in. I talked to my congresspeople. They enthusiastically said, 'My goodness, you're right. That levee's a disaster just waiting to happen. We'll get back to you.'" A bitter laugh escaped her throat. "I've been checking messages for four years. But zip." She grew somber. "I heard a family died. Their SUV got washed away."

"No, we saved them."

"Thank God for that."

The relief of someone who just learned she had not committed murder? Or was the reference just a way to brush up her patina of innocence?

In the reward business you learned to read people, and Colter Shaw was talented at it. But Annie Coyne remained a mystery.

And how had she known they were in an SUV.

She asked, "You know disaster response. So how do the trenches look?"

His only experience digging one was prior to a gunfight. Like a foxhole in combat. He said, "Never relied on one to stop a flood. And nobody has any idea how deep the water'll be by the time it gets out here."

"How much of the town has evacuated?"

"It's about ninety-five percent. They've gone to Hanover College."

Coyne was nodding. "Good choice. If that goes, well, it's time to start looking for the Ark."

"You know if Gerard Redding's evacuated the mine?"

"Hope so, for his workers' sake. As for him, don't much care. His name's not on my dance card." She said this sourly.

Shaw lifted a brow.

"We don't see eye to eye, Redding and me."

"That right?"

She sighed. "Water. Goddamn water. It's the new gold, Colter. The earth is mostly water but nearly all of it might as well be Play-Doh. The water that counts? It's vanishing. In Africa, the Middle East, South Asia . . . There, if it's not droughted away, it's being weaponized. A warlord who controls the water controls the people." Her gaze grew dark. "And I have a feeling it's the same thing here. Gerrymandering around water sources to keep the voters under a politician's thumb."

Shaw had not heard of this, but it was right up his father's alley—a man who never met a government conspiracy he didn't brake for.

"Fresh water in California." A shake of her head. "It's like playing a dozen games of chess at the same time. All the Salad Bowl farms—from Sacramento down to Bakersfield—fighting for every drop. Small ones like me and huge agra-com operations. Back in the old days they fought over land and claims and gold. Now we fight over water." She scoffed. "Of course, now I've got to worry about too *much* of it."

"If the land flooded, what would it do to the farm?"

"I'd lose a year's crop. It would wash away topsoil and the seeds I just sowed. And the water would unbalance the nitrogen and phosphorus. But worse than that, I'd lose all my research fields. Here, take a look."

She walked toward her desk and he followed her. On it were hundreds of sheets of paper, folders, books, magazines. Though it seemed highly unlikely to be the case, he took the opportunity to see if there was any evidence she was preparing for the flood ahead of time, proving she was behind the sabotage. But it was all scientific in nature, financial spreadsheets, technical data.

Besides, she didn't seem like the sort of woman who was foolish enough to leave evidence lying around.

"Hobby of mine. I farm because I love it, and it's a family legacy. But I stumbled on something a few years ago and it's become a passion. Phytoremediation."

"I'm not generally passionate about things I can't pronounce."

A smile eased onto her face as their eyes met. "You're funny, Colter. Phytoremediation is the science of removing toxins and chemicals and other crap from the soil through plants. Certain types of vegetation absorb the bad stuff, break the poisons apart and dispose of them in the air. Stuff that'll kill us and animals doesn't affect them at all. And what they off-gas isn't bad either."

Interesting idea. He'd have to mention it to Dorion. Because of her job she was acutely aware of the effects of chemical spills. The process Coyne was describing would not be an immediate solution to an incident, but maybe plants could be sown in affected soil to mitigate long-term pollution.

He told her this.

"That's exactly what it's about. I think it's the wave of the future."

She stretched and stifled a yawn.

Shaw gave it one more shot. "Must've gotten up early for the trenching."

Coyne gave him a look. Did she suspect something?

"Started digging the minute we heard. About seven or so. But you're talking to a farm girl, sir."

Shaw cocked his head.

"If we're still in bed at five a.m., that's known as sleeping in. Now, I got some ditches to dig. You best scoot."

31.

The entrance to Redding Mining looked more like a prison than a business.

An acre of gravel—and today, mud—was encircled with a six-foot-high fence of thin metal posts sharpened like old-time Prussian army helmets and painted gray. Entry was via an electronically operated chain-link gate about twenty feet wide. Inside the forbidding barrier were administrative offices to the right and factories and workers' buildings to the left. Straight ahead were the three mine shafts themselves.

Colter Shaw rolled his bike to a stop just outside the gate and squinted to make sure he was correctly reading the signs above the entrances.

INFERNO

HADES

HELL

A man with a perverse sense of humor, this Gerard Redding.

In the hills behind the mines were two smokestacks a hundred feet high, with fumes wafting from them. Scaffolding and fencing and pipes and conduit and relics of old, rusting machinery were everywhere. Mining apparently did not require tidiness.

A skeleton crew was working today and their efforts had nothing to do with copper. While Annie Coyne's battle technique was digging trenches, Gerard Redding's men and women were filling and stacking sandbags. To gain access to the office you had to climb up and down sandbag "stairs" assembled at the gate. All the workers' vehicles were parked outside this perimeter, except for a late-model Mercedes and a Lexus, which were inside the protection zone. The owners of those vehicles weren't going anywhere.

He climbed off the bike. There was an armed guard in a small shed beside the gate. "Can I help you?"

"I'm working with Mayor Tolifson. I'd like to see Mr. Redding."

The guard looked him over as he made a phone call and explained Shaw's presence. He seemed to stand slightly to attention as he listened to the response—though this might have been imagination. He disconnected and said, "Wait here."

Shaw recalled that Tolifson and Starr had not spoken kindly of the man.

That's putting sugar on it . . .

Shaw reflected that the attack earlier by Bear, while it might technically have been on the Redding Mining property, was a long way from this location. Was that significant?

He looked at the sandbagging operation. It was an impressive wall. Had they started building it before the levee's collapse? Maybe, though they were moving quickly. It was not impossible that they began their work after the witching hour of 6:15 a.m.

A few minutes later a man in his seventies appeared from one of the buildings He was stooped but in fit shape, and clearly muscled. His face was weathered, and thinning white hair was combed back over the top of his narrow skull.

He walked with a stride, and climbed the improvised stairs to join Shaw. "It's okay, Fred," he said to the guard.

The man retreated to the shed.

"Gerard Redding."

Shaw identified himself.

The miner glanced at the Yamaha and Shaw looked for any indication that the man was familiar with him or the bike—and therefore had heard a report from Bear about the earlier encounter.

None that Shaw could see.

He handed Redding another Shaw Incident Services card. Unlike Coyne he stuck it in his rear slacks pocket without as much as a glance.

"You know about the levee." Shaw nodded to the sandbagging workers. Did they fill and stack just a bit more quickly now that the boss was present? He added, "The city's overwhelmed, so our company's helping. The mayor's ordered a mandatory evacuation."

A breezy laugh. "He the police chief now?"

"Acting, yes."

"Hm. Well, sir, you're standing in *unincorporated* Olechu County. So *mandatory*'s not a word that means anything."

"Then 'requesting.'" Shaw looked around. "Your employees might want the option. Though it looks like you sent most of them home anyway. Or told the shift not to come in."

Was it the latter? That could be incriminating, depending on when he'd issued the stay-at-home order.

But Redding did not step into the trap. "No, the whole shift was here. But as soon as I heard about the collapse, I got 'em out. These boys—and gals—volunteered. Hugh and me, the operations manager, we've been helping with the bags too, in between moving the electronics and paperwork records to high ground. In case the whole levee comes down."

"You moved fast."

"I started yesterday."

Ah . . . an admission!

The miner continued, "I thought something like this might happen. I know the Never Summer. It's been part of my whole family's life for nearly two hundred years. I check the weather daily. Here and up north, at the source. Snowpack—how deep? Last winter—how cold was it? Was there any melt in January or February or is the mountain still loaded with the snows from October, just waiting to melt and flood? And now, record heat? I knew it was going to swell. I always keep sand and bags ready." He nodded to a huge pile.

How good an actor was he?

"So we'll stay put."

"Your workers?"

"You notice anything about their cars?"

Shaw had not.

"They're all pointed at Hillside Road. Which, yes, goes up the hillside. And look at the exhausts. The engines're running. We hear the levee goes entirely, they can be out of here in thirty seconds."

He squinted as he looked over Shaw. "I suppose you talked to the *Petticoat Junction* girl."

"Annie Coyne. Yes."

"I'll bet she's not leaving either."

When Shaw said nothing, Redding chuckled. "Of course not. She's afraid I'll sneak in and turn her faucets on. Flood her out from the inside. Or burn her spread down. That woman needs to chill. She's convinced my family's been stealing water from hers for generations. A barn owl spooks and it's because I'm poisoning crops late at night. A combine breaks, it's sabotage. The price of soy goes down, I'm pulling strings."

Shaw looked at the wall of sandbags that had grown higher as they'd spoken. It was now about four feet tall and the way the workers were moving, it seemed likely they'd have the front of the mining operation covered in the next hour.

Shaw's eyes scanned the mine, the refinery and the surrounding hills.

Then the wall of bags.

"You think this'll hold?"

"I'm an engineer, Mr. Shaw. I calculated estimated velocity, volume, dispersion per hundred feet from the levee, grade of the land. And temperature—everyone forgets about temperature. Bad mistake." He examined the bags. "It will hold. Let's hope the fore-cast's wrong, and we get some overcast on the mountain up north. Slow the melt. Now, I appreciate your visit and you can thank Mayor Tolifson for his concern. Of course, you know he's of two minds."

"How do you mean?"

"He wants me to evacuate so he doesn't need to allocate re-sources to save assholes like me who don't *feel* like evacuating." He looked at Shaw wryly. "Then there's the other aspect. He doesn't want us to stop the sandbagging. If my mine gets destroyed or has to shut down for a year, that means layoffs. And you know what unemployment means in places like Olechu County."

"I see a lot of small towns in my work. It means drugs and crime and overdoses."

"You've got that one hundred percent right, Mr. Shaw. And I suspect that that's more than *acting* police chief Tolifson can deal with. Anything more I can help you with?"

"No. Just wanted to deliver the message." His eyes scanned the hillside above the offices, the road to the refineries.

"Consider it delivered."

Shaw turned to walk back to his bike.

Redding called, "One thing."

Shaw looked back.

"Here you are, Paul Revere, riding around warning everybody, 'The water is coming, the water is coming,' on that horse of yours. You better figure out where you're going to get your own ass to when you see that tidal wave coming your way. If it's easier to come back here than it is to get to high ground, feel free."

"Appreciate the offer. With all due respect, I hope I don't have to take you up on it."

"With all due respect, so do I."

32.

As Colter Shaw parked his bike near the command post, he noted that Officer Debi Starr had risen from the table and was walking to him.

"Hey, Mr. Shaw."

"'Colter,' remember."

"Oh, right." That bashful look again. "Colter. You find anything at the farm or mine?"

"A few things. I'm going to tell the crew." He nodded toward the tent.

"Sure. Just wanted to catch you here first. Just me. Mayor Tolifson's kind of new to this business. He's learning a mile a minute. But he was talking about getting a warrant if it looked like Ms. Coyne or Mr. Redding had started prepping for the flood before they learned about the levee collapse."

He said, "There'd be no basis for a warrant. No exigent circumstances, no probable cause."

"Oh, you know about that?" She looked relieved.

"I was thinking of being a lawyer. I read a lot on the subject growing up."

"You read . . . what, like Perry Mason?"

"No, law books."

When Ashton and Mary Dove fled the Bay Area the most well-represented items in the rental truck were books, including an entire set of Supreme Court and Ninth Circuit—the federal appeals court that embraced California—decisions.

She snickered. "Reading books like those growing up? Surprised you didn't spend your time on a team. And dating." A smile.

"I was homeschooled. No team, and a half-hour drive on mountain roads to get to the closest girl."

"Gotcha. Well, just didn't want us to go approaching Magistrate Dundee with a funky piece of paper. That man does not take kindly to those who don't do their homework. He will cut your legs right out from underneath you."

"I think we're pre-warrant, Officer. I'm curious. Is policing in your blood?"

"No. Outlawing is."

"Not an admission you hear much."

"I'm descended from Belle Starr. Not a hundred percent sure but the locales and family trees line up. Besides I'm claiming it 'cause I want to. And the twins get some mileage out of their mom being related to a bandit out of the Old West."

"I've heard of her." Shaw knew about Starr from Ashton, who read the children books on American history—the gospel and the unorthodox. He recalled Starr was a larcenous, rather than murderous, outlaw who had a winning sense of style, wearing velvet riding gear and a plumed hat. She carried two pistols and was a good shot. Her violent death remained unsolved, though a romantic triangle was likely involved.

He told her about his own connection with early America. "I was named after John Colter, a pioneer explorer and mountain man. Dorion—it's spelled D-o-r-i-o-n—her namesake is Marie Aioe Dorion, supposedly the first mountain woman. Our older brother Russell's named after Osborne Russell. He was among the first settlers in Oregon."

She tsk'ed her tongue. "Any stinkers give you trouble for your collective ancestors' less-than-correct history?"

"I personally didn't abscond with anybody's land. And if someone's upset because of a name I didn't give myself, that's their burden."

"I like your attitude, Colter."

In the tent Tolifson, Dorion and Olsen looked up at him as they entered. TC McGuire and Gutiérrez were not present; they were on evac detail.

He glanced at the levee. No, it wasn't his imagination. It was definitely thinner. And beginning to look fragile.

"Our friend Katz call? From the electronic, not the potato, chip company. With bags of cash?"

Dorion's sour laugh was his answer.

He asked Olsen, "The bomb curtains?"

"Effing weather. They think forty minutes to an hour. And after sunset, nobody flies, not on a mission like this."

His lips grew tight, then he asked, "And evacuation?"

"Still a couple dozen remainers we know about. But a lot of the houses are dark—we don't know about them. Nobody answering the door. Mrs. Petaluma is still ignoring everybody too. Mary Dove called her twice. No response." She looked to Starr. "And everybody on our list of disabled and home care?"

"They're out."

"Good," Shaw said.

Starr muttered, "And now some kids are playing in the caves on the hillside." An angry expression on her face, she pointed up the valley.

Dorion added, "That's on Eduardo's list, to pry them out."

Shaw looked to those around the table. "Now, the Hatfields and

McCoys . . . Annie Coyne, the farmer? No sense that she's behind it. She started trenching after the levee came down, she claims, and I think she was telling the truth. And it was a used machine with no rental sticker on it. Probably hers, so she didn't get it in anticipation. And she's doing environmental research. It means a lot to her. A flood would destroy her work. Also, she has sentimental attachment to the farm.

"She admitted the feud with Redding. If she was guilty, she'd steer us away from any grudges she had. Of course, maybe it was an act . . . But I'd take her off the list as a suspect to the tune of, say, ninety percent.

"Now, Redding. He and some men were sandbagging. He had a big supply of sand and bags. He said he kept them there as a regular matter. He *did* anticipate there'd be a problem with the levee, but said it was because he followed the weather reports in the mountains and knew the levee was at risk. That seemed credible too."

"So he's innocent," Starr said, sighing.

"I didn't say that," Shaw offered.

Tolifson frowned. "How do you mean?"

"Because as I was leaving, there was an employee I saw in one of the buildings behind the offices. He was trying to stay out of sight, but I caught a glimpse of him. I said 'employee,' but I'm really going to go with independent contractor."

"Ha," Starr muttered. "He means muscle."

Shaw nodded. "It was Bear, the man who tried to beat me to death with a shovel this morning."

33.

Shaw watched TC McGuire climb the hill to the command post. The big man was fit but was walking slowly. It had been a long day—the time was after 5 p.m., though it seemed as if the levee collapse had happened days ago.

Tolifson had pulled him off evac detail and briefed him on the assault suspect having a likely connection to Gerard Redding.

Shaw said, "We'd like to get some surveillance on the mine—from someplace safe, of course. You know the area?"

"Like the back of my hand. Hell, yes."

Shaw asked Tolifson, "You have any telephoto surveillance cameras?"

The mayor in turn looked to Starr, who said, "Hm. Speed guns are about as high tech as we get. And they're two years out of date. That's it."

McGuire said, "Got my phone. It's a new one. So you're looking for that guy with the beard, right?"

"Yes."

And the officer was nodding. "You hoping for some shots to use for facial recognition?"

It was Starr who answered—absently, as she was staring at the map of the town and the surrounding area. "Don't think we can pull that together, TC. I'm guessing Colter just wants a video of Bear and Redding together. Hopefully, a shot with Bear's vehicle make and model and, if Santa's good to us, a tag number in our stocking."

Starr had summarized exactly what he wanted.

"I'd still think about facial rec, but I'll aim for what you're saying," McGuire said. He rose and sauntered off.

Starr leaned close. "He'll do a good job. He's the best hunter in town, so he can stalk like nobody's business. And for fun, you can believe it, he writes computer code and does AI with his kids. Can you imagine?"

Olsen asked, "That man you're talking about? Bear? Ex-service?"

"You usually teach better hand-to-hand, but yes, could have been."

"So he could have a source for explosives."

Starr responded, "If TC comes through for us, Colter, you do an affidavit that this Bear attacked you—sounds funny saying that seeing as how a real one did come after me once. Different story. You do an affidavit he tried to brain you. Show the picture of him and Redding together. We'll get that warrant, sure as shootin'. Open up the Jumanji box of Redding's phone records, texts. We may get all sorts of goodies. I'm thinking—"

She was interrupted by the squeal of tires above them, a car braking to a stop beside the Winnebago.

Shaw at first thought the Chip Man, Katz, had returned. But this was a late-model Lexus SUV.

"Hey!" a man's urgent voice called as a door slammed hard. "Police? I need the police!"

He was in his late thirties and wearing a rumpled, though to Shaw's eye, expensive suit.

The man radiated concern, not danger, and Shaw's gun slipped from his mind as he saw the arrivee run to the breach in the levee and stare at it, dismayed.

Good-looking and with the body of a health club aficionado, he sported thick hair that probably brushed up into a stylish cut but that was now rain-messy and unattended. No shave that morning, and a thick growth further darkened his troubled face.

"Sir?" Tolifson called. "Help you?"

He hurried down the hill to the command post tent. "Up the highway, where the road's blocked off. They said there were some police here for the accident. You have to help, please!"

Shaw was examining him clinically. "You need medical attention?"

"No, no, it's not me. My fiancée. She was going to be driving this way earlier today, going to a spa in Fresno. She never showed up, and she's not picking up her phone. I heard the news that the dam had collapsed and a car went into the river. Is that true?"

"An SUV, and we saved the people inside. There was no one else."

He lowered his head and muttered something. Maybe a prayer of thanks. Then he looked up. "But something must have happened. I mean, I told her not to take her car on a day like this. But she insisted."

Shaw and Starr looked each other's way. She said, "Sir, did it happen to be a Chevy Camaro?"

"Yes! A blue one. How did you know?"

34.

His name was John Millwood and he explained that he and his fiancée, Fiona Lavelle, lived in Reno. He worked for an investment firm and she had recently left her teaching job to take creative writing classes and work on a novel.

"I told her not to come this way. To stick to the interstate, but she wanted scenery."

Tolifson pointed to Louis Bell's pickup truck, of which only the top of the bed and half the cab were visible. It was sinking into the levee as the mud softened further. "Fellow in that F-150 was right behind her. She gunned the engine and made it onto the highway before it collapsed."

His voice rose, almost angrily. "Then what happened? Something must have happened! She's disappeared."

Shaw had done this business for long enough to know that courtesy went out the window when a loved one was missing. The tragedy was everyone's fault, from God down to the man delivering coffee to a search-and-rescue task force. He'd learned not to take it personally.

Millwood added, "She never even got to Fort Pleasant."

"You know that?" Starr asked.

The businessman nodded fervently. "Yes, ma'am. Officer. When I didn't hear, I looked over this map. You know, Google Earth . . . And I found the first gas station you come to going south from Hinowah. At Hadleyville Road. I called the manager. I asked if they had video and if it showed the highway. There was one. I begged him to scan through it to see if she passed by this morning. She didn't."

Exactly Colter Shaw's idea.

Millwood continued, "Sure, another car might've blocked the camera or she turned into another entrance to stop for coffee or food. And maybe he didn't even look, just said he did. But then there's her phone . . . And you know, I have a sixth sense she's in trouble."

With a nod toward Shaw, Starr added, "This man here's a tracker."

Tolifson filled in, "Like with bloodhounds. Only he didn't bring any."

Shaw would have to correct his job description at some point.

Shaw asked, "Is Fiona a good driver?"

"Good enough. Careless sometimes." Millwood sized Shaw up. "What kind of tracker are you, police?"

"No, I go after rewards offered to find suspects and missing family members, friends."

"Hm. Never heard of that. But I'll pay you five thousand to find her."

"I—"

"Seven five."

Shaw was thinking about the situation. There were other tasks that needed attending to. The evacuation, helping Eduardo Gutiérrez dig the kids out of the caverns in the hills above town, and following up on the criminal investigation to determine if the miner Gerard Redding and Bear were behind the sabotage.

But he simply could not turn away from Millwood.

Finding people who had disappeared and were possibly in danger was Colter Shaw's essence.

Now that he'd made the decision to look into her vanishing, he moved into a different place. Mentally, emotionally. Time became the enemy. And the possibilities of a dire fate expanded exponentially. Car crash, snakebite, a spill into the Never Summer for whatever reason . . .

There were human threats too.

Bear, for instance.

If Fiona had skidded off the road, and he came up to "help"?

Shaw could easily imagine what might be on the man's agenda.

"I'm not here professionally. I'll help you out if I can. No reward necessary. But I can't do it full-time. I'm helping Mayor Tolifson and Ms. Shaw. Disaster response . . . Let me look into a few things."

"Oh, sir, I can't thank you enough! Anything you can do! Anything!" His eyes were wide. Anger morphed into pure, powerful gratitude.

Shaw withdrew his notebook and unscrewed his expensive Italian fountain pen. Everyone except Dorion looked at it with varying degrees of curiosity. She was familiar with the tool. For one thing, Ashton had used one in his correspondence, when the children were growing up. For another, it was his sister who'd given him this particular model; it was to replace one that got incinerated in the same inferno that destroyed his most recent Winnebago.

The pen was not an ego thing, as it was for some. For every job Colter took voluminous notes—supplemented with maps and, occasionally, sketches, and a fountain pen was much easier on the hand than ballpoints.

He opened a notebook, but before jotting any notes, he pulled out a chair beside Millwood's and swung around the laptop on which the map of the area was displayed. Together they looked at the highway from Hinowah to Hadleyville Road, assuming that Fiona had not slipped past the gas station and was lost somewhere beyond that point. The stretch of highway was about fifteen miles long. To the east of Route 13 and running roughly parallel to it was the Never Summer. To the west of the highway were forest and rocky hills and towering Copper Peak, which rose about five or six hundred feet above the landscape.

Shaw eyed the dark brown line of 13 south, noting a half dozen side roads.

He asked Tolifson, "Mining trails?" Tapping them on the monitor. "Yessir. And lumber."

"Do they lead anywhere but back to Thirteen?"

"No. And those that don't, they just end at abandoned mines. Or lumber mills. Old ones. All closed up decades ago. Some a hundred years or more."

He began to ask Millwood questions, as if this were any other reward job, and recorded the results in his small handwriting, perfectly straight, though the paper was not ruled.

—Could she swim? *Yes.*

—Were there any flotation devices in the car? *No.*

—Was the Camaro mounted with slicks or regular tires? *Regular.*

—Miles on them? *I don't know.*

—Was there a two-way radio in the car? *No.*

—How many phones did she have with her? *Why, one. She only had one phone.*

—Weapons in the car? *No.*

—Food and water? *Snacks and beverages. I don't know what kind or how much.*

—Medical supplies in the car? *No.*

—Was the car in good shape? Brakes and engine? *Yes.*

—How much horsepower? *It was the six, not the eight, but big enough—330 or something.*

—She in good shape? *Well, pretty good. She was going to a spa to work on that, lose a few pounds. Not that she had to, of course.*

—Tools in the car? *Just tire changing.*

—You said she was a moderately good driver; had she ever had accidents? *Yes, fender benders and they were her fault. Not paying attention.*

—Was the tank full? *I don't know.*

—Did she have warm clothing? *Whatever you'd normally take on a visit to a spa.*

—Matches or cigarette lighter? No. *She didn't smoke.*

—Liquor? *Definitely not.*

—Did she get scared easily? *Like snakes?*

—Anything. Do snakes scare her? *I don't know. I guess no phobias.*

—Medications? *No.*

—Any enemies? Ex-boyfriends or stalkers who were
problems? *Why would you ask that?*

—These are relevant questions. Please answer. *No.*

—A find-my-phone or computer location app? *Yes, but
none of them worked.*

—Any emotional or mental issues that might affect her
ability to cope? *What are you saying? . . . No. Of
course not.*

Answering these questions and a few others took only minutes.
It was a short list, but it didn't need to be as comprehensive as on
some jobs. If a missing person had vanished somewhere in the state
of Maine, say, well that reward job would have required consider-
able research.

But Fiona Lavelle had disappeared somewhere on a fifteen-mile
stretch of highway. Shaw needed only a minimal amount of data to
begin his investigation. He looked over the notes, assessing the situation, calculating the likelihood of possible occurrences:

She had in fact driven past the gas station at Hadleyville Road
and the manager had not seen her because the view was blocked. Or
because he simply hadn't bothered with the request. She hadn't picked
up when Millwood called because her battery was dead or the phone
was silenced.

—Eight percent.

Gone into the New Summer from the levee?

—Zero percent.

Gone into the retaining pond with the Suburban?

—Zero percent.

Gone into the river someplace else? He'd driven Route 13 earlier and the surface was slick. Braking fast to avoid a deer, even with ABS, she might've skidded off the road and into the Never Summer. Or ended up there because she tapped the accelerator too hard. But in that case the drone would probably have picked up the wreck. And there were very few places where the river came close to the highway.

—Five percent.

Skidding off the road in the *other* direction, into the forest? Route 13 was largely straight but had some serious drop-offs from the right lane. She might have flown off the asphalt for the same reasons as the above likelihood.

—Twenty-five percent.

Sleeping off the fright? On reflection, napping wasn't as likely as he'd first thought.

—Five percent.

Pulling onto one of the trails to wait out the storm, her phone battery dead and no charger cord with her?

—North of 50 percent.

And the Bear risk, capital *B*?

Had he noticed the bright blue car and flagged her down?

The odds?

—Unknowable.

Consequences if he did?

Not good.

They returned to the main tent. He asked Starr, "TC have eyes on Bear?"

She called and Shaw could tell from the conversation that he was at the mine but could not locate the man.

The officer said, "You want me to tell him anything?"

"If he does spot him and he leaves, text me right away. I need to know where he is."

She relayed the information.

Shaw told Dorion, Tolifson and Starr he was going to look for the woman.

No one objected, which he'd half expected. Then again he was here, risking his life, as a volunteer—and he *had* saved the Garveys. There could be no problem with him saving someone else.

If he could.

He told Millwood, "I'm going to start where she was last seen, after she got off the levee." He nodded to the pile of sand and the burlap bags on the far edge of the levee. "I'll go south from there."

"I'm coming with you," the man said firmly.

Shaw said that wasn't necessary. He would do the initial search and then decide if Millwood and a search party would be of any help.

"It's my fiancée. I'm going with you. I'll just follow you if you don't agree."

Shaw had a rule that offerors never accompany him.

It added unnecessary complications to the search.

Shaw looked into the man's eyes. The word *desperation* didn't come close to describing what he saw.

"All right," he said. "Let's go find her."

35.

Colter Shaw was speeding toward the other side of Hinowah, with the shadow of the levee on his left.

Shadow was figurative, as the rain clouds had excised every bit of sunlight from the village. But the earthworks nonetheless cast the presence of an ominous dark force.

He glanced up at the towering mass, rising close to a hundred feet above him, covered with the sheen of flowing water, gray and glistening like fish skin.

He tugged the throttle a little higher.

And then he was on the other side of the spillway bridge and shooting up the steep road to Route 13. He caught a bit of air, then skidded to a stop near a pile of sand, going perpendicular to the direction of travel, which afforded a good view of the waterfall from a different perspective. Looking north—in the direction of the command post and his Winnebago—was a far more dramatic perspective. The levee seemed particularly fragile, the Never Summer particularly hostile.

The sand truck was gone and so were Sergeant Tamara Olsen's corporals. He'd learned from Dorion that the trio had rooms at a motel in Fort Pleasant, and Williams and McPherson had gone there to change into dry uniforms.

He glanced down the hill he'd just shot up and noted John Millwood approaching the spillway bridge. He would soon begin the four-wheel-drive low-gear climb to where Shaw was.

Given that Fiona Lavelle might be in peril . . . and that Bear was presently unaccounted for, Shaw would not wait for the man to arrive. He walked slowly back and forth, studying the asphalt.

The rain had been relentless but had not removed the fresh skid marks from the front and rear tires of a sedan. He speculated that they had been left by Lavelle's Camaro as she had, maybe, heard the pickup behind her honking in alarm and had glanced back to see the levee melting, then instinctively gunned the engine. Tolifson had suggested as much.

But were these marks in fact from her vehicle? Or had they been left by some kids playing drag race on a recent Friday night?

Shaw knew a number of people in law enforcement. A crime scene team could easily have measured the distance between left and right tires—called the "track"—and gone on to one of their databases and found the answer in sixty seconds. A match wasn't definitive. Manufacturers had learned the economic genius of sharing platforms. In one reward job he'd run, he'd learned that the Acura MDX and Honda Pilot shared a 113.8-inch wheelbase.

In this day and age, Colter Shaw could do his own forensic work almost as quickly. After deslinging his backpack he removed a tape measure, crouched and checked the distance between the center of one skid mark to the center of the other. About sixty-two inches. A fast search online showed that the track of a late-model Chevrolet Camaro came in at sixty-two and a half inches.

Good enough.

Millwood crested the hill far less dramatically than Shaw had. He parked on the shoulder and joined him.

Shaw pointed. "Skid marks. It's a Camaro's track dimensions."

"How do you know?"

"Measured them."

"Yeah? You're like Sherlock Holmes."

Then Millwood was brushing his dark hair absently as he looked down at the black streaks. "They don't go straight down the highway."

No, they didn't. The skid streaks indicated that the car was pointed about forty-five degrees to the right. Shaw squinted as he examined the shoulder. "Look."

He was nodding at some green shrubs with broken tips. The men pushed past them and into the woods. Before them was an overgrown trail that descended for a long distance—at least a quarter mile—until it disappeared in the dark woods. Near the shoulder, the path—probably one of the logging or mining trails Tolifson had mentioned—was stone and gravel, but the men didn't have to go very far before they found a patch of mud with fresh tire prints. They had the same track, so it was most likely Fiona's car.

"She came this way?" Millwood was puzzled, clearly. "Why would she do that?"

"You said she wasn't an expert driver. Probably she sped off the levee so fast she lost control and drove through the brush and started down. It's about a twelve-degree incline, slick leaves and mud. No way she could stop."

"Let's go," Millwood muttered urgently.

"Wait," Shaw called, not to discourage him pursuing the search—they'd already settled that issue—but to give them a chance to assess and find a safe way down the incline.

Never hurry into an unknown environment.

But the man didn't hear, or he chose to ignore him. Millwood ran back to the highway and a moment later the Lexus crashed through the brush and started down. Shaw actually had to step back. Walking to his bike, he climbed on, fired up and followed.

As they descended the grade grew steeper and rockier yet and Shaw—a dirt bike motocross racer—drew on his skills to sway around the obstacles. Soon they bottomed out on a flat area of stone and mud. Ahead of and above them was Copper Peak. It was a miniature version of Yosemite's Half Dome, with a sheer, almost vertical face to the north and a rounded side to the south, pitted with caverns and ledges and cliffs.

To the men's left, southwest, the mining trail continued into the woods. To the right was a cliff below, which they could hear the turbulent mini version of the Never Summer, formed as the runoff from the spillway raced through the gulley.

Both men looked up the muddy and brush-filled trail.

Millwood voiced his opinion. "She controlled the skid, then decided she couldn't get back up the hill in a rear-wheel-drive car and kept going into the forest."

Made sense to Shaw. "And she's stuck in the mud somewhere, her cell battery gone. With the rain, she didn't want to hike out, and's waiting for it to clear."

He decided against telling the man that it was in that very direction, several miles farther on, that he'd been attacked. In a minute or two he would speed that way on the bike, his pistol grip exposed—just in case—and have Millwood follow.

But Shaw then glanced behind him—toward the cliff and the sound of the runoff torrent.

He saw a tread mark.

Millwood noticed too. "No!"

So, Lavelle's car had not proceeded straight down the mining trail from Route 13, as they had driven, but had swerved right, toward the river.

The men walked forward to the edge.

Millwood froze, choking. "My God!"

The Camaro lay upside down in about six feet of water. It was clear to Shaw that she had gotten stuck in the mud near the edge of the cliff and had tried to work her way out. She must have hit the gas too hard, and wheels spinning, the car skewed sideways—tumbling over the edge into the stream, which was here about eight feet wide.

He noted the doors were closed but the window nearest to where they stood—the passenger side—was partly opened. Though the vehicle was too close to the side of the gulley for an adult to climb out.

The other side?

He couldn't tell.

Shaw dropped his backpack, opened it and reached inside for rope. He got as far as saying, "Here's what we're going to—" when John Millwood stripped off his jacket—the name Armani briefly visible—and flung it aside.

"No!" Shaw called.

The man paid him no mind but kicked his shoes off and leapt into the water.

He was instantly caught in the fierce current and his efforts to grip the car were useless, as he was carried past it into the whitewater torrent in seconds.

"Help me!" Millwood cried, grabbing momentarily onto a rock outcropping.

As he lost his grip and was swept away, he shouted some additional words in a desperate, choking voice.

He could not swim.

36.

Keep the boss happy.

Never piss off the boss.

Never disappoint the boss.

Despite what absolutely fucking *awful* circumstances you've found yourself in.

Hire Denton drove the hobbling Jeep along a strip of mud, gravel and rocks that passed for a trail.

Which it really wasn't.

It was a strip of mud and gravel and rocks.

Trails were more or less smooth and more or less obstacle free and wide enough so that—unlike here—you didn't fall off the side and tumble fifty feet into a gulley if you as much as sneezed or looked away for a half second.

Careful.

Hire was his legal name. Being on the mission he presently was engaged in, he thought again how it would look on his tombstone. Like an advertisement for a day laborer.

Thank you, Mom and Dad.

He could always leave instructions for the undertaker to make it "H. Denton."

Or just change it.

But that meant going to a lawyer or going to a courthouse and filling out papers and it was really just too much trouble.

Hire was a pool ball of a man. *Round* was the only word that fit his physique—body and nearly bald head.

"You ready, boys and girls," he called. "Almost there." And hummed a song whose name and lyrics he did not recall. Something from a soft rock channel.

Hire continued slowly up the wannabe trail in the rocks and found a flat area, wider, like the landing in a stairway going up to a second story in a tall house. He climbed from the vehicle and looked at the rain-swept landscape.

Desolate.

Overcast sky, rain, mist.

And gray cliffs.

Oh, and mud. A lot of mud.

He knew for a fact it had rained for about ten hours, but he could have been told it was thirty and he'd've believed the person doing the telling.

He tapped the gun on his right hip to make sure he knew exactly where it was in case he needed it. He didn't know that he would, and didn't know that he wouldn't.

But Hire Denton was a man who took very few chances.

Just ask his boys and girls.

He walked to the back of the Jeep and scanned the area again to make certain he was alone. He was. But who the fuck would want to be here anyway?

He opened the liftgate and leaned close to a camo backpack.

"How we doing in there?" he whispered. "Comfy? Glad to hear it."

The boss knew he talked to his friends. But so what? That was his business and his alone.

grease or other fat as insulation—and one should do the same in a survival mode—was wrong. The fat was merely to prevent chafing. Serious extreme swimmers wore wet suits or acclimated their bodies to the cold slowly.

Neither of which was feasible at the moment.

He tied a bowline around his waist—the preferred knot for this task—and looped it around a smooth-barked birch. Paying out line, he descended. Colter Shaw was not unaccustomed to cold water. The first half of his daily shower in the Winnebago's tiny stall was searingly hot, the second nothing but the coldest in the tank. And so the initial shock was not unexpected. The body is a powerful furnace, and his heart began its frantic revving, forcing warming blood to every square inch of skin. The breath vanished from his lungs.

The worst, as anybody braving chill water knows, is when the shoulders dip below the surface.

Now, just do it.

An audible gasp and the shock and pain.

The water, after all, had recently been mountaintop snow.

Shaw considered his priorities.

If Fiona were in the car, which was wholly submerged, she was dead. There'd be no air pocket like what had saved the Garvey family in the retention pond. Nothing could have kept her alive for three hours—and if water in the lungs didn't kill her, the hypothermia would have.

Save Millwood. His only mission.

Easing out more line, he fought to keep himself more or less upright as he moved downstream.

Their father had taught the children survival swimming—in tidal currents, in frozen-over lakes, in hurricane-tossed open oceans (a field trip, of course; the Sierra Nevadas were not visited by named storms). But, he'd taught that the most difficult type of water survival was in a flood. The water speeds up, slows down, changes direction, drops into basements and wells in a city, and gulleys and caves in more rustic areas. It was generally not hard to stay afloat in lakes or ocean—if you relaxed and didn't panic. But floodwaters were pure muscle and would slam you into any number of blunt objects: walls, trees, vehicles, debris . . . corpses.

Or, as in this case, one of the dozens of rocks jutting out from the water and just below the surface.

More line . . .

He approached the rock that the pale, terrified man was clinging to.

Shaw's plan was simple. He would grip the man's belt, tell him to take a deep breath and let go. The rope would act like a pendulum and swing them to the shore. Millwood would clamber up the bank to dryish ground and Shaw would follow.

Shaw was now about eight feet away, kicking hard to remain midstream.

Six feet.

Four . . .

Three . . .

He wrapped the loose end of the rope around his left wrist and reached for the man's waistband.

He was inches away when Millwood lost his grip.

With a choking scream he went under the whitewater and vanished downstream.

Ah . . .

Being just above the surface himself Shaw had only a limited view ahead. And the river wove in serpentine curves; he could view nothing past the next bend.

Paying out more rope, kicking himself away from the endless sharp rocks.

Soon he reached the end of the rope—two hundred feet of line pulleying around a birch tree gets you only one hundred feet of distance. He climbed out, shivering, and dropped the loose end of the rope and gathered it to him.

Sprinting downstream along the path, under the towering face of Copper Peak, he spotted Millwood clinging to another cluster of rocks midstream.

This also was just out of reach.

And ten feet farther on the walls narrowed, creating a flume, through which the water accelerated to twice the speed it was here. The banks were lined with more rocks and Shaw could see stony steps that water cascaded over through the narrow slot. Slipping into it would mean a thirty-foot ride over scores of jutting razors. And if a rocky blade didn't slice a jugular, a collision could easily break a neck.

He did the rope trick again, this time using as the improvised pulley a scrub oak. Not the smoothest of barks, but the only option.

Then once more into the water, which had not, he thought acerbically, gotten any warmer in his brief foray onto land.

Millwood was in an odd configuration. His legs were drawn to the left, not downstream. The surface of the water was flowing toward the flume but, beneath, the current was tugging him in a different direction.

Shaw knew why, and the answer was troubling.

He recognized an underwater cave entrance.

The opening was not big enough for Millwood's entire body to fit through, but it would hold him snug, under the surface, like a swimmer stuck in a pool drain. If he lost his grip now, and was pulled into the entrance, even all of Shaw's strength could not free him.

Holding the rock as best he could, his knuckles white, Millwood was struggling desperately to keep from being pulled to his death.

Shaw eased closer. Once, his feet slipped and he pinwheeled in the water but finally he brought himself under control. He sucked air and continued toward the man. He didn't bother to yell, "Hold on," or the like. Unnecessary or obvious instructions were a waste of breath.

"Please, please! Help me. I can't—"

Speaking of which . . .

Shaw shouted, "Quiet!"

He was now five feet from him, gripping the rope with hands beginning to cramp from the cold. He knew his core temperature was dropping and he had only ten or so minutes until hypothermia began its inevitable process of confusion, followed by debilitating exhaustion.

Breathing hard, more rope, and yet more.

Nearly there.

A shout: "I'm going to let go. I can't keep it up. I—"

And Millwood did, slipping under the surface as he was tugged toward the cavern's opening.

Just before he got there, Shaw lunged and caught the man by the wristwatch, whose leather band he doubted would hold for very long.

"Grab my waistband."

Millwood did so, and hand over hand, Shaw pulled them both upstream. Slowly, slowly, in the face of the relentless flow.

They came to a tree whose roots had been exposed by the patient onslaught of water. Using the tough tendrils as handholds, he helped Millwood out. The man in turn offered his hand to Shaw and assisted him to the bank. Millwood dropped to his knees. "I'm sorry! I'm sorry! I wasn't think—"

Shaw waved his hand to silence him. "I'm going to check out the car. Call nine-one-one."

38.

The men jogged upstream, where Millwood found his phone to make the call and Shaw slipped the rope around the smooth-barked tree he'd originally used.

He paused, though, taking stock. He was lightheaded. Hypothermia can, of course, be fatal—simply freezing you to death. But it can also disorient you to the point of making very bad decisions, which can also kill you.

But, yes, he decided, he could function.

Now, next to the inverted car, he took a breath and went back into the water.

The passenger side was closest to shore and that was the door and window he'd seen earlier—the one too close to the rocks to escape through. So he made his way around to the other side of the vehicle.

Ah, the window was open and there was a large enough gap between the car and this bank that a person could have squeezed out.

But had she?

Now, to find out . . .

Reaching inside. No one in the front seats.

And the rear?

He—

Slam!

Shaw jerked under the impact.

And the big gray fish—a muskie—swam indignantly away after grazing his face.

He tried again.

Fiona Lavelle was not here. The car contained only some plastic bags and luggage. Fast-food wrappers. A Starbucks cup. Suspended in space.

He pulled himself to shore and climbed out. "She got out."

Millwood's eyes were wide and he looked around. "Where? Where is she?"

"I don't know. Nine-one-one?"

"I called and somebody's coming."

"The Lexus." Shaw nodded, shivering. "The heater."

"Oh . . . Right. I didn't think." He ran to the big SUV and turned on the engine, and then hit the controls on the dash. He opened the liftgate, rummaging through bags. He changed clothing.

Shaw walked to his bike and opened his backpack. He too stripped off the wet clothing and pulled on dry attire. The wet items went into a pile. He'd get to them later.

Finally dry socks and his boots.

He began carefully coiling the rope. The world, Shaw had learned, was made up of two kinds of people—those who coiled rope and those who did not. There was no doubt which side of the line he fell into. All survivalists did.

"How much does she weigh?" he shouted to Millwood.

"How much?"

"Fiona? Her weight?"

"One twenty-three. That's why she's going to the spa. To lose a—"

Shaw ignored the rest of the words. His question hardly was about her svelte figure; he was asking if she could have been sucked into the cave.

At that weight, no.

So where?

Shaw was looking forward to the blasting heat in the luxury vehicle.

But he realized he couldn't indulge just yet. He noticed a glint from a nearby ridge of rock. Under an overhang was a mobile phone, backward facing.

The lenses were aimed toward where the Camaro had been, according to the marks in the mud.

The woman had been recording herself.

The device was locked but the screen showed twenty-two missed calls.

He took the phone to the Lexus and climbed into the passenger seat, where the heat cascaded over him.

The sensation was consuming.

"Found this."

Millwood gasped. "It's Fiona's!"

"She was taking a selfie video, I think, about getting the car out of mud, for YouTube or something. It's not open."

"I know the passcode." He typed it in and found the most recent video. He hit PLAY.

What Shaw suspected was right. Lavelle was determined to rock the car out of the mud trap—and record herself doing it.

About four minutes in they saw the rear end leap over a branch under the doormat and carpet and slide sideways over the brink, as Fiona screamed.

Then the sound of her choking. Briefly. Then nothing.

"The hell was she thinking?" Anger flushed Millwood's face.

Shaw said, "She did everything right. Just one of those flukes."

Millwood was silent for a moment, looking at the phone. In a diminished voice he offered, "I don't know what to say. I wasn't thinking, jumping in."

"No, you weren't." Shaw's voice was staunch. This was not a moment for *Oh, it's all right.* "Now, I'm going to go looking for her.

You're going to get a motel room and take a hot shower. A long hot shower. And stay there and get some rest. Wait until I call you. Understood?"

The man nodded meekly. "Sure, anything, you say." Millwood shivered. "Mr. Shaw, what do you think happened to her?"

"I can't speculate. I'll look for her and the county officers will too. Now, I want to get started. You go get that shower. You need your core temperature up."

"You?"

"Later."

A hot shower beckoned irresistibly.

But resist he did.

Now, he needed to follow the first clue as to where Fiona Lavelle—or her body—might be.

A clue he had already spotted.

A makeup bag.

About twenty-five feet downstream from the underwater cave.

The dark blue accessory was circling frantically in an eddying pool at the base of the flume.

Shaw was on his bike, driving in low gear along a four-foot-wide path paralleling the torrent, bordered to his left by the towering face of Copper Peak.

After the flume the waterway widened and proceeded west—still quickly but with less frantic energy.

Ten feet later a white sweater sat half onshore, half waving excitedly in the water.

More clothing and a running shoe. And within arm's reach was a wallet. It contained money and credit cards in Lavelle's name.

Another item of clothing—a blouse.

And then a windbreaker.

Stained with blood.

The path ended at a cliff, over which the water poured, a smaller version of the Never Summer cascading over the injured levee.

Shaw walked to the edge and peered down at the ground about forty or fifty feet below. He was careful, and kept his center of gravity low. He did not believe in that adage that being on unprotected heights somehow ignited a desire to throw oneself into the abyss.

He did, however, believe in gusts of wind, and today they'd enthusiastically accompanied the rain to Hinowah, California.

He believed too that, though it was unlikely, Bear might be vindictive enough to trail him. TC McGuire had not called to report he had located the man.

A glance back, though, revealed he was safe from the last of those risks.

Looking down, he saw the water cascading into a pool. From there another tributary had formed and flowed on toward Annie Coyne's farm and Gerard Redding's mine.

The water was covering a railroad track, and sitting idle on it was a freight train—a long one with oil tanker and coal carrier cars. Three crew members, in orange Carhartt overalls, were standing on high ground, examining the flood and probably debating whether or not to proceed. A true expert in all things train, his sister had explained that today's locomotives were not powered directly by their diesel engines, but by electric motors; the diesels ran huge generators to provide the juice. Maybe the men were concerned about electrical shorts.

The newly formed river took their entire attention, hands on hips, eyes down.

One thing they didn't seem the least curious about were colorful items of fabric lying on the ground and in the branches of two nearby pines, as if articles of women's clothing descended from the heavens onto their route on a regular basis.

He walked back to the bike, fired it up and returned to where the drowned Camaro lay.

He assessed the forest and rock formations around him, noting that not a single officer had yet responded to Millwood's 911.

No problems there. In fact, he was pleased by their absence.

Colter Shaw always worked better alone.

39.

Time to pull the trigger for real.

Waylon Foley had enjoyed eyeing the poor assholes in the command post with the spotter scope, aiming at Motorcycle Man in particular (his shoulder still stung, his nose still ached).

But the circumstances that he found himself in hadn't allowed him to actually take a shot.

That had changed.

Foley was presently in a wall of rocks dotted with pine and scrub oak, aiming at his target and reflecting that his task was not going to be that easy.

Because his intent was to *wound*. Not kill.

Destroy the man's knee or ankle. Take him out of commission.

This would also slow down the others, keeping them on edge, worried that they'd be next.

Foley had been hired to murder sixteen times in his career (and he was successful each time). In the service of committing those crimes he had wounded or badly injured around forty people (no exact number because twice he hadn't stayed around to count body parts after the bombs).

Every one of those victims except the magic sixteen had been collateral damage.

Now, hilariously, Foley was thinking, since he was intending only to injure, killing a target would make the *death* collateral damage.

Topsy-turvy . . .

Using the spotter scope, he was watching the man follow a trail up a rocky hillside.

Foley burrowed into an indentation in the rocks and trees. In the tan and green camo, he was nearly invisible, though he scanned the area to make sure no one was nearby. He was above that part of Hinowah known as Misfortune Row. Apparently, it was where the silver miners in the mid-1800s moved after their claims dried up and they had to downsize to a tent city on the site and make their living serving miners who were successful.

And, good news, there was nobody to witness the shooting; the neighborhood was deserted.

He watched the target make his way around rocks, over paths, looking at dirt and mud at his feet.

When hunting game, you never wounded, of course.

And if you did, by accident, you moved heaven and earth to track the creature and put it out of its misery. You *never* let an animal suffer. Animals had no concept of the future. They had no hope, they had no fear of disappointment. They didn't live past the next leaf or groundhog or salmon. So taking their life was nothing to them. But pain they experienced for as long as pain persisted.

Foley had once cut off a man's little finger because he'd caught him throwing stones at a dog (later reflecting that making him swallow the digit was probably over the top, but he was just in one of those moods).

He pulled a piece of gray polyester cloth from his pocket (cotton and burlap left telltale fibers) and rolled it into a thick shooting rest for his rifle. It was an old one, a Savage, and it had been in his father's inventory of weapons when the man died. Foley had descended

on Dad's house just after hospice called and he grabbed this particular weapon before his brother even knew the old man had passed.
Twenty thousand in cash too, but it was really the gun he wanted.

Windage, gravity, a muscle tremor (because some asshole took
your shovel away from you, for instance) . . . all of those factors and
a dozen others could conspire to make the mission to wound prob-
lematic.

You aimed for the shoulder, you hit the heart.

You aimed for the leg, you hit the femoral artery.

Or you aimed for the ankle and missed, and the damn target
shot back.

Foley wasn't overly concerned, however. He was the best shot he
knew of. While other kids in school were aimlessly running into one
another playing football, swinging bats at baseballs, or getting hot
and sweaty in the backseats of cars with Mary Jean Phelb, he was
shooting.

In the army, shooting.

After the army, shooting.

Reloading his own ammunition, pouring lead for the bullets.
Studying the physics of wind and gravity, the dynamics of airflow
over copper and lead and Teflon.

Shooting . . .

At twenty-four Waylon Foley had gotten married. And it was
okay. For a while. Until the desire to kiss his honey on her forehead
and head out into the woods with his gun became a *need* to kiss his
honey on her forehead and head out into the woods.

He'd rather have been there than at the movies, or the dinner
table.

Or bed.

The divorce was mutually agreed upon.

And so he began to spend nearly every weekend with the Savage
rifle. He recalled an article he'd read once about the actor Daniel
Day Lewis. While shooting the film *Last of the Mohicans* he had

reportedly lived the life of his frontiersman character so he could become the person he played. Part of that process was sleeping with his rifle.

Foley loved that.

He didn't exactly sleep with the Savage, but he kept her in the bedroom, not far from his pillow.

He now pulled the caps off the Nikon scope—the one atop the rifle—and laid the crosshairs on his target.

Thinking: Shoulder, leg, hand, foot.

He mentally flipped a coin—if you could flip a coin when you had four choices.

Then circumstance, not chance, won. At this distance, the leg was probably best.

He'd take the risk of hitting the femoral artery.

In went his camo-colored earplugs.

Now . . .

Come on . . .

Would the man *please* stop moving?

Yes, at last. He must have received a text. He paused for a moment and fished his phone from his back pocket. He read the screen and sent a reply.

Foley worked the bolt with that delicious click-click sound, putting a long, narrow, golden bullet into the comfortable weapon's receiver and centered the crosshairs on the man's right leg.

All right, girl. It's up to you.

A squeeze of the trigger, slow, slow.

Then the huge bang, a kick to his aching shoulder.

He peered through the scope.

The slug had gone directly where he wanted it to, into the man's lower calf, and he tumbled down a low hillside, mouth wide with a scream Foley could not hear.

"Thank you." Alone and not on a shooting range in front of anyone else, he planted a kiss on the warm blue-steel receiver of the rifle. Leaving the spent shell inside—why help out the police?—he slipped the caps back on the Nikon scope and the rifle into its case. He rose.

He knew he should leave.

But he used the spotter scope to spend a few wonderful additional seconds watching the target writhing on the ground, desperately ripping off his belt to make a tourniquet.

He wondered if he'd accidentally struck a critical vessel.

Wound, not kill . . .

Yet, he reflected, if things had gone slightly wrong, and the man died?

Well, you could hardly blame him.

If his client didn't like it, he could come here and do the dirty work himself.

40.

"Mommy, what was that?"

The answer was: a gunshot.

But Dorion Shaw said, "I don't know."

And gave no visible reaction, though she was of course troubled by the sound. She was presently FaceTiming with her eldest daughter, Rebecca.

Back to the problem at hand. "It has to be somewhere. It can't have vanished. That is physically impossible," she said to the eleven-year-old.

Rebecca had misplaced her drawing tablet, and Dorion was presenting her case, which was based on the laws of the physical world, as well as personal knowledge of the facts of the situation.

Logic.

It was how Dorion ran her life.

How every Shaw sibling ran their lives.

"But I can't find it!" the girl's voice implored.

"The sunporch."

"I looked."

Dorion was standing beside her brother's Winnebago, umbrella in one hand and iPhone in the other.

What was the gunshot?

She looked down to the command post tents.

On the small screen was the small face, brows knotted in worry.

She said to Rebecca, "The porch was the last place you were playing with it. Last night. I saw you."

Digital art was Rebecca's preference. She excelled in all media but Dorion and William were exceedingly grateful that she preferred the sort that did not leave pastel chalk dust or linseed oil and turpentine scents throughout the house.

When they'd FaceTimed last night, the girl had showed her mother a piece she was working on that had more than a little Picasso in it—angular people, angular pets. The distortion was intentional (if pressed, the girl could do a portrait in colored pencil that approached photorealism).

Becca had been in the family's sunroom. Dorion had praised the work, told her to put the device away—it was bedtime—and to pick a story for Mommy to read. Her sister, Mary, summoned, they'd curled up in bed and listened to some Dr. Seuss. Dorion admittedly had poor performance skills when it came to prose narration—especially the different character voices, which the girls still liked—but she could hold her own with children's verse.

After several encores, they'd handed the phone over to her husband. Their children had a bedtime pardon while the parents conversed, then it was lights-out for everybody, William included, as the three of them were on East Coast time.

Just moments ago, her phone had given a FaceTime chime. Those who had children and those who had their own businesses always answered their phones. Dorion fit both descriptions.

The girl now claimed that no magical conditions existed that would result in the wizardly disappearance of the tablet but the search her mother sent her on was proving futile.

"If Uncle Colter was here, he'd find it."

The daughters of two engineers with a slurry of degrees between them, both daughters were heirs to their mother's nickname within the Shaw family, the Clever One. They were aware of what their uncle did for a living and when he visited would often ask him about his business of seeking rewards. (Thank God, she and William agreed, they did not know what their *older* uncle did—a man who looked and behaved like the clandestine military operative that he was. That day would come. Rebecca was already asking about conflict zones and had recently queried, "What does 'weaponizing food' mean?")

Then her eldest brought a smile to her mother's face by adding, "I'd offer a reward."

Thinking of her brother, she crooked her umbrella between chin and shoulder and dug out her other phone. No message from him. He was going to look for that woman whose fiancé had reported her missing.

"What's that noise, Mommy? Like a bathtub."

She reversed the camera on her iPhone to the back lens and aimed at the levee, over which the Never Summer spewed like an open Washington, D.C., fire hydrant on an August day.

"Oh! That's awesome! Are you going swimming?"

"It's a little cold."

Both girls loved the pool at the neighborhood rec center and Mary was taking lessons. At eight years old, she was built like a swimmer, had good technique and a competitive edge. Dorion and her husband were pleased that she took to this particular sport, which did not involve body slamming or large blunt objects being swung or pitched toward heads.

Then she heard some words on the other end of the line, growing heated. Rebecca had to move the phone so that her mother couldn't see what was transpiring.

Some shouting.

Dorion had learned not to be alarmed. Children were little geopolitical centers and conflicts arose and vanished. And growing up in the Shaw household rearranged your priorities and concerns in a big way.

"Mare took it," Rebecca announced.

"You said I could!"

"No, I didn't."

"Last week. You said!"

"Did not!"

Dorion told Rebecca to be forgiving and told Mary that permissions were not indefinite—and taught her what the word meant.

Détente ensued, though it did not rise to the level of the girls working together on the tablet to "draw a picture for Mommy," as she had suggested.

Then they both got tired of the dispute and said they were going to go play *Stardew Valley.*

Her husband came on the line. William Sharpe might have been a leading man, with trimmed black hair, a square face and endlessly dark eyes. "Hey. How's it going?"

She gave him a rundown of the levee collapse case, adding that her brother had found evidence of sabotage.

"My God . . ."

He would understandably be concerned, but it was not in Dorion's nature—or any of the Shaws', for that matter—to avoid the truth about their professions. (As for personally? A different story. She thought grimly of her secret half-sister, Margaret.)

"Any ETA?" William asked. He worked as an infrastructure engineer mostly from home, so Dorion was free to grab one of her go-bags and jet off to a disaster site at any time, with no need for major parental schedule juggling. He was not only an expert at the esoteric discipline of applying the "wisdom of crowds" to solving engineering problems . . . he was far better at cooking and cleaning and laundry than Dorion would ever be.

She was just telling him that she had no way of knowing if the levee was still at risk when she stopped speaking, as her phone pinged with a text from Debi Starr.

It began:

Need you. County medical center. ER.

"I have to go love you." All one word.

And she disconnected without waiting to hear her husband's own words of farewell.

41.

Now, the despised guards on the other side of the wall, Arana Braveblade walked to the far edge of the garden, the spot from which if you stood tipatoe you could see the village and—thrillingly—Fraeland, to the East of Central Realm. The wind bathed her skin, the sun graced her hair and shimmered it golden before the broodclouds returned.

She had spent hours here in the garden, avoiding Thamann Hotaks and his minions—and most everyone else in the castle. She would tend the herbs, practice spells and look through the foul air that hung like a stale cloak about the village in hopes of catching a glimpse of those lands.

And dream of her escape and reunion with her brother and the other villagers Hotaks had kidnapped, each because of his or her special talent that he jealously coveted.

Was Nathon still alive? His skill at steel shearing was unparalleled. But he also had a way of speaking his own mind—to his detriment.

And the others?

A faint rain had arisen and it whispered, "Wait no longer, wait no longer!"

She stuffed the herbs she needed into a pouch and crushed them together. This velvet bag she slipped into the forbidden pocket of her blouse, just over her heart.

She recited the incantation—and in uttering these particular words, committed a death-by-steel offense.

Would it work?

Yes!

Shimmering and humming, a Blue Strayer appeared before her, resembling the sleigh in which she and Nathon would gleefully ride down the hillsides in the snow when the family went to the mountains for the LowSun holiday.

The Old Times.

The Happy Times.

She inhaled deeply and climbed inside. She felt an odd sense that it was grateful for being conjured. She wondered if it was aware of existing in the OffState tired of its condition and impatiently awaiting materialization. Or did it sleep, dreamless like the dead, until brought to life?

Whatever was the case, the Strayer now closed the sides tightly around her, as if a hug of gratitude. Did she hear a voice?

Some said Strayers had a heart and soul.

And could be more intelligent than many people.

She bent to the ground and retrieved what she'd hidden here one stormy night, when even the guards were sheltering. She gripped the sword's hilt and lifted it, still in the scabbard, and slipped the weapon into the Strayer beside her.

She now looked to the horizon.

To the place where she could be herself, out from under the heel of Thamann Hotaks.

There would be no need to be a Somewhat Person any longer.

She leaned forward and whispered, "*Mym Vayantos!*"

Take me away!

The Strayer rose slightly off the ground, as if studying the wall, and then with no warning surmounted it like a horse taking a jump.

Arana Braveblade inhaled a deep breath as they plummeted straight down, toward the cluster of buildings that was the village, growing bigger and bigger with every passing fraction.

All right, hold on, Fiona Lavelle thought, gazing down at the passage in her notebook, which was twice the thickness as when she'd bought it, because of the ink and coffee and soda stains—a few ketchup blotches too.

The pages were filled with her handwritten prose—and also many angry and frustrated and exasperated cross-outs. One thing about writing by hand, and not on a computer: your limitations stared you in the face; they weren't banished into the ozone like bits and bytes when you deleted on Word.

Lavelle had loved what one of her professors had told the class: Ernest Hemingway said there were no great writers, only great re-writers.

While she didn't care much for the American novelist, she knew that was true, though she also guessed that some people didn't have to revise quite as much as others.

The way she had to.

The wind bathing skin?

How can wind bathe anything?

And: *Gripping a sword hilt?*

No.

You know better. The hilt is the handle plus the guard plus any ornamentation.

You grip the *handle*.

And you have the *rain* speaking.

If you get it wrong, you're going to hear about it!

Then her thoughts slipped from her fantasy world to return to the present.

Arana Braveblade could, with the right spells, and the right tweaking of her plot, resurrect the Blue Strayer.

But could she save Big Blue, her beloved Camaro?

She guessed that was impossible, with damage that bad, lying in the bottom of a gulley filled with torrenting water.

She guessed her set of wheels was—to use a very un-Braveblade word—toast.

A burial by river.

Then she perked up. Hm, interesting idea. Like the Viking's burial by sea. She jotted the words in her *Idea* notebook. Someone would be honored in a burial by river. Arana would lead the group in a heartfold she herself would write.

She now lifted her coldtorch—a Braveblade term, which translated here and now into a reading halogen attached to a USB battery pack—and shone it around her new home. It was a dingy cave that had once been the entrance to the shaft of the Good Luck and Fortune Mine, which closed in 1875. By then, according to the Olechu County website, it had been shut down after producing "untold" tons of silver and a slight bit of gold, though the big gold veins were farther south. The Good Luck was one of a dozen mines in and around Copper Peak. There had been some talk of turning them into tourist attractions but in reality this had no appeal whatsoever. It was nothing more than a thirty-by-thirty-foot damp chamber with a black and spooky shaft disappearing down into the heart of the earth. The shaft was grated off with chain-link.

Beside Fiona were two gym bags and a backpack, containing dry clothing and quick-mart provisions of the sort that Arana Braveblade, who lived in in the year 2243 A.E. in EverWorld, could not have imagined: jerky, cheese sticks, salt-and-vinegar potato chips, dried salami, saltines, Coke, Sprite.

Oh, and Hershey bars.

Some beer too. Which Arana did partake in, though it was forbidden by Thamann Hotaks for women to drink alcohol (even though he plied female visitors to his wing of the castle with tea he had secretly laced with Willing Nectar).

She had some first aid equipment too and she now sprayed some more Dermoplast on the cut on her forearm. The bleeding had stopped but the wound was open enough so that there was a brief sear of pain before the anesthetic part of the spray took hold.

She gasped briefly.

Feeling a chill, she opened one of the gym bags and pulled on another sweatshirt. UCLA.

This was not a school that meant anything to her—the institution itself, the team. But at the thought that she might just jump on an airplane and go visit the place—to attend a lecture or enroll in a course—she began to cry.

Possibility . . .

And then she froze.

A sound.

Which might be the grit of a footfall. She quickly extinguished the reading lamp, plunging the entire front of the mine into near darkness.

Please no . . .

For a moment, she was weak. For a moment she was the old Fiona Lavelle.

Then she thought: No way.

It was Arana Braveblade who picked up the five-pound rock. And rose.

One edge was jagged. It would easily cut flesh and crack open a skull.

She kneaded it in her hand.

As if she were gripping the *handle* of a Rendingsword.

Yes, definitely steps, getting closer.

Then she paused.

She took the reading light in her left hand and with the rock in the other she stepped a few feet closer to the entrance.

The light would blind him.

Could she actually strike him?

Fiona couldn't.

But her hero could.

All in a day's work for Arana Braveblade.

And so *she* could too.

Then she started at the sound of a man's voice.

"Fiona? Hello. It's all right. I'm a friendly."

Something about that word, *friendly*, made her more comfortable than if he'd said "a friend," because that would have been a lie. She had no friends here.

She was silent.

"I have a flashlight. I'm going to turn it on. But I won't shine it in your face, just at my feet. I don't want to fall, and my eyes aren't accustomed to the dark. I don't think you have a gun. Do you?"

"Yes, I do."

"What kind is it?"

A pause. "All right I don't have a gun. But I do have a big fucking rock."

"I'm not a threat. I'm coming in now. Don't hit me."

A light came on and the beam swept across the floor and grew brighter as he approached.

Then he was inside. While he kept the beam at his feet, as promised, she turned the reading light on and hit *him* full in the face.

He was a handsome, athletic blond man in his thirties, with blue—now quickly blinking—eyes. Though his face was unthreatening, there was something ominous about his clothing—all dark. She gripped the rock more tightly.

"Fiona, my name is Colter Shaw." He swung the beam over her nest—the bags and backpack and notebook and pens, the food and drinks. "I'm here to rescue you, though I have a feeling you don't really need rescuing, now, do you?"

42.

Martina. He'll be all right."

Dorion preempted the conversation immediately with that sentence. No niceties, no greetings. Just take care of the reassurance first, the instant the woman answered.

"What, Dor?" Martina Alonzo, Eduardo Gutiérrez's wife, had a low voice. Normally calm, the special-needs teacher was understandably alarmed.

"We're in California. On a job."

"But, the conference . . ."

"This was unexpected. Now. Ed was shot."

"Mio Dio!"

She and Han Tolifson sat in the waiting room of the Olechu County Medical Center, ten miles southwest of Hinowah. A typical such room in a rural county. The only decorations were an eye exam chart and a My Pony poster, in a corner where undersized furniture sat.

She said, "It's his leg. Not life threatening. He's in surgery. I've sent you credit card information. I know you're planning to get here tomorrow. But you'll want to come now. Get a flight, first class to Fresno. I'll have a car pick you up and bring you here."

"What happened, Dor? Was it, what? Cartels? Gangs?"

"We don't know. There's some sabotage on a levee. We've been investigating it. My brother's here, and it may have been mistaken identity. The suspect might have thought he was shooting at Colter."

"My God . . ." Now panic gave way to consideration. "All right. I'll take the boys to my mother and get the first flight I can."

"And, Martina. There's a highway patrol officer here. He's keeping guard. There's absolutely no reason for Ed to be in any more danger, but I've made sure he'll have somebody here around the clock."

"*Gracias* . . ."

They disconnected.

She texted her brother again. He hadn't replied earlier and he didn't reply now. She was growing concerned.

But only moderately. If anyone knew how to stay alive it was him.

She asked the mayor firmly, "There some underground shit going on here that you're not sharing? Meth operation? Gunrunning? Human trafficking?"

"No! I swear!"

Dorion didn't know whether to believe him or not. Her disaster response took her to many different locales. Big cities, small towns, military bases, corporate campuses, swamps, deserts, forests, ports . . . And in every one of them there'd been politics at work. Sometimes about who got FEMA aid. Sometimes about who wanted to point fingers at lack of disaster preparedness.

Sometimes about nothing to do with the disaster. The hurricane or earthquake or fire had simply laid bare shenanigans that certain individuals had hoped would stay hidden . . .

But never had any of her employees been targeted.

She looked at his mortified face.

And decided that, no, he didn't *know* of any such activities.

But largely, she assessed, because he suffered from the sniffles of oblivion.

A doctor emerged with an update. The woman, in blue scrubs, reported that Ed Gutiérrez was in good condition . . . and lucky. The bone had not been touched. There would be rehab and a long time of healing but he would regain most use of the leg.

She said gravely, "It was a large hunting rifle round. But this wasn't a hunting accident, was it?"

"No."

The doctor's head, crowned by an Afro tucked into a bonnet, nodded slowly. She asked Tolifson, "You have anyone in custody?"

"No."

"A quarter inch to the left, and the leg would be gone. Sixteen inches higher and he'd be dead." A stern voice now. "Whatever's going on, just keep that in mind."

She turned and left.

Dorion rose, leaving Tolifson, and walked outside. She opened the liftgate of her SUV and unlocked a metal suitcase. From it she took a small black semiautomatic that was the same brand and model as Colter's, a Glock 42. Both of the younger Shaw siblings had coveted California concealed carry permits. Russell, being a government employee, didn't need one.

She chambered a round, slipped the weapon into a Blackhawk inside-the-belt holster and clipped it against her waist. Into her left pocket went a second magazine.

She'd never thought she might need it on a disaster response job.

But one of her father's most important rules was in her mind.

Never be unprepared for anything.

43.

Fiona Lavelle was wearing several layers. Smart. This space, an entrance to an old mine, had to be forty degrees. The stocking cap was probably a fashion statement.

She was definitely on the defensive. Her right hand continued to grip the rock, her left the light. He blinked once more and she backed away and aimed the beam elsewhere.

"Who are you?"

"I'm a professional tracker. I look for missing people. Your fiancé wanted me to find you. Though you're not engaged, are you?"

"No. He just says that. So he's here." Her eyes closed briefly in dismay.

"About an hour ago. When you didn't show up at the spa."

A grimace. "Where he sent me to lose weight and get in better shape. He came looking for me when I didn't pick up like I'm supposed to. He lets two calls go by unanswered and I'm in violation."

And then what? Shaw wondered. He'd worked a number of jobs involving domestic abuse runaways. The abusers were infinitely clever in establishing rules.

And devising, and delivering, punishments.

Shaw told her, "And he's here because he had an AirTag or tracker in the car."

"That's right. He hides them in very clever places. After I got stuck in the mud I went through the trunk and found it. I broke it but it was too late, I guess."

"He called a gas station on Route Thirteen, south of Hinowah, on the way to Fort Pleasant. The manager looked over the security video and didn't see your car. So he figured you must've had an accident here between the town and the crossroad."

"Are you a private eye?"

"Sort of. I'm helping with the levee situation. When he was talking to the police, he heard what I did and offered to pay me to find you."

She gave him a cynical glance. "How much?"

"Five thousand. Then he went up to seven five."

She gave a laugh. "Didn't even jump to ten. And he's worth twenty-five million. At least." Her eyes grew troubled. "But—"

"I didn't tell him. Don't worry. He believes the accident was real and that you survived and you're lost in the woods somewhere, probably injured. His concern is real. But it's like a bank robber's concern is real—for his loot, if it goes missing."

She gave a cold laugh. "Good way to put it. You didn't say anything, so you must have suspected. Why?" She realized she was still holding the rock and dropped it.

"A few things. Why wouldn't you pick up twenty calls? Excessive calling, even before he knew about the collapse. Typical domestic stalking behavior. And earlier, when I was asking him questions, to get a profile of you, he was patronizing."

"Oh, one of his specialties."

Shaw continued, "Then the skid marks on the asphalt just south of the levee? Where your Camaro ended up just after the collapse. There were both front- *and* rear-wheel skid marks. The front were brake marks. The rear were from acceleration. You made it off the levee and hit the brakes. Then I'm guessing you debated for a minute, made a decision, hit the gas and drove down that old trail to the base of Copper Peak."

She lifted an eyebrow, clearly impressed with his deduction. "You're like a detective."

Sherlock Holmes, her non-fiancé had called him.

"I found your phone—where you *meant* it to be found. It looked like you were doing a YouTube or Instagram video. But the camera was pointed at the rear wheels. If it had been legitimate you would have included yourself in the driver's seat, looking at the camera, narrating. But you couldn't have any footage there—since you weren't *in* the driver seat. You were standing outside the open window and using a stick to push the accelerator after you turned the wheel to the right. I saw those footprints.

"Another thing that made me suspicious? He had your passcode. Husband and wife, longtime married, maybe. But a younger couple, engaged or not. No. Passcodes would be secret. By the way, he leapt in after you."

"*What?* That river? Jesus. He can't swim. Not very well. We go to the Caribbean and mostly he struts. He shows off in front of the women. I'm not allowed to talk to anyone, but he can flirt all he wants."

"He's obsessed with you."

Lavelle scoffed. "A bank robber's loot. You saved him?"

Shaw had to smile at the hint of regret in her voice.

"I can't believe I'm baring my soul to you." A shrug. "But there aren't a lot of people I can talk to."

Shaw heard this often. Successful tracking required good listening, and he was fortunate that doing so was a talent he came by naturally.

He looked at the cut on her arm. "Part of your act, the blood on your jacket?"

"Nail file. Stings like hell."

"Let me see it."

Superficial.

"Bandages?"

"Band-Aids. In there." She nodded to her gym bag.

"Cover it. You'll be fine."

"My car . . . can it be fixed? I'm writing a fantasy novel." She gestured to a notebook. "About a magic sleigh my hero was riding in. I have a subplot where it's injured and she saves it. But what about my real car?"

"Probably. But you'll have to leave it there for now. Keep up the fiction for the time being."

"I figured."

He nodded. "What exactly was your plan?"

"Originally, I was just going to the spa to get away. He let me go because I told him I was going to work on my weight. He's been after me for that."

"He hinted as much when I interviewed him."

Her jaw clenched in anger. Then she said, "What I was going to do was eat donuts and popcorn and write my book. Get away from him for four days.

"But then the more I drove, not answering the phone, not hearing his voice, I felt free. And then the dam collapsed. It was like a sign. And I thought: What an opportunity! I jumped at the chance. It would seem like I'd died in a natural disaster. One more victim of the flood. My body disappeared. The car found at the bottom of a river. It'd look real.

"I needed to find a place to be out of the storm . . . I couldn't get a motel room. He's on all the credit cards. I read about these old mines on the county's website. This was one of them. Look, I know, Mr. Shaw—"

"Colter."

"It all sounds so weird. But I was desperate to get out." Her voice choked. Tears started to fall. "I was so goddamn stupid. Getting myself into this mess. At first, he was so kind, and interested in me and so romantic. Not much humor. That should've been a clue. He was too . . ."

She was thinking of the right word.

Shaw said, "He suffered from the disease of the literal."

Lavelle laughed. "Ah, that's good." The smile faded. "Then little by little he worked his way in. He got me to quit my job. I was teaching. High school English. He kept asking me about the other faculty members. Questioning me about field trips, who came along with me. Did I really have to stay late? He'd show up at the school, surprising me. He kept saying I didn't need to work. I could stay home, write my novels, we'd go to country clubs. Go to his firm's events—he's an investment advisor—meaning he coerces people into paying him to invest their money." She sighed. "I could argue and fight . . . and win sometimes, but it was just exhausting. Easier to just surrender. I wanted to write anyway." A nod toward her notebook.

"You're not in grad school?"

"Ha, like he'd let me be around other men? He says that." She wiped tears. "You know how terrible it is to be worshipped day and night?"

"Not a condition I've ever suffered from. Being worshipable."

Another hollow laugh. "There. Funny! See. Humor. Ah, how I missed that." She shook her head. "You know how bad it's gotten? Last month we were having a nice dinner. John was behaving himself. No cross-examination about what I'd done all day. None of that. I thought maybe he'd changed. It was the old John. I thought maybe he was going to surprise me and tell me he was seeing a therapist.

"And you know what he does? Helps me clear the dishes and tells me to find a movie on Netflix and goes to the bathroom. I'm all hopeful . . . And when he comes out, his hands are bleeding! He cut his own palms with the steak knife I'd used at dinner—which he'd pocketed in a napkin when I wasn't looking."

"Defensive wounds." Shaw understood.

"And just then the police show up. He'd called them from the bathroom, nine-one-one, and said I attacked him." Lavelle shivered in rage. "He was all, 'Oh, thank you for coming, Officers, but I'm all right. It's okay now. She's calmed down.' He didn't want to press charges. After they left he said now I was on record as being an abuser. And when he quote 'punished' me next time, he could always claim it was self-defense."

"And he did?"

"Oh, yes. Every month or so. My sister-in-law sent flowers for my birthday. He was convinced it was some man who'd talked her into doing it for him. I got alcohol sprayed in my eyes for that. Sometimes it would be boiling water. A fall down the stairs . . . And every time I packed to leave, I'd find him on the phone with my mother or sister-in-law, saying he'd be in the neighborhood and wanted to stop by for a visit. And looking at me with this expression that said, 'They're next.' How can one person be . . . the embodiment of evil, like that? Sounds like a terrible cliché, but it's true."

"A sociopath."

"I saw an online therapist for a while—until he found out. That's what she diagnosed. Sociopathic narcissist. I probably knew who he was sooner than I admitted to myself. But, the thing is, Colter, we want somebody in our lives so much. So desperately. And we open up the spiked gates and wave them cheerfully inside."

One of the reasons his very career existed.

"So. Me. Dead to the world. People like him need somebody to possess. I thought he'd move on, find somebody else. Oh, I felt bad about that. But I needed to survive." A cock of her head and a wistful smile. "It's not going to work, though, is it?"

"A hundred years ago, maybe. But the world's different now. Mobiles, facial recognition, social media, pictures and videos everywhere. And your video selfie of the car? There's a sound-analysis program that can tell you hit the gas *before* you put the car in gear.

And, there'd be a manhunt. And responders do not like wasting time on people who don't need rescuing."

"Unlike you . . ."

Shaw didn't smile. He added, "And now, after trying to trick him? Nothing's going to stop him from coming after you."

Her face resigned, she said, "Well, it was a good few hours I had, thinking maybe I'd made it to Fraeland."

As she dabbed at her eyes, he was thinking of one reward job he'd had—in which a young woman had vanished and her parents offered him six figures to find their daughter.

He did.

But too late.

The abusive boyfriend she'd run away from had found her first.

Shaw would always remember the couple's face as he broke the news.

Lavelle nodded around the cave. "You think I'm in danger here?"

"No. He's the sort who can't imagine someone would trash a fifty-thousand-dollar car and run off to a dank cave just to escape from him. He thinks you're in the woods trying to find your way out. I have some things to take care of. Sit tight here for the night. You've got food and water and battery power. You have a phone?"

"A burner. He doesn't know."

"Take my number." He recited it and she punched it into the mobile. "You're up high enough so that if the levee does go, you won't be flooded out. I'll be back in the morning."

He glanced at her notebooks.

"Work on your novel. I know a few writers. They'd give anything for a few days with no interruptions. Even in an abandoned mine shaft."

Colter found Dorion and Tam Olsen in the command post. He parked and joined them.

"How is he?"

"He'll live," his sister told him. "Working again? They don't know. The doctor said 'most use' of his leg. Ed liked to get out into the field. He was never good with desk work."

Colter noted that Olsen's face was particularly troubled. She was a soldier, yes, but army engineers were construction professionals for the most part; violence and gunplay rarely knocked.

"That's where it happened?" Colter asked. He nodded to caverns on the hillside where the CP sat, about three hundred yards west.

"That's right. He was getting those kids out of there." Dorion, rarely bitter, muttered, "It was all a lark for them. And my friend took a bullet to save them from getting their asses drowned."

Olsen asked, "He was only shot once?"

"That's right."

"I heard three. He missed twice, I guess."

Dorion said, "No, there was just one. The others were echoes."

"The valley, the hills," Colter said. Then he did something they ought to have done an hour ago: he pulled the rope to release the flap of the tent. Protecting them from the sniper.

If he was shooting at one investigator, why not more?

His sister asked, "What're we up against here? You don't talk much about your jobs. You been involved in anything like this?"

He thought for a moment. "Ashton's death. It was about a lot more than just that. But the truth stayed a complete mystery until a long time later. This reminds me of that. Not the facts, but the . . ." He sought for a word. "Tone."

He then turned his attention from the levee and from Gutiérrez's shooting. "We have another wrinkle. The woman whose fiancé drove here from Reno?"

"John Millwood?"

"It's a domestic. He's abusive and she engineered the whole thing to escape from him."

He explained about Fiona Lavelle's plan.

"Fake her own death?" Olsen said. "Sounds like the plot of a bad thriller flick."

"Her idea was to buy some time. Probably hoped he'd move on from her."

"He won't," Olsen said. "They never do." Spoken from experience, darkly.

"She's where?"

"Hiding out in an old silver mine."

"He suspect anything?"

"No, he believes the accident was real and county deputies and I are looking for her. He's in a motel in Fort Pleasant. I left her with chocolate, jerky and beer. And she's writing the great American novel. Or the great something kind of novel. She's got my number if there's a problem."

And there were plenty of dangerous-looking rocks at her disposal.

"We'll deal with that situation later."

Olsen asked, "Gutiérrez's shooter, was it—?"

"Bear," came a woman's voice behind them.

Debi Starr walked into the tent.

The siblings and Olsen turned to her. "I found the shooter's nest in the rocks on the south side of the valley."

It was a huge area, he was thinking. How on earth had she found exactly where he'd shot from?

She explained. "I nailed the slug. Good news it went through soft tissue—both good for Ed *and* for the forensics—and ended up in the dirt. I stuck a straw in the bullet hole in the ground and sighted up it. Adjusting for elevation and a little wind, I found the nest pretty easy. If he had a rest for his rifle it was silicon and not a cloth sandbag. No fibers. And no brass. He's a pro, no doubt about it now. Remember what I said about not having anything personal on him?

"He tried to walk away from the nest careful and was pretty good at it, but he planted a foot right in a bit of soft mud. Probably didn't bother to clean it because he was in a hurry—*and* because he doesn't think much of us poor small-town constables.

"But he's in for a surprise. I drove out to the bridge where you got attacked this morning, Colter. Found matching boot prints. So Bear's the sniper. I'll write an application for a warrant and, you"— a nod toward Colter—"do an affidavit putting the shooter at the copper mine earlier today. And we pay Mr. Redding a visit."

44.

Gerard Redding surveyed the sandbagging around the fence and decided it was as good as it was going to get.

Five of the six feet height were protected. And any flooding this far from the Never Summer—about a mile—would probably rise no more than a meter or so.

He was standing in the circular yard of the front of the company. He had always thought of this portion of his business as Cerberus, mythical three-headed dog guarding the entrance to the underworld.

This entryway was the body.

The three shafts—Hell, Hades and Inferno—were the necks.

The rock faces, a half mile down, the snarling heads.

It was a labored metaphor but he liked it.

He called to his workers. "Okay. That's good! You can go home now." He repeated the message in Spanish. He held up envelopes, each containing a hundred dollars in cash.

The half dozen men and women walked up to the fence and took the bonuses gratefully. They then hurried to their idling cars and made their escapes.

Hugh Davies, the operations manager, walked out of the office, looking over the barricade as well. "It's good, don't you think?"

Davies, a foot shorter than Redding, had a dapper, distinguished air about him. Even today—a day of alarm and extremes—he wore a white shirt and tie.

Redding nodded.

The manager continued, "She'll get the flooding worse than us." Eyes cutting across the highway, which separated the mine from Annie Coyne's farm.

"Bitch," Redding muttered.

At least, he had the satisfaction of knowing her frustration and anger every time she saw the north four hundred—the huge plot of farmland her father had lost to Redding's sire in that fateful poker game. Redding was a miner, not a farmer, so he'd let the property go to seed. All he cared about was the mineral rights and that particular parcel had exceeded the old man's expectations. He could have leased agrarian rights to her. But hell no.

"Everything secure?" he asked Davies.

Referring to moving the computers and paperwork to a safe location.

"As long as it doesn't turn into Niagara Falls."

It wouldn't. Redding's calculations had confirmed this.

"You want to leave?" Redding asked. "We can move the barricade."

"If you're not, think I'll stick around too. In case your ass needs bailing out."

"Ha."

He believed that Davies had a crush of sorts on him. But it was as nebulous and unformed as it would forever be.

They gazed around. "Odd, the place looks funny with nobody around, no trucks, no sounds of machinery."

"Like we had a snow day."

"What's that?"

"You don't know?"

The manager shook his head.

Redding explained about schools up north closing because there was too much snow on the roads. He'd lived in Rochester getting his master's in engineering at RIT, and the woman he lived with, briefly, had children.

Davies said, "Hm. Think it would teach the kids to toughen up."

"Might get hurt. Parents would sue."

Every person involved in mining was aware of one thing above all else: liability. It was far too easy to be hurt or killed in the profession.

Davies nodded. "Learn something new every day." He walked off toward the office on the north side of the mythical dog's body.

Redding glanced at Annie Coyne's farm once more, then continued on to the workshop. He unlocked the door with a keypad and stepped inside. The place had no windows, of course. The building was visible from the highway and he knew competitors in the copper-mining world would love to cruise by and take a dozen digital high-definition pictures of what Redding was up to, from the research and development perspective.

Paranoid?

Maybe a little.

But he had many reasons to be cautious.

He now looked at one in particular.

It was a device he himself had invented and was as yet un-patented, resembling a moon lander—four legs under a gray metal box. Its height was about three feet, its width two.

On the right side was the drill, which would dig a hole in the earth beneath it, where a blank rifle bullet would be placed. On the other side was an armature that ended in a round metal plate resting on the ground.

The robot would then fire the bullet and the shock waves would drive down into the earth and then return to the sensor. This was typical of many devices in the industry, but what was revolutionary about his was that the software could differentiate between the types of ores the shock waves discovered and the quality of the vein.

He'd recently tried it and had spectacular results.

Redding wanted to make sure the device was safe from floodwater, on the off chance the sandbagging didn't work. The machine was too heavy to lift. He would dismantle it into the component parts and store them high on the metal shelves in the back of the workshop.

First, the brain.

Using a tiny Phillips-head screwdriver, he removed the plate on the top of the robot. He set this and the four screws on a plastic examination tray a few feet away. He played a flashlight inside, nodding to himself with approval at the cleanliness of the design. And then he unplugged the green motherboard that measured three inches by six. This went into a Ziplock bag.

For the rest of the machine—motors and gears mostly—he didn't need to be so delicate and so he would use a large cordless drill fitted with a screwdriver head. He opened the desk draw where he kept the Black & Decker.

He calculated that—

The fiery ball, which Gerard Redding never saw, of course, was about ten feet in diameter. The explosion turned every glass beaker, pipette, jar and dish nearby into glass dust. It converted any object made of thin metal, like wastebaskets and rulers, into bits of shrapnel. It removed the acoustical tiles from the ceiling and pushed the sheet metal walls outward a good twelve inches, ripping the door off the hinges and sending it frisbeeing into the chain-link fence fifty feet away.

It also removed Redding's head and detached his arms and shoulders from the rest of his torso, which was flung into the front wall.

Curiously despite the flame, the fire detectors overhead didn't function; they had been rendered useless by the force of the blast. So instead of the room filling with the gentle fire-extinguishing rain from the ceiling pipes, what appeared instantly was a thick haze.

Which was notable in that while the fumes from plastic explosives are generally gray-white, this particular mist was red, a hue that matched the shade of still-damp human blood perfectly.

45.

What a time . . .

Noah's flood, a nearly dead family, a missing girl from an overturned Camaro, a shot-up disaster response worker and now a horrific explosion at a mine. And not down a shaft, which had happened once before.

But in an office.

Awful . . .

A terrible accident.

Or a terrible murder.

Hanlon Tolifson was reflecting that the CHP was darn well going to *have* to pry investigators and Crime Scene loose and get them down here from the Olechu barracks.

Sitting in the command post, he was presently on hold, waiting for a captain to come back on the line and respond to his request.

As he waited, he reviewed his performance during the Test so far.

And was satisfied. He gave himself a solid B.

This was important.

Confirming, for certain, that he would take on the job of police chief of the incorporated village of Hinowah, California.

He liked the work.

Liked the puzzle solving, the protecting the innocent. The respect.

And that gun thing too. He liked the way it sat on his hip, how it felt in his hand, the idea it was always there . . .

Clint Eastwood, Kevin Costner, *Yellowstone*.

The command post was now less wet but more breezy, a wind coming up from the north, blowing in the direction of the Never Summer's flow. He occasionally peeked out, looking south, feeling that creepy sensation on the back of his neck at the thought that Eduardo Gutiérrez's shooter—the man nicknamed Bear—was still free.

Colter Shaw was here, along with his sister, both on their phones. Colter had said they didn't need to be concerned with Fiona Lavelle. She was all right, but not to say anything to her fiancé, if he called. He had not gone into details. But that was okay with him. One less thing to worry about.

Sergeant Tamara Olsen was on the other side of the levee with her two corporals, Williams and McPherson. Could they get those bomb curtains here soon?

All of that to think about.

Ah, Gerard Redding . . . The sight in Workshop One had been described by Hugh Davies, the mining company's operations manager, as "unimaginable." There came muffled sounds after that. And he believed Davies was crying. Then, likely, puking.

Debi Starr and TC McGuire were present at the mine, taping it off as a crime scene and making sure people stayed clear.

"Mayor?" CHP Captain Diego Rivera was back on the line. "Okay. Here's what I can do. I'm getting our bomb squad people in from Sacramento. And two Major Crimes folks, one of the rotating teams. They're outta Oakland."

Neither very close.

"Uh-huh. And I'm just kind of wondering when."

"I told them to prioritize it."

"Okay. But, like I said, I'm just kind of wondering when."

"Hold on. It's Sacramento."

No click. Just silence. His eyes went to Dorion Shaw. Tolifson had long ago retired "DRB," as being not only disrespectful but unfair considering that her iron-lady approach was saving lives. He decided that as chief he would need a bit more of that edge, like her. More police stuff to work on. Like his quick draw and boning up on the California Penal Code.

Rivera was back. "Five, six hours. Probably less."

No, probably more, Tolifson thought. This was not sour cynicism, just a realistic thought given that as a mayor of a small town he had become familiar with how slowly the gears of state government ground when you were in the bush league.

"Well, we're thinking it's not an accident. That means there's a perp somewhere out there."

Rivera: "Could've been a gas explosion. Happens a lot in mines."

"Gas? It was in a laboratory. Nowhere near a shaft."

"They have gas in labs."

"Not this one."

"With the storm, Mayor, it's a busy day. As you can imagine. They said secure the scene. They'll be there as soon as they can."

"Well, Captain, the site *is* secure. Nobody's going anywhere near where it happened—and could, maybe, happen again, which is why we really want somebody expert to take a look. Secure isn't the issue. The issue is finding out what the heck is going on here."

"You know what happens, Han." A pause. "Not with *you* of course, necessarily, but *somebody*. They go trooping through the scene, evidence gets messed up. The lawyer at trial gets the defendant off."

Tolifson didn't like the "necessarily."

Looking toward Dorion and Colter Shaw, he called, "He's saying secure the scene. They'll get some people here as soon as they can."

She asked, "How soon is that?"

"He doesn't know."

Dorion's face darkened and she approached, hand outstretched for the phone.

It looked like DRB was back.

Good.

She asked, "Who?"

Tolifson smiled as he handed it to her and whispered, "Captain Rivera, CHP."

She took the phone.

"Captain, this is Dorion Shaw. I own Shaw Incident Services. I'm running response with Chief Tolifson."

He liked the way that sounded.

"We have a situation maybe you can help us with . . . It's the press. They're becoming a problem."

Press? Tolifson wondered.

She listened. "Well, I don't know who called them. But a couple of the reporters are asking why there's been no police response to a suspected high-explosive sabotage on the levee and now what appears to be related incidents. A wounded response worker and an IED death. They're wondering if it's being taken seriously in Sacramento. Now, I'm on your side, Captain. I know how strapped you are. I want to help you out. Is there something I can tell them about the delay in your response . . . Yes, I understand there's flooding in Fort Pleasant. A newswoman brought that up, and well, fact is, her reporting is that it wasn't so bad. Now she's onto the explosion at the mine. She's doing a story for the nightly news. I wish we could preempt that."

Go get him, DRB.

"A solution? Well, I'm thinking we could have the town officers here do a preliminary. We've got good people. I've seen their credentials . . . Yes, I'm sure that'll keep the reporters happy. That's part of our job at Shaw Incident Services: press relations. Always good to have them on our side . . . All right."

She handed the phone back.

"And she is who again?" Rivera asked bluntly.

"She's a consultant."

"Consultant." As if the word was synonymous with venomous snake. "You're green-lighted to work the scene. Just be sure you preserve every damn bit of evidence. Custody cards for every molecule of skin and bone."

"Will do, Captain."

He disconnected before the man added more qualifiers or changed his mind.

"Thank you," he said to Dorion.

Tolifson now hesitated, realizing he'd just gotten what he'd asked for. The chance to spend time in a place that would be horrific beyond his imagination.

Molecule of skin and bone . . .

He found himself staring at the levee.

Then he heard a voice behind him. "Mayor."

It was Colter Shaw speaking.

He turned.

"Dorion told me you got the okay to start investigating the Redding bombing on your own."

"That's right."

"For what it's worth, I've done demolition investigations as part of my job. I know you probably want to run the scene yourself, but if you don't mind, any chance I could do it? I know what to look for, and it'll cut the time down considerably."

A frown. "Well, now, Mr. Shaw, Colter, you're right I'd rather do it myself. But if you think it'd be better for the case, I'll stand down." He shrugged. "We all have to make sacrifices for what's best."

46.

The truth is a thing of percentages too.

Because truth's building blocks—facts—don't always stand up the way we'd like.

People grew sick from wind and vapor and spirits—a one hundred percent fact—until germs were spotted by a rudimentary microscope.

A human being couldn't fly. Fact. Until two brothers demonstrated otherwise on a beach in North Carolina.

Then there are the more subtle underpinnings of the truth.

What would the shattered metal and glass and plastic—and human tissue and bone and blood—in a copper mine workshop say about what happened there?

Would what Colter Shaw was about to find support an answer that rated a truth factor of one hundred percent?

Or zero?

Or somewhere in between? (It took a while to link those crawly little microscopic things to the flu.)

The rain had largely stopped but the surface of the highway to the Redding mine was still slick and when Shaw arrived he skidded long, stopping just shy of the gate. The sandbag barrier was down

260 : JEFFERY DEAVER

here, allowing the ambulance and two official cars—Debi Starr's and TC McGuire's—inside.

Shaw took in the grim mine—made grimmer yet by the awareness of what had just happened in the workshop shed not fifty feet away, the door blown out and burn marks in a corona around the frame.

Shaw walked to two people who were having a conversation near the entrance: Debi Starr and the man Shaw had met earlier, the operations manager, Hugh Davies, looking pale and distraught and actually wringing his hands.

Without a greeting, he turned to Shaw with hollow eyes tinted with red skin from crying. "I saw it." He whispered, "I'll see it forever. He . . . I mean you can't even say 'he' or 'him' anymore. It's a thing. That's what the explosion did."

Starr was holding a notebook and she'd already gotten some information, he could see. She was saying to the man in a kind, motherly voice, "There are some people you can talk to. They're like counselors. Trauma. They can help. They really can." She wrote some names and numbers—from memory, Shaw noted—and tore off the slip and handed it to him. He stared at this too.

Shaw supposed that being the town traffic detail, she had had occasion to see tragedy on the highways and would want to set up a fatality's family with those who could help during those impossibly difficult times. For his own business he'd done the same on rare occasions. Teddy and Velma Bruin maintained a list of such professionals.

Two more vehicles arrived.

Tolifson and Dorion. The mayor walked up to the three of them, while Dorion made a call, possibly to Ed Gutiérrez who was out of surgery. The slug, which Debi Starr had dug out of the earth on the hill near town where he'd been hit, was a hunting rifle caliber, a big one, .308.

Shaw looked around for Bear, notably sniper nests where the man might be sighting on them.

No sign.

McGuire was searching the grounds for him, Shaw knew, but had reported that he'd found no evidence of his presence.

Starr said to Shaw and the mayor, "I asked Mr. Davies about that employee, the man with the beard, the stocky one, and he's not familiar with anyone of that description."

Her eyes told him that she believed he was telling the truth.

So maybe Bear wasn't on their payroll after all.

Which didn't mean Redding hadn't hired him on the sly.

Tolifson said, "When Ms. Shaw asked about explosives earlier, to blow part of the spillway, Redding said they didn't have any."

Davies responded, "That's right. We use an outside service. Demo work is specialized."

Starr asked, "They never leave explosives here, Mr. Redding told us."

"Nowhere to keep 'em safe. But I'll call the service and double-check." Davies took his phone and with shaking hands made the call. He left a message and stood with slumped shoulders as he cradled the silent mobile.

Shaw noted Tolifson was once again fiddling with his pistol.

That was enough.

He gestured for the man to step aside with him. The mayor frowned but did so.

Shaw lowered his voice, so as not to embarrass him in front of anyone. "You've got to understand that that weapon of yours has a five-pound pull. It's not as light as some, but it's low enough. A twitch can fire it. There's a rule: Never touch your weapon until you need to draw, and never draw until you see a threat."

Shaw didn't know how this schoolmarm stuff would be received.

Gratefully, as it turned out. "That's helpful. Appreciate it. You're right. I'm new to this game, but I'm a fast learner. And I'm soaking up stuff right and left." In an odd move, he shook Shaw's hand enthusiastically and returned to the others.

Davies explained that Redding had been in the building by

himself, working on one of his inventions. The man frowned. "It used a blank rifle shell to send sound waves into the ground. For identifying ore. You think that could have anything to do with what happened?"

Shaw said, "No, that's C-four in there, not smokeless powder." The scent was unmistakable.

He couldn't help but notice the names of the mines once again.

Hades, Inferno and Hell . . .

Davies got a call and had a conversation. He disconnected. It had been from the demo company. He said, "They use only gel here—not plastic. And they didn't leave any here anyway. But for what it's worth, the guy I talked to said that there was a notice on the Interstate Dangerous Substances Network that four kilos of C-four were stolen from a land-mine manufacturer outside of Seattle. Three days ago. They have no idea who and the police don't have any leads. Sounds unrelated."

Never assume there's no connection when confronted by seemingly unrelated events or individuals.

Ashton Shaw got a lot of mileage out of that one.

Tolifson said, "Maybe we should follow up on it."

Starr held up her phone. "Already sent an NCIC request." She then pointed to the front of the workshop. "Look."

A series of footprints. Somebody had either walked from the door to the fence and back, or the other way around. He and Starr walked closer and studied them, as she taped the trail off with a yellow ribbon.

"No way to tell the sole mark," she said. "But big enough to be Bear's."

"There." Shaw was pointing up. "Security camera. It might've caught him."

Davies was hesitating. In an unsteady voice he said, "The disk is in the workshop. A separate hard drive plugged into the desktop. To the left as you walk in. The videos are stored for forty-eight hours. Then they're overwritten."

Shaw said, "I'll get it when I search the room."

Tolifson was looking away. Then he said, "I appreciate this, Mr. Shaw, but I'm thinking. You wonder if maybe the bomber left another IED in there? You know, to stop investigators?"

"I give it fifteen percent."

"How do you figure that low?"

"It's just logical. Assuming it was murder, which I think it's safe to do now, then it wasn't a timed device. The killer couldn't know exactly when Redding would be inside. The trigger was rigged to something that Redding touched, stepped on or sat down in."

"Okay, but how are you going to avoid setting another one off?"

"There's an easy rule for that."

"What?"

"Be careful what you touch, step on or sit down in."

47.

He had learned to go to a different place.

When faced with a situation impossible to witness yet witnessing was unavoidable, Colter Shaw flipped some kind of switch in his psyche.

After all, if a reward was offered for a person who could not be found, then one possible explanation was that they were dead, either of natural causes, accident or criminal intent. Or their own hand, of course.

And in his mission to discover them, he occasionally found the person he sought was no longer of the living—and, accordingly, altered in terrible ways. Perhaps by time and the elements. Perhaps by weapons. Perhaps by scavenging animals or insects.

Shaw was not a spiritual man, but he'd heard of people claiming that in near-death incidents, they had floated above their body, and looked down in a state of utter calm.

Shaw did not believe in that, but he stole the metaphor.

And that's what he did when he confronted horror.

He floated above it.

He did this not to avoid being sick or stave off nightmares. No, he did this to ply his trade. Simple as that. To survive you needed to

observe and assess dispassionately. And whether that involved noting footsteps in a beautiful garden that smelled of violets, or observ-
ing the angle of hacksaw blades on a victim's ankles, he had to be as
distanced as a surgeon.

He now, wearing blue gloves, found himself in that mental place
as he surveyed what had once been a man—one he'd spoken to just
a few hours before. Examining the organs, the shattered and burned
black and red skin, the bones . . .

The stains of blood.

Indicators of the how and the where of the explosion.

Normally Shaw would document his findings in another one of
his notebooks dedicated to the job, but that would take too long and
he wanted to get the hell out as soon as he could. He had his phone
to record the details of the incident. He lifted it now.

"How 'bout if I handle that," someone said behind him.

He turned to see Debi Starr approaching, a digital camera in
hand. "Just easier and better if we don't have to play bucket brigade with the evidence. Photos're in the chain of custody too. Oh,
and here."

She handed him booties.

"I'm the footprint queen, remember? The tales they tell . . ."

Shaw slipped them on.

He glanced at her as she took in the gore, noting her face was as
neutral as his. He wondered where *she* floated.

Starr was aware of the direction of his gaze. "Aw, seen this before. Nab Wilkins—born Arthur, so don't know where the nick
came from. He took the bend at Lumberton Road doing eighty. It's
a forty zone. You know those numbers are on those signs for a *reason*? Seatbelt wouldn't've saved his life, but at least he wouldn't've
gotten smeared all over both sides of the highways. Cut clean in two.
Never did figure out how that happened. So this?" A gesture toward
what remained of Redding's desk. Then a shrug. "I mean the head
is a bit unpleasant. And people forget that along with blood there's

a bunch of shit inside people. Particularly true here. But other than that. All in a day's work for Traffic Girl. You look like you've done this before too."

"A few times. You know, I put the percentage low for another device, but low is not zero. You sure you want to be here? You have family, right?"

"*Everybody's* got family, Colter. And if we can find out what the hell's going on in this town, then maybe they'll be all the safer for it. What do you think happened?"

"That thing of his he was working on."

Starr examined it. "Looks like a robot."

"All its components go to the left, not everywhere. So the bomb wasn't in there."

"No."

The desk was in pieces, the chair blown against a wall and embedded in the Sheetrock. Most shelves—and the equipment they held—were on the floor.

Not a single piece of glassware had survived.

Shaw studied the pieces of desk scattered around the front part of the room. He shone his light on what had been a drawer. "It was in there."

Starr looked at it and nodded.

He closely examined what remained. "See the bits of circuit board? That could be from the detonator. Cell phone. Two circuits with different numbers. So you can arm it from a distance. Just in case there's a similar frequency that trips the main circuit."

"*Professional*," she said, and glanced around. "There's the hard drive." The security camera disk—pale blue—wasn't big. She walked carefully to it, looking at the floor as if land mines studded the concrete.

Starr slipped the drive into a Ziplock bag. "Prosecutors like special evidence bags. We don't have any. These'll have to do, and if a defense lawyer's a stinker about it, on the stand, I'll ask him to describe in detail the difference between official twenty-nine ninety-nine CSI bags and these, and watch him come up short."

Shaw said, "My theory is get your perp's ID first and worry about his trial later."

She considered this with a glint in her eye. "You mean something might happen to 'em, and they don't make it to the courthouse alive?"

"No, I do not mean that."

"Hm." She continued to look at him for a moment. "Now, sir, *I've* got a badge and you don't, but I know for sure that you've done this more than I have. So what else are we looking for?"

"One of two things happened here. A murder for its own sake. Or a theft, and the bomb was meant to cover that up. If it's the first one, then all we can find is a footprint, or tool marks."

"And the second?"

"Look for someplace ransacked."

She laughed, looking around. "Hell, Colter, this is the definition of ransacked."

"There'll still be something you just sense is out of place—where he was searching for the hidden treasure."

He shone his brilliant light around the walls of the room, which was about thirty by forty feet. "You go left, I'll go right. And let's move as fast as we can. If there's something here that gives us a clue about the risk to the levee, we need it ASAP. But remember—"

"Step, touch, sit."

The two began the search. The made their way through the circuit slowly, placing their feet onto the floor only after they shone their respective lights at the concrete and, reassured there were no trip wires, continued on, looking to the right and left and up and—especially—down. Pausing frequently. They repeated the process again and again.

Slow . . .

They returned, after their full circle, to the remains of the desk without finding anything either of them considered helpful.

Shaw then was looking at a small gray metal file cabinet on its side next to site of the bomb. It was badly damaged but more or less intact.

Starr said, "It's been moved."

The base had left marks on the floor from where it had originally been. "It's like the bomber moved it there next to the bomb. He wanted it destroyed, along with Mr. Redding."

"And look. The lock." Starr pointed.

"Jimmied with a screwdriver. Bomber broke in and did a sloppy job of it, because he didn't think it would survive the explosion. That's the ransack. Whatever he took—that's our answer."

The drawers were both partly open and Starr shown her light inside. "Papers. Don't see any wires or timers."

Shaw mused, "The perp found what he needed, moved the cabinet, set the bomb and then left."

"What was so important he needed to put this all together to steal whatever was inside?"

"Or *wanted* to steal, but didn't manage to find," Shaw said.

"How's that?"

"Look." He shone his beam on the underside of the top drawer, where a sliver of paper was visible.

"Something taped up there."

They regarded each other and Shaw knew she was thinking exactly what he was: weighing the odds that the paper was booby-trapped versus the value of what it contained.

From it they possibly could deduce the identity of who was behind the levee sabotage—presumably Bear's employer—and save more lives.

A closer examination revealed it was a large white envelope, about 8 by 10 inches.

"See any wires?" he asked.

They both looked.

None. He reached down and tugged. It came away with nothing more than the sticky sound of peeling tape.

"Phew," Starr said. Then she opened it, and tugged out the half dozen documents.

Shaw stepped close and together they read.

The documents made clear who was behind the sabotage.

And what the reason was.

And, most important, that it was only a matter of time until the rest of the Hinowah levee came tumbling down to earth, unleashing a deadly flood.

48.

Lithium.

The new silver, the new gold . . .

That was what the levee destruction was about. And why Gerard Redding had been so horribly murdered.

In the command post once more, where the team was assembled, Shaw watched Han Tolifson, wearing latex gloves that were a size too large, reviewing the documents that had been recovered from the bombed mine office.

Shaw was explaining to Dorion, TC McGuire and Sergeant Tamara Olsen, "Redding had some new machine that could detect different types of ores below the surface of the earth. He was testing it and he found Hinowah was sitting on top of a bed of lithium."

Tolifson gestured to the documents in his hand. "This's paperwork for mineral assays." He handed them to Starr, who tucked them into an oversize Ziplock bag. The mayor added, "Looks like the deposits are pure enough for electric vehicles."

McGuire said, "I thought lithium was only found in South America and Africa. Not here."

Starr said, "I just looked it up online. There's a caldera—a depression left over after a volcano—not far away. On the Oregon-

Nevada border. It's got the biggest lithium deposits in the world—thirty to forty million metric tons."

Tolifson was frowning. "Never knew. Why haven't we heard about it?"

She explained, "Looks like there're prohibitions on mining up there. A lot of it's under Indigenous land. In Olechu County? No restrictions at all." She looked toward Dorion. "So. The reason for the flooding was exactly what you said at first: Vultures. Redding was sabotaging the land to drive people out, then he'd buy it up cheap." She glanced at the baggie. "There're also drafts of letters to people who might not be inclined to sell. Very subtle. They say if they want to stay, that's great, Redding Mining will sell discounted respirators and water-testing kits."

She shook her head. "Lithium extraction isn't like deep-shaft copper mining. It's pumped into big ponds on the surface. Then as the water evaporates the lithium is skimmed off."

Tolifson said, "What a mess."

Tamara Olsen said, "He blows the top of the levee to scare everybody into evacuating. Then, when they've left, he blows the rest. Minimizes injury and death. When the dust—well, the water—settles, he starts buying up the property. Which means there *are* more explosives inside." She looked to Shaw. "On a timer, you think?"

"Probably not. He'd need to control when it happens."

Shaw was not surprised to hear Starr's trademarked "Got a question."

Tolifson nodded her way. "Go ahead, Debi."

"So. Why was he killed?"

The very inquiry that had been in the forefront of Shaw's mind. He suggested, "A lithium-mining cartel doesn't want any competition."

Dorion was nodding. "The assay company is offshore. In the British West Indies, I saw." A glance at the baggie docs. "Less than reputable, maybe. They're being paid by a cartel to report any big finds."

Then Colter picked up on the theme. "They like Redding's plan to buy up land in Hinowah—but they want to cut him out. Bear wasn't working for Redding. He was hired by *them*, whoever they are. Or, possibly, he was *originally* hired by Redding but he turned. People like that, it's usually a question of the highest bidder."

Dorion sighed. "All of which means the levee's still at risk."

True, Maybe Redding wouldn't push the button. But his new "partners" would.

TC McGuire looked up from his laptop. "I got the video of the security camera from the mine. The drive you collected, Debi? That our boy?"

He spun the Dell around. The camera mounted on the outside wall of the building that contained the workshop that had proved to be Redding's death chamber revealed a man, head down, baseball cap on, in a dark jacket and slacks. He wore a backpack. On his hands were leather gloves. He was walking toward the fence surrounding the mine.

"That's him," Shaw said. The build and beard were giveaways. "Bear."

The next shot showed him throwing a rope with a grappling hook on the end over the sandbagged fence surrounding the mine entrance and climbing it.

He vanished from view. Fifteen minutes later he returned, used the rope to climb the fence and walked to the road, disappearing into the woods on the other side of the highway.

"Any car?" Shaw asked.

McGuire scrubbed through the video. "No, sir."

Shaw asked, "That forest. It's on Annie Coyne's farm?"

Tolifson said, "That's right."

"I'll follow up on that."

Tolifson asked Sergeant Olsen, "It's too late for the bomb curtains?"

"Right. Under other circumstances maybe, but not with the overcast and mist."

The mayor asked the others, "Plans now?"

Dorion said, "I think the town's pretty well evacuated. But I can drive through and see if any lights are on. That'll mean remainers. I'll pry them out."

After that, she said, she would get a few hours' sleep at the motel outside of town.

After his "crime scene" work at Annie Coyne's, Shaw would return to the camper and rest up briefly.

Shaw's phone sounded. He glanced at the number on the screen and told his sister, "It's Tony."

Together they walked outside, away from the others.

"Tony. I'm here with Dorion."

"Is Mary Dove there yet?"

Dorion explained that she'd left the Compound but was spending the night at a motel on Route 44, until a mudslide was cleared.

The lawyer then said, "Good, so she's safe."

His tone was one of relief. It was curious and Shaw looked to his sister.

Tony continued, "Now, I found something you should know."

"Go on."

"In another letter I found, Sarah's sounding more and more unhinged. I'll read some of it. 'They're after me. They want to put me in the hospital. They want to erase my mind, cut off my tongue. And people are helping them. People I thought I could trust. But you can't trust anybody, only fools trust. And what do they get? They get betrayed. But I'm ready. Yes, Eddy Street. You told me not to, but I had to go there—and buy a gun. I heard all your arguments against it. But there has to be a reckoning for betrayal. There has to be justice.'"

Tony said, "Eddy Street? Gangs?"

"That's right," Shaw said.

So Sarah had been armed.

From now on, they would have to assume that mother had passed down to her daughter not only a searing resentment of the Shaw family.

But a firearm as well.

49.

Colter Shaw cycled up to the COYNE FARM sign.

The Yamaha's bright beam caught the trencher. It sat idle. Shaw could see why.

Annie Coyne had dug dozens of channels as deep as the machine was capable of and the troughs now covered the entire front area of the land. It was like a diorama of the First World War, the Germans and the Allies facing each other across no-man's-land, in their protective burrows.

Which reminded him of the rivalry between the Coynes and the Reddings.

A conflict that fate—in the form of high explosives—had just resolved.

He rode over the plank drawbridge at the front gate and on to the farmhouse, parked and walked toward the doorway.

Annie Coyne had heard him coming and opened the door just as he got to it.

"Colter. The levee?" Her face was wary, though she was also likely thinking that if disaster was imminent, a phone call would have been more appropriate.

"No. Hasn't collapsed. Still at risk, though."

They stood on the front porch—the level plane of old wood that sat on the west side of the house, from which you could see marvelous sunsets, Shaw was sure, though it was hard to imagine any sun whatsoever on a day like this.

"Come in."

They walked inside the scented, frilly living room.

Bordello . . .

"Gerard Redding is dead."

She spun around, brow furrowed.

"He was murdered. A bomb in his workshop."

"Bomb?"

"And something I didn't tell you before. The levee didn't collapse on its own. It was sabotaged. Also with explosives. The same kind, or very similar."

She took the news with a mixture of shock and confusion.

"And Gerard was behind it?"

"Yes. It's not public knowledge about the levee."

"I won't say anything . . . But why on earth?" She swiveled her gaze. toward the window and her eyes narrowed. "My farm. He wanted me out of business and wanted my property! He was going to flood me out."

"No. Nothing to do with you. There are lithium deposits under Hinowah. For batteries. He wanted to flood people out and was then going to buy up the land, turn the town into a pit mine. But if there's lithium under your property, then he'd want that too."

"But who murdered him? Why?"

"We don't know. Maybe competitors. Rival lithium mines."

"Why isn't the levee safe, if he's dead . . . Oh, wait . . ." Her eyes widened slightly in understanding. "Somebody *else* wants to take over what he had planned?"

"It's likely. There's a lead I want to follow up on. We have the bomber on video getting away from the mine into your property."

"*My* property?" Her sun-brushed, freckled face grew troubled. "Where?"

"There's a post-and-rail fence along Route Fifty-eight, near the entrance to the mine. Is there a place where somebody could park and not be seen from the road or the mine?"

"Probably. I think there's an old tractor trail. Do you want to go look for it?"

He nodded again, noting that she was looking out the window at his bike, maybe wondering if he had in mind they ride together. But few dirt bikes were meant for two passengers, and the Yamaha was no exception. Especially on a windy, dark evening.

"Your Jeep?"

A faint smile. "Sure."

She grabbed a navy windbreaker from a hook near the door and tugged on a baseball cap with UC DAVIS on the crest.

Outside they walked to the vehicle. He glanced to the barn. "How's your second-story cow?"

"Confused. But that's pretty much the waiting state for bovines."

Making their way as best they could through the yard, skirting around puddles and patches of mud, they got to her Jeep. The vehicle was an old model, roofless, though today, with the storm, she had snapped into place sheets of yellowing plastic for a roof and side panels.

She fired up the engine and clicked on the headlights and powerful spots mounted on the top frame. She snapped on her seatbelt. A glance at his. "You better."

He strapped in and she sped off.

Under her urgent hand, the vehicle bounded along, sometimes on paths, sometimes off-road. Mud flew in their wake and raindrops appeared like coldly iridescent fireflies in the fierce beams from the lights.

He tugged out his phone and, as best he could with the turbulent ride, consulted a map of the area.

"That way," he said and pointed, directing her toward one of the spots where Bear might have parked.

In five minutes he said, "Here's good."

Coyne skidded to a stop and they climbed out. They were in a weedy clearing and ahead of them was a thick band of trees. Through them he could make out the flashing lights of an emergency vehicle at the mine entrance. The Olechu County Sheriff's Office had finally arrived. They were probably a perfectly competent law enforcement agency but Shaw sensed they would move methodically—read slowly—and that wasn't good enough for Shaw. He wanted Bear. And he wanted him now.

Coyne asked, "What're we looking for?"

He pointed to the fence with his tactical flashlight. He handed his spare to her and she turned it on. "The bomber disappeared into this part of the woods. We want footprints, tire prints."

Eyes on the ground, sweeping the beam, Shaw walked toward the road, looking for a muddy patch. There was a lot of ground cover here and he could find no tire treads. Coyne joined him. "And who is this guy?"

"We know he's professional. Mercenary probably. I thought he was working for Redding—I saw him at the mine. But now we're thinking he's on somebody else's payroll. Whoever writes his checks writes big ones. He uses high-end aftershave."

She turned his way but he offered nothing further on the subject.

"There." Shaw had found treads of a parked vehicle. And shoe or boot prints leading from the driver's door to the rear, where presumably, the IED had been stored.

He examined the tire treads and measured them, jotting the results in his notebook. You couldn't narrow down the make and model, but Shaw deduced he was in a pickup truck. He took a picture of the tread marks but there probably wasn't enough detail to nail the brand.

He then retraced the steps from the tread marks to the highway, staring down at the bright disk of halogen.

"Looking for anything in particular?"

"If he dropped something. Doesn't happen often but after perps commit the crime they're more careless. They want to get away fast. I've found business cards and hotel room keys. But Bear—what I'm calling him—apparently not."

"You *are* like a cop. I mean, I guess you have to be, in the reward business, looking for escapees and fugitives."

So. She'd looked him up.

He called Debi Starr.

"Hey, Colter."

"I found where Bear parked." He sent the picture to her. "Here's a tread mark. Not very detailed."

A pause. "No. Can't make the brand. The track? A pickup, right?"

"I'm guessing."

"My, that narrows it down to . . . Let me think. Oh, right . . . One hundred and twelve percent of the county. Anything else?"

"No."

She thanked him and they disconnected. Coyne and he returned to the Jeep.

Coyne was saying, "I was thinking of you being a cop. I remember my dad and I used to watch the old detective shows, like *Matlock, Hill Street Blues, Law and Order*." A sad laugh. "Nice times."

They climbed in and drove back at a less frantic pace.

Coyne seemed thoughtful, and Shaw supposed she was reflecting on her history with Redding. Maybe thinking of the poker game where Redding's father took advantage of hers. Losing that four hundred acres probably changed the entire nature of the farm, shifting it from comfortably profitable to a challenge to stay afloat every season.

And what would happen now that her rival was no more?

They returned in silence to the house and she drove over the drawbridge, parking beside the Yamaha.

She swung out and stood for a moment, hands on her hips, looking up at the sky. Then her gaze dropped to the trenches. Now that she'd learned that there was a real possibility that the levee would still blow, she was assessing.

She seemed confident they would save the farm from disaster. And turned to him with a smile. "That beer now?"

"Sure."

As they walked to the house, Shaw noticed that they were the only ones on the property. "Your workers? They'll be all right?"

"None of them live in the area. It's way cheaper outside of Olechu County. Doesn't seem like it would be, but those big companies in Fort Pleasant? They bring in employees from Silicon Valley, the Bay, L.A. And up go the property values."

"A representative from one of them, a computer chipmaker, said he has a lot of residents of Hinowah on the payroll."

"Well, he's lying. I know the company. They brought in their own employees. Some locals have middling jobs, low-pay, while the property values and taxes keep climbing. It's gotten so crazy, my people have to live thirty, forty miles away. Sometimes farther."

Shaw thought of the developer, Theo Gabris, the huge houses he was building.

Inside Coyne's home, with the interior lit in warm yellow and rosy shades, they took off their jackets, hung them and wandered into the kitchen, which was outfitted with scores of appliances and utensils, a number of which Shaw couldn't begin to identify. Dominating the room was an old, unevenly planed farm table, which had hosted many, many meals, he sensed. Had she ever been married? The mantel pictures were inconclusive.

As she got the beers, he called Fiona Lavelle, in her escapee cave. She was fine, was getting a lot of work and was actually enjoying her time in "Nerworld," which, she explained was a massive network of cities and roads and even lakes and rivers under the surface of the earth in her novel. He decided that his nieces, Rebecca and Mary, would enjoy the story.

When she brought the beers, Shaw asked a question that had been nagging. "Big companies in Fort Pleasant, you said. Plural? I only know about the chipmaker."

Coyne handed him an Anchor Steam. "The other big one is a bottled water operation. The second or third largest in the country. Even more controversial than computer chips."

He lifted an eyebrow.

"They don't use the Never Summer water—under the Law of the River, they have no rights. But what they do is just as bad. They pump up groundwater from the aquifers. It's basically theft, even though there's no law to stop them. They purify it, mark it up a thousand times and say fuck you to the people of the county . . . and farmers like me. I don't use just Never Summer water. I need groundwater too. The aquifers around here aren't going to last forever. My wells? Six hundred and seven hundred feet. The way it's going, I'll be tapping into the lava in the earth's core pretty soon."

She took two large swigs of beer and walked to a large window looking over plowed fields, lit by bright spotlights on the roof of the house. Shaw joined her. The two of them were standing close, their shoulders brushing briefly. "You know, Colter, I can run this spread pretty much by myself. A thousand acres? A lot of work, but I can manage it. I've got the suppliers, the equipment, the chemistry. But it's useless without the one magic ingredient."

"Water."

"Water's to farming what light is to photography. It's not the main thing but the main thing wouldn't exist without it."

"Why did the Coynes settle here, and not San Joaquin Valley or Sacramento?"

"Why does anybody settle anywhere? Maybe my great-great-greats were tired of pushin' west. And back then the Never Summer was a real river. Plenty of water for a copper mine and a two-thousand-acre farm.

"Ah, it's getting worse and worse everywhere. All the rivers in the U.S. are drying up. The Colorado you hear about mostly. But also the Arkansas, Red River, Rio Grande, the South Canadian. Shrinking, shrinking, shrinking . . . Hey, Colter, this reward business of yours doesn't work out you can make a mint as a C-fifty-seven. A licensed driller in California."

She fell silent.

Shaw was aware their biceps now pressed together. Firmly.

He thought of the glance they had shared earlier.

You're funny, Colter . . .

Simultaneously they set their bottles on the table, each noticing and each smiling at the sort-of coincidence.

Then they were in the other's arms, kissing fiercely, hands finding buttons. Hands finding flesh. And zippers.

The rarest of moments, these. When, miraculously, all the elements come together. The time, place, the sensibilities, the desires—that indefinable but certain and perfect alignment like the pins in a tumbler lock and the teeth of the key.

Click . . .

Clothing dropped as they made their way to the bedroom.

Then they were inside the spacious room, which continued the theme of rococo as if some settler from the East Coast had carted with them this warm and gaudy Victoriana as a foil against grim, dusty and muddy pioneer life.

Though this reflection lasted less than one second.

Colter Shaw had in his mind only one thought.

How to get the towering array of satin pillows from the bed as fast as possible without flinging them to the floor.

He needn't have worried.

Annie Coyne swept them off the comforter with one hand and pulled Colter Shaw after her with the other.

THURSDAY, JUNE 21

50.

f you were wondering," she said.

Shaw was just floating out of sleep. The time, he noted, was 6 a.m.

Coyne, it seemed, was as wide awake as she had been before.

She had pulled up the gold chenille comforter, it just covering her breasts.

Shaw tugged it down.

Only an inch.

Made all the difference.

He kissed her once more. She kissed him back but it was of a different species. And he knew the moment last night—which had been about as perfect as moments like that could be—wouldn't repeat itself. Not at this moment.

There was an agenda.

The "wondering" part.

He looked at her quizzically and opted for the comforter too. Nothing to do with modesty. The house was old and drafty.

She pointed to the corner of the room.

There sat two gym bags and a wheely suitcase. A man's suit in a dry-cleaning wrapper was draped over the bags. And two pairs of shoes—running and oxfords, in a man's size.

"I wasn't wondering. I am now."

"Danny and I were together a year. He works in Fort Pleasant. Teaches environmental science. Not a thing in the world wrong with him. Not. A. Hair. So I didn't have a damn reason in the world to sit him down, take both his hands and tell him it wasn't working."

"And his reaction?"

She thought for a moment. "Perplexed first. Then hurt. Then problem-solving. His solutions didn't take."

Obviously. Given where she and Shaw presently were.

"His last stage of grief was gallantly backing away. If I ever need a friend . . . that playbook."

Shaw was thinking of Fiona Lavelle, whose personal life he had also come to learn about. This was not uncommon in his job. There's a certain intimacy in the act of posting a reward: offerors' guards come down and they confess to failings and limitations and mistakes.

And express—sometimes desperately—hopes.

Coyne rolled toward him. Her hand was on his chest and she twirled a bit of his hair. He liked it that each of her nails was a different color. Her toes too? That was one of the few parts of her physique that he had not paid any attention to last night.

She repeated, "Not a flaw about him. But you know my real love?"

"Dirt."

"Acres and acres of dirt." She kissed his shoulder. "With him I was facing a life of faculty dinners, small talk, movie dates, playing charades." She squinted. "You don't strike me as a charade player, Colter."

"Never tried."

"You draw a card and act it out, see if your partner can guess it. I drew one that said 'SpaceX.' Didn't even know what it was." A brief nod. "Then . . . there was the baby thing, but that's a whole 'nother issue."

"And yet . . ."

She noted he was looking at the clothing. "I'd say he's eighty percent out."

Shaw had to smile to himself at her choosing the numerical analysis. That was his forte.

"He said he's coming back to collect them. But it's been a month."

Shaw looked over the pile. "Hm. Second-tier fashion. He doesn't need them. Left them accidentally on purpose. An excuse to come back."

"You think so?"

"Though maybe he's just lazy or forgetful."

She laughed. Another kiss.

"So what's the story with you? A different damsel in every town you visit, Colter?"

"A lot of towns, not so many damsels."

He thought instantly of Margot, though she resided in a past that, if it were a verb tense, would be called permanent perfect. Had he been forced to pick one soul whose path crossed his it would be Victoria Lessner. Their first interaction was a knife fight, and they'd grown close immediately after, though whether the relationship between the steel blade and their romance was causal or merely a coincidence, Shaw could not begin to say. They still saw each other some—though only if their respective jobs—she was a security consultant—happened to be contiguous. Neither had ever boarded an airplane for a visit and Shaw suspected they never would.

Coyne broke the ensuing silence with: "You know you can read the body language of crops?"

He didn't. "So corn has been lying to me all along, and I don't know it."

"They still tell you what they hate and what they like and what they need—growing toward the sun, drooping from thirst or lack of nitrogen. I can read them better than people. Men, at least."

"I'm an open book." He moved to kiss her but stopped suddenly.

"What?"

"Vehicle."

"I don't hear anything."

She probably had, on the periphery, but hadn't paid attention to the subtle stimulus.

Colter Shaw was unable *not* to focus the senses.

"You expecting anyone?"

"No."

Bear?

He rolled out of bed and dressed quickly. She did too. Her eyes grew wide as she saw him checking his gun—dropping the mag to make sure all six rounds remained and tugging the slide to confirm the chambered round.

No reason for the weapon *not* to be in order but you did this anyway. Always.

"Colter," she whispered. "The bomber?"

"Don't know. You have any weapons in the house?"

She nodded to a shadowy spot behind the bedroom door, where he saw a pump shotgun, twelve gauge. Short—an eighteen-inch barrel. The perfect home-defense weapon. Often all you needed to do to scare off a home invader was to work the pump. The metallic *chuck-chuck* was enough of a warning that an unwanted visitor was about to die a particularly unpleasant death to motivate them to flee.

"Should I get it?"

"Not yet."

Staying low, he moved into the living room, and avoiding the lace curtained windows, he picked one with an opaque pull-down shade and peered through the crack between it and the frame.

Nothing.

But he now definitely heard an engine and tires on gravel behind the house.

"Colter!" Coyne pointed to the kitchen. A shadow was moving past the curtain.

He was gesturing for her to join him in the corner of the living room—her office, which had the fewest windows and was the most defensible spot in the room. He did consider having her get the scattergun, but he didn't know her level of skill. Some farmers are good shots—those who raise livestock mostly, and have a need to kill predators—but others, crop farmers, rarely shoot as part of the job.

Just as she joined him, he got a text.

He read the screen.

It was from Debi Starr.

Colter. Don't touch your weapon. I'm serious. Keep it holstered. Whatever happens. Don't touch it.

He knew she wasn't going to answer and so he didn't bother to type the obvious query that came to mind.

"What is it?" Coyne asked, seeing his face.

He shook his head, hearing the crunch of gravel.

She looked toward the shotgun.

"No. Keep your hands out. In plain sight."

"What are you—?"

The front and rear doors burst open simultaneously—Starr coming in through the kitchen, and Tolifson and TC McGuire from the front. Their guns were drawn. Shaw noticed that Tolifson held his awkwardly but that his finger was nowhere near the trigger.

It was a solid tactical assault, and Shaw wondered where they'd learned it. He suspected the choreography might have come from one of Starr's podcasts.

The officer holstered her weapon and drew cuffs in a smooth gesture that told him she rehearsed often.

Then, in a voice laced with true regret, she said, "I'm sorry about this, Annie, but we're placing you under arrest for the murder of Gerard Redding. And we've got some other charges we're going to have to add too. But we can get to them later. Could I ask you to turn around please?"

"No, no, no . . ."

"Annie, they matched the others around town, the ones in the assay reports that Gerard Redding supposedly ordered, making it look like he'd come up with this plot to open a mine."

Shaw was thinking: Nowadays, with deliveries made down to the minute, all the perp would have to do was wait for a text message that the samples were about to be delivered and get to Annie's mailbox just before the truck. But he tucked that thought away and continued to listen.

Tolifson said, "The same time Bear planted the bomb in Redding's workshop, he hid the assay reports in the file cabinet to implicate him—on your orders."

"And what," Coyne spat out, "was the fucking motive—other than we didn't see eye to eye."

Starr said, "The north four hundred, the land your father thought Redding stole."

Annie Coyne stiffened.

"Redding dies, the levee comes down and ruins the mine. His estate inherits property it'll take millions to get in shape again while having to pay taxes on the land. You sue to get the four hundred back and they settle. And you can negotiate more water from the Never Summer, to boot."

"And ruin my farm too?"

"You've got those trenches." Starr nodded toward the front of the property. "Looks to me like you'd have some flooding but most of the water'd go south into the marsh."

Shaw said, "And how does Annie supposedly know Bear?"

"Your military days. You were overseas. Combat deployed."

A look of disgust crossed her face.

"Now, Annie," Tolifson said, "work with us. Where can we find him? Bear? And how can we disarm the other bombs?"

The woman seemed to shiver in anger.

"I'm not saying anything more."

Starr sighed. "That's your right. Now we're back to invoking the Fifth again?"

"Yes."

"We called the magistrate in Olechu. We can get you arraigned later. The county lockup's been evacuated because of the flooding. We've got a van we use for transporting prisoners to county. We'll keep you in there for the time being. It's air-conditioned. We'll get you to a restroom if you need it. And there's water in there too."

"Come on, Debi. Are you thinking this through? You really think I'd believe I could get away with a crazy idea like this?"

"Fact is, Annie," Starr said, "you almost did. Except for two things." She glanced at Shaw. "Colter here. And a half dozen honeybees."

52.

TC McGuire had put out a BOLO, a be-on-the-lookout-for bulletin, describing Bear, including screenshots from the mine security footage.

Sitting across from him in the command post, Debi Starr asked, "Did you say he's wanted in connection to a capital murder case?"

McGuire said he had not but would revise the announcement.

California still had the death penalty for certain homicides—like this, committing murder-for-hire, though the state had not in fact executed anyone in years.

But the designation was an attention-getter.

Starr said to Tamara Olsen, "You ever do demolition?"

"Some."

"Mind looking at some tough pictures?"

"I guess not."

The officer displayed what Shaw could see were images of the deadly workshop she'd taken with the digital camera. With the flash, it was as if she had used a vivid setting; the blood was particularly bright, the scorch particularly black.

"Hm. The head . . ." The sergeant was clearly taken aback. As Shaw had guessed, she had little, if any, combat experience.

Starr asked, "How much C-four would you think could cause that?"

"Half kilo. Maybe little more."

Shaw would have thought the amount would be less, but his knowledge of explosives was largely theoretical. He'd set dynamite charges to blow snowbanks for controlled avalanches. And he'd disarmed a bomb once. It had been fake—used as a diversion—but he hadn't known at the time it wasn't real.

"And how much was used on the top of the levee this morning?"

Olsen now looked over the waterfall. "Two ki's."

Starr said, "Assuming that this was part of the batch stolen from the armory, that leaves more than two kilos for the lower part. Would that be enough to bring it all down?"

It was Dorion who spoke now. "It could. But remember, it doesn't have to blow the whole thing. One big V-shaped notch would still produce the same level of flooding."

Olsen said she agreed. Her phone hummed and she took a call. After a brief conversation, she disconnected. "The first chopper'll be here in about forty minutes, with the bomb curtains. I'm going back to the motel to pick up the rest of the gear we'll need."

Starr asked, "Anything we should do?"

As she walked away, she gave a faint laugh. "Pray for no short circuits in the detonators."

Just after she cruised down the hill in her SUV, a dark gray pickup made its way to the command post and stopped.

"She's here," Dorion whispered to Colter.

It was Mary Dove. The vehicle rocked to a stop. The lean woman, with the same silver braid as yesterday, climbed out. Usually dressed in a long skirt, today she wore jeans and a work shirt under a black leather jacket. Cowboy boots. The F-150 featured a rifle rack in the back window and Shaw noted that her favorite weapon, a Winchester .308—the same as Bear's gun—sat beneath a Ruger cylinder-fed .22 carbine, silver and black.

There was no greeting other than nods among the Shaw family. They had, after all, breakfasted together just yesterday. Shaw made introductions, and Mary Dove took in the names of those present. Shaw knew she would be memorizing them and making minute observations about each one.

She would also be noting in particular her son's own grim expression, its genesis: Annie Coyne's arrest.

Absurd.

And yet Debi Starr presented sufficient probable cause to the difficult magistrate to justify the warrant.

He recalled too the blaze in Coyne's eyes when the subject of Redding and his father, and the old man's "theft" of the farmland years ago at a poker table, was brought up.

He chose not to play the percentage game as to her innocence or guilt.

Mary Dove was regarding the levee. "My. It looks fragile. What's the prognosis?"

The word came to her naturally. She was, after all, a medical doctor.

Dorion said, "We just don't know."

Tolifson offered, "And there could be another IED inside."

Colter said, "We're getting bomb curtains to drape over the top. Army Corps of Engineers. The woman you passed on the way up here. Forty minutes."

"And what's our percentage that'll work?" she asked her son.

Everyone in the family knew his numeric approach to decision making (even his nieces, who recently estimated the odds that he could be talked into buying ice cream on any particular visit at eighty-two percent).

"Have to keep that one blank for the time being. Not enough data."

The woman looked down at the village. "And your remainer is still there? Mrs. Petaluma."

Dorion nodded and pointed to the house and the garden.

Starr grimaced. "And just so you know. She's armed."

"Has she shot anybody?"

"Not in recent memory," the policewoman said

"And you speak the same language?" Starr asked.

"I speak Ohlone and some Miwok. And I would think, her being from around here, she speaks mostly Miwok. But they're related languages. She'll understand me well enough."

Tolifson said, "As long as we can make her appreciate the danger. But I was thinking you could appeal to her heart. Say the town thinks of her as a valuable resident. We'd be devastated if anything happened to her. And—to be frank—if the levee does go, we're going to have our hands full . . ." His voice faded, as often happened, when Mary Dove turned her gaze toward someone.

"With all respect, Mayor. I'm not asking about language for accurate translation. She understood everything you've said to her and everything she heard on the TV. This is something different." She eyed the man closely. "There's an expression *allinik liwwap*. It means 'white people talking.'"

"Not trusting what we're telling her."

"Partly that. Also, you're not getting where she's coming from. Now, I'll see what I can do." Mary Dove walked to the truck.

"No," Dorion and Shaw said simultaneously.

She looked back.

"You'll have to do it by phone."

"I've already tried her," their mother pointed out. "She didn't return the calls."

"You can't go down there," Colter said. "Because of the levee."

Dorion said, "Water like that, you can't outrun."

She debated. Then pulled her mobile out of her back pocket and hit a redial button.

A tilt of her head. "Voicemail." After a moment she said into the unit, "*Kučí hiéma. Hópopi kan* Mary Dove Shaw."

She left a brief message in both Indigenous and English and then her number.

Slipping her phone back, she said, "We'll see."

"Any other remainers?" Mary Dove asked.

McGuire said, "A couple of families we think have some meth or opioids they don't want to lose. Then a couple of crazy survivalists. Those people. Wacky, you know."

The Shaw family regarded each other with varying degrees of smiles on their faces.

Then Colter noted the transport van, in which Annie Coyne was being held, drive up the hill and park about a hundred yards south of the CP.

Colter's phone hummed and he glanced at the text. After reading it, he gazed out of the town for a moment and then asked, "TC?"

"Yessir?" McGuire responded.

"You know computers pretty well, I've been noticing."

"Some. For an old guy like me."

"I've got a job for you." Shaw turned the man's laptop his way.

53.

Waylon Foley watched her SUV—the black Expedition with government plates—squeal to a stop in the River View Motel outside of Fort Pleasant.

It was a weathered, non-chain place, dressed drown in peeling paint, sporting greasy windows and serviced by vending machines whose contents he would never even *think* about consuming.

The motel, however, lived up to its name at least. Every room offered a kick-ass view of the Never Summer River, presently raging past at what he guessed was about forty miles an hour. It would slow soon as it continued south, to Fort Pleasant itself, where it flushed into a floodplain.

He watched the woman park and climb from the SUV, pushing back her thick red-black hair, zero attention paid to the surroundings. Foley glanced at the olive drab uniform and the Army Corps of Engineers patch on the shoulder. The name on the ample breast: T. OLSEN. The uniform and insignia had an effect on him. Foley killed the engine of his pickup and, more careful than her, looked around slowly. He *had* to be cautious. He'd been seen in person and on tape. And though his appearance now was not what his appearance would soon become, enough people were looking for someone of his general description that prudence was vital.

The River View nestled up against a defunct service station on one side and a self-storage operation on the other. One cat, three buzzards, a dead squirrel and zero humans were present. No police patrols cruising by either. The authorities had their job—finding the leg-shooting sniper and mine-owner bomber—but they also had a hundred-foot levee that as far as they knew was about to detonate into a flood. They were, in other words, preoccupied.

The parking lot was gritty and decorated with trash that couldn't melt even in today's torrential rains—like beer bottles—and trash that could: paper and cardboard and food, now piles of mush. A thoroughly unappealing place. The smell of rot and the smell of garlic from a Chinese restaurant fifty feet away and the smell of crap—dog or human. He strode across the asphalt now, moving silently on his rubber-soled boots, following her route from the Expedition to the rooms. She stopped at 188 and fished for the key, undid the lock and stepped in.

He got to the door just as she was swinging it shut.

"Hey, there, Soldier Girl," he whispered.

She gasped. "Jesus."

A moment passed between them, their eyes locked.

Then Alisette Lark—aka Sergeant Tamara Olsen, her fake name in this operation—gave a coy smile as she looked down at the telltale bulge in the front of his slacks.

Her voice was amused as she said, "Don't tell me, Waylon. Not the uniform?"

Foley grinned then nodded toward the bed. "Leave it on. Well, just the top. Not the rest of it. Obviously."

54.

The center of his universe was alive.

John Millwood's heart was thudding—and not from the effort of trooping through the woods like an Eagle Scout in pursuit of a merit badge.

Fiona was alive.

He was about two miles south of Hinowah, and a half mile west of where he'd parked on Route 13 a half hour earlier, when he began pushing through viny and dense woods. He paused and gazed about him in a slow circle.

Green and brown, green and brown . . .

Then he kept trooping along, secure in the knowledge that she was safe.

He would soon find her!

In fact, he didn't mind a brief delay.

It would give him time to refine her punishment. Something appropriate, to assure that she would never, ever pull a stunt like this again.

Millwood had taken the advice of that man Shaw for as long as he could: shower, warm up in the motel room. He'd sat at the cheap desk, reading emails and making some work-related calls. He'd gotten some sleep, but then wakened, agitated. And finally the impatience and antsiness got to be too much.

He *had* to get out of the room and hunt for her himself. And so he had driven back toward Hinowah to the spot where he and Shaw had found her car. Below the highway, down the steep hillside, he could see flashing lights. The workers were probably trying to get the car out of the water.

Damn her. Responsible for losing a fifty-thousand-dollar car? True, Fiona had bought it and she had made the payments, but every penny in a family belonged to the man—the head of the household. That was just the natural order of things.

And so it was in effect *his* car that she'd destroyed.

He was going to ask the emergency workers if they'd seen her but he first ran into a man in a battered pickup, parked on the shoulder of Route 13, two hundred yards from the dissolving levee. Wearing coveralls and a safety vest, he was, it turned out, part of a sandbag-filling group of volunteers that had been told to stand down and keep way back from the levee for some safety reason.

Had he, by any chance, seen a young blond woman in the woods?

The man had turned down the volume of a country-western station and said, "Well, yesterday, yessir. There was a woman. She was wearing a stocking cap, so I don't know what color hair, but yessir."

He'd pointed to a ridge of rocks to the south of that miniature mountain Millwood had learned was named Copper Peak. Where he'd gone for his goddamn swim. (Her frigging fault too, of course!)

And then the bombshell: She had been carrying a couple of heavy gym bags, the worker had told him.

Millwood felt the emotion unleashed within him.

First, elation that she was alive.

Second, undiluted rage. The sneaky little whore had some plan. She'd taken her luggage from the car *before* it went into the water. And that meant she'd planned it all out. She'd driven the car into the river on purpose.

The video was to trick him.

God, the sense of betrayal had been almost overwhelming.

Now, he pushed along the overgrown mining trail, looking for any sign that she'd passed this way.

He paused and took a hit of whisky from his leather and silver flask. Bushmills. His favorite. Fiona hadn't liked Irish whisky at first but then he kept pushing her. (One time she'd said, "Don't be a nag," and he'd given her his "hurt" look—he really perfected it—and she could see he felt bad about it. She'd taken one sip, shivered, then another, as he kept insisting. Finally, she said yes, he was right. She *did* like it.)

If only she'd listen to him the way she should!

More slogging through the leaves and the mud. His poor Ferragamos would never be the same.

Thank you so very much, Fiona. You'll clean them. You'll make them shine like new.

Looking at the ground, doing his own tracking, like Shaw. No prints yet. But he'd find them.

As he trudged, he considered various scenarios about what might have happened.

Most likely this was a trick so she could run off with someone, get to a motel and . . .

He shivered in rage at how that sentence would end.

It occurred to him that Shaw found the car pretty fast. Maybe he was a good tracker but then again maybe the two of them engineered the whole thing.

That's why he'd sent Millwood to a motel—to get him out of the way so the two of them could shack up in a room of their own.

He was a good-looking guy, and younger than Millwood.

A thought that made him want to scream.

Then, though, the holes in that conspiracy began to emerge. For one thing, Shaw had seemed genuinely concerned about her.

And how could they have met previously?

It would have to be somebody else.

But who?

Months ago he'd gone to the dark web and found a hacker, whom he gave five hundred dollars by way of a gift card number for instructions on constructing a keylogger—malware to record her passcodes.

The instructions were:

USE VISUAL BASIC OR BORLAND DELPHI TO WRITE A CYCLICAL
INFORMATION REQUEST, OR A SYSTEM HOOK, YOU GOTTA USE C
LANGUAGE, I LIKE FILTER DRIVERS INSIDE THE KEYBOARD STACK . . .
U WANT OTHER BOXES WHICH IS ALWAYS GOOD GO WITH DLL . . .

At which point, Millwood had thought: Screw this. And simply hid a tiny spy camera in the vent over her desk, videoing her typing in her passwords.

A lot easier.

Last night, at the motel, the emails he read were not about his work; they were hers. And there was nothing suspicious about them— though they could have contained a code. The word *recipe* might mean "motel room." The word *groceries* might mean "condoms."

But even if not, she still had to be punished for putting him through all this.

And he suddenly had a thought.

What if the punishment had a second purpose? Something that brought them closer, tied them together forever?

Ah, yes . . . He liked that.

It centered, of course, on dependency.

The end result of the punishment was that she would have to depend on him completely.

Say, she lost her hearing.

Or went blind.

He liked the last one best. If she was deaf, she couldn't hear his orders or his corrections.

How could one become blinded?

Acid in her eyes? No that pain was too much. But more important, he couldn't disfigure her. It was her angelic appearance that made him obsessed.

Maybe there were blinding poisons. Or, wait . . . There'd been something on the news about a man who went blind because a baseball had hit him in the back of the head. The occipital portion of the brain. He would do some research into it. Yes, he liked that idea.

He could control a blind woman completely.

Then John Millwood froze.

There, in a patch of muddy earth were her prints. They were her shoe size—6½, which he knew because he'd bought her a dozen pairs of sexy high heels (which she rarely wore, bitch).

He followed them for a short distance but then they disappeared. As if she'd tried to obscure them.

Or someone had.

A lover . . .

Fury surged through him, then it dissipated.

He needed to focus.

And studying the ground carefully, he started forward once more after the love of his life.

55.

Waylon Foley was the first to admit he led a good life.

When he wasn't running jobs like the one he was currently in the midst of, or hunting in Montana or Utah or, well, name your state, he spent much of his time in Key West, not far from Ernest Hemingway's home, ever populated with tourists and six-toed cats.

He had a small villa looking in the direction of Cuba, which he'd been to—undercover—several times on assignments. Lots of palm trees, lots of rocks decorated his full acre—good sized for the neighborhood. Security was good. Electronics, of course, and a minder he hired from Miami. Rodrigo was a man of loyalty that went beyond compensation for the significant money Foley paid him. He would do little things like stop when on an errand and bring Foley a Cuban coffee and a guava pastry. All on his own.

The little things mattered in his life.

His Savage rifle.

Guava.

The blouses of military uniforms worn by former porn stars doing a damn fine job in a new role.

Beside him, Alisette Lark stirred.

Their liaison had been a mere twenty minutes but that was enough for him.

He had seen her in the uniform. He had thought of her thin, taut legs and round chest, and he had wanted her. Immediately.

But the instant it was over, like when he was married (well, often before it was over) he found himself thinking of the fields, the smell of gunpowder.

The blood.

His rifle.

Lark stretched. He smelled her. All the smells. Had she been satisfied?

It had seemed so. And Lark was not a woman to fake anything—unless it was a role she was playing, in a porn flick or for one of his jobs.

She lit a cigarette, despite the motel's prohibition—a two-hundred-dollar fine—and she said, "I did what you asked. About coming on to her."

"The disaster response girl."

"Her, yeah. Dorion. But I didn't ask her. I asked her brother *about* her. Colter. If she was seeing somebody. You were right—from the beginning. He's the one we have to worry about."

Which turned his attention to his aching shoulder and nose.

Prick . . .

Her coming on to the woman, through her brother, was yet another element of the plan, a way to misdirect them. To humanize the woman they thought was Sergeant Tam and to put any suspicions to bed—so to speak.

"I would've done it."

He knew. She did everything he asked. She was making a lot of money. And, besides, he knew she was a switch-hitter. You had to be in the adult film industry.

At the thought of the Shaws—Colter in particular—he felt a sting of anger.

Would there be time to get even?

Maybe. More people would die today. If Shaw was one of them, fine, but Foley was too professional to deviate from one of his plans simply for revenge.

He took the cigarette from her long fingers and drew hard, then handed it back. "Update?"

"The cute little officer thinks that the farmer's guilty. Her boss, the one playing police chief—"

"The mayor, right?"

"Yeah, Tolifson. He's a bozo, but it'll look good for him to get a collar—I think he wants to be chief when this is over with—so he's drinking the Kool-Aid that Annie's guilty. Shaw? No, he doesn't believe it. He's fucking smart. He might as well be a gold shield. He thinks she's being set up."

"Hm."

When he took on the job, Foley had bolted together a plot that he was pretty sure would work, with a lot of moving parts. But damn elegant, he'd thought. They'd use two explosive charges—first to take the top off the levee and scare the asshole inhabitants out of town. Then Alisette and the fake corporals—from a criminal crew in Oakland—would show up to monitor everything. If it was going according to plan, the second charge would destroy the levee completely, and unleash the flood.

But there had to be a contingent plan—in case the responders learned the levee collapse was not natural.

Which they had.

Thanks to gold-shield Motorcycle Man . . .

And, apparently, a bunch of fucking honeybees.

The contingent plan was that the mine owner, Gerard Redding, had orchestrated the sabotage to destroy the town to mine lithium. But then the authorities would discover that *that* was bogus, and Annie Coyne was the real guilty party. She had wanted to ruin Redding and his mine because of some feud between them and because she wanted his allocation of water.

He watched Alisette Lark stub out the cigarette on the top of a soda can and drop the butt in. She stretched and walked into the bathroom. She was completely nude but it was an unselfconscious walk, not surprising for someone who had had sex with probably a thousand men and women over the past decade.

They had met under odd circumstances. She herself had been running a scam to defraud a Boston businessman—some neat plot, involving crypto—when Foley had been on-site coincidentally to shoot the man in the head for some other infraction. He'd waited to kill him until she got her money. Professional courtesy. They started talking and he noted her intelligence and grit and blasé attitude about blood, and unquenchable lust for cash.

He hired her two, three times a year for front work. Sexy and smart. She did her homework. In her gym bag now were a half dozen books she'd devoured for the job, including *Flood Plain Management* by the University of Minnesota, the *U.S. Army Manual of Dams and Waterways* and the data sheet on Hydroseal by the manufacturer. The last she'd discovered on her own. That the goo was used on hard surfaces, not dirt like the levee, was a question that woman Dorion Shaw had raised. But, damn, Lark had finessed it, without raising any suspicions.

Now, in this unfortunate motel room, Foley too rose and, not bothering with the shower, dressed fast, reflecting that only two aspects of the job remained.

Destroying the levee with the remaining set of charges.

And the other, his immediate goal: to kill the farmer girl.

She would protest to the police firmly that she wasn't guilty and she'd probably do a credible job. People might start to believe her, and do some serious investigating.

But if she was killed by the "mercenary" she'd hired, so she couldn't dime him out?

Well, case closed.

56.

She had been smart.

But not smart enough.

John Millwood was looking at the soupy ground in front of the huge formation of rocks to the south of Copper Peak, about four or five football fields' length from where the worker had spotted Fiona.

No footsteps, but curious marks in the mud, as if someone had taken a crude broom—made of branches and leaves—and obscured them. Did she do it?

Or her goddamn lover?

Millwood continued in the same direction.

He was enjoying the Blind Fiona scenario.

Probably unlikely. What if he killed her or damaged her brain, and he had to take care of her in that injured state?

Well, it was a fun fantasy.

Ah, there!

Definitely footsteps!

Then they stopped, where a rocky trail led upward into the hills. It was mostly stone but there were some muddy patches, which too had been brushed to obscure the prints left in them.

But not completely.

And the tracks did not return down.

She was up there still.

Gazing into the hills, he got the impression this was an old mine.

She might have found it online. Or maybe her lover had told her about it.

He started to climb.

Panting against the effort—another reason to punish her—he made his way higher yet. At about fifty feet above the ground, the path leveled out. Yes, it *was* the opening to a mine. Someone had made a half-hearted attempt to board the place up. But the sheets of plywood had been pulled down—long ago. They were covered with mud and rock. Two large warning signs had been graffitied to near obscurity.

He walked to the entrance and froze, looking down.

Two used condoms.

His skin seemed to boil with jealousy at the sight.

Were they her lover's?

Slow down, he told himself. The condoms were covered with mud and sat near a variety of cigarette butts. This would be a place for local teens to sneak off to.

Keep your head about you.

Quietly, he started inside.

Yes! She was here! He could smell her perfume. He knew because it was the same as his mother wore. He'd given her a bottle for her birthday. It had taken a few passive-aggressive reminders for her to wear it but finally she'd given in.

The name of the scent was Passion.

Another ten feet, twenty.

Then he eased silently into the large space. Yes, it was what he'd thought: the entrance to an old mine, the shaft, in the back, covered with chain-link.

There she was!

And what the hell was this? It looked like she was on a goddamn camping trip!

At the far end, she sat bundled up and writing in one of those stupid notebooks of hers. A small LED reading light plugged into a battery illuminated the area.

Instantly, the rage vanished. His heart swelled with unrestrained love. She was so beautiful!

"Want some company?"

A scream burst from her lips. "John! No!" Scattering cans and bottles of water and the notebook, she leapt to her feet. She charged for the cave entrance, trying to dodge around him.

But he was faster.

He stepped in front and, with a hard shove to her chest, pushed her back to her little nest. She fell but didn't hit her head.

Her oc-cip-i-tal.

Maybe the vision idea was not such a bad one after all.

Meet my wife, Fiona. She's blind. But what a trouper . . .

"John, for God's sake. Leave me alone!" She started to cry.

She was upset? Look at everything she'd put him through over the past two days!

"Look, I'm begging you! Just leave me alone . . ."

"Why are you wearing that stupid hat? You know I don't like it."

"Please! I don't love you."

Millwood clicked his tongue. "Oh, you'll get there, honey. You just have to try a little harder . . ."

57.

John Millwood felt so relieved that he'd found her—and found her alone, not in flagrante—that he forgave her.

Typical of how generous he was toward her.

Running from him, destroying his car, his shoes, his Armani jacket . . .

It was a sign of his wondrous kindness, forgiving her.

"Isn't it funny—I don't mean ha-ha funny—I mean confluential. That's a word I made up. 'Confluence' like things coming together and 'coincidental.'"

She was staring with an odd expression. Dismay, he believed.

He forgave her for that too. He found his lust expanding and he remembered the first time they'd made love. It was so beautiful . . . After, he'd just sat and stared at her, while she slept. Every inch of her body, from the pores of her hair to the freckles on her thighs. He didn't get a minute's sleep that night.

He was tempted to re-create that now—on the blankets she'd brought in her effort to escape from him. There would be some justice in that.

But no.

There was a time and a place for everything.

nfluential . . . I don't want to say we're soulmates. That's a
hat cheapens the concept of what we have. We transcend that."

Fiona's voice choked. "Please, just leave!"

As if he hadn't heard a word. "You went a little crazy in the
d. That's all. Let's get all this stuff packed up. We'll take the spa
the table, why don't we?"

He'd work on her weight himself back in Reno.

And for now, he'd reward her: "We can stop at Denny's on the
way."

"John. Listen to you! I just want to be left alone."

"Ah, you don't really mean that. You're just upset. Writer's block,
maybe."

Her shoulders slumped, but her eyes blazed. "You're troubled!
There's something wrong with you."

Ooo. That wasn't good. He bristled.

She continued, "Don't you think that if I went to all this trouble,
hiding from you? That's a message!"

"A message," he mocked. "Message . . . I think it's a message
that maybe you're the one who isn't quite right."

"I've had it. No more."

"There are ten million women in this world who'd give their
eyeteeth to be loved the way I love you." He moved closer. "You
must be cold. Denny's. Hot cocoa." She'd ordered it once at another
chain restaurant, where they had a Saturday lunch. She had seemed
unhappy—among the first indications that she was confused about
her love for him. She hardly said a word for the entire hour he'd
made her sit at the booth. But he remembered she liked the cocoa.

He took a look over her things. There was a lot to carry. But he
didn't want to leave anything behind.

"You're not going to hurt me again, are you? You're always hurting me."

He felt indignant. "That only happens for a reason. I don't do it
because I enjoy hurting you. But there are times . . ."

Times she disobeyed, times she looked at other men, t
didn't reply "I love you too" fast enough.

"John, you're a good-looking man. You have a fine job. F
somebody else."

"I don't want anybody else. We've been through this a million
times. It's you I love."

"You don't love me. I know you've been sleeping with Sophie in
your accounting department."

He laughed triumphantly. "See, you *are* jealous! You *do* love me.
And Soph? That's nothing. Physical gratification. It's just what I saw
you doing by yourself in the shower."

She gasped.

He'd drilled a hole into the bathroom wall.

"All right, pack up. Let's get out of here. We'll hit that Denny's.
Cocoa and burgers. There's one with a motel nearby I passed on the
way here. We'll have some food. You could use a shower."

Then disaster struck.

"Fiona!" a man called from the tunnel entrance. "It's me, Colter."

A flashlight beam swept the floor.

Millwood turned to Fiona, making a fist with his right hand and
touching a finger to his lips with his left.

She looked horrified but nodded.

Shaw continued, "John's SUV's parked on the highway. He's
somewhere near—"

As he stepped into the space, Millwood turned the flashlight of
his phone on and shone it into Shaw's face. The man blinked and
froze. He quickly switched the flashlight to his left hand. And started
to draw a gun.

But Millwood lunged forward and slammed into Shaw, who
stumbled to the ground, dropping the pistol. Millwood grabbed it.

He didn't know much about weapons. There didn't seem to be a
safety latch. Apparently, all you did was point and shoot. Shaw's
reaction bore this out. "Wait, Millwood. Careful . . ." He climbed

to his feet and, palms forward, walked to Fiona, asking, "You all right?"

She whispered that she was.

The nightmare had become real. He raged, "I knew it! Knew it all along! You've been fucking her. You were part of the whole thing! Did you help her crash the car? Help her put together this little love nest?"

"Millwood, put the weapon down. You don't want to get into more trouble."

"John, please—"

"Don't be a fool." Shaw hesitated. "Everybody knows she's here."

A lie. Millwood could tell—he could read people like books. One of his special talents. And the truth was *no one* knew she was here. Of course Shaw wouldn't say anything. He wanted her all to himself.

"Quiet!" he raged. And shoved the gun her way.

"Millwood! It's got a hair trigger!"

"Shut up," he muttered. But he did take his finger off the trigger—and was relieved to know that if he *did* shoot, there'd be nothing complicated about it.

Millwood was looking at the mine. The chain-link covering the shaft, in the dim back, was not complete. There was room to push a body through and down into the shaft. In the shadows he believed he saw an ancient pulley, which meant that the shaft was a vertical drop. He could simply shoot Shaw and shove the body into the darkness. Then—

No, wait . . .

That wouldn't work. The sandbag man in the pickup truck had seen Fiona, and Millwood had asked about her. If Shaw went missing around here, Millwood could be linked to the death.

Then an idea: Shaw attacked *him*, and he fought back, getting the gun away. But Shaw grabbed a rock and kept coming. He was forced to shoot him.

Self-defense.

Fiona wouldn't dare contradict him. If she did, he would explain, the first stop he'd make after getting out on bail would be to her mother or sister-in-law.

"Whatever you're thinking, Millwood, it's wrong."

"Wrong? Fiona's in the mine. You're in the mine. You knew she was here. The facts speak for themselves."

"I was helping her get away from you. She's afraid of you. You've hurt her."

That again.

"Only when she deserved it. People are fine when parents spank their children. Why shouldn't a man be able to do the same with his woman? It's only logical."

"You cut yourself—fake defensive wounds. And lied to the police about it."

Millwood shot a cold smile to Fiona. "Oh, sharing our secrets now, are you? That's not very nice."

Fiona whispered, "John, what are you going to do?"

A stunningly beautiful woman . . . but slow sometimes.

Millwood lifted the gun to Shaw's chest and pulled the trigger.

In the dimness of the cave the flash from the muzzle was nearly blinding.

58.

For a moment no one moved.

Then Colter Shaw stepped forward. A nod at the gun. "I'll take it."

The man's eyes went wide.

He pulled the trigger again.

Now, nothing. Not even a click.

Before he'd ascended into the mine entrance, knowing Millwood was here, Shaw had pried the Hornady Defender slugs out of the shells—liked he'd done on the bee project—but left the primer caps in, so that if Millwood knew guns and pulled the slide back to look at the chamber, he'd see brass and believe it was loaded with live rounds.

Shaw shook his head. "That was not wise." He pulled the gun from Millwood's hand, hoping he'd make a move.

It was unprofessional. But Shaw wanted badly to take him down, plant the man firmly on his back, knock the breath out of him. Have pain radiate the way pain did in a moment like that. Efficient and unstoppable.

But sadly, John Millwood was in gaping mode. Frozen.

Shaw swapped the fake mag for a real one, and worked the slide, ejecting the brass in the chamber and loading a live round. The gun went back into his holster.

"Now, turn around."

"You can't do this! You're not a cop."

Shaw removed zip ties from his right rear pocket.

"Bullshit. That's illegal."

Not true. Citizen arrests were authorized under California Penal Code Section 837, if someone saw a felony committed in their presence.

"Turn around."

Millwood gave a cold smile and his hands curled into fists. He stepped forward.

Ah, thank you, Colter Shaw thought.

It didn't turn out to be as much fun as he would have liked.

Millwood was probably a very good domestic abuser but when it came to somebody who fought back, well, he didn't do so great.

After his first swing, Shaw simply ducked, stepped in and performed a variation of the takedown he'd been thinking of just a moment earlier: left forearm against Millwood's chest, right sweeping into the back of his knee. Then a swift push and lift.

Down he went.

The fun was over all too fast, but there *was* a delightfully hard landing.

Wheezing and gasping, the man clawed at his chest.

Fiona Lavelle looked on with some pleasure.

Shaw rolled the debilitated man over and zip-tied him.

"Too tight?"

"Ah, ah . . ."

But that wasn't in response to the ties. Shaw assessed they were fine.

He walked to a pile of rocks near where Fiona had set up her little home. He lifted his burner phone from where he'd set it earlier, before Millwood's arrival. The unit was in live-stream selfie mode so he was looking at himself. In the lower right-hand corner was a miniature TC McGuire.

"How'd it work out?" Shaw asked.

"Hollywood," the man offered. "As they say, it's in the can."

The text Shaw had received forty minutes earlier, as he'd stood in the command post, was from the desk clerk at the motel where Millwood was staying. Shaw had given him a hundred dollars to text if the man left his room and drove off.

Then Shaw had slipped two hundred to one of the town sandbag volunteers to hang out in his pickup truck on Route 13. If someone matching Millwood's description in a white Lexus SUV had showed up near the scene of the Camaro accident, inquiring about a young woman, he was to direct him toward the cliffs.

Shaw said to Lavelle, "They got it all. Hi-def."

Millwood muttered, "You are in so much trouble . . ." His voice faded as he struggled to take in air.

"You're insane." Lavelle's voice was a cold whisper.

His mood flipped instantly. "Oh, honey, I'm so sorry . . . Really. I am. I was only doing it for you! Maybe I pushed a little too hard. Please forgive me!" It was eerie how quickly he jumped from one state to the other.

"Shhh," Shaw said. He turned to Lavelle. "Bring the important things with you. We can come back for the rest."

She gathered up notebooks and her electronics, placing everything in a big yellow backpack.

They walked outside, Shaw leading Millwood by the arm.

"I'm going to sue you." Millwood was gasping, wincing at the pain too. The limp was impressive. And gratifying.

Shaw said, "Save your breath. I mean that literally. You'll feel better if you don't talk."

They walked—and shuffled—down the mining trail. At the

bottom, Debi Starr was standing beside her Public Safety Office pickup. Squinting, she examined Millwood's zip ties. They passed muster and she led him to the backseat and helped him in.

"I was watching the stream," she said. "We've got battery, menacing, brandishing. And attempted murder. That's the ace in the hole."

In California firing a weapon at someone, even a toy, is attempted homicide if you believe it's real and loaded.

Starr turned to Fiona. "You all right, miss?"

"I'm fine."

The deputy said, "You know every domestic I've answered, it's always: he said/she said and we've gotta figure out which wound came first, the iron burn or the serving fork. Now, we've got evidence that's pure gold. And may I add, Ms. Lavelle, you are a fine actor."

"Thank you. I told Mr. Shaw the situation and he said me hiding out from him wouldn't do it. People like him, sociopaths, you have to put them away."

Through the partly opened rear window of Starr's cruiser came the words: "This is entrapment, you assholes!"

Without even turning her head, Starr called, "No, it's not. All right I'll read him Miranda, and hand him off to the sheriff's office. The stinker can cool his heels there until county intake opens up again. I'll need statements from you both but they can wait. We've still got a levee that's debating whether or not to come down."

59.

t's Colter. I'm here with Dorion."

The siblings stood outside the lockup transport van. There were no windows, but in the back was a plate with louvers, for ventilation. The boxy vehicle was parked down the hill from the command post. Whoever had situated it here had courteously parked it under a thick oak, so the machine-gun rattle of rain would not drive the occupant crazy.

"This is goddamn insane," Annie Coyne muttered.

Shaw said, "I've called a lawyer I used to work for in San Francisco. He'll get somebody to Fort Pleasant as soon as he can."

Dorion added, "I know him. He's one of the best criminal attorneys in the state."

"I didn't do any of this. I was set up."

"We know. What we don't know is why and who did it. We need your help."

From Dorion: "Day before yesterday, when Bear got into your Wrangler to pretend to get the payoff money, did you see a vehicle behind you?"

There was silence while she thought. "No. But who thinks they're being followed?"

Colter said, "This whole thing's been carefully planned. And fast. And it would have to have started as soon as reports about the record snowmelt came in and it was predicted the Never Summer would flood. Make that, what? Three days. They'd need time to fake the lithium documents and find samples to plant in your barn."

Dorion asked, "Did you see anybody parked near the farm?"

Shaw added, "A pickup. Like the tire treads we found on your property near Redding's."

"Maybe. But it's planting time for some crops, and then trenching in case the levee came down. That's all I was focused on. He could have strolled right past me and had a cup of coffee in my kitchen and I wouldn't have noticed."

Disappointing they didn't have the truck's tag; Shaw really wanted a car registration. They were better than fingerprints because prints weren't always in the system. Cars were ninety-nine percent of the time.

"Can I use your phone? Is that all right?"

Shaw didn't care whether it was all right or not. He slid his through the small gap.

She placed a call and Shaw heard her speak in Spanish. "Manuel, it's me. I need help. Can you ask everyone on the crew if they saw a pickup truck parked near the property in the past few days? A truck you didn't recognize. It's important. Call this number. Thank you."

She slid the phone back.

Shaw asked, "You want to call Bedroom-Clothes Guy?"

"No." A pause, then, "Look, Colter, last night—"

"Annie, don't think I formally introduced you to Dorion. She's my sister."

Coyne fell silent, though Shaw believed she might have chuckled, even under these circumstances.

He was also aware that Dorion was regarding him with a look that could be described only as wry. She'd been after him for years to settle down. She knew perfectly well that he was the Restless One in the family, though she also would be thinking: People change.

He asked, "You have the money for bail?"

"No. And the property's mortgaged to the hilt."

"I can loan it to you."

"Colter, no."

"I know you're good for it. What're you going to do, take your dirt and skip town?"

Waylon Foley drove through the deserted village of Hinowah.

No, not quite empty. A few people remained. He noted several faces peering at him as he made his way to the woods on the north slope of the valley. Reluctant to leave their homes, suspicious of the government telling them what to do, he guessed. They tended to live in houses that needed painting and repair, lawn art in the form of broken auto parts.

And there were still some stragglers evacuating, taking their precious possessions with them. *Their* faces were dark with concern. A couple of these looked his way warily. Were they wondering: Is he crazy, not getting the hell out of town? Isn't he worried about the flood?

And of course the answer to that was: There won't be a flood until I decide to blow the second set of charges.

He drove partway up the hill at the top of which was the command post, but turned off before he got near it. He edged into the woods, parked and climbed out. He was behind a tall cluster of gray rocks, out of sight of the CP and anyone nearby.

Crouching, he scanned the area and spotted his target: a white transport van. At the moment, two people were outside, at the back. Colter Shaw and his sister.

He had a brief fantasy of Alisette Lark and Dorion together.

Military uniforms were involved.

Then, back to business.

A few minutes later Colter and Dorion left the van, and started walking uphill toward the command post, talking between themselves.

Which left the van, with farmer girl inside, unguarded.

He assessed. The battered white vehicle was big enough for about eight or nine people. No windows. Just vent louvers at the back, pointed downward. He couldn't see in.

Was somebody else inside with her?

He just wondered this in passing; collateral damage, again, was not Foley's problem.

Okay, get to it.

He needed to move on her now, fast, and get back into hiding on the south hillside above town, where Lark and the Oakland gangbangers waited.

Given who he was—a gun man, through and through—Foley was disappointed that he couldn't shoot Annie Coyne.

No windows.

Besides, the vehicle was surely bulletproof.

But, he reflected as he returned to his truck for the three-gallon container of gasoline, it definitely wasn't fireproof.

60.

Colter Shaw and Dorion walked up to the command post and sat across from Fiona Lavelle and Mayor Tolifson.

Lavelle was on the phone with her sister-in-law, who was driving over from Nevada to pick her up and collect the rest of her possessions from her hideaway cave. She was relaxed and there was a light in her eyes, and Shaw couldn't help but think of one word: *survival*. It comes in all forms. There was surviving by avoiding avalanches and standing tall and aggressive to scare off mountain lions, and there was surviving by tipping a sports car into a flooded gulley and making a hidey-hole in an old mine shaft to escape abuse.

The woman disconnected. And looked his way. "You know, Mr. Shaw . . ."

He tilted his head with a smile.

"*Colter* . . . I've never heard of this reward-business thing. But I have an idea. You should open a subsidiary: helping people *hide*. You might make more money doing that."

Dorion gave a smile too.

In fact, it was not a bad idea.

Looking over the levee, the woman added, "It looks a lot thinner than when I drove over it this morning."

Dorion replied, "It is. The water's eating away at both sides. Like planing a board."

"Has it crested yet?" Lavelle asked.

"No. There's continued high temperatures predicted up north," Dorion said with a grimace. "More snowmelt. If somebody doesn't believe in climate change, have them come to Hinowah and start stacking sandbags."

The woman was looking through her notebook. Shaw noted that unlike his naturally small and precise handwriting, hers was loopy and bold and, well, sloppy. But, it got the job done. She'd filled scores of notebooks, first page to last.

"What's your book about?"

"Fantasy. My hero's a woman spell-caster in this mythical world. She's been kidnapped by an evil king. Thamann Hotaks . . . 'The man who takes.' Get it? Based on guess who?" She shook her head. "It's a simple story. And it's like hundreds of other novels in the genre. But why write something different? There's a reason they sell. People want stories where good wins out over evil. That never gets old."

And Colter Shaw—a fan of Tolkien—could hardly disagree.

He noted the corporals were pacing back and forth at the opposite end of the levee. The second SUV pulled up and Tamara Olsen got out. They were looking at the river and having a discussion. He guessed the helicopter with the bomb curtains was nearby.

Debi Starr pulled up in her cruiser. She parked and joined them. "Eduardo? Have you talked to him?"

Dorion said, "He's doing all right. His wife's flying in. They're going to get him up walking today."

Tolifson asked, "That soon after getting shot? Maybe they want to make sure they have hospital beds if . . ." A nod toward the levee.

Shaw might have told him that a full jacketed round—not hollow point—piercing only muscle tissue was not a very big deal, if it missed the important highways of blood vessels.

He glanced around, and realized his mother was not present. "Did Mary Dove step away?"

"Last I heard she finally got a call back from Mrs. Petaluma. She'd talked her into packing a bag and leaving. I was on a call to Sacramento and when I hung up I noticed she was gone."

Shaw glanced toward Mrs. Petaluma's house down in the valley. "Look."

"No!" Dorion whispered.

Their mother's gray pickup truck was speeding through downtown toward Mrs. Petaluma's home.

Shaw grabbed his phone and hit speed dial.

He saw Mary Dove's head turn sideways momentarily but she ignored the call as she skidded to a stop, climbed out and strode to the woman's doorway. Even in a hurry, she maintained her upright posture and elegance.

Brother and sister regarded each other, both understanding that there was nothing to be done. Mary Dove was aware of the risk. She too had learned the art of survival from her husband and analyzed dangers in the same way Ashton had. She had probably calculated the odds were low that the levee would collapse in the twenty minutes it would take her to collect the woman and get her to safety.

The flaw, however, was that calculations were only as good as the objective facts you fed into the computer. And no one, not even an experienced engineer like Dorion, had those facts and figures at hand.

The levee's fate was closer to the spells and magic of Fiona Lavelle's hero.

Dorion offered, "Well, she's not going to stop and have tea. They'll get away as fast as they can."

"Come on," Shaw whispered to her. "Come on."

Fiona Lavelle distracted Shaw from those thoughts with a scoff. "Glad *he's* not there."

Shaw glanced her way to see the young woman looking at Olsen and the corporals, standing beside one of the SUVs across the valley.

"Who's that?" Shaw asked.

"This gross dude. When I made it off the levee yesterday morning and stopped? The driver in one of those SUVs didn't even ask if I was okay. He looked me over and was sort of licking his lips. Reminded me of John."

Shaw nodded sympathetically. But only for an instant. The understanding hit Shaw like a blow. He cut his gaze to Lavelle. "That SUV was there *while* the levee was coming down?"

"Yeah. Another one too, a black one just like it. They were parked on the shoulder. That's why I wasn't worried about calling nine-one-one. I knew they would report it, so I could escape down the trail."

Colter asked Tolifson and Starr abruptly, "The army engineers? Did you call *them*?"

The two regarded each other. "No," Tolifson said. "Marissa Fell? In the office? She said they'd called and said they were on their way."

Starr understood. "Damn. They're fake! We let a fox into the henhouse."

Tolifson blinked. "What's all this?"

Starr said, "They were here *before* the bomb. Which means they're the ones who set it. Who the heck are they?"

Colter asked, "Describe the guy you just mentioned."

"I just saw his head and shoulders. Big, round face, red hair and beard."

Colter leaned into the computer, typing fast, to load the screen grabs of Bear. He swung the screen toward her.

She squinted. "Yeah, that's him."

"Stolen SUVs and fake government plates. Which they could have made in ten minutes."

You could buy surplus uniforms for a song online. Corps of Engineer patches too.

Olsen—or whoever she really might be—was working with Bear.

Colter said, "There's no bomb curtain coming. In fact, they're getting ready to blow the rest of the levee. And it's going to happen any minute."

"You're sure?" Tolifson asked.

Dorion answered, "She told us the curtains would be here in forty minutes or so. We'll start to ask questions when they don't show up, so they have to blow it before that happens."

Debi Starr blurted, "We need backup!" She grabbed her mobile.

Colter was studying the trio across the valley, trying to see side-arms. The phony corporals wore Colt 1911 .45s. Powerful and ac-curate, and because they were so heavy, they offered little recoil, which meant that you could fire fast with good aim.

He could assume that Olsen had a concealed weapon of some kind.

"Now!" The voice was Debi Starr's, speaking into the phone. "I want Prescott Moore on the line now. We've got lives at risk in Hinowah . . . Well, let me tell you, miss, I am sick and tired of hearing excuses about Fort Pleasant. Get his butt on the phone this minute."

"Debi!" Tolifson whispered.

She ignored him. "Well, I wouldn't need that tone if you'd unclog your ears and listen to me. Moore. Now." She sighed. "Then con-nect me to Sheriff Barrett." A brief pause. "Sheriff. It's Debi Starr, Hinowah Public Safety. We've got three people in our sights, armed, and they planted the bombs here in Hinowah. They killed one per-son and shot up another. We need a full county and highway patrol response *immediately* . . . SWAT and bomb squad. I mean *now*. And no more 'poor Fort Pleasant' crapola."

"Geeze, Debi," Tolifson muttered.

Colter called, "Tell him we have an active shooter. That always gets attention."

"Active shooter?" Tolifson asked. "But there isn't one."

Colter Shaw said, "There will be. In about sixty seconds."

61.

A nother thought landed hard in Colter Shaw's mind.

If Annie Coyne *was* the fall person, which he knew was true, she had to be eliminated.

It was the only way the plot would work. Alive, she would deliver credible alibis, counter evidence and witnesses to prove she *wasn't* behind the levee explosion or the planting of lithium samples.

But if she were to die, the authorities would be inclined to follow the path of least resistance in the investigation: assign the guilt to her and close the case.

He drew his weapon.

"Colter," Starr began, "what . . ."

"Bring the keys to the van."

"Heck. Of course!" Nodding, she clearly understood.

She started after him, fishing in her pocket, as the items on her service belt bounced sideways and up and down. The woman was getting quite a spoonful of law enforcement today, the sort that had surely never been seen in a small town before.

More activity in a single day than any true crime podcast could offer up in a month.

He sprinted through brush down the hill toward the van. Just as he broke from the bushes he saw Bear, holding a gas can in both hands. Their eyes met and Colter aimed in his direction. Bear was strong but a three-gallon container weighs about twenty-five pounds. He was straining to hold it. The cap was off.

"Down. Careful." Colter didn't want it to tip over and spill. The engine of the van was running and the hot tailpipe might set off a blaze.

The man nodded. And began to crouch and do as told. "Okay, Mr. Shovel. We're all good here."

Starr ran up and targeted him too. The big gun was held steady in her hand.

"Have to ask: You know how to use that thing?" Colter whispered.

"I plink pennies with my twenty-two on the range. Make souvenirs for the twins and their friends. Twenty-five and fifty feet."

Hitting coins at that distance? Hell, she could outshoot him.

"Lie face down on the ground!" she called.

Bear was crouching, the can now resting on the grass. His hand rested atop it, and he wasn't doing as she instructed.

Starr said, "I'm considering that a deadly weapon and you should understand that that authorizes me to use force to stop you."

Nothing.

"Sir, that translates into I am about to shoot you in the face."

"All right!" He released his grip on the can.

A breeze blew it over.

No!

He'd been faking the weight. The gas was already under the van. And in his left hand was a cigarette lighter.

Without a word, Starr fired but just as she did, Bear dropped fully to the ground and touched the lighter to the pool of gas.

It erupted in a huge tower of orange and blue flames and a cloud of smoke. The man probably lost hairs on his forearm and maybe some skin but the tactic worked. He had put up an effective smoke screen. They heard two shots from the other side as the man fired, but he had no better target of them than they did of him. Glancing back to the command post, Colter saw that Tolifson, Dorion and Lavelle were crouching but none had been hit.

He and Starr didn't return fire.

Never fire a weapon without a clear view of your target and what's behind it.

The two ran forward to the van, and he skirted the flames to the left, Starr to the right, both staying low. But the man was gone.

Starr could get nowhere near the rear door, the only one accessing the prisoner compartment. Colter glanced into the driver's seat; there was a small grille-covered window between the driver's and the prisoner's areas. It was, however, only eight inches high.

Annie Coyne's screams cut through the air—piercing even from inside the enclosed space.

Starr tried again but had to back away. "Colter, what should I do? I can't get close! Can we shoot the lock out? She's dying in there. Jesus!"

"No. Locks don't shoot out."

"Henry and the fire truck, they're at the evac station. I don't know—"

Colter squinted at the van and the surroundings. He said calmly, "Drive it away."

"What?"

"Just get in and drive away from the flames. Fifteen feet, twenty." He pointed uphill toward the CP.

"Oh." A why-didn't-I-think-of-that grimace. She ran to the driver's side, leapt in and started the engine, then sped forward.

Colter looked underneath. The flames hadn't spread far or enthusiastically, because of the soaked terrain, and the vehicle had not caught fire.

Starr stopped abruptly, slammed the transmission into park and jumped out, running to the back door.

Covering her as she opened the lock, looking for Bear, Colter called over of the roar and crackle of the flames, "You understand she's innocent."

"Yeah, yeah, Colter. All good. We'll get it taken care of."

She flung the door open.

Choking, Annie Coyne stumbled out.

Colter called to her, "Stay low and get to the command post."

Coyne oriented herself and began to stagger there.

The officer started in that direction too.

"No," Colter said. "Stay with me, Starr. Better shooting vantage."

He was watching Bear's F-150 pickup skid into downtown and race for the bridge over the spillway. It was a tough shot for their pistols and there was a risk they'd hit one of the houses that Bear sped past—houses that might be occupied by remainers.

He and Starr stood down from firing.

Then the man was over the bridge and disappearing into the forest on the road that led up to Route 13.

As soon as that happened, the corporals started firing toward the southern hilltop, basically covering shots to keep Colter and Starr down and stop them from hitting Bear's truck when it emerged. Clearly, their operation had gone to hell and they needed to escape.

Colter and Starr crouched, though the slugs came nowhere close.

She placed a call—sheriff's department again—and told whoever answered that the shoot-out was ongoing and they needed to get a roadblock on the south end of Route 13.

Colter didn't disagree but he believed that would probably not be their escape route. He told her, "I think their plan is to head down one of the mining trails to a clearing, a chopper'll pick them up. We have to stop them here, now."

"You think they have a . . . Never mind. Whoever they're working for has money. Of *course* there's a helicopter." She squinted at the Expeditions. "Okay, grilles and tires. Here we go."

Colter nodded at his small pistol. "Not much good at this range. Shoot some pennies for us."

The officer grinned, then did something that he'd never seen. She stepped back a few yards, walked behind a tree and rested her left hand on a branch, palm up, and placed her right, holding the pistol on it. You always fired a long gun on a rest, a pistol rarely.

There followed a stunning fusillade of shots from the big weapon. A pause between each one to reacquire, but no more than a second. Soon the slide locked back and she reloaded. He noted four extra mags. Twice what most cops carry.

"Glad I'm not a coin downrange from you," he said, shouting since they were both partially deafened.

The grille of one vehicle was perforated and steaming, and two tires of the other were flattened.

Bear's pickup—their escape vehicle—remained hidden in the brush; Starr had no target toward it.

Olsen and the fake corporals were now trapped on the east side of the highway, hunkered down behind the SUVs, which were nothing more than bullet-resistant barricades at this point. One of the men started across, shooting as he went but Starr fired his way—Colter let go a couple of rounds too—and the fake corporal dropped. He probably didn't get hit, but his mind had been changed. He crawled back under cover.

Tolifson shouted, "CHP called me. They're on the way. But they're saying thirty minutes."

A puff of smoke appeared from a tangle of brush behind which Bear's truck was hidden. A big slug—a hunting-rifle bullet—suddenly snapped over Colter's head.

He and Starr dropped.

Dirt kicked up behind them.

It would be the rifle Bear had used to shoot Ed Gutiérrez. And he clearly knew what he was about when it came to weapons.

Two more rounds followed the first. A pause.

Olsen and the corporals started across the highway but Starr rose quickly and fired, driving them back.

She dropped just as one of Bear's slugs slammed into a tree very close to them, and two more followed, digging up dirt a few yards from them.

Another pause. Another trio of shots. They were getting closer.

"Internal mag," Colter shouted.

She nodded.

Bear had a hunting rifle, which unlike an assault weapon had a fixed magazine that held only three rounds. After every third shot he would have to reload, which took maybe four or five seconds.

Colter said, "Count the rounds. We've got to get out of here. No cover."

"I'll draw him out," Starr said. She rose fast, fired a few shots at the lead SUV, and when she dropped, they counted three rounds from Bear. The boom of the last shot had not subsided when she and Colter started sprinting to the command post.

Just as Bear reloaded and let go with another three, they tumbled to the ground, where Tolifson, Dorion and Fiona lay behind a berm of earth in front of the tents. McGuire was behind the department pickup.

"A standoff," Colter said, still shouting.

Starr said, "There's one way they can change that."

Colter Shaw had figured this out too. "They're going to blow the levee, so we'll have to break cover and try to save the remainers."

Colter glanced quickly into the valley and saw Mary Dove crouching with Mrs. Petaluma behind an open doorway. No more than fifty yards from the black bulwark of earth that was soon to unleash a tide in their direction.

Rotund bombsmith Hire Denton was sitting in his Jeep, a quarter mile from the levee, listening absently to the gunshots. Wasn't his problem.

He was on a website, shopping for more Bob, good old-time black powder.

He was squinting at the price—a little high—for something you could buy in gun stores for reloading ammo, but your average clerk at, say, Frederick's Gun Shop, might not be inclined to step into the back and wheel out a hundred-pound keg.

He decided to go ahead and make the purchase, of which the payment was the easy part. Delivery of even low explosives like Bob took some logistics. He was about to send the info when—

Ding . . .

Ah, it was the Go message from the boss.

He'd been wondering if he'd ever hear, and if his efforts in the cold water to plant Charlie at the Never Summer would have been a waste of time—though he would of course be paid whether Charlie met his fate or not.

Here was the answer.

And so it was goodbye, my friend, enjoy your last few seconds on earth.

Charlie, an exceedingly *high* explosive, was meager on smoke but big on destruction.

He took his other phone, the one he would use to call the two numbers. First, the arming circuit, then the detonation circuit. The phone was passcode protected, and ten digits—so it could virtually never be guessed.

Hire Denton, however, had no trouble remembering it. The string of digits was the phone number of his local Wendy's, where he placed an order at least three times a week, the 20 Nuggs Combo being his favorite.

62.

The gunshots had started three or four minutes ago.

Mary Dove Shaw instinctively knew they were at first coming from small arms, being traded back and forth over her head and that of Mrs. Petaluma.

Some rounds were from the hill to her left, where the command post, her daughter and younger son were. And some from the right where she could just see the tops of a few black SUVs. Then longer rolling booms from a hunting rifle, the shooter on the SUV side, hidden somewhere in the trees.

"Stay low," she said to Mrs. Petaluma, who nodded. Her eyes revealed not panic but concern. A bit of anger too. She was the sort of woman, Mary Dove assessed, who did not like her life to stray far from where she had tucked it into a high-fence corral.

They crouched behind the open driver's side door of Mary Dove's pickup.

A lull in the gunfire.

Broken by an altogether different—and more horrifying—sound.

Her eyes, and her companion's, cut fast to the Hinowah levee.

Whose midsection blew outward under the force of powerful explosives.

A huge U-shaped portion from the top to the river bottom gave way, sluicing downward, tumbling into town, an avalanche of black mud and rock and water.

"Shit," Mrs. Petaluma muttered.

Mary Dove looked for cover, and finding none, turned her eyes back to the earthwork. She couldn't help it—she marveled as the huge thing collapsed, dissolving, a mythical animal dying.

And at the wall of water that cascaded out directly for them.

There was nothing to do.

Nowhere to hide.

The flood would strike them in fifteen seconds.

Snap their necks probably, so powerful would be the force.

Certainly, if that was not their fate, it would slam them into any number of the blunt objects that sat behind them.

She had a fast memory of Ashton Shaw lecturing the children on surviving shark attacks. "It was simple," he said. "Never go in the ocean."

Ah, as troubled as the man was, he certainly had a sparkle from time to time.

How she missed him . . .

She glanced toward where Dorion and Colter were, hoping for a last look at her children.

No. she couldn't see them.

Ah, well.

She braced for the impact.

Then something odd happened.

The wall of water deflated.

As it surged into town, the depth dropped fast, from ten feet to five to three to one.

The flood became an inch-deep pool, the sort that might ease into your backyard after an ordinary rainstorm.

They regarded each other, and then Mary Dove scanned the scene in front of them.

She understood what had happened.

There had been *two* sets of explosions. The first had destroyed the levee and started the flood. But almost simultaneously another explosion had brought down a wall of rock upstream, filling the narrow notch the Never Summer flowed through just north of Hinowah. It effectively created an impromptu dam, cutting off the current entirely before it even got to the levee.

No time for elation, though. After only a moment, the gunfire began again.

63.

From cover near the command post, Colter Shaw nodded to his sister.

Dorion's plan had worked.

Earlier in the day she had hired her own demo expert, a quirky guy named Hire Denton to get to Hinowah as fast as he could. He'd arrived several hours ago, along with a sizable inventory of various explosives.

Dorion had sized up the notch the Never Summer flowed through and the canyon just north—upstream—of it. Denton would plant five kilos of C-4 in strategic places where she had determined an avalanche would dam up the river almost entirely before the water got to the Hinowah levee. He was to be ready to detonate the packages the minute she texted him.

When they had concluded a few minutes ago that it was likely Bear and the fake soldiers were going to blow the levee to help their escape, Dorion had signaled Denton that it was time to detonate the charges he'd set.

The resulting dam meant the land to the north would fill up quickly but the lake would cover only abandoned fields and a swamp.

There was enough empty space to contain the water until the county or state—or the real Corps of Engineers—got a new levee in place. Then Dorion's dam would be slowly dismantled and the Never Summer would begin to flow again.

But the aquatic state of Hinowah and its surroundings were not foremost on Colter's mind.

Bear, Olsen and the corporals had lost their leverage and—whatever they felt about the failure of the levee's destruction—all that was left for them was to escape the traditional way: in a getaway vehicle, notably Bear's pickup, still hidden in the woods.

That meant that the crew's earlier problem persisted: crossing Route 13 under fire from Colter and Starr and others at the command post.

Olsen was the first to start, but Starr forced her back with a half dozen shots.

"Damn," the officer muttered. Presumably because of her dismay at missing the woman, but even getting slugs close enough to drive her back to cover was an accomplishment. That was a hell of a range for a sidearm.

Then too she could rise to a firing position only very briefly; Bear had zeroed in with his telescopic sight and was placing rifle shots exactly where he wished them to go.

Colter too returned fire but his gun—with a barrel length a half of Starr's and a tenth of Bear's—was pretty useless for distance shooting like this.

Mayor Tolifson, who had been huddling under cover, terrified, inhaled deeply a half dozen times and, his face filled with resolve, rose fast and lifted his own Glock. Before the mayor could pull the trigger, though, Bear parked a slug right beside him, spattering rocks and dirt. The slim man whimpered and dropped to the ground.

Starr called, "Mayor. Gimme your mag."

He stared.

"Bullets. I need your bullets!"

He wasn't quite sure how to get the magazine out of the gun. Colter scrabbled to him, and grabbed the weapon.

Starr shook her head. "No, you keep it, Colter."

A nod. He checked the weapon.

It was unloaded.

Grimacing, Colter called, "Tolifson, ammo? You have any ammo?"

He blinked, stared at the gun, then closed his eyes in dismay. "The office. I . . . I forgot to check."

His weapon was now a paperweight.

It was then that Bear laid down covering fire for the two corporals, one of his slugs striking the gas tank of the Public Safety pickup directly behind Dorion and Lavelle. The women rose to get out of the path of the streaming liquid. Lavelle made it to cover, but Dorion slipped and slid about ten feet down the hillside, completely exposed to Bear's weapon.

Starr called, "I'm out, Colter." He saw the slide of her Glock was locked back.

Colter was too.

Then Bear stepped out from cover, looking toward the CP tent, understanding that his enemies were out of ammunition. He'd looked through a spotter scope and seen the locked-back receivers. He worked the bolt and aimed toward Dorion, who climbed onto one knee and drew her own pistol, a small Glock like her brother's own. She aimed carefully at Bear, who paused.

He actually seemed amused.

She fired six fast shots the big man's way, emptying the weapon. They all missed.

Colter sprinted to her and helped her to her feet.

Bear aimed slowly.

Who would he target, the brother or sister?

His and Dorion's eyes met. He squeezed her hand.

"Damn it, Colter. Remember the rule: Never get sentimental. Ashton told us—"

Her words were cut off by the huge rolling boom of a hunting rifle.

Dorion gasped.

Colter froze.

Neither had been hit.

She said, "Look."

Pointing to the hillside where Bear was standing.

The big man was wincing in pain—and dismay. His rifle had been shot out of his hands. A slug had slammed into his receiver and splinted the stock, sending it flying. His hand appeared broken.

His face was eerie. He looked as if a friend had just been shot. He stared at the corpse of the rifle, shattered, on the ground near his feet.

"Who?" Dorion called.

Mary Dove. That was who. Her shot—from her .308—had hit the stock of the big man's rifle.

She was shaking her head—a message to the man.

Bear was frozen in position, staring down at the woman.

A moment passed during which neither of them moved.

No, Colter thought to Bear. Don't.

He crouched, drew his Colt pistol and began to lift it.

He didn't even get ten degrees to target before his mother's rifle bucked again.

The bullet struck Bear in the middle of the chest.

The man looked confused. Betrayed. He dropped to his knees and picked up his own wounded rifle . . . He didn't lift it in an attempt to fire the gun. He clutched it to his chest and then fell forward. He went still.

"No! Don't shoot." A woman's voice. Olsen—or whoever she really was—had shouted.

Apparently, Mary Dove's shooting had convinced her and the corporals that more police would arrive.

"Don't shoot!" she called again. "We're surrendering."

Apparently she had no idea that the reinforcements did not involve a phalanx of SWAT officers but a woman in her sixties, who weighed at most one hundred and ten pounds.

Mary Dove replaced her Winchester in the rack, thinking of the hundreds of times she'd used it to put food on the table in the Compound.

In all her forays into the autumn fields over the years, she had never felt the least emotional about bringing down a buck, merely concentrating on aim to make sure the creature didn't suffer.

And she had not felt any emotion now. From the glove compartment, she retrieved her pistol, resting in a ruddy holster she herself had tanned, cut, and stitched. She'd stitched the gun belt too, which she now strapped on.

No one was more devoted to the concept of gender equality than Mary Dove Shaw. She nonetheless felt there was something unladylike about semiautomatic pistols, especially the profoundly ugly black Glocks.

No, a woman should pack a revolver. In addition to the aesthetics, she believed that six shots were plenty if you knew what you were doing. (And the one she wore was a Ruger .44 Magnum, firing a slug so powerful that it would go straight through an assailant on its way to disabling the engine block of his getaway vehicle.)

"Those were good shots." Mrs. Petaluma nodded approvingly as she replaced her own gun, the old cap-and-ball Colt Dragoon.

The women shared a smile and they climbed into the pickup.

Mary Dove fired up the engine and motored along the street in the direction of the levee. As they passed the mudslide, she noted three trout flopping on the ground in a shallow puddle.

She stopped and climbed out. Knowing how slippery such creatures could be, she took out a pair of canvas work gloves from the toolbox affixed to the back bed, and collected the fish one at a time, depositing them in a cooler in the back of her truck and covering them with water from several bottles.

After police statements, and helping in any other way she could, she would ask to borrow Mrs. Petaluma's kitchen to fry up the trout for the woman, Colter, Dorion and herself.

Mary Dove had her own Never Rules. And one of the most important was:

Never miss a chance to have a meal with friends and family.

64.

We're good. Six feet of stone and gravel."

This pronouncement was from Ordell Balboa, who was a real sergeant in the real Army Corps of Engineers. The man and his team of eight had helicoptered in from a base near Sacramento. (He'd reported, with a confused frown, that, no, there had been no aviation groundings yesterday anywhere in the area. That was yet another fiction spun by the mercenaries.)

Colter stood with him and Dorion on the north side of Route 13. They were examining the dam.

He asked, "Who did the demo? Good work."

"Man I use from time to time. Hire Denton."

"That's not a name."

Dorion chuckled. "He's a private explosives consultant and facilitator."

Colter decided that would be an attention-getter if he had the job description written on his business card. He'd met Denton a few times. He was amused that the only way he referred to his sister was his "boss."

Balboa was nodding as he examined the rockwork again. He

glanced back to Dorion. "How'd you get the authorization to do the blasting so fast?"

"I didn't," Dorion said. "I just ordered it. Paid for it myself."

She offered nothing more.

There was a pause as he digested this.

Colter knew that any demolition work involving explosive materials needed local and state approval. The feds too, since the levee, as small as it was, still fell under the purview of the army engineers.

"I guess I don't need to put in my report anything other than a rockslide being the cause of the damming obstruction."

"Appreciate it."

"But give me that man's number. I could use him from time to time."

Colter wondered how the U.S. military would respond to a man who named his explosives.

And apparently also had conversations with them.

The soldier shot a look at the remnants of the levee. "We can have a temporary one up in a week and a permanent one in a month. Then blast out Denton's work, start the river up again."

Colter glanced at his Winnebago.

Hell.

A slug from the phony soldiers had smacked into the windshield, spidering it, and ended up in the passenger seat headrest.

Expensive to fix. And he'd have to have it done soon. If police were inclined to write you up for a mere crack in a windshield, which they were, they would *definitely* do so if the damage was caused by a .45 projectile.

Dorion and Shaw left Balboa to his engineering work and walked down the hill to her SUV.

The case was not, of course, over. Bear and the phony engineers were merely hired guns. The latter had been arrested, but their boss was still at large, ID unknown.

And it was time to find out who that was.

The two skirted the command post, which had been hermetically sealed off by Officer Debi Starr, who had strung more yellow tape in the past six hours than had been used in the hamlet of Hinowah in the past six years, he guessed. Starr had also used the metal detector that had found the slug traversing Eduardo Gutiérrez's calf to discover the burial sites for scores of bullets fired by the mercenaries. These were marked with plasticized playing cards. Clever idea if your small-town police station didn't have enough yellow numbered evidence sandwich boards in its inventory to go around.

It had taken two bombs and a lethal shootout, but the Olechu County Sheriff's Office had finally decided Hinowah was not crying wolf. They had a crime scene team running the workshop at the Redding mine and they would soon tackle the levee, the command post and the black Expeditions. The FBI's experts also were en route.

Colter and Dorion walked past the prisoner transport van that had very nearly been Annie Coyne's crematorium. It too was festooned in yellow.

They joined Han Tolifson at the bottom of the road where it curved left and descended into the town proper. He looked their way with raised eyebrows.

"So it's solid?" he asked.

Deadpan, Dorion replied, "You could call it a 'boulder' dam."

Though stern in her disaster response work, Dorion probably had the best humor of all the siblings.

It took a beat, then Tolifson smiled.

"We'll convene at the office." He gave directions.

Colter got into Dorion's SUV and they drove into the village center.

As they approached the modest one-story Public Safety building, which had government architecture written all over it, Colter spotted on the sidewalk beside the front door his mother, Annie Coyne, Mrs. Petaluma and a gray-haired woman in a purple dress—a friend of the Indigenous woman, Colter guessed.

Their mother noticed the siblings and waved. The foursome on the sidewalk hugged one another, then split up, Mrs. Petaluma and her friend walking away toward the town square, and his mother and Coyne heading toward the front steps of the PSO, where they waited.

Dorion parked and she and Colter, along with the two women, walked inside.

The office was part of a government complex, not a stand-alone building, so you couldn't judge the size from the outside, but Colter was surprised to see how small the law enforcement operation was.

It was clear somebody loved houseplants.

Immediately inside the front door was a reception desk, presided over by Marissa Fell, a large brunette in her mid-thirties. Her heart-shaped face, light olive in complexion, and mass of curly hair gave her an alluring air. Had she been on duty throughout the day, even during the worst of the flood scare? Colter guessed she had been. Her eyes and expression told him she was that sort of person.

Tolifson poked his head through a door in the back, gesturing them to follow. As they walked down a short corridor, he said to Colter, in a low voice, "I tell her it's unprofessional, the place looking like the Garden Center at Home Depot, but her position is that we're in charge and we shouldn't pay any mind to the opinions of others. She's not wrong there."

Colter noted a particular tone in the mayor's voice. He had seen too the absence of wedding rings on his and Fell's hands. The percentage they had more than a working relationship?

Sixty plus percent. Part of the proof: she'd won the houseplant dispute.

They now entered an office pen of six desks, only three of which showed signs of habitation. One belonged to the town's third patrol person, currently on vacation, L. BROWN. The second was TC Mc-Guire's, who was at the moment sitting in front of a large computer screen, keyboarding in a clattery blur, his big head looking straight forward instead of where his fingertips were striking. On the screen was the reality-show tape of John Millwood pointing the Glock 42 in Colter's direction at the Good Luck and Fortune Mine.

The other occupied desk was Debi Starr's, the name plate reported. He noted a number of framed pictures, the subjects primarily a handsome blond man about her age and twin boys, presumably around ten, with blond crewcuts.

Windows into another world.

On the wall was a bulletin board featuring mug shots and security cam images of fugitives and suspects. As most wanted notices were digital, these printouts seemed from a different era, almost decorations, though the dates were recent. He couldn't help but note a reward for one suspect in particular, a mean-looking man with a broad, flat face and narrow eyes, resembling a predatory whale. The reward was for $25K, and as the crime was domestic kidnapping, Colter was tempted to pursue it. Maybe he would come back here after all was said and done.

He wouldn't mind an excuse to stay in the area a bit longer; Colter Shaw was very aware that Annie Coyne was three feet behind him.

Tolifson directed them into a conference room, big enough for just about as many people as their party made up. They found seats in mismatched chairs. On the floor were dusty boxes of file folders and stacks of documents without cardboard homes. In the corner was an ancient minifridge, whose hum suggested it still worked, and on a counter a coffee maker that had clearly surrendered long ago.

Debi Starr smiled a greeting, though it was a harried offering. She'd been poring over notes in scrawly handwriting and making tick marks next to some entries.

Tolifson sat at the head of the table and said to Dorion, "Maybe your associate could join us."

"Of course." She pulled out her phone and dialed a number. A moment later the screen morphed into a FaceTime call.

Eduardo Gutiérrez, in a blue robe, was peering into the camera from a green-and-beige hospital corridor.

"Ed. We're with Colter and a few others, including the entire police force of Hinowah." She slowly panned the camera.

"How are you, sir?" Tolifson asked.

"They're making me walk. Asking nicely, but still."

"Your shooter's gone," Dorion said. "He's probably in the same hospital you are. But in the basement. In a bag. Want to meet the SWAT officer who took him out?"

"You bet I do."

She swung the phone to her mother.

Gutiérrez gave a laugh. "Mary Dove!"

"Eduardo."

"You're the one who . . ."

She nodded.

"Well, thank you for serving the writ of habeas corpus."

The term literally meant "producing the body," though it referred to a *living* one, pursuant to a legal proceeding.

Tolifson opened a file and skimmed it, nodding. Then he looked up. "I need to brief the CHP and County Sheriff Barrett. He'll be taking over. So . . ." He put his hands flat on the table. "First of all, I'll need AB Fifteen oh sixes from everybody who fired a weapon today."

Colter noted Starr hesitating. She frowned and pressed her lips together, about to speak. He sensed something delicate was coming. She cleared her throat and said, "Actually, Mayor, that form applies only to law enforcement. So TC and I are the only ones who need to file one."

A blink. "That's what I meant. I'll need *statements* from the civilians."

Dorion said, "We'll get those done, Mayor."

He lifted a pen over a yellow pad. "Now, any leads on who hired them?"

Colter said, "Only that they're probably local."

A frown. "How'd you figure that out?"

Without looking up from her notes, Starr said, "I'm just thinking: Because the feud between Annie Coyne and Gerard Redding was part of the scenario they concocted. Doubt anybody outside Olechu County would know a thing about it."

"Sure. Makes sense. But local . . . who?"

Marissa Fell stepped into the room, then handed out sheets of paper. "Their IDs. From prints and facial rec in NCIC, Sacramento, San Francisco and Oakland."

She had done a comprehensive summary of each perp.

If Tolifson ended up police chief, she'd be key in helping save his ass when it needed saving.

Which Colter suspected would be frequently, at least during the first year.

Through the phone, Gutiérrez asked if he could get one too.

Dorion took a photo of hers and sent it to him.

Colter looked over the sheet.

Bear was Waylon Foley, forty-three.

COMBAT IN THE MIDDLE EAST, DISHONORABLE DISCHARGE FOR STEALING SMALL ARMS AND FREELANCING AS A MERCENARY ON WEEKENDS. WITNESSES RECANTED SO THEY JUST KICKED HIM OUT, HE WASN'T COURT-MARTIALED. LIVES MOSTLY OFF THE GRID. USED TO OWN A FIREARMS RESTORATION SHOP IN MONTANA. BUT THE PAST TEN YEARS HAS BEEN SUSPECTED OF PUTTING TOGETHER TEAMS FOR HIGH-PRICED HITS—AND A FEW HEISTS. NCIC HAS QUITE A PROFILE. INTERPOL AND EUROPOL BANK ACCOUNTS TOTAL

TWO MILLION. OTHER ACCOUNTS PROBABLY BUT THEY'RE HIDDEN.
HE LIKES ELABORATE PLOTS, SETTING UP FALL GUYS.

Impressive plan indeed, Colter reflected. Two layers of misdirection. He led everyone to think that the levee sabotage was put together by Redding, who wanted to destroy the town for lithium. But in case the team tipped to that, he had a backup: setting up Annie Coyne.

The memo added:

FOLEY'S MO IS THAT HE OPERATES ON A NEED-TO-KNOW BASIS.
NEVER TELLS THE PEOPLE HE HIRES WHO THE ULTIMATE CLIENT IS.
HE'S KNOWN FOR HIS WATERTIGHT COMPARTMENTS.

Interesting metaphor under the present circumstances.

"Tamara Olsen" was in reality Alisette Lark, thirty-four. She was a former adult film performer, a profession not known for fine acting skills, though she was clearly an exception.

Colter read:

MARRIED AT 19 TO HER QUOTE "MANAGER" THEN GOT DIVORCED
TWO YEARS LATER AND QUIT THE BUSINESS. SHE WENT ON TO
PURSUE A VERY DIFFERENT CAREER. SHE WAS NEVER ARRESTED BUT
RECORDS SHOW SHE'S BEEN QUESTIONED IN A DOZEN SCHEMES
INVOLVING EXTORTION, INTERNET FRAUD, CRYPTO FRAUD, FELONY
LARCENY, CONSPIRACY TO COMMIT HOMICIDE. ALL SUSPECTED.
NOTHING HAS EVER BEEN PROVEN.

Fell's report also disclosed the IDs of the two corporals. Lawrence Williams was really Devon Smith, who worked in a gym in Oakland and ran with the Fifth Street Bloods. Robert McPherson was Trey Coughlin, a small-time drug dealer suspected of two hired killings, also in an East Bay crew.

Tolifson said, "If the profiles're accurate, the watertight thing, none of them know who's the boss." He added absently, "Too bad Foley's dead. He's the only one who could finger the ultimate perp."

Mary Dove smiled pleasantly. "He *was* trying to shoot my children."

Gutiérrez spoke from the phone. "I have a thought."

"The floor is yours," Tolifson said.

"Dorion was telling me about that guy who came to see us, Howie Katz. From the chip company."

Colter explained to those in the room who weren't aware. "Community relations, GraphSet Chips in Fort Pleasant. Offered anyone displaced from town by the flood a payment or interest-free loan to rebuild. I see where you're going, Ed."

Gutiérrez nodded. "Blowing the levee and diverting the river could mean less flooding in Fort Pleasant, less risk of damage to the company."

Annie Coyne said, "But destroying the town just to save your inventory?"

Tolifson said, "An inventory that's probably worth a billion dollars."

Colter: "So Katz comes to Hinowah, talking about helping the town out after the levee goes, but it's just an excuse to check out the progress of the erosion firsthand. If it wasn't enough he'd order Foley and the others to blow the second set of charges."

Then another thought occurred. He said, "Water."

Those in the room looked his way. He said to Coyne, "You were telling me about the bottled water company in Fort Pleasant. One of the biggest in the country?"

"Olechu Springs," Tolifson said. "Three dollars a bottle retail, and that's one hell of a markup when you don't pay for your raw materials."

Dorion asked, "Would they have an interest in diverting the river? Was it polluting the source?"

Gutiérrez said, "Or maybe flooding would damage *their* process-ing plant and wells. A water company destroyed by water."

Annie Coyne said, "There was a big controversy when they were looking for a place to build their plant."

Tolifson added, "That's right. Remember it well."

"The company made a pitch to everybody in Fort Pleasant about selling the town's water rights. Half didn't want to, the other half did. And the way the town charter was set up, the county board was the sole decision maker. I remember Prescott Moore, the supervisor, did a full-court press and it got approved. Checks went to everybody who had well water in town. From the get-go, they regretted it. The checks were a lot smaller than they'd expected—and they lost all control over their water—there were guarantees that personal sup-plies would be protected, but the lakes and rivers vanished. And then sediments started to appear in the town tap water."

Annie Coyne said, "You know, water transit works the other way too. You take it out of aquifers, but you can also add it back."

Those in the room—and Gutiérrez from afar—were looking her way. She continued, "During a rainy season farmers pump water underground to save it for dry ones. Here, the Never Summer's ninety-nine percent pure. But as it moves south of Nowhere it starts flowing past residential areas and companies. It picks up pollution. By the time the water gets to Fort Pleasant it'll fill up the aquifers with all kinds of crap."

Tolifson said, "You're saying they need to divert the flow so it doesn't pollute their product."

"A possibility."

Starr said, "We'll put them both on the suspect list. The water company and GraphSet." She frowned as she doodled a daisy on the yellow pad. Then she looked up at Colter. "This reward business of yours. You do interrogations, right?"

"I call them interviews. But yes."

She said, "I know those kids from Oakland, the muscle, don't know diddly. They're willing to squeal like whatever animal squeals—some pigs do and some pigs don't. But that Lark woman, she's not talking either, but seeing her reaction to Foley getting killed, I got this feeling we could call her Mama Bear."

Dorion asked, "Sleeping together?"

"Dollars to donuts. Which means she could've picked up *something* about who the client is. She shut down completely with me and the mayor. Want to have a go at it, Colter?"

He nodded.

Starr and Colter rose and left the conference room. They walked to a security door, and she punched in the code to get into the lockup, which consisted of four cells and an interrogation room.

The metal doors had small head-high windows and Colter caught a glimpse of two Oakland thugs sitting sullenly on beds. They continued to the room at the end, where a weapon lockbox was mounted by the door—you never met with a suspect armed. But Starr couldn't find the key. She shrugged. "She's shackled."

"If I can get out of shackles, she can get out of shackles." He handed her his Glock.

"You can do that, really? The shackle thing?"

"I'll teach you how if you want."

"'Deed I do."

Starr opened the door and he stepped inside.

65.

Alisette Lark.

As Colter Shaw sat across from her, she looked at him with narrow eyes.

It was a gaze very, very different from the ones she'd shot his way earlier in the day.

"So, reward seeker." Her voice was husky. She'd apparently been softening it earlier. "There many of you around the country?"

"Not enough to make a union."

"You don't take over a Hyatt for your annual convention, hm? Sessions and keynotes and boxed lunches?"

He set his pen and paper in front of him. Sometimes the people he was interviewing balked at his recording their conversation on his phone, even the offerors—whose side he was on, of course. But no one ever had a problem with taking notes.

"You were never military, Alisette."

Always let the subject know right off that you've done your homework.

"But you get the chain-of-command concept, obviously, considering this job."

She regarded him with eyes that now reflected boredom.

Shaw continued, "Waylon was the general in charge. You're, well, a sergeant. Or captain, if you like."

"And you want the commander in chief."

"Of course we do."

"As I told Barbie out there—"

He frowned.

"The officer."

"Officer Starr's name is Debi."

She sighed. "Barbie's a doll."

He shook his head.

"A toy? . . . Where did you grow up, Mars?"

Might as well have.

"As I told *her*, Waylon believed in insulation. I never met the person who hired us. Him or her. I never heard a name. A location, a make of car. A size of shoe. A preference of food or wine. Nothing. It was for everybody's safety. His—or hers. And ours. *You're* not going to torture me, but there're people who would. When they know the ground rules, that I'm completely ignorant, they'll realize that there's no reason to proceed with the pliers or blowtorch. We go our separate ways. Or they shoot me in the head. Either way, painless."

Encouraging that she was talking. Getting the first word out of a suspect's mouth was often the hardest part.

"No dead drops?"

A shake of her head. "Not that I heard of."

He'd seen her behavior when she was being deceptive—which had been nearly every minute they'd been in each other's company. That was her untruthful kinesic—body language—baseline, how she behaved when lying. The tilt of her head, the pauses when selecting a response, the tap of foot, the squint of eye, a gesture, a verbal tic—or the absence of a verbal tic.

Now the behavior was different. Not drastically so, but evidence to Shaw. He believed it was ninety percent the case that she was being honest.

"How did they communicate?"

"Like everybody else in this business. Burners."

"What did Waylon do with them?"

"I repeat my comment. He broke them in half and threw them out. You didn't see the *Barbie* movie. I suppose you haven't seen *Breaking Bad* either?"

No clue.

"Where did he toss them?"

"Sewers, lakes, dumpsters, garbage cans. Half the world's cold cases could be solved with enough people to go through every inch of the local sewage systems and trash dumps."

He gave no reaction, but he'd had the same thought on more than one occasion.

"The most recent phone Waylon used? Where did it end up?"

Her eyes were now back to flint. "There's nothing in it for me, Colter. The sentence's mandatory. Conspiracy to commit murder, special circumstances. I may not get the death penalty. But I'm definitely never getting out. I tell you anything at all, whoever the client is, I'm dead. They'll have unlimited funds. And that means a long reach—even into Q."

San Quentin, one of the most secure prisons in the country.

"Point us in the right direction. We could recover a phone on our own. Crime scene. Nobody'd know the lead came from you."

"Again, why? Nothing's in it for me."

He studied her for a moment.

Shaw rose and walked to the video camera sitting on a tripod near the door. He shut it off.

Which engendered a frown.

He returned and sat. "What if there *was* something else we could offer you . . . *I* could offer you."

Now she looked curious.

"You'll be in prison. Granted. That's your future. But what about your past?"

She shrugged.

Shaw said slowly, "The past . . . It's never erased. Is there anything I could do to . . . clear up some questions you might have? Something you've been wondering about over the years?"

Her eyes widened momentarily, then grew inscrutable once more.

He leaned forward, smelling her sweat and perfume—and, he was pretty sure, a scent of Waylon Foley's expensive aftershave. "I find things, you know. I find people. It's what I do. And I'm good at it."

This time the crack in the stone was wider.

"Would there be anyone in your past you might want to know about?"

She inhaled and exhaled an unsteady breath. Licked her lips.

Shaw had read in the brief bio Marissa Fell had prepared about Alisette Lark that, at nineteen, she had gotten married. And, two years later, divorced.

Shaw was thinking of several rewards he'd pursued under circumstances with some parallels. Rewards posted by women in their thirties or forties, who had married young and then divorced after several years and moved on to very different lives.

Women like Alisette Lark, though without the criminal angle.

As a general rule Colter Shaw did not pursue rewards to find birth mothers or adopted children. Most often, each in their own way wished to remain anonymous. But there was one exception: when the birth mother had been diagnosed with a genetic illness later in life and she felt her child should be made aware of it.

Shaw had then tracked down the adoptive parents and delivered the information on the medical condition.

Lark breathed deeply and lowered her head to wipe a tear away with fingers of her shackled hand.

Shaw said softly, "I'll find your son or daughter, tell you about them. What they're studying, the family they're part of now. I won't tell you where they live or give you enough information to find them on your own. That's set in stone. But you'll know something."

He pushed his notebook and offered the fountain pen. "Draw a map of where you think Foley might've pitched the phone."

She stared at the implement for a long moment, then picked it up and started to draw with a steady hand. She was talented. As she sketched, she said, "Even if you find it, remember, Waylon broke it in half."

"Let us worry about that," Shaw said. "Keep going. You're doing great."

66.

Outside the Public Safety Office, Colter Shaw and his mother were walking toward the parking lot. Annie Coyne was with them. Dorion had gone to visit Ed Gutiérrez and his wife, Martina, who had landed in Sacramento about an hour earlier.

Shaw involuntarily looked at the fallen levee. Clearly his sister's odd demolition man, Hire Denton—how *had* he come by that name?—had calculated correctly as the dam was holding. A half dozen army engineers, armed with surveying equipment and tablets, were walking around in the muck of the riverbed where the gap was.

They seemed to think all was secure, but it never hurt to keep an eye out for oneself, and Shaw looked casually for possible escape routes, just in case.

Very few risks in life clock in at zero percent.

Foremost in his thought was the conversation he and Dorion were about to have with Mary Dove at the hotel the woman had checked in to between Fort Pleasant and Hinowah. Nice and private.

How would his mother react?

She was a scientist, which suggested an absence of emotion, or at least the willpower to master dismay. She had always had a stoic quality about her.

Yet in his reward-seeking jobs, Shaw had witnessed any number of offerors who were men and women of steel in their professional lives but who became inconsolable, sobbing and frantic, when confronted with hard personal truths.

Shaw had already been rehearsing.

I found something in Ashton's papers. It's tough, but you need to know . . .

Or possibly:

You know toward the end, Ashton wasn't really in his right mind . . .

This looming conversation dominated his thoughts, but it was not the only thing on his mind.

He was also thinking about Annie Coyne. His sister and mother would stay in the motel that night.

But Shaw?

The Winnebago was one possibility.

The other was a cozy bedroom in a certain farmhouse, filled with lace and stained glass, a bit gaudy for his taste. But he would gladly cope.

A firm voice from behind them disturbed his thoughts.

"Ms. Anne Rachel Coyne?"

The three stopped and turned.

"That's me, yes."

The pudgy man wore a three-piece suit, a rarity in general and hardly the sort of garb one would see in Hinowah. The natty jacket, brown, was tight and the white shirt a size small. Neck flesh bulged. The red-and-gray-striped tie was broad and shiny. His cuff links might or might not have been real gold doubloons.

"My name is Myron Nash, I am an attorney representing the Redding Mining Company. Mr. Redding's brother and his wife are flying in to take over operations, at least temporarily. They're the primary beneficiaries of his will."

"Okay." Annie was squinting her cowgirl look at him, as if to say, It's been a long day. Please get to the point.

"I'm here to inform you that the police searched the workshop where Mr. Redding died. They found some documents in one of the walls that was blown open in the explosion. Probably left for safe-keeping ages ago and forgotten about and sealed up during renovations. They're relevant to the dispute between you and Mr. Redding over water rights to the Never Summer. Here's a copy. The original document will be tested but I have every reason to believe it's authentic."

Frowning, she took the sheet. Over her shoulder, Shaw read:

TERRITORIAL GOVERNOR

OLECHU COUNTY, CALIFORNIA

THIS IS TO CERTIFY THAT THE EZEKIEL REDDING MINING COMPANY FIRST USED WATER FROM THAT RIVER KNOWN AS THE NEVER SUMMER IN ENGLISH AND THE TLAMATI IN INDIAN ON MARCH 4 OF 1848. ALL USES SUBSEQUENT TO THAT DATE WILL BE DEEMED SUBORDINATE.

The yellow, crisp document was signed and dated.

"No!" Annie's eyes closed briefly.

The lawyer asked, "Your ancestors first use was when?"

She whispered, "After that. In March of 1848, they hadn't even staked a claim here. They'd wintered near where Grand Junction, Colorado, is now. They didn't get to Hinowah until June."

"You're sure?"

"I've seen the original deed of trust. Yes."

"I'm sorry to have to deliver this news then." He didn't seem particularly sorry but neither was he triumphant. "Here's my card if you or your attorney have any questions."

She slipped the copy of the territorial order and the card into an inside pocket of her jacket.

The man turned and walked back toward the parking lot, his gait nearly, though not quite, a waddle.

Looking from Shaw to Mary Dove, she said, "After the snowmelt flooding's gone, the drought'll be back. I'll lose *all* the water. And that'll be it."

"Annie . . ." Shaw began.

"You two go on," she said. "I think I'd like to be alone."

67.

An hour later, Shaw and Debi Starr were behind the shabby River View Motel, just outside Fort Pleasant, with TC McGuire, all wearing crime scene booties and latex gloves.

This was where Waylon Foley, Alisette Lark and the two fake corporals had stayed—their base of operation.

The three were walking back and forth. Shaw and Starr were searching visually, with McGuire manning the metal detector. The hunt was difficult; the scruffy field—soaking wet but still drought-yellow—was home to hundreds of items: beer and soda cans, broken toys, auto parts, melting cardboard containers, a huge belt buckle that seemed fairly new and had been found—tellingly—beside three large used condoms and bagged trash, much of it around a NO DUMPING sign.

Lark's map had indicated where she recalled Foley had been standing when he broke and tossed away his phone. But the big man presumably had a good pitching arm and they were having no luck spotting it.

The woman's concern about Bear breaking the phone was, as Shaw had suggested, not a problem. The gesture, apparently a technique in a popular show on TV, might have rendered the screen useless but it had no effect on the guts: the circuits and chips. Provided, of course, Foley had not wiped all the data first.

Kicking at a clump of muddy weeds, below which were more muddy weeds, Debi Starr said slowly, "Had another thought. The hoopla about the town selling water rights to the company? Ick." She was looking down at more condoms. "What do you think about this: Some anti-bottled water group is behind it. They want to drive the company out of business. There were plenty of protesters against them too, just like the anti-frackers. Maybe they assume that Olechu Springs is getting the water from the river, but they don't know it's tapping into the aquifer."

Interesting idea.

He asked her, "Does the Never Summer flow near the bottling company?"

"I don't know. You have a map?"

Shaw reached into his backpack and removed his tablet. Pulling off the latex gloves, he called up a map of Fort Pleasant and the surrounding area.

"That's the water company. There." She tapped the screen. "And the Never Summer . . ." She traced the blue line as it meandered past several restaurants, a school and the county government buildings. But it wasn't close to Olechu Springs bottling. No, protesters would likely not think the water came from the river—certainly they would not risk murder on the unlikely possibility they would disrupt the evil corporation.

"Kaput, I'd say. My theory."

Shaw was then frowning, staring at the screen. With two fingers he zoomed out.

"Debi! Hey. I found it!" McGuire was holding the body of a flip phone in a gloved hand.

"All right!" she said, smiling.

Shaw continued to study the map then looked up.

Starr offered, "Now, we have to talk our way into the county lab without the sheriff knowing about it."

McGuire had joined them. "Why's that?"

She said, "Barrett's good, no argument there. But we need to move fast. He'll think he needs to run the op through the system. He won't like it that we cut him out, but as long as we get results he'll live with it. Especially if we let him take some of the credit."

Officer Starr was not only a talented investigator but she was a pretty decent practitioner in the art of interagency politics, which was often trickier than solving crimes.

Did podcasts deal with that topic?

Shaw asked, "Where's the technical services operation?"

"On Delroy Street," Starr said. "Not far." She then asked Mc-Guire: "How long will it take to get inside the phone?"

Slipping the discoveries into a plastic bag, he replied, "Depends— if he used the default password, about ten seconds. If he made up one, it'll take longer. With six or eight random digits, it could be a hundred thousand years. Give or take."

Apparently, this was not a joke.

68.

"You're really hungry?"

"Hungry? Yes."

"It's not part of the act?"

"No."

Several hours after the scavenger hunt behind the motel, Shaw and Starr were at Maureen's, a bar and grill in Fort Pleasant. The inconsequential remains of what had been a fine hamburger sat in front of Colter Shaw.

"I thought you were just ordering to, you know, look normal."

"Hm."

Yes, he *was* hungry. When the waitress had come by, Shaw had suddenly realized he had eaten nothing that day.

An iced tea sat before Starr, with no food. And she wasn't sipping.

Under other circumstances customers here would have been treated to a view of the Never Summer as it coursed past, across the street, but presently it was a tepid stream.

He offered Starr his plate. "Fries?"

She glanced at them as if they were insects in a collection jar. "Don't see how you can eat at a time like this."

He didn't recite his father's words:

Never forego sustenance or restroom breaks when you have the chance.

He ate a half dozen fries. He'd salted liberally.

Starr asked, "Are there a lot of people like them?"

"Them?"

"Waylon Foley, Alisette Lark? What would you call them? Hit people but more than that. Like hit *strategists*."

A good expression. He'd hold on to it.

"No. Most killers for hire are dim. They advertise on Craigslist."

"You're kidding."

"And they're genuinely surprised when the wife hiring them to kill her husband turns out to be FBI. But who we were dealing with? Targeted demo work, fall guys, misdirection, costumes, stolen government plates. That's rare."

She grimaced. "And there's collateral damage too. Redding, Ed Gutiérrez. Anybody in the path of the flood."

"All still good?" He was facing the window, his preferred location in any public establishment. That revenge-minded enemy thing.

Starr scanned the interior of the restaurant. "Yep." Then she ventured some tea. She said reflectively, "I always figured my first homicide case would've been one of those stupid ones. Mr. X takes out Mrs. X for nagging, or Mrs. X takes *him* out because he belted her one too many times after his second six-pack. Professionals? In Hinowah?" She clicked her tongue.

"You called it," Shaw pointed out. "The shovel man with the empty pockets and nice aftershave. When all is said and done, you should do a podcast about it."

"I *listen* to pods. I don't *do* pods. You think this is going to work?"

"No way of knowing. You can only run numbers if you have all the facts."

"You want to take a guess?"

"I don't guess."

Starr was looking past him at the suited man. "At last. The woman he was with? She's gone to the john."

Shaw took a last hit of coffee and wiped his face. "TC?"

"He saw her too. He's looking our way."

Shaw, Starr and McGuire rose. The two cops met in the middle of the bar. Shaw hung back. He was here mostly as what Starr had described as a "strategizing consultant."

Starr hit a button on her phone.

She was dialing the number that a self-described "geek" in the Olechu County Sheriff's Department Technical Services Division had managed to extract from Foley's broken burner. It had been one of the "right away" passcode situations, not the six-figures-of-years one.

For a moment nothing happened, as the signal went from Starr's hand to the stratosphere or beyond and back down to earth.

Then it landed—in another phone, one that sat in the suit jacket pocket of the large man who was hunched over the table Starr and McGuire stood near. He hesitated a moment, put down his fork and pulled the mobile out. He flipped it open, barking, "It's about time you—"

Starr drew her pistol and stepped quickly toward the table, aiming toward the man's chest, while McGuire, who was wearing blue latex gloves, lunged and ripped the phone from the man's hand.

Patrons froze, patrons scattered.

Starr took center stage. "Theodore Gabris, you're under arrest for homicide and conspiracy to commit homicide. We have a warrant to seize all electronic devices in your possession."

The man gaped. "What?"

"Please stand up and put your hands behind your back."

"This is bullshit! I didn't do anything. Nothing at all!"

"Stand up. Hands behind your back."

The real estate developer rose fast, his chair falling backward. His reaction changed from shocked to huffy. Disgust filled in at the edges. "You've got the wrong person."

He was one of those people for whom misfortune was always someone else's fault.

"I'm suing you. You'll lose your job." Then he gasped when he saw Shaw, realizing the Mr. Stone from Silicon Valley interested in a Windermere home was not who he'd seemed to be.

While TC McGuire went into the phone and disabled the lock to keep it open, Starr nodded to Shaw. "Do the honors with my cuffs. I want to keep him covered."

He did as asked, and it was a good, efficient job, which included a double lock. In the reward-seeking business, he mostly zip-tied people. But he had experience with cuffs too.

Mostly on the receiving end.

But a skill is a skill, however you learned it.

69.

That Debi Starr and TC McGuire had acted alone in Theo Gabris's takedown had indeed ruffled some feathers, just as she'd
predicted.

Colter Shaw, Starr and Han Tolifson were in the office of Olechu
County Sheriff James Barrett, who looked to be around forty-five.

Also present was County Supervisor Prescott Moore. Dorion
had described him as "pudgy," but that had been based on a video
call, and Shaw knew the camera fattened you up some. He didn't
look too bad in person.

As for Barrett, he was as stiff and scrubbed as his uniform.

This was not a criticism. Law enforcers who were part robot
were among the most efficient. Shaw tended to be suspicious of the
absent-minded, the grinners, the backslappers and the whiners who
wore badges.

"You were a bit huffy earlier, Officer Starr." Prescott now fixed
her with a look.

"And I apologize. But we were under fire."

"Understood. I suppose."

The sheriff took over. "And regarding your takedown of Gabris, we *could* have liaised." His back was perfectly perpendicular to the floor.

She said, "Thought about everything and decided we needed to move fast. Only had minutes to act."

Tolifson added, "It was with my okay." The man was full-on police chief now. Two nine-millimeter magazines on his left hip, both loaded. Forest green uniform, Sam Browne belt and all the accessories one would need to arrest a vehicle full of uncooperatives.

Moore asked, "What *was* the big hurry?"

Starr said firmly, "We had a reasonable belief that the person behind the Hinowah levee collapse and the related murder of Gerard Redding was in possession of a burner phone he used to communicate with the deceased suspect, Waylon Foley."

For a law enforcement newbie, Debi Starr had certainly mastered formal cop-speak.

She continued, as if testifying in court, "We kept Foley's death out of the press, and so it was likely Gabris hadn't yet disposed of the burner he used to communicate with Foley. We planned to call the last outgoing number on Foley's phone; whoever answered was probably the boss who'd masterminded the plan. Mr. Shaw's theory was that Gabris was the most likely candidate. We followed him to a restaurant, called the number, and it paid off. His phone rang."

Barrett had only four items on his desk. A laptop. A pad of yellow paper. A mechanical pencil. And a mug of coffee printed with a slogan: WORLD'S GREATEST DAD on one side; WORLD'S GREATEST SHERIFF on the other.

"You had other suspects?"

"GraphSet Chips and Olechu Springs."

"Never liked anybody connected with them," Barrett muttered. "Outsiders. *And* exploiters."

Starr looked at Moore. "To be honest, sir, we did have a few suspicions about you."

"*Me?*"

"Mr. Shaw's sister found somebody had been in your house recently. We wondered if there was a reason you might want it destroyed, after your wife's passing. My sympathies, by the way."

"Thank you," he said dubiously. "You thought I might . . . have had something to do with her death."

"Not really."

Hardly a phrase to take the sting out of being offended by the tacit accusation.

"Who was in the house, do you know?"

"Josh, our teenage son. It's the reason I haven't sold the place. He can't let go of his mother. Someday he'll move on." The supervisor gave a faint laugh. "And if I was a suspect, I'm surprised you didn't wonder about my business—I wanted to destroy the records in my mortgage brokerage company because I'd been, I don't know, laundering money or skimming clients' funds."

Starr said, "Oh, that was part of it too, sir." A nod to Shaw.

He said, "But I had my private eye in Washington, D.C., do a deep dive into your business. It was legit."

There was very little that the beautiful and stern Mack McKenzie could not find when she put her mind to it.

The supervisor's laugh this time was of astonishment.

Now Barrett picked up the pencil and in precise handwriting recorded the details of the takedown, as Starr recited them. Finally he finished.

"All right, Officer Starr, and Mayor or Chief. And you . . ." He looked at Shaw briefly then continued, "How'd you end up with Gabris?"

It was Shaw who answered. "Officer Starr and I were looking at the map of where the river was in relation to the bottling plant, and we noticed something else. Railroad tracks. I had driven my dirt bike here to meet with Gabris yesterday. I rode over some tracks—you steer a bike differently when you cross rails, so I was aware of them. The only railroad around here—running straight to his development from Hinowah. On the map, I followed the line north. They were the same tracks I'd seen beside a pond at the foot of Copper Peak, filling up with the runoff from the levee spillway. There was a freight train stopped there. The tanker cars had an oil company logo on the side but—"

Barrett squinted as he took in the ingenuity of the idea. "The cars were empty, and the crews were pumping the water *into* them."

"That's right. I remembered seeing well-drilling crews in Gabris's development. And a farmer in Hinowah had just told me about the difficulty of finding groundwater around here. The drilling was going deeper and deeper and a lot of times coming up short. Gabris could hardly sell houses without inspectors reporting a good water supply. And the farmer? She told me you can pump surplus water into the aquifers to store it for dry seasons."

Prescott Moore said, "Gabris hired Foley to blow the levee and divert the water to the pond. The tankers would suck it up and then pump it into the ground underneath the development."

Shaw nodded.

Starr added, "Explains why the sand for the sandbagging got to Hinowah so fast. Gabris had it sitting in his construction site, ready to go."

The sheriff asked, "Wouldn't he know there wasn't enough water on the land before he decided to put a development there?"

Debi Starr said, "Sure he would. That's why he could buy the land so cheap. He built multimillion-dollar houses, and when they sold he'd take the profits and skip the country before the water dried up. His companies've built other developments in California and Arizona. All in arid locations."

Barrett jotted. "I'll have my counterparts down there look at the situation. Maybe he's stealing water in other places too to fill up those aquifers."

When the meeting concluded, hands were shaken and cards exchanged. Shaw, Starr and Tolifson left the sheriff's office.

As Starr continued to the Public Safety pickup and Tolifson started for his private SUV, Shaw stopped him. "Can I talk to you for a minute."

"Sure."

Shaw asked, "You're in the process of filling the police chief's job, right?"

"Oh." The non sequitur surprised him. "Well, correct. But I'll tell you, I've decided to pin this old thing on permanently." He tapped his chest, where the badge sat on the uniform blouse under his jacket. "I had some doubts at first. But, you know, sir. It feels good. And the six-gun isn't bad either. After what happened at the command post, I learned my lesson. Won't ever forget those bullets again. And no more fiddling. I know I have to bone up on the law some too, but I'm a whiz at Roberts Rules of Order and the Hinowah Muni Code. I'm sure it's a pretty short jump from there to the California Penal Code."

Shaw was looking at the low soupy bed of the Never Summer. And damn if he didn't spot a side-by-side refrigerator-freezer half buried in the muck.

He turned to Tolifson. "Don't."

The man blinked.

"Don't take the job."

"What're you talking about?"

"I've worked with law all over the country. Police chiefs, detectives, patrol. It's not you, Mayor."

He looked indignant. "I can learn."

"The technical aspects, sure. But there's instinct and intuition. Things I can't really describe, but you know it when you see it."

"I might disagree with that, sir."

Shaw steamed ahead. "You've got somebody in the department right now's perfect for the job."

A knowing smile. "Debi. I get it. You've enjoyed working with her. She's cute, she's funny, she's a whiz with the coffee. And a hard worker. You want to help her out."

His words riled. The inappropriate *cute* and *coffee*, of course. But it was also the man's utter misunderstanding that Debi Starr was not a woman who needed any helping out whatsoever.

"She's a natural."

"And you can tell."

"That's right."

Tolifson muttered, "She's a third-grade teacher who's taking a joyride at wearing a badge."

"She's a cop who happened to spend a little time teaching grade school."

No smiles now. "We could debate this forever."

Shaw gazed at him levelly. "Han, I've been attacked with a shovel, been shot at and nearly drowned. My sister's associate got shot. She was nearly killed too. And she and I saved Nowhere from Noah's flood. Her fee and my reward? Those normally would cost a quarter million dollars and you're not being charged one penny. You're a good mayor, I can see that. People like you and respect you, and you stood up today when the town needed you. Stick with what you're good at."

His eyes on the trickling river.

Shaw could read his face. The debate.

Finally, a sigh.

"All right, Mr. Shaw. All right . . ."

He unenthusiastically reached out and shook Shaw's hand.

The men parted ways. As Shaw walked to the bike, his phone chimed. A text from Dorion:

Problem. Tony's camera caught a blue SUV, Oregon plates,
driving to and from Compound. He went to check. Mary Dove left
a note on door. She was expecting a delivery. She said please

redeliver. And gave the address of motel she booked here. If it was Margaret and she saw it, she's on the way to Hinowah. We're at Mrs. Petaluma's.

He replied.

Leaving now.

70.

Colter parked the Yamaha outside Mrs. Petaluma's house.

Mary Dove's pickup was nearby, as was Dorion's SUV.

There was another vehicle too. Annie Coyne's Jeep Wrangler, back to its topless state. The forecast was in. No rain was predicted. One weatherman said that the recent inundation would have virtually no effect on California's drought.

Colter walked to the front door and rang a bell.

"Come in." It was his mother's voice.

He slipped off his shoes—protocol, it was clear—and stepped inside. He studied the cozy place, filled with mismatched furniture, in many different styles, from mission to JCPenney house brand to contempo black leather. Family pictures and Indigenous decorations and paintings and drawings. Comfortable in the way that Annie Coyne's house was, and in a way that his house—he actually owned one, in Florida—decidedly was not.

He smelled cooking fish and upon entering the kitchen he found Mary Dove in charge of the stove, and Dorion, Mrs. Petaluma and Annie at a round table that dominated the space. Mrs. Petaluma was shelling peas. It wasn't harvest season, but Colter had seen a hothouse on the south side of the property. Crops all year round.

Annie looked his way. She was pleased to see him, as he was her, but there was a pall in her eyes. He recalled the slim piece of paper that foretold the likely end of her generations-old farm.

He whispered to Dorion, "Tony's text."

She nodded. "I saw it. We'll have to warn her before we go outside again. At least she's got her weapon."

Colter noted the big Ruger on their mother's hip.

He wondered again. What was their half-sister's mission?

Mary Dove took the colander holding the peas and boiled them, then drained the pan, and added butter and some herbs from a small window garden. Mrs. Petaluma removed a potato casserole from the oven. Colter asked about the location of the china and utensils, as he, Coyne and Dorion set the table.

The plates were handed out and each person filled theirs to near the breaking point.

"Need a levee to keep the sauce in," Dorion remarked.

Laughter.

Mary Dove occasionally said a type of grace in the Colter household before meals. It was not spiritual, but simply a recognition that the family was together. It often ended with "And another day has passed, and we've survived."

This often drew a smile from everyone, even—until his last months—Ashton.

Today, though, the meal was ceremony free, and they dug in. The hamburger had dented but not derailed Colter's appetite.

"The fish is great," Coyne said to Mary Dove.

"Fresh as can be," the woman responded.

And Colter wondered when on earth his mother had found the time to go shopping.

They talked about the cases against the suspects and how Colter and Debi Starr had deduced that the real estate developer was the ultimate perp.

"He was stupid. His triggerman, Waylon Foley, went through

burner phones every six hours or so. Gabris kept the same one he'd had for days. The call log has dozens of other numbers the police are checking out. Mostly untraceable burners, but there's a landline in Calexico."

Annie Coyne gave him a questioning look.

"Town on the, yes, California-Mexico border. Small place, not much happening there. The only thing of note is that it's near the All-American Canal. That's the only source of water for all of Imperial County, east of San Diego and L.A. Runs from the Colorado River to the Salton Sea. Eighty-two miles. Longest irrigation canal in the world. If that canal's sabotaged, or the Colorado runs dry, a billion tons of agricultural products disappear. FBI and Homeland are very interested in what Gabris's connection is to the place."

"Water," Annie Coyne whispered, as if the word were an obscenity. She had eaten the least of all of them.

After they had finished and were clearing the dishes, Mary Dove's phone lit up with a text. She looked at Mrs. Petaluma and asked, "Can I use your computer again?"

"Of course."

Mary Dove said to the others, "Come with me." A curious tone in her voice. Mysterious and important.

Dorion and Colter shared a glance.

They all walked into the den, which was even more jam-packed than the rest of the house with memorabilia and art, most of it involving Native people and sites. Mrs. Petaluma sat at her crowded but orderly desk and turned on a computer. A large flat-screen monitor came to life. She began typing quickly.

The woman glanced up at Colter, who stood nearby. She said, "I see that expression, Mr. Shaw. Is this where you tread into a minefield, thinking, oh, an elderly Indigenous woman using the internet?"

"No," he said, gently pushing back. "What I'm thinking is, you don't often see *anyone* running Linux as an operating system."

A shrug. "Open source. So much better than Windows or Apple. Mary Dove? What's the URL?"

Their mother held up her phone, displaying the text she'd just received.

It turned out to be a Zoom invitation. Mrs. Petaluma typed in the URL and then rose, giving her seat to Mary Dove, who sat and, seeing herself in the camera, smoothed an errant strand of hair.

A moment later they were looking at a man wearing a pale shirt with the top button undone and the collar spread wide, a loosened gold and black tie hanging low. His hair was the opposite of Mary Dove's—frizzy and disordered.

"Mrs. Shaw."

"Mr. Grossman. I have some other attendees." She gave the names of those present.

"Hello, everyone."

The office was that of a lawyer, Colter could see. The back wall was lined with case reporters—in their distinctive beige and red hue that every law student and lawyer in the country would recognize instantly. He could see too that the man was in San Francisco; Colter caught the Bay out one of the man's windows. The view featured a sliver of the Rock—Alcatraz.

Mary Dove said, "Barry handles many of my legal matters. Now." Nodding to his digital form. "Your text said you have some information for us."

"I do. Now, no lawyer on earth is going to give you a one hundred percent answer to a legal issue, but I think we're in the ninety-fifth percentile on this one."

Again, Shaw and Dorion shared a questioning glance. She lifted her palms, as if to say, "I have no idea."

Their mother said to the lawyer, "I haven't said anything to my friends and family. Perhaps you could fill everyone in."

"Of course. Mrs. Shaw became aware of a potential legal situation today, and she asked me to look into it. Now, you mentioned Ms. Coyne's presence. Where are you hiding, Ms. Coyne?"

The woman frowned in curiosity and stepped in front of the camera.

"Hello." Her voice was uncertain.

"Greetings. Now, have a seat. If there's a seat to have."

Mrs. Petaluma pushed one forward and Annie sat.

"Mrs. Shaw was explaining that until today your farm and Redding Mining Company had an informal arrangement to divide the water in the Never Summer River fifty-fifty since neither of you could prove superior rights."

She sighed as she repeated, "Until today."

"Mrs. Shaw told me a lawyer for the mine found a certificate of first use that predates your family's arrival in Olechu County."

"That's right. And it looks authentic."

"It probably is. The water board records don't go back that far, but those certificates were not uncommon and the board and local authorities have upheld them unless there had been an obvious forgery."

"It didn't look forged." Her voice was filled with discouragement.

Grossman absently brushed his crazy hair, making it all the crazier. "Now, a little history about Hinowah. It was originally populated by a settlement of Native Americans from the Miwok Nation. By the way, I have to thank my paralegal for this. Rashid is a miracle worker. He dove into records going back hundreds of years. Found a treaty between tribal elders and the army. The tribe would supply fruits and vegetables for the soldiers, and the army would protect them from warring tribes.

"And do you know what else Rashid found? Maps of irrigation ditches from the Never Summer to the Miwok farmland, as part of that treaty. Dated 1841. I understand from Mrs. Shaw that you're Miwok, Mrs. Petaluma."

"Yes. And my family has been on the land here since 1837."

The exact date seemed curious to Shaw, until she continued with an edge to her voice. "The year our family ancestors fled—after the Amador Massacre. Mexican colonists attacked their village and executed two hundred of our people."

Colter, Dorion and Russell had been homeschooled, and as part of the history "track," Ashton had taught how, throughout the 1800s, the California government, as well as white settlers, engaged in systematic genocide and ethnic cleansing, forced labor and child separation. The Indigenous population was 150,000 in the 1830s. In 1900, it was around 15,000.

The woman scoffed bitterly. "Fort *Pleasant* . . . it was anything but."

Grossman grew somber. "I am very sorry for that, Mrs. Petaluma. Now, to the matter at hand. According to the Law of the River, the Hinowah Miwok tribe can claim first use of the Never Summer. And since you appear to be the sole successor in interest, Mrs. Petaluma, that water's yours. Every drop. One hundred percent."

The woman took this news without any emotion. After the briefest moment of hesitation, she tilted her head toward Annie Coyne. "So if I want, I can give her as much as she needs."

Coyne gasped. Her mouth was agape.

Grossman nodded and said, "It's yours to do with what you want."

"Can we get a ruling on that?"

"I'll draft the petition today."

"And also a codicil in my will to make sure my heirs do what I direct with the water."

"Of course. Just send me a copy of your original will. Mrs. Shaw will give you my email."

"*Mi'we'lu takmu*, sir. Thank you."

The call ended.

Then Annie Coyne was on her feet and throwing her arms around Mrs. Petaluma, who—Shaw was not surprised—endured the gesture awkwardly. Mary Dove received the next embrace.

Then, instantly, it was back to business. Mrs. Petaluma rose and headed for the kitchen, saying, "We have peach pie and rhubarb. I commend them both."

As if anyone who dined in her house would be committing a sin to forego dessert.

71.

Shaw was on his Yamaha, returning to the Winnebago.

His sister and mother were now safely in their new motel, miles from the one Mary Dove had mentioned in the note taped to the front door. Dorion had checked into the new place using a fake name, no ID and paid cash. This was not exactly according to the rules but she paid $200 for a room that went for $49.99 with the story that she was escaping an abusive husband and had her elderly mother in tow.

The clerk had reached under the counter and lifted a baseball bat in her substantial fist and said, "If he comes by, just let me know."

Shaw now powered his Yamaha up the hill where the infamous gun battle had occurred earlier, crested it, and then continued up the shallower incline to the shoulder where the camper was parked. He mounted the bike on the back and walked to the front to see if the bullet hole spidering had gotten worse.

It hadn't.

But there *was* a wrinkle.

A traffic ticket sat beneath a windshield wiper.

For real?

He snatched it off and read.

VIOLATION OF CALIFORNIA VEHICLE CODE SECTION 26710.
DEFECTIVE WINDSHIELD.

Then he looked at the bottom of the ticket.

See other side.

He turned it over.

Just kidding!
LOL!
Text me. Want to stop by.
D.S.

Shaw sent the message and Debi Starr replied.

Be right there.

This would be about thanking him for his role in getting her the chief's job. Shaw hadn't intended that she find out about his involvement, the pressure on Han Tolifson, but had forgotten to tell him to keep mum.

Starr would be a few minutes so he made another call, gazing at the canyon that was now the rocky, largely water-free bed of the Never Summer, brilliantly illuminated by high-power work lights set up by the army engineers as they were going about their methodical efforts in preparing the ground for the new levee.

A click on the line.

"Colter!" Annie Coyne's breezy voice flowed through the phone. "Hey."

She choked. "My God, I can't thank you enough for what you did. You, your mother, your sister. For everything."

He could only think of flippant quips. Like: all in a day's work.

Never banter.

He got right to the reason he'd called. "Just wondering. I know it's late, but if you're interested in another beer, I could go for one."

The pause was brief, but it was like a zipped computer file. Compressed but filled with mega data.

"Actually, I'm having someone over." Another pause. "It's sort of about the clothes . . . that got left."

He noted the structure of the sentence, the word choice. Passive voice was always a tell—a way to communicate when you didn't want to say something directly.

Coyne might have been offering that her professor friend was picking them up and taking them back to his place.

Or she might have meant that she was going to help him hang the items in one of the spacious closets in her bedroom, slipping both the running and dress shoes under the bed.

Not much doubt about which.

"No worries," he said lightly.

"But, Colter, really, I hope we can all get together at some point. That'd be real nice."

"It would be," Shaw said. "Take care now."

"You too. And really, I mean it. Thanks."

"'Night."

He hit disconnect, knowing without a vapor of doubt that those would be the last words the two would ever share.

A moment later the Public Safety pickup arrived, and Debi Starr got out.

She shook Shaw's hand warmly.

"Like your ticket?"

"Funny."

"We'll have statements for you and your sister to read and sign. Your mother too. She is one heck of a shot. Was she ever in combat?"

Being the wife and partner of Ashton Shaw meant that, in a way, yes. She'd been instrumental in dealing with threats to her husband and the family at the Compound. And she'd done this efficiently and without emotion. But he shook his head no. "She hunts a lot."

"Well, whole 'nother matter: I want to say something. Han said that you talked to him about me being the chief of police and all. Darn if that wasn't nice of you."

"You're a natural at this business." Shaw said nothing more. He was not good with gratitude.

"Ah, thank you for that too. But I wanted to tell you, I'm passing."

Shaw was nodding slowly. "You're . . ."

"Not taking the job."

"But, look, traffic detail in a small town—"

"No, no, no. I guess I never explained. Jim and me're moving now that the twins're out of school. We're going to San Francisco." She tapped the Hinowah Public Safety patch on her biceps. "I just took this job temporary. I passed the civil service tests at San Francisco PD and I'm going to be fast-tracked for detective."

Shaw could only laugh. "You'll be an even better gold shield than a small-town police chief."

"Here's hoping."

"And Tolifson?"

She gave a wry look. "He's entertaining candidates and took himself off the list for chief."

"All right, *Detective* Starr . . . Get us those reports, and we'll sign 'em and send 'em back."

He extended his hand, but she stepped in and hugged him hard.

After she'd left, he put a square of Gorilla Tape over the bullet hole in hopes that it would contain the cracks—this rarely worked, but he was less likely to get a real ticket if the officer saw he was making an effort.

He couldn't take the camper through town—the valley roads were too narrow and the crest onto the south side of Route 13 would never work, so he made a three-point turn and drove ten miles in a loop around Hinowah, past the defunct fracking operation and then east again.

Picking up on 13, he continued for about a mile through the misty night until he could see the garish red and yellow lights of the motel's neon sign in duplicate: above the structure itself and, distorted, on the wet asphalt before him.

He pulled into the parking lot and slammed on the brakes.

Three vehicles sat in front of him. Mary Dove's pickup truck, Dorion's Pathfinder.

And a blue SUV with Oregon plates.

The vehicle that Tony had seen arrive at and leave the Compound, after scoring Mary Dove's destination.

No! Margaret had found her prey!

He pulled the camper to the side of the lot and pushed outside fast.

Time was the critical factor now, not subtlety.

Mary Dove and Dorion each had separate rooms but only one that showed activity—shadows moving across the curtains.

He hurried to this door.

A deep breath. Hand on his pistol's grip.

Then he pounded hard. "Open up. Now."

Sounding like a police officer.

It seemed a strategic role to play at the moment. And he could think of nothing else to do. Motel doors are far harder to kick down than most people think.

The door swung open. Mary Dove stood there, frowning. "Oh, Colter. That was dramatic."

Dropping his hand, he looked past her. Dorion sat in one of the cheap armchairs and in the other was the older woman he'd seen outside the Public Safety Office talking with his mother and Mrs. Petaluma. She now glanced at him and offered a pleasant smile.

He took an instinctive glance around the room.

There was no one else.

Shaw tugged his jacket close to hide his weapon.

Dorion gave him a complicated look.

Mary Dove closed the door. "Colter, I'd like you to meet someone." She nodded to the older woman. "This is Margaret Evans." A brief pause, and a smile. "Your half-sister."

72.

Colter took a beer.

A Sierra Nevada.

When on a reward job, he liked to drink a local brew, and it didn't get any more local than this brand.

The women were drinking pinot noir. It was Oregonian and he wondered if Margaret had brought it from wherever she lived in the state.

The woman had an elegance about her. Her straight gray hair, parted in the center, fell to the middle of her back. She wore a simple chain necklace. Three rings, subtle, small, were on fingers tipped in polish-free but carefully trimmed nails: tiger's eye opal, a diamond and a twisty gold band, like a puzzle ring, on her heart finger. She had changed from the country dress she was wearing earlier and was now in a long denim skirt, white blouse and brown leather vest.

Not dissimilar from what Mary Dove occasionally wore.

Her eyes were dark and sharp and didn't seem to miss a single thing in the room, including those in it. She was older, yes, but attractive by any standard.

He caught a glimpse of the pistol that had been mentioned in his father's correspondence, the one from Eddy Street in San Francisco.

A 1911 Colt. But she wasn't carrying it holstered; the gun weighed two and a half pounds and featured a lengthy barrel. The weapon sat in a colorful macrame bag at her feet.

In a soothing voice, tinted with a European accent, she said, "We should dispose of the big question first. Yes, you and Dorion and I *are* legal half-siblings. We share Ashton as a father."

Mary Dove seemed unable to contain the smile when looking at Colter's expression.

"My husband, Robert, and I met him and Mary Dove when we were both guest lecturing at Berkeley. We were journalists and had taken up the cause of writing about the rise of totalitarian movements in the world, the U.S. included." She sighed. "We felt it was our mission to bring these movements to light. World War Two and Hitler's coming to power began a mere hundred years ago—and death camps were only eighty. That is just a splinter of time in the history of the world. Would we like to believe we have quote 'cured' that type of dementia and sadism? Of course. Have we? No. Absolutely not.

"Your father helped us immeasurably. He was researching an aspect of the problem that we had not thought about: the relationship between corporations and totalitarianism. That was a mistake on our part. Of *course* companies can facilitate fascism and nationalism. Look at the Krupp weapons company, which helped rearm the country under Hitler—who also leased state-of-the-art computer systems from America to identify and track Jews. Some historians believe the company was aware of that." She took a sip of wine and looked knowingly at the Shaws. "And then some corporations are totalitarian entities themselves."

"BlackBridge," Colter said evenly.

The corporation their father exposed, with disastrous consequences.

Margaret grimaced and continued her narrative.

"Some of his research led us to a company in our home country."

A sour laugh. "On the surface it was a humanitarian aid nonprofit. It seemed to be doing good things, but in reality? It was an intelligence agency identifying dissidents. I continued to focus my research here, and Robert went overseas to interview someone inside the company."

"He was there no more than a week before . . ." Her voice caught. "An accident. A car accident. On a straightaway, dry asphalt, and Robert never sped or drove dangerously."

"I'm sorry."

"I learned that I was in danger too. I do not know who in the U.S. government received what, but someone sold me out. And my visa was revoked. If I did not leave voluntarily I would have been deported—into the arms of the Ministerstvo Vneshneekonomicheskikh Svyazey. That's the Ministry of Foreign Economic Relations."

She laughed bitterly. "How is *that* for a pseudonym? It was really a brutal state security agency—the one responsible for Robert's death. If I had gone back I would have been killed too. But you know your father—he was always thinking of ways to outwit Them. 'Them' with a capital 'T'—the enemy that Ashton could see and so many others could not. And he came up with plan."

Colter said, "He *adopted* you."

She offered an amused glance his way.

Dorion said, "And you became a citizen?"

"Not automatically. There were still hoops to jump through. But it stalled the deportation, and eventually I did get citizenship. And then I went underground. New identity. My real name is Sarah."

Ah, the Sarah in the letters. Ashton's friend. Not his lover.

"I changed it to Margaret—after Margarete Momma. She lived in eighteenth-century Sweden and is considered the world's first woman political journalist. I wanted to keep writing, but I knew I had to wait. In the meantime, Ashton got me a job as a teacher in a private school."

Colter shared a glance with Dorion, who whispered, "We found the letter."

"We thought it was about you getting *admitted* to a grade school as a student."

After a beat of a moment, both Margaret and Mary Dove laughed.

Then their mother cocked her head. "So you thought Ashton had an affair with Sarah, and they had a baby, Margaret?"

Neither of the pair replied.

Mary Dove was not dismayed or disappointed at their assumption. "Understandable. It was a time when Ash was starting to slip away from us all. Besides, what was one of his most important rules?"

Dorion answered. "'Never ignore the facts.'"

Their mother offered, "You heard he had a daughter, and you had no indication of her age, other than he'd apparently helped her get into elementary school. And he never mentioned anything about a Sarah or Margaret. Your assumption was logical. Of course . . . if you'd been less concerned about sparing my feelings and just told me about it in a phone call . . ."

Partly good-natured chiding. Partly gentle rebuke.

And, as always, she was right.

"So," Margaret said, "that is the story of how I became your half-sibling and the daughter of a man three years younger than I was."

Colter said, "The angry letters you wrote. The gun?"

"Oh, you found those too? I told you that somebody here—in the States—had betrayed us. After my husband was killed I went crazy, I will admit it. I wanted to find them, get revenge. I bought the gun from a street dealer on Eddy Street. I'd written a story about the gangs there and had some contacts. I played Hercule Poirot, trying to track down who had done it. But your father convinced me not to. He said revenge was not why God put me on earth. I was a journalist not a soldier. I gave up that idea and started reporting again.

Carefully, of course, under various pseudonyms." A wry, knowing glance. "But of course I kept the gun." A glance toward her bag.

Margaret now looked him over carefully. "Which brings me to our reunion." A sip of wine. "I had to find the Compound. I knew about it, but not where it was. And I was too paranoid to use a computer or phone to contact Mary Dove or you. One of the reasons I've survived this long is because of what Ashton taught me." She paused a moment. "And the reason I wanted to find the Compound was . . . because I needed you, Colter."

He could see where this was going and he gestured encouragingly.

"In my reporting I learned about a company based in Brussels. A chocolate manufacturer, what else? Their confections are quite good. Popular throughout Europe. But that is merely a cover. Their main function is to engineer misinformation campaigns. And, far more troubling, the company employs one particular individual to identify and murder those exposing totalitarian and anti-democratic threats. Activists and journalists like myself. He's killed at least five in Russia and other Eastern European Countries. Two in the Middle East.

"I learned that last week he was given the assignment of killing a person or persons within the next month here in the U.S. My source had only limited information. The assassin is a man, middle aged, and he works in the bookkeeping department of the company. That's what he's known as, his code name: the Bookkeeper. No one outside the organization knows his identity but the rumors are he is obsessed with balance sheets—and numbers—and is quite good at that job. As good as he is at murder."

She smiled. "Yes, yes, Colter. You understand now. The Institute for the Freedom of Journalism has offered a reward for information leading to the identity and arrest of this man. And yes, this *is* the man who killed Robert. Now, I must say—"

"I'll do it."

"You don't want to know about what the Institute is offering?"

If ever there was a reward-free reward job this was it.

"No."

"Thank you, thank you," she whispered as relief and gratitude flooded her face. "No one has the resources or the desire, frankly, to pursue anyone with no known record—and no known identity. MI5 and -6, the FBI, the State Department, Homeland, the SDECE in France . . . If we could give them a name and location, proof of past crimes, maybe some evidence of what he has planned, then they would start a file and assign investigators. But until then, we are on our own."

"Do you know the targets?"

"No, just that they're in or near the same city in the U.S.

"The institute has several safe houses they use for at-risk journalists. They will set you up in one there, if you'd like. I'll meet you there and—"

"No," Colter said. "It's time for you to go back underground. It's what"—he smiled—"*our* father would have wanted."

A sigh. "The truth is, I am tired. Endless fighting finally catches up with old bones. The damn body. It simply does not always cooperate." She dug into her purse and pulled out an envelope. "Here's the address of the safe house and the phone number of the institute."

He opened the envelope and glanced at the details of the place that would be his new home for—well, however long it took to find the Bookkeeper and report him to the authorities.

Or come up with a different, perhaps a more efficient, solution to bring him to justice.

In his work, Coler Shaw had learned that sometimes one person's survival means another person's demise.

Margaret added, "The Institute will get you more information if they can find any."

Shaw nodded, then he noted the hour was nearly midnight and he knew everyone was feeling the same exhaustion he was.

This had been a long, long two days.

He said good night and returned to the camper. Walking over the damp gritty asphalt, he was thinking about where the institute's safe house, for which he would leave at first light, was located.

Colter Shaw's profession had taken him to some exceedingly inhospitable and dangerous locales.

He wondered if this particular destination would prove to be the *most* inhospitable and dangerous of any he'd yet worked.

Those were the rumors, at least.

But then he'd never been to New York City.

And he recalled one of his father's most important rules.

Never judge a place until you plant your feet on the ground.

EPILOGUE

***Publishers Monthly* Reviews in Brief**

★ Starred Review—*The Blue Strayer: Arana Braveblade, Book One*,
By Fiona Lavelle

The year is 2243 of the Altered Era, and Arana Braveblade, a talented spell-caster, is snatched from her home in Fraeland, along with her brother and a half dozen others by the soldiers of Thamann Hotaks, the evil leader of the Central Realm, the largest region in the continent of Hemifond in EverWorld. Braveblade engineers an escape from Hotak's castle with the help of a Blue Strayer, a sort of magical sports car with a mind—and sense of humor—of its own. Her mission is to rescue her brother and the other kidnappees and form an army to take on Hotaks.

This debut novel is a delight. Author Lavelle avoids the clichés that can mar fantasy writing the way Braveblade and her band skirt the deadly vapor pits of Millwud Gorge. Her writing is crisp and to the point, not bogged down with overwrought prose and tedious narrative. Both the storylines and the cast of characters spring from a truly vivid imagination and we find ourselves transported to the world of Hemifond with the same gentle but sure hand with which J. R. R. Tolkien guided us through Middle-earth, and C. S. Lewis, Narnia.

A second book is in the works, and a streaming series is in development.

JEFFERY DEAVER is the #1 international bestselling author of more than fifty novels and one hundred short stories, a nonfiction law book, and an album of country-western songs. His books are sold in a hundred and fifty countries and translated into twenty-five languages. His first novel featuring Lincoln Rhyme, *The Bone Collector*, was made into a major motion picture starring Denzel Washington and Angelina Jolie. He's received or been short-listed for a number of awards around the world, including Novel of the Year by the International Thriller Writers and the Steel Dagger from the Crime Writers' Association in the United Kingdom. In 2014, he was the recipient of three lifetime achievement awards. In addition to writing the Lincoln Rhyme and Colter Shaw novels, he and coauthor, Isabella Maldonado, write the Carmen Sanchez–Jake Heron series, the first of which is titled *Fatal Intrusion*. He wrote the original radio play *The Starling Project* for Audible.com, starring Alfred Molina, and his Colter Shaw series is the basis for the CBS primetime drama *Tracker*, rated the number-one show in America last year. A former journalist, folk singer and attorney, he was born outside of Chicago and has a bachelor of journalism degree from the University of Missouri and a law degree from Fordham University.